MW00846756

HACKNEY

Kingsland · Hack. Downs · Dalston · Homerton

Victoria

London-Fields

Victoria Park

Old-ford

Shoreditch

Str.

Bethnal Green

Bow

D O

Liverpool-Str. St.

Broad Str.

·gate Str.

CITY

N. St.

Fenchurch St.

TOWER HAM

Stepney

Tower

London-Dock

Tunnel

W.I. Do.

UPPER

POOL

Rotherhithe

Surrey Commercial Docks

Isle

THWARK

Spa Rd.

Southwark Park

H

Sth. Bermondsey

Dockyard

D.

The Frozen People

Also by Elly Griffiths

ELLY Griffiths

The Frozen People

QUERCUS

First published in Great Britain in 2025 by

QUERCUS

Quercus Editions Limited
Carmelite House
50 Victoria Embankment
London EC4Y 0DZ

An Hachette UK company

The authorised representative in the EEA is Hachette Ireland,
8 Castlecourt Centre, Dublin 15, D15 XTP3, Ireland (email: info@hbgi.ie)

Copyright © 2025 De Rosa-Maxted Ltd

The moral right of Elly Griffiths to be
identified as the author of this work has been
asserted in accordance with the Copyright,
Designs and Patents Act, 1988.

All rights reserved. No part of this publication
may be reproduced or transmitted in any form
or by any means, electronic or mechanical,
including photocopy, recording, or any
information storage and retrieval system,
without permission in writing from the publisher.

A CIP catalogue record for this book is available
from the British Library

HB ISBN 978 1 52943 333 3
TPB ISBN 978 152943 334 0
EBOOK ISBN 978 1 52943 335 7

This book is a work of fiction. Names, characters,
businesses, organizations, places and events are
either the product of the author's imagination
or used fictitiously. Any resemblance to
actual persons, living or dead, events or
locales is entirely coincidental.

3

Typeset by CC Book Production
Printed and bound in Great Britain by Clays Ltd, Elcograf S.p.A.

Papers used by Quercus are from well-managed forests and other responsible sources.

For Andy

The earth has bubbles, as the water has,
And these are of them . . .

Shakespeare, *Macbeth 1.3*

'Dear me,' said Mr Grewgious, peeping in, 'it's like looking down the throat of Old Time.'

Charles Dickens, *The Mystery of Edwin Drood*

Chapter 1

Ali

Alison Dawson can never cross the Old Kent Road without thinking of Monopoly. The brown square nobody wants. She used to play it with one of her husbands, she can't remember which, offhand. He'd thought it a sexy, Ali MacGraw/Steve McQueen type of thing when, in reality, it had just been a board game played – rather self-consciously – on the grubby carpet squares of a Travelodge. Hugo. That was the one. None of the others would be mean enough for a Travelodge.

It's a grey, unpropitious day. The start of a new year, the old one still visible in the shape of dying Christmas trees lying in the gutter, awaiting collection, and the words 'Ho ho ho' in cotton wool on the window of a Turkish barber's shop. It's not a scenic route to work but Ali hardly notices that anymore. Chicken Shacks, vape shops, boarded-up houses, graffiti promising that the Second Coming is on its way. About time too, thinks Ali. If she looks up, it's a different matter: she'll see Georgian windows, moulded cornices, the occasional surprising glimpse of a phoenix or an angel standing guard on a rooftop. Ali does not look up today. She's late but not enough to worry about. She knows that time is a relative concept.

Ali is fifty, something that still surprises her when she says it aloud or when she has to scroll back on online forms to find 1972. She makes it a point of honour never to lie about her age or to say 'thank you' when someone says she doesn't look it. All the same, it's a shock to acknowledge that she has lived for half a century, has chalked up three husbands, one son and a career in the police force. In many ways, she feels the same as she did when a teenager in Hastings, standing looking out to sea in a self-consciously troubled way, thinking: when is my life about to start?

She waits for the lights to change, something which always amuses her son, Finn. 'You're not in sleepy Sussex anymore,' he tells her, 'you have to take your chances with London traffic.' Ali moved to the capital when Finn was only four. She was a single parent by then, working as a cleaner and living in a one-bedroom flat in Stratford, an area that hardly seemed part of the metropolis then but is now famous for hosting the Olympics. Ali crosses the road. She's heading towards a cliff face of office buildings, grey and featureless. There are shops at ground level and, above them, floor after floor of business premises. What do these people do all day? Ali often wonders. She catches sight of herself in the window of Bilal's Bagels. Bright red hair, black jacket, jeans and trainers. 'Not bad for fifty,' Ali tells herself and then changes it to 'not bad'. You have to watch ageism, even in an internal monologue.

The East End has changed since Ali moved here twenty-seven years ago but real Londoners, like her colleague John, say the skyline is almost unrecognisable now. The space-age buildings with their homely names – the Gherkin, the Cheesegrater – overshadow the Victorian churches and sixties tower blocks. But the building that houses the Cold Case Unit – so cold they are frozen, Bud says – wouldn't appear on anyone's list of memorable examples of city architecture. Number 14 Eel Street is so anonymous as to be almost invisible: plate-glass façade, featureless lobby with two lifts, one of which is permanently out of order, signs for Fire Exits and Toilets. There's an old-fashioned noticeboard, the type with removable letters, that lists the businesses spread over the five storeys. Ali's office, the Department of Logistics, a title that is both weighty and vague, is on the third floor. Ali considers the lift but pushes open the door to take the stairs. She threw her Fitbit into the Thames two weeks ago, but she still likes to get her step count in. 'Can't be unfit in our job,' says Geoff, despite not having seen his feet in living memory.

Ali takes a break on the second-floor landing and checks her phone in case anyone thinks she's out of breath. A reminder from her book group. They're meeting tonight and Ali hasn't got around to reading *Conversations with Friends*. And there's a text from her son, Finn: 'Terry fine. Bit me once. Now under table.' Finn is looking after Ali's deranged cat, Terry. She texts back, 'Thanks love,' and steels herself to finish the climb.

Dina is the only person in the office. She's eating microwaved porridge in a pot.

'This stuff tastes like death.'

'It's good for you. It's not meant to taste nice.'

'Isn't anything that's good for you nice?'

'Sex?' suggested Ali. 'Want a coffee?'

'Coffee's meant to be good for you these days, isn't it?' says Dina. 'I can't keep up.'

'In moderation,' says Ali. 'It's always in moderation.' A concept she struggles with, to be honest.

Dina and Ali are sometimes called 'the twins', although there is a fifteen-year age gap between them and Dina is black and Ali is white. Their only physical similarity is that they both have a small gap between their front teeth, but police nicknames are like that.

'How's Terry?' asks Dina, as Ali collects their mugs on her way to the kitchen.

'Much better,' says Ali. 'He bit Finn this morning.'

'Poor Finn,' says Dina, who always takes Finn's side.

'He's a Tory. He's used to it.'

Finn would say that he isn't a Tory, he just works for them. Sometimes that distinction doesn't seem quite enough for Ali. As she waits for the kettle to boil, she washes the cups in a half-hearted way. Sometimes Bud has a real blitz and cleans everything with bleach, which Ali says is more unhealthy than germs. The kitchen is as dreary as everything else in Eel Street: Formica cabinets, chipped tiles, stained sink with only one tap working. But Ali hardly notices because this is home, even down to the poster for a comedy night Bud attended in 2018. He loves stand-up although, amongst the team, he is often several minutes behind on a joke.

Ali makes the coffee adding an extra spoonful of Nescafé for herself – she has a serious caffeine habit – and carries the mugs back into the open-plan area. Her desk is at right angles to Dina and faces John. It's a view she's grown used to: John's West Ham water bottle, the underwater mural on the building opposite, the venetian blinds that are never quite straight.

'Thanks,' says Dina, when Ali puts the mug on her desk, avoiding Tom, the spider plant.

'Is Geoff in?' Ali nods towards the closed door of their boss's office. 'Should I have made him a coffee?'

'He was here earlier,' says Dina. 'He was asking for you.'

'What did he want? Do you think it's another case?'

'I asked if we were going through the gate again and he said, "It's a fucking five-bar gate."'

'Geoff swore? Shit.'

'Yeah. I tried to make him put a pound in the swear box but he pretended not to hear me.'

'Come in, Alison.' Geoff waves at the visitors' chair with a lordly gesture that dislodges his 'World's Best Boss' mug, an ironical present from Ali that she fears was taken literally. Luckily, it's empty. Geoff often misses out on the coffee run. Ali picks the mug up and puts it back in slightly the wrong place, just for the fun of it. Geoff moves it back.

'Alison,' she says. 'This must be serious, Geoffrey.'

'It's interesting,' says Geoff, and tries a smile. His husband, Bobby, once told him that smiling releases molecules that fight stress but, in truth, Geoff's face is made for tragedy. All the lines point downwards.

'Am I going through the gate?' asks Ali. If it's tonight, she won't have to go to book club.

'It's a different gate,' says Geoff. 'A gate to the nineteenth century.'

'The nineteenth century? But that's Tudor times.'

'Do you say these things to annoy me, Alison?' says Geoff. 'I thought you had a degree in history.'

'I do,' says Ali. 'From Queen Mary's.' She waves in the vague direction of the Mile End Road.

'Then you must know the Tudors were the sixteenth century,' says Geoff.

Strictly speaking, the Tudor reign started in the fifteenth century, with the Battle of Bosworth Field in 1485, but Ali doesn't think that Geoff is in the mood to be contradicted.

'My degree was mostly about the Married Women's Property Act,' she says. 'Did you really say that we're going back to Tudor—sorry, Victorian times?'

'Let me explain,' says Geoff, settling himself in his chair. Please do, thinks Ali.

The first two words are a surprise though. 'Isaac Templeton.'

'*Who?*' Ali, who had decided to hear Geoff out in silence, can't resist an exclamation.

'Isaac Templeton. The justice minister.'

'I know. My son works for him.'

Geoff has met Finn several times. He even gave him some advice when Finn was thinking of applying for the civil service, Geoff being an expert on institutional form-filling. But, for a moment, the boss looks genuinely confused.

'Your son?'

'Yes, Finn. He's a spad. A special advisor.'

'That's . . . well . . . that's interesting. Because Isaac Templeton's great-great-grandfather was suspected of murdering three women in the 1850s. There wasn't enough evidence to convict him, but it's always been a stain on the family honour. Isaac is writing a book about his family and he wants to be able to present evidence of his ancestor's innocence. That's where we come in.'

Geoff leans back as if all is explained whereas, in Ali's opinion, all he has done is invite more questions. And did he really say, 'a stain on the family honour'? Are they in the nineteenth century already?

'How did Isaac Templeton find out about us? I thought only the Prime Minister and the home secretary knew.'

The Department of Logistics, or the frozen people, as Bud calls them, was set up by Geoff ten years ago. Ali joined in 2015. When she was recruited she assumed they were working on cold cases and she still remembers her shock when she realised that their goal was actually, physically, to travel in time. Then she met Jones and it all seemed possible. The government have given them limited resources, all contained within the grim façade of Eel House, but Ali has never been sure exactly who knows what.

'Some higher-up members of government are also aware of our operations,' says Geoff, sounding pompous, as he always does when challenged. 'Templeton is, of course, the secretary of state for justice.'

'I know.' *Minijus*, Finn calls it, which sounds like a particularly unpleasant diet drink.

'As such,' says Geoff, at his most pontifical, 'Templeton has followed our work in the Mulholland case.'

Laura Mulholland disappeared in 1976. Her adult children were convinced that she was killed by her second husband, Steven, but there was no evidence. Until Ali and Dina visited and saw Steven burying Laura in the back garden of their house in Chiswick. In 1979 the house was knocked down and flats built in its place. Geoff is trying to get permission to dig up the car park, but the case is no longer seen as a priority. Steven died in 1992. They haven't even been able to tell Laura's children but, as Jones says, '*We* know and that's something.' It doesn't always seem enough though.

'The Mulholland case was a genuine miscarriage of justice,' says Ali, remembering the blood and dirt on Steven Mulholland's hands as he washed at the outdoor sink. 'Isaac is only writing a book. Are we really going to use the gate just to help him sell more copies?'

'It's an opportunity, Jones says.'

That explains a lot. But not everything. Jones still sees the team primarily as research assistants.

'We're waiting for Jones's report,' says Geoff. 'In the meantime, Isaac wants to meet you to put you in the picture.'

'He wants to meet me?'

'He's asked for you especially, I believe.'

Ali is surprised into silence. Outside she can hear Dina singing, 'Enjoy yourself, it's later than you think.'

Chapter 2

Ali has met Isaac Templeton before, although she's pretty sure he won't remember. Finn invited her to a reception at the House of Commons and, during the course of the evening, introduced her to Templeton.

'Ah,' said the MP, when the family connection was explained, 'the Creator.'

'That's right,' said Ali. 'I did it all myself.' She'd been aware of Finn shooting her warning looks, just as he'd done one school parents' evening when she'd started singing 'Sister Suffragette' from Mary Poppins with the history teacher.

'HA HA,' said Templeton, in capital letters, before moving on.

Ali had been only half joking. She'd married Declan when she was nineteen and pregnant. They'd tried their best, living first with his parents, then hers, and finally being approved for a council flat on the outskirts of Hastings. They divorced four years later and Ali moved to London. She probably gets on best with Declan out of all her husbands but she's not about to give him much credit for Finn's upbringing. She was the one who worked as a cleaner to pay for his school uniform, who sat with him over homework and encouraged the ambition that led to a degree at the LSE and Finn's current elevated employment status. Declan wasn't a bad dad, he attended football matches and was even supportive during the traumatic French horn period, but he wasn't the Creator. Sometimes Ali says that Elvis was Finn's father, a joke that comes from a Lana Del Ray song and appeals only to her.

It feels odd, crossing London in the middle of the day, as if she's skiving or on holiday. Ali spent a lot of her time at school skiving, hanging around with Declan on the beach or in the amusement arcades. It was never as much fun as she thought it would be. But today she is legitimately going about her work, albeit work that she can't discuss with anyone. She'd like to text Finn, 'Guess where I'm going?' He doesn't always answer but, sometimes, he's up for quite a virtual gabfest: jokes, memes, pictures of Terry wearing devil's horns. Now Ali sits on the almost empty Tube train, trying to read *Conversations with Friends*, and wishing she could tell someone where she's going. I'm meeting Isaac Templeton! At his flat! I'm going back in time!

Isaac Templeton lives in one of the new apartment blocks built as part of Battersea Power Station's rebirth. Ali hasn't been to the area in years and it's as disconcerting as any time slip: a whole new Tube station, residential piazzas appearing out of nowhere, landscaped walks lined by saplings still wrapped in plastic. She's not surprised that Templeton's address is one of the smartest, with a doorman and a terrifying lift crawling up the mirrored outside wall. Ali is in the process of moving from Mile End to Bow (it's why Finn has temporary custody of Terry) and had thought she was moving up in the world because her new house has a small garden. But this is moving upwards at speed. She emerges from the lift feeling distinctly shaky.

Templeton meets her at the door, obviously alerted by the doorman. He's wearing tracksuit trousers and a T-shirt. It's a surprise. Templeton is always formally dressed, in dark suits that set off his Ken Doll good looks. He's often described, by the tabloids, as 'dishy'. Ali disapproves of objectifying a person by their looks but it's quite enjoyable to see a man at the receiving end for once. Also, she has always thought that Isaac Templeton's dishiness was only in relation to other Members of Parliament. Who was it who described politics as 'show business for ugly people?' But, close up and in casual clothes, she's sorry to say that Isaac Templeton is very handsome indeed.

'Ms Dawson. How good of you to come.'

'No problem. And it's Ali.'

Does Templeton know of her link to Finn? Finn has Declan's surname, Kennedy. Ali went back to her maiden name after divorce number two. She bitterly regrets all the passport-changing, bank-card-altering nonsense that she went through with her first two marriages. She hadn't bothered with Lincoln on the third. Partly because Lincoln's surname was Scrubb.

She follows Templeton into a room so bright that she almost shields her eyes. The effect comes partly from the stunning view of the Thames, showcased in a wall of glass, but also from the predominance of chrome and white marble in the room. The sun has emerged, and the light beams on myriad glittering surfaces. It's like walking into a trophy cabinet.

Templeton offers coffee, which Ali accepts. She's sure he'll have the latest Gaggia machine somewhere and is curious to see if he'll prepare the drinks himself. It seems so. Templeton pads away – his feet are bare – and Ali looks out of the window towards Chelsea Bridge and wonders how to broach the fact of being Finn's mother. She needs to tell Templeton. Apart from anything else, it will be embarrassing if he finds out another way. But she doesn't want the MP to treat Finn any differently because he has a weird time-travelling mother with startling hair and a nose ring.

But, when Templeton appears, carrying a tray with coffee and biscuits, almost the first thing he says is, 'So you're Finn's mother. He's great. One of my brightest advisors.'

Ali can't help responding to anyone who praises her brilliant boy. She can feel herself thawing. The excellence of the coffee helps too.

'He's very clever,' she says. 'How did you know he was my son?'

'I was introduced to you a few years ago. At a reception.'

'I didn't think you'd remember.'

'You're very memorable.'

'Thank you,' says Ali, though she's not sure if it's a compliment. Once again, she blesses the day she dyed her hair the colour of a London bus. Even though Finn hates it and Terry had actually hissed when she first got back from Kelly's salon.

She goes on. 'My boss says you have a mission for us.'

Templeton is silent for a minute and then he fixes her with a stare. His eyes are grey-blue with surprisingly long eyelashes. 'I'm sorry. I'm just having trouble coming to terms with it. The fact that you actually travel in time.'

'*You're* having trouble coming to terms with it. Think what it's like for us.'

'I really can't imagine.'

'When Geoff told me I thought he was joking. But he doesn't joke much. Well, he doesn't now.'

When Bobby died of cancer two years ago, Geoff had outwardly coped well. After nursing his husband through his dying days, Geoff said openly that his passing had been a relief of sorts. Geoff came back to work after only a few days of compassionate leave. He was his old self – pedantic, kind, infuriating – but often seemed to be only partially present. Geoff was never much of a joker – only Bobby could really make him laugh – but now he's even later to a punchline and the laughter, when it comes, seems almost shocking.

'When did you join the team?' asks Isaac.

'I joined the police in 2005 as a graduate trainee. I went to university as a mature student. I joined CID in 2007. I came across Geoff – Geoff Bastian, my DCI – on another case. We got on well, he's a bit stuffy but he's always fair. A few years later, Geoff told me that he was setting up a new unit and asked if I'd like to join. He said they were doing interesting work. I had no idea how interesting. On my first day, he sent me to talk to Jones.'

'I've heard a lot about this Jones. But who is he?'

'Her name's Serafina. She's a woman. Her surname is really Pellegrini but she used to be married to someone called Jones. It's a kind of joke. Jones thinks she gets more respect if she has an androgynous name.'

Rightly, judging by the look on Isaac's face.

'Jones is a physicist. She graduated in Italy and moved here when she married Jones. Anyway, for years she'd been working away in a lab somewhere in London trying to come up with a method of time travel. Well, she managed it.'

'Just like that?'

'No, of course not "just like that". Though Jones would say the time involved is immaterial. But she developed an actual way of moving atoms in space. I can't explain it – no one can really – but it's as if you create a space and then fill it with that exact person. So, after many attempts and lots of mockery – mostly because she's Italian and a woman – she managed to get someone in government interested. They gave her a team, led by Geoff. I'm part of the team.'

The idea is that each member has a special skill. John is a celebrated murder detective; Dina is a computer expert; Bud is a physics whizz. Ali still doesn't know what her special skill is meant to be, unless it's a surprising willingness to take risks (except when crossing the road).

'And have you,' Isaac lowers his voice, although there's no one to overhear apart from a whirring police helicopter, silent behind the triple glazing, 'have you actually travelled in time?'

'We call it going through the gate,' says Ali. 'And yes, I have.' This still seems such an amazing thing to say that she pauses, out of respect for the concept as much as anything.

'The first time was March 2020. It was lockdown, you see. We only had to go back to before the twenty-third to see the difference – no masks, busy streets, et cetera.'

'Weren't you worried about taking Covid back in time?'

'Jones didn't think it was an issue and we tend to believe everything she says. It's a problem really. We've made a few trips since then, me and two colleagues, Dina and John. Last year Dina and I went back to 1976 to get information on a murder case. That's the deal. You do know that? We collect evidence. We don't *do* anything.'

'Is that because anything you do in the past might affect the future?'

'That whole killing Hitler thing? You need Jones to explain why that's a fallacy. No, it's more that we're flimsy. We can't interact with people. We can't really be seen, except in certain lights. Jones is working on a way of making us more substantial. It's to do with the displacement of matter, apparently.'

'And when you go . . . through the gate . . . do you come back to the same minute that you left? Has no time passed at all?'

'No, that's Narnia,' says Ali. 'Time passes as it usually does. If we're away an hour, an hour has passed in the present too.'

Ali remembers, the first occasion, being scared that she wouldn't get back in time to feed Terry. The larger fear – being trapped as a shadow for ever – had simply been too big to contemplate.

'What's the longest you've been away?'

'We were in 1976 for two hours.'

Isaac Templeton rubs his eyes. 'I'm sorry. It just sounds so extraordinary. Hearing you say it like that.'

'Yes,' says Ali. 'It is.'

After a pause, Templeton says, 'Why don't I tell you about this case? I'll think about the other stuff later, when my brain stops spinning.'

'Good idea,' says Ali.

Templeton produces a cardboard file, which must have been concealed under the fur throw that covers the white sofa.

'I need to explain to you about my great-great-grandfather,' he says. 'He was a collector.'

'What did he collect?'

'Women.'

'He collected women? What does that mean?'

Ali and her friend Meg are preparing themselves for the book club, which involves drinking wine in Ali's house. But at the moment it is full of packing cases and black plastic bags – she's moving at the weekend.

'Isaac Templeton's great-great-grandfather was a patron of the arts, apparently,' says Ali. 'He supported artists and their models. Of course, all the artists were men and all the models were women.'

'And all the artists were middle class and all the women were working class?'

'Naturally.' This is often where Ali's conversations with Meg begin and end. As far as Ali can tell, Meg's claim to be working class rests on the fact that she went to a rather posh comprehensive in Surrey. But Ali isn't going to argue. For her part, she can't see what's wrong with being middle class. For most of her life, she has aspired to be middle class. Ali and Meg met at Queen Mary's which, for Meg, cements her proletarian claims and, for Ali, represents a considerable step upwards. Everything's relative.

'Anyway,' says Ali, squinting at her reflection in the kettle since all the mirrors are packed, 'it starts with an artist's model called Ettie Moran. She was killed in a building used by artists and owned by Cain Templeton, Isaac's great-great-grandfather.'

'Cain? Talk about nominative determinism.'

'Oh yes. Cain and Abel. The first murderer. I think it's quite a cool name though.'

'You just like single-syllable names.' Meg's children are called Sebastian and Arabella. Come to think of it, she *is* middle class.

'To go on with the story,' says Ali. She often has to do this with Meg. Their conversations have so many diversions that Ali is sometimes tempted to present an agenda. Meg, who teaches English at a secondary school, might appreciate this.

'People suspected Cain but he was an influential man, so it seems that no one actually accused him. But there were rumours that he was part of a club, a really gruesome group called The Collectors, and that, to be a member, you had to kill a woman.'

'Jesus. How do you know all this stuff?'

'Isaac's been researching his great-great-grandfather. Not much has been written about him but I think there are references in some art books. I don't know where the stuff about The Collectors comes from but I looked online and I found something called the Templeton Collection, which is kept – guess where?'

'The British Museum?'

'No, the People's Palace at Queen Mary, University of London.'

'QMUL? That's a bit of a coincidence.'

Jones has a theory about coincidence and déjà vu being proof that time travel is possible, but Ali doesn't think that it's the time to share this. Ali would love to tell Meg about the unit's true purpose, but she knows that her friend would never believe her or, if she did, keep the news to herself. Besides, Ali has signed the Official Secrets Act.

'Quite a few Victorian philanthropists left things to the People's Palace,' says Ali. 'Including Wilkie Collins. Although his library somehow got lost in transit.'

'Was Cain Templeton a philanthropist?'

'According to Isaac he was. He supported the arts and let impoverished artists live in his house rent-free.'

'And killed women?'

'He was never charged,' says Ali.

'Of course not,' says Meg. 'He was rich. Did they even have a police force then?'

'The Metropolitan Police was founded in 1829,' says Ali. 'I remember going to a talk about it when I first joined up. They were called Peelers after Sir Robert Peel who was home secretary and they mainly dealt with petty crime. The detective branch wasn't formed until 1842. They were working-class men, labourers mostly. There was no formal training.'

'And no women detectives.'

'Of course not,' says Ali. 'It's no job for a lady.' They grin at each other. It's an old joke, a line once uttered by a professor in reference to bar work and now used by them as shorthand for all the many injustices that make up the patriarchy.

'I bet those detectives still didn't investigate rich, powerful men,' says Meg.

'I'm sure you're right. At any rate, no one seems to have investigated Cain Templeton but, according to Isaac, there started to be rumours about him, about other women who mysteriously vanished in his vicinity.'

'Why are you involved?' says Meg. 'I mean, I know you deal with cold cases, but this is ancient history.'

'It's because of Isaac Templeton,' says Ali. 'He wants to clear his ancestor's name. And it seems that he's got enough influence to recruit a lowly detective sergeant.'

'He must be very charming,' says Meg, draining her glass and standing up. 'Just don't marry him.'

'He's married,' says Ali. 'And I'm really trying to get out of the habit of marrying every man I go to bed with.'

Chapter 3

When Ali arrives at the unit the next morning, there's an excitement in the air, a faint electric hum that means Jones is in the building. Dina jerks her head towards Geoff's closed door.

'The doctor is *in*.'

John is at his desk, writing notes in his italic handwriting which is both beautiful and illegible. He's a tall man with greying dark hair and a face that looks slightly battered by life and a youthful rugby career. He looks up as Ali hangs her coat on the rack.

'I hear that something exciting might be happening.'

'What have you heard?' Ali sits on the edge of Bud's desk and a voice from the coffee room says, 'Get your ass off my iPad.'

'Ass?' says Ali. 'You're sounding more American by the day, Bud.' But she shifts slightly.

'I heard that the gate might be very wide open.'

Ali looks at Dina.

'OK. I told him,' says Dina. 'It was too good not to share.'

'Is it even possible?' says John. 'To go back so far?'

'I guess that's why Jones is here,' says Ali.

Bud appears, carrying his *Dr Who* mug (David Tennant era). 'What's everyone talking about? Why am I always left out?' Bud is twenty-eight, the baby of the group, but sometimes sounds even younger. He's tall and skinny with a penchant for T-shirts with slogans like 'I'm with stupid' or 'I'd rather be reading'. Jones says he's a brilliant physicist but that doesn't stop the others sometimes treating him as if he needs subtitles.

'Geoff wants me to go back to the 1850s,' says Ali.

'Cool,' says Bud. 'What was happening in the 1850s?' Bud sometimes likes to pretend that he's never heard of history.

'Crinolines, horse-drawn carriages, men in beards,' says Ali.

'Sounds like Hoxton,' says Dina. 'Will you have to dress up, Ali?'

Dina has an unfortunate addiction to fancy dress parties. Over the years, Ali has been forced to impersonate a nun, a pirate and Servalan from *Blake's 7*. Dina has recently broken up with her boyfriend Liam, which was a relief to most of her friends but has curtailed her party spirit. Despite her personal preference for remaining in her own clothes, Ali hopes that Dina's sociability resurfaces. She'd even welcome an invitation to 'Dress as your fantasy' or 'Come as your star sign'. At least she's Leo, clearly the best of the bunch.

'Maybe,' says Ali. 'I don't know if I'll be visible, but I suppose we shouldn't take any chances.'

'You know the rules,' says John. The team's protocol, what Geoff grandly calls their 'Charter', is pinned on the wall in the kitchen.

1. *Watch*
2. *Bear Witness*
3. *Don't Interact*
4. *Stay Safe*

'Does Jones think you'll be visible?' asks Dina.

'I don't think she knows. We almost were in 1976, remember?' says Ali.

'We weren't able to interact though. I hope I'll be able to chat to people in 1966. As long as it's not all about football.'

'What's football got to do with 1966?' asks Bud.

'They think it's all over,' says John. 'It is now.'

Dina is currently working on a cold case involving suspected victims of a serial killer who died last year, aged ninety. It's thought that his murderous career, which involved vulnerable young men whom he befriended and housed in the many flats that he owned, began in 1966. If Dina sees Ross Canterbury being abducted by Sir Martin Grantly (the knighthood was taken away when he was convicted) then she will, at least, have some answers for his mother, herself in her nineties.

'Jones is perfecting the process,' says Ali. 'Apparently.'

'What does that even mean?' says Dina.

'It's to do with the particles,' says Bud vaguely.

'You'll have to dye your hair,' says John.

Ali pulls a strand of Ferrari-red hair in front of her face. 'Never,' she says.

'You'll have to dye your hair,' says Jones. 'Or wear a wig.'

'Typical,' says Ali. 'The first thing we're talking about is hair.'

'That's the patriarchy for you,' says Jones.

Jones's hair is jet black and cut so short that it's almost a skull cap. When Ali first met her, Jones had black curls tumbling down her back. She's beautiful enough to make the crew cut glamorous but there's no doubt that she looks more serious now. Jones is tall and slim with large brown eyes that can look meltingly sympathetic. Ali has learnt not to be fooled.

'You'll have to lose the nose piercing too,' says Jones.

Ali touches her diamond stud. This will be a wrench. She has had this particular piercing since she was fourteen, her first act of teenage rebellion. She'd been sent home from school with a letter for her parents. Ali's mum Cheryl had replied that Ali's nose was her own business. Ali had been proud of her for that.

'Will they be able to see me?' she says.

'I hope so,' says Jones. 'I understand you were more visible in 1976 than before.'

Steven Mulholland had seen them; Ali is sure of it. He had stopped, in the process of washing his Lady Macbeth hands, and stared wildly at the shrubbery. She hopes that the two shadowy figures reminded him of divine retribution. She hopes they haunted him until the end of his days.

'How much more difficult is it to travel so far back in time?' asks Geoff.

'It's just making a loop,' says Jones, as she has done many times before. She picks up her leather jacket from the back of Geoff's chair and holds the material taut between both hands. 'If a small insect wants to go from here to here' – she nods her head to the left, then right – 'what a tedious journey! But if you do this' – she brings her hands together – 'it happens in an instant.'

'I know,' says Ali. 'We square the square and enter the fifth dimension. All I want to know is, will I be safe?'

'When have I ever failed you?'

'The very first time.' That had been during the lockdown trip. Ali and John were so elated to find themselves in a world where life was going on as usual, they moved too quickly. They left the side street where they had materialised and drifted along Oxford Street. On this first trip they had been little more than wraiths, their reflections hadn't shown in the windows of any shops and they were able to move unseen through the bustling pre-Covid crowds. Occasionally they'd see someone shiver or look round, as if a shadow had passed over them, but to all intents and purposes they had been invisible. They could see each other, though, and exchanged delighted glances as they checked the date on newspaper stands and watched the billboards warning of the new killer virus. They had half an hour, Jones had told them, but their phones had stopped working. The blank screen was a surprise and strangely terrifying. But they checked clocks outside department stores and were back in good time. The problem was that they couldn't find the ingress point, as Jones called it. They hadn't realised that they had to be standing in the exact same spot, the position of their feet correct to the millimetre, in order to return. Several anxious minutes were spent moving from paving stone to paving stone, trying to recreate the exact place and precise stance. Now they always mark the spot by spraying special paint – visible only in UV light – around their feet.

'We were all learning then,' says Jones. 'You're a pro now.'

'If you say so,' says Ali. 'But do you really think that you can take me back all that way? To 1850, wasn't it?'

'Time is relative.'

'So you keep saying.'

Jones ignores this. 'I'll need a few weeks to prepare. And I imagine you'll want to do some research too, Ali.'

'I've got an appointment at Queen Mary's this afternoon. It's where I was at uni,' Ali explains to Jones. 'I'm still in touch with my old history tutor. I thought she could tell me about the nineteenth century. Plus, the Templeton Collection is kept there.'

'The Templeton Collection?' says Geoff.

'Apparently Cain Templeton collected historical artefacts as well as women. He donated them all to the People's Palace.'

'The People's Palace,' says Jones. 'I like the sound of that.' She's a communist, albeit one that likes designer clothes.

'It's pretty cool,' says Ali. 'It was built in 1887 to provide East Enders with their own library. Apparently, it also employed the first female librarians. Some of the original building burnt down in 1931 but there's a new People's Palace next door. Art deco.' It was where Ali graduated. She remembers standing with Finn and her parents, feeling ridiculous in her cap and gown but also giddy with the achievement of being the first member of her family to gain a degree. Even her brother, Richard, had been there.

'Is it worth all this trouble?' says Geoff. 'For a crime that happened nearly two hundred years ago?'

Ali looks at him in surprise. 'It was your idea.'

'Well, strictly speaking, it was Isaac Templeton's idea,' says Geoff.

'It's important to keep the government onside,' says Jones. 'They fund us, after all. And it's an exciting challenge. To go back so far.'

'It's not my job to please the government,' says Geoff. Although it is, really. 'The welfare of my staff must be my priority. I wish you didn't have to go alone, Ali.'

'Me too,' says Ali.

'I think it will be too difficult to send two people so far,' says Jones.

'I still can't understand why Isaac Templeton asked for me personally,' says Ali.

'You're quite famous in government circles,' says Geoff.

Ali didn't know this; it must be the hair.

'I think it's just because you're a white middle-aged woman,' says Jones. 'You won't stand out so much.'

'*Grazie*,' says Ali. She's learning Italian on Duolingo but it's hard to be sarcastic in another language.

Chapter 4

Ali loves going back to Queen Mary's. She can never get over the fact that you can turn from a busy London street, pass through a gateway and find yourself in the centre of a campus university. The mixture of old and new buildings includes halls of residence, lecture theatres, shops, cafés and a launderette, bisected by the Regent's Canal. Students are wandering across Library Square, carrying laptops and take-away coffees. They are a vibrant and inspiring sight, the diversity of QMUL is one of Ali's favourite things about it. Clement Attlee, whose statue stands outside the cafeteria, would surely have approved.

Ali gives old Clem a nod as she passes. She also takes a detour to look at the Jewish cemetery. This square of ground, surrounded by modern buildings, was fascinating to Ali as a history student and more interesting than ever now that she's a time traveller. The Novo Cemetery, which dates back to the 1700s, was once the final resting place for London's Portuguese and Spanish Sephardic Jews. Ali is not sure how Queen Mary's acquired the site but she knows it was a controversial decision. The human remains were moved elsewhere but reburial was said to contravene Jewish law and a proposed new memorial never materialised. The university apparently committed to the upkeep of the flat tombstones but, today, they look some-what sad, surrounded by weeds and wind-blown rubbish. Even so, Ali thinks that the graveyard symbolises the many different people who found a home in the East End of London. It was a Dutchman who drained the marshes so that houses could be built this side of the Thames; it was French Huguenots who brought the skills to start the local silk-weaving industry. The people once buried in this patch of ground, surrounded by student accommodation blocks, would have been fleeing from the Inquisition. Even here, they would have to practise their religion in secret. It wasn't until 1656 that the first synagogue was built within the City of London.

Once, returning from Drapers, the student nightclub, in the early hours, Ali had seen a shadowy figure crossing the graveyard with a peculiar dancing gait. She'd put it down to her first experience of hash brownies but, later, someone had suggested that the figure was the ghost of Daniel Mendoza, the boxing champion of the 1790s, commemorated by a bronze plaque on the wall of the library. His bones no longer lie in the Novo Cemetery, but Ali likes to think that she glimpsed his shadow-boxing spirit.

Ali makes her way past the graves towards the Queen's Building, the elegant classical edifice that once housed the People's Palace. It's where students gather on graduation day, having their pictures taken on the steps or posing on the lawn with the giant letters QMUL. Once again, Ali remembers that day. Since then she's attended two graduation ceremonies for Finn, for his bachelor's and master's degrees, and marvelled at the casual attitudes of some parents. 'We've got two graduations this week,' she overheard one mother saying. 'Bit of a bore really.' These people had always expected their offspring to move smoothly from GCSE to A levels to university. But Ali had left school at eighteen with indifferent A levels. By nineteen she was married to Declan, pregnant and working in a shop. She will never take it for granted, even for Finn, who'd been lucky enough to ride that smooth escalator upwards.

And now Ali is returning as a successful alumna on police business. She walks up the steps and into the lobby where, hovering between mock-classical pillars, Ed Crane, the museum's curator, is waiting for her.

'Alison, good to see you.'

'Ali, please.'

Ali remembers Ed. He's a tall man with receding hair and a slightly anxious look, as if he's afraid of doorways. Ed gallantly pretends that he recognises Ali too, but she doesn't think he does. She didn't have red hair when she was at QMUL, was simply another mature student, diligent and self-conscious, carrying her books in a Lidl carrier bag. She'd caught Hugo's eye but only because he was a predator. Hugo had annoyed her on graduation day by taking all the credit for Ali's first. 'We got there in the end,' he said to Ali's mum. But Ali knew that it had been despite, not because.

'Thank you for seeing me,' Ali says to Ed. 'As I explained on the phone, I work for the police now.'

'It's not what I would have expected,' says Ed, which seems a rather odd remark.

'I work on cold cases,' Ali continues, 'and I'm researching the Templeton family. I understand Cain Templeton left his archaeology collection to the People's Palace.'

'He did,' says Ed. 'It's upstairs, in the attics. You don't mind the stairs, do you? The lift's broken.'

'I prefer stairs,' says Ali.

These are worse, though, than the three flights to the Department of Logistics, twisty and uneven, lit only by sporadically placed light bulbs that flicker in an unhealthy way. Ali is very aware of Ed behind her, treading lightly for such a tall man. She wishes she could have gone at the back. At least then she could stop to catch her breath occasionally. Eventually, they reach a door marked 'Private' and Ed moves past her to unlock it.

'We used to have the collection on public display,' he says, 'but there are some sensitivities . . .'

'Really?' Ali's ears twitch. 'What sort of sensitivities?'

The room is in darkness but there's a faint glimmer here and there, greenish like phosphorescence. Ali thinks it's coming from the glass cases that line the room. She takes a few steps, aware that her breath is still uneven. The lights come on and she realises that she is staring at a skull with a nail hammered into the centre of its forehead. She backs away.

'It's all looted,' says Ed, just behind her. 'Quite common in Victorian times. Rich people went to archaeological sites and just took what they fancied. That skull is Roman but there's a mummified cat from an Egyptian tomb. Several *shabtis* too, and burial goods. It's doubtful whether Cain Templeton knew the value or provenance of any of it. He was just a magpie, picking up glittery objects. I said as much to Isaac Templeton.'

'Isaac Templeton came here?'

'Yes, about a year ago. You know he's a Tory MP?'

'I'd heard.'

'He was just after publicity. He wanted us to put the objects on display again. You can imagine the headlines. "Public treasures restored after being hidden away by woke museum staff." Of course, I had to say no.'

It sounds as if Ed very much enjoyed saying no. Ali thinks he's probably right in his assessment of Isaac. According to Finn, Isaac likes to portray himself as a simple fellow, chivalrous in the old-fashioned mould, bemused by so-called 'cancel culture'. This despite trying hard to cancel most of his political opponents.

Ali walks slowly through the room. It's a long, low attic with peeling paintwork and creaking floorboards. The glass cabinets are thick with dust. It's hard to believe that the public was ever allowed up here. The overhead fluorescent lighting flickers like the bulbs on the stairs. Ali stops to look at a case containing a necklace made of dark stones, each bead shaped like a small tooth.

'Bronze Age,' says Ed. 'From the Isle of Man, I believe, although the jet is from Whitby. Found in a burial mound.'

The jewellery has a baleful gleam. Was it a funeral decoration? An ornament for a sacrificial victim?

'Can you return any of this?' she says. 'Send it back to Egypt and Greece or the Isle of Man or wherever?'

'We've tried,' says Ed. 'On their own, none of the objects are that valuable or worth the trouble. As a collection, though, it's quite a curiosity. Have a look at this.'

He shines his phone torch into a dark corner of the room. It illuminates a vat of golden liquid with a sponge-like object suspended in it.

'Murderer's brain,' says Ed. 'Preserved in formaldehyde.'

'Murderer's brain?'

'The Victorians thought you could tell a murderer by the shape of his or her brain. No idea where Cain Templeton picked up this particular example.'

'I can see why you wouldn't put this on display,' says Ali.

'Exactly,' says Ed. 'And then there's the curse.'

Ali looks at the mummified cat, whose painted eyes look back at her. Of *course* there's a curse.

'The whole collection is rumoured to be cursed,' says Ed. 'I don't know what form it takes but it probably can be summed up as: if anything happens to the exhibits – the person responsible will die.'

'Who's that?' says Ali.

'Almost certainly the curator,' says Ed.

Ali takes photographs of all the objects though she can't see how they will help with the case. They do tell her something about Cain Templeton though. He was a collector through and through. On the way back down the twisty stairs, she asks Ed if he's ever heard of The Collectors.

'It was a club for men who collected women. The rumour was that you had to kill a woman to be elected.'

'Bloody hell,' says Ed. 'And Templeton was a member of this club?'

'Allegedly.'

In the lobby, Ed looks at her curiously. 'You're investigating this? From all that time ago?'

'In a way.'

They shake hands and Ed says, 'I really do remember you. I wasn't just saying that. You used to feed the stray cats in the cemetery. You had a Lidl carrier bag.'

Ali doesn't know whether to be pleased or slightly unsettled.

★

Ali's next visit is to Elizabeth Henderson, lecturer in nineteenth-century history. Elizabeth was Ali's personal tutor and, once Ali got over her fear of tutorials, essays and university in general, was one of the best things about QMUL. They've kept in touch since Ali graduated in 2005, mostly through email. What with lockdown and life in general, it's been almost five years since they've seen each other in person. Ali's first thought is that Elizabeth hasn't changed. Her hair was grey when Ali first met her and it's still in the same uncompromising bowl cut. Ali assumes that Elizabeth is in her sixties but she could be much younger or much older.

They sit in chairs by the window. Familiar campus sounds drift past: jazz from the music rooms, laughter and the quack of ducks from the canal. Elizabeth makes them both coffee from her special machine and asks, 'So what's this sudden interest in the nineteenth century?'

'I've always been interested in it,' says Ali, slightly stung. 'My thesis was on the women's suffrage movement. You should know, you were my tutor.'

'And very good it was too,' says Elizabeth. 'But you're a police officer these days, not a history student.'

'I work on cold cases,' says Ali, echoing what she told Ed Crane, 'and I'm researching something that happened in 1850.'

'Whatever for?' says Elizabeth.

'You're the one who says the past helps us understand the present.'

Elizabeth just stares at her. Ali remembers that she always knew when a student was bluffing.

'I just thought,' says Ali at last, 'that if I understood the nine-teenth century more, I'd understand this case better.' It's almost the truth.

'What, exactly, do you want to understand?'

'If I could time travel,' says Ali, 'how would I fit in to society? What would I do? What would I wear?'

Elizabeth leans back in her chair. She always sits very firmly, legs apart, and now it almost looks as if she's trying to anchor herself to earth.

'It's not a question of what you wear,' she says at last. 'The problem is up here.' Elizabeth taps her smooth grey bob. 'In your head. You, Ali, are a very modern woman. You can't just become Victorian by wearing a big skirt. You have to believe in God, in England, in the Royal Family. You have to believe that the shape of your head determines your character and that wearing divided skirts makes you a lesbian. You have to believe that the dead can talk and that men are superior. You have to be able to make a posset, sew a seam and recite the Lord's Prayer. Can you do any of those things?'

'Our Father, which art in Heaven . . .' begins Ali, but she can't get any further. Declan, a lapsed Catholic, would have managed it, even adding a pious sign of the cross at the end.

'Exactly,' says Elizabeth. 'You're an atheist, feminist, socialist. They'd burn you at the stake.'

'Isn't that more of a seventeen hundreds thing?'

'They still believed in witches, trust me.'

'People still believe in them today. I've been married three times. All my ex-husbands think I'm a witch.'

'I'm sure that's not true. Well, Hugo perhaps.'

Hugo had been Elizabeth's colleague in the history department. His affair with Ali didn't break any official rules – they declared it so that Hugo wouldn't get to mark any of Ali's papers – but it wasn't exactly a popular move. Hugo and Ali got married straight after she graduated and Hugo found another job.

'There were Victorian feminists,' says Ali. 'I know about this. Barbara Bodichon, Bessie Rayner Parkes. Mary Wollstonecraft was even earlier. When was *A Vindication of the Rights of Woman* published? Seventeen nineties?'

'Seventeen ninety-two,' says Elizabeth. 'It's good that you remember something from my course. Mary Wollstonecraft was born near here, actually. In Spitalfields. But that's just my point, they were *Victorian* feminists, or pre-Victorian. You're the modern kind. It's very different.'

'Will you teach me all these things?' says Ali. 'All the things that make you a Victorian? You're a brilliant teacher. You can manage it.'

'Well, to start with,' says Elizabeth. 'They were all mad.'

Chapter 5

'Where do you want this, Mum?'

Finn stands in the hallway carrying a large vase that looks as if it could once have held the ashes of a favourite elephant. Ali can't think where it comes from or why she has it.

'Oh, just leave it there.'

'There are already two chairs and a broken exercise bike here. It looks like the overflow from a junk shop.'

'In my bedroom then. Thanks, love.'

Ali's new house is a two-up, two-down in Bow. The downstairs is all one room, open-plan kitchen and sitting room with French doors onto a small back garden. There's also a tiny loo that was probably once outside. Upstairs there are two bedrooms and a bathroom in dire need of modernisation. It's like a child's drawing of a house but Ali bought it because it has stained glass in the front door, original sash windows and an apple tree in the garden. The front is concreted over and Ali sees Finn eyeing it disapprovingly. At least there isn't fake grass, one of the many things he feels passionately about. Ali assumes that the paved area is for a car but that's no use to her because she doesn't have one.

The removal men have completed their work, taking with them a large tip and a bag of mini Snickers. Now it's just Ali and Finn trying to make sense of her possessions, which seem mysteriously to have doubled. Finn has brought Ali's cat, Terry, a perpetually angry Siamese, who is now sitting on top of her kitchen cabinet, vibrating with resentment.

Despite the long day and the backache which is beginning to make itself felt, Ali loves spending time with Finn, especially when they are both involved in practical tasks which show them at their best. If they have too much leisure time, over a meal or a day out, they start bickering about politics or Ali asks one too many personal questions. She knows that Finn has split up with his girlfriend Cosima but she has virtuously refrained from asking too many details. Ali liked Cosima but avoided getting too close because she knew that this day might come. Finn met Cosima at work and they were together for four years. Ali doesn't know why they broke up, but Finn is now living alone in the Pimlico flat. 'He's fine,' Declan said when Ali raised the subject, 'don't worry.' Ali hates her ex-husband telling her not to worry. For years, worrying was her *job* while he was swanning around trying different jobs before eventually becoming a website designer. But, all the same, he's probably right.

'Shall I put the exercise bike in the pile for the dump?' says Finn, swinging on the door frame in a way that used to infuriate Ali but which she now finds rather endearing.

'Or put it outside and leave a note on it saying "free to collector",' says Ali.

'Yeah, they'll be queuing round the block.'

'It only wants a few screws or something,' says Ali.

'Did you ever use it?' Finn smiles rather patronisingly. Recently, to Ali's surprise and slight discomfiture, he's become very keen on fitness. He goes to the gym three times a week and cycles around London in alarming Lycra clothes. Finn is tall and slim, like Declan. He never seemed unfit but now he looks almost dangerously lean. Wasn't there a Shakespearean character who had a 'lean and hungry look'? Ali will have to ask Meg. For some reason, she blames Isaac Templeton for the bike.

'Of course I used it,' says Ali. 'Where else would I hang my clothes that are too clean to be washed and too dirty to go in the wardrobe?'

Finn laughs and heaves the bike outside. Then he puts the spare chairs in the kitchen and opens the back doors. It's been one of those balmy days that you sometimes get in January, full of the promise of spring, but now it's almost dark and the air is cold. A security light comes on and illuminates the skeletal tree. Ali jumps as Terry weaves around her feet. She picks him up.

'I don't want him to go out yet.'

'He'll be king of the neighbourhood before long,' says Finn. 'The godfather. The don.'

'He'll enjoy having a garden,' says Ali. Although, to be honest, the space doesn't look much fun at the moment. The grass is threadbare and the flower beds are empty. But the previous owners have left a rusty wrought-iron table and it's not too much of a leap to imagine sitting out here with a glass of chilled wine.

'It'll be lovely in the spring,' she says. Since working with Jones, she no longer takes the future for granted.

'You can have parties here,' says Finn. Ali smiles at the thought, although even her colleagues on their own would make the place look crowded.

'Shall I order us a takeaway?' she says.

There had been a selection of flyers on the doormat and, at random, Ali and Finn choose 'Taj Mahal, Indian cuisine to your door'. The food takes its time to make the journey – Ali reckons she could have reached the 1970s quicker – but, when it arrives, it's delicious. By this time, Ali and Finn have drunk most of a bottle of red wine and, perhaps due to its effects, the house is looking quite homely. There are three vases of flowers in the empty fireplace, sent by the unit (tasteful, so probably chosen by Dina), Ali's parents and Meg. Ali has lit the lamps and, in the kitchen, the downlights make the grey cabinets look quite stylish. Ali's precious collection of mismatched glasses and china is displayed in an open unit.

Ali and Finn eat at her new kitchen table, just big enough for two. Terry puts up a stealthy black paw and snares an onion bhaji.

'You won't like that.' Ali takes it away from him.

'Want a bet?' says Finn.

Terry starts to patrol the kitchen in stalking pose.

'Do you think there are mice?' Ali asks.

'Probably,' says Finn, tearing off a piece of naan. 'There are mice everywhere in London. Rats too.'

'Great. Now I'll sleep easily at night.'

'Do you want me to stay?' asks Finn.

'No, love,' says Ali, touched. 'I'll be fine. And aren't you working tomorrow?'

'Yes,' says Finn. 'Isaac's having an awayday. Just an excuse to show off his country estate.'

'Where is it?' asks Ali.

'East Dean in Sussex.'

'Sounds like a Victorian melodrama.'

'Piers says it's a bit like that. A big Gothic mansion on the cliffs. Near Beachy Head. Apparently, it's a popular spot for suicides.'

'Fun,' says Ali lightly, although the word always chills her to the bone. She knows the statistics about young men and suicide.

'How are you getting there?' she asks.

'I'm driving down with Chibu and Piers.'

These, Ali knows, are Finn's fellow special advisors, both Oxbridge and posh although Ali imagines that Isaac thinks Chibu's Nigerian heritage gains him some extra points somewhere.

'What's the awayday about?'

'Supposedly immigration but, really, it's the same as every meeting. How quickly can Isaac become PM?'

Ali thinks of Isaac Templeton, padding barefoot around his glittering apartment. *I need to explain to you about my great-great-grandfather.* Part of her wishes that she could tell Finn about the meeting although she thinks he might not like the thought of her visiting Isaac at his home, drinking coffee prepared by him.

But Finn says, tipping more jalfrezi onto his plate, 'Isaac mentioned you the other day.'

'Did he?' Ali fills their wine glasses whilst telling herself to be careful.

'Yes. He remembered meeting you at that reception. He was asking about your job. I said you were a police officer and he asked if I ever worried about you being in danger. I said that you were only working on cold cases.'

'So cold they're frozen.' Ali finishes the line. She's slightly jolted by Isaac thinking that she might be in danger. 'You can tell Isaac that danger and me don't mix.'

'He also said he liked your red hair,' says Finn, in the expressionless tone that means he's uneasy. Finn got on fairly well with Hugo, who became his stepfather when he was fourteen. Declan had married again by then and presented Finn with two half-sisters. Finn had shuttled quite happily between his two families, with a stoic good humour that had made Ali want to weep. But he had openly disapproved when Ali divorced Hugo and married Lincoln. Ali's third marriage had coincided with Finn going to university and had been the most strained year in their relationship. Finn can't suspect Ali of wanting to marry Isaac, who is years younger and has a fragrant wife of his own, but he doesn't like men being interested in her. Oedipus, phone home.

'I'm thinking of changing my hair,' says Ali.

Chapter 6

'Are you sure?' says Kelly.

'It's my boss,' says Ali. 'He suddenly says it isn't suitable.'

'What a shame.' Kelly picks up a fiery strand of Ali's hair. 'It really suits you. What's your boss's hair like?'

'He's bald.'

'Typical. Well, red's the most difficult colour to change. We'll have to use a neutralising shampoo. That'll restore the natural pH balance and get rid of some of the dye. Then we can put an ash brown over the top.'

'Won't it be my natural colour?'

'I think your natural colour is too light. The red will show through. This will look natural, if that's what you're after.'

Is that what she's after? Ali looks gloomily at her reflection in the mirror at the hair salon. In her opinion, natural is overrated. Natural family planning doesn't work. Natural mineral water is boring. When she first dyed her hair, she felt invincible. This woman doesn't care what you think, said the almost fluorescent locks.

People smiled at Ali in the street, stallholders in Hackney Market recognised her. 'It's Ginger Rogers,' said an admittedly drunk man on the night bus. Now she'll be just another brown-haired woman trying not to let the grey show through.

One of the juniors leads Ali to the sink where she tilts her head backwards and feels the water trickle down.

'Is this temperature OK?'

It's slightly too hot but Ali doesn't have the heart to say. She's been coming to this salon for ten years. Before that, she used to cut her hair herself. When she was nineteen, she'd gone platinum blonde. It's there in the wedding photos. Ali in a red dress and Doc Martens outside Hastings Register Office. Declan in jeans and a leather jacket. Both sets of parents had wanted them to get married in a church but both had been relieved that the deed was done before Finn was born. He's there in the photos too, a slight swelling beneath the red lace. Ali shuts her eyes and lets the junior massage her scalp. It hurts a bit but, once again, Ali doesn't say anything.

Two hours later she emerges into the street with brown hair that comes to just below her shoulder blades. Kelly wanted to cut it shorter and add some layers but Ali suspects that she will have to wear her hair up so it's better to have some length. Ali doesn't recognise her face in shop windows. She looks dowdy, she thinks, the straight strands make her face look thin and pale. When she buys a *Big Issue*, the seller doesn't make his usual comment about redheads having more fun. Ali sighs and takes refuge in Dunkin' Donuts.

'You look great,' says Dina.

'Where's Ali?' says John.

'Ooh, doughnuts,' says Bud.

Geoff hears the D-word and appears in the doorway. Bobby was always making him go on diets but, now that he's a widower, there are often tell-tale crumbs on his shirt. Ali found a Crunchie wrapper in his office once and Geoff said, unconvincingly, that he'd found it on the street.

'Have a doughnut?' Ali offers the jam-stained cardboard box.

'The hair's good,' says Geoff. 'Very nineteenth-century.'

'Just the look I was going for,' says Ali.

'It makes you look younger,' says John. That must be something his wife taught him to say.

'Oh, I was going to say it makes her look older,' says Bud, surprised.

'How's the research going?' Geoff asks Ali.

'I'm going to the London College of Fashion this afternoon,' she replies, 'to be fitted for my clothes.'

'I can't imagine you in a big skirt,' says Bud. 'What are they called? Crinolines?'

'I'd love to dress up as a Victorian,' says Dina. 'What did you tell them? Why do they think you need the clothes?'

'One of the lecturers is a friend of my old lecturer, Elizabeth,' says Ali. 'I told her that I needed the clothes to help me research a case. She was a bit sceptical but she put me in touch with this Dulcie. She does a lot of dressmaking for films so maybe she won't think it's that strange.'

John has been listening to this with a deepening frown. He turns to Geoff.

'Is Jones really sure about taking Ali back to the 1850s?' John has been asking the same question ever since the trip was first mentioned. He is a great worrier, which is one reason why he left CID after a stellar career as a murder detective. That and the alcoholism and subsequent breakdown. John credits the unit with helping him to rebuild his life. They come second only to his wife and adult children as objects of his fierce devotion.

'She's confident it will work,' says Geoff, sounding as if this confidence is not contagious.

'We travel in time every day,' Dina launches into her Jones impersonation, 'it's just that we go forwards not backwards.'

'Is like going upstairs.' This is Bud's contribution. He overdoes Jones's Italian accent, which, these days, is really only audible on some vowel sounds.

'She doesn't know though,' says John. 'No one has done this before. Ali shouldn't go alone. I should go with her. Like I did the first time.'

'Jones says that's too complicated,' says Geoff. 'She says that she has to cut a hole in the space-time continuum and, the further back you go, the harder it is.'

'If it's so difficult, we shouldn't be doing it,' says John, who can be stubborn when he wants to be.

'I'll be OK,' says Ali, wondering, as she does so, why she is so sure of this. 'Jones says I'll fit in just fine, being old and white and all that.'

'Yeah, can't say I'm looking forward to nineteen-sixties racism,' says Dina. 'It'll be like going on Twitter.'

'When are you going through the gate?' asks Ali.

'It was meant to be next week but it's been put off for you,' says Dina, which makes Ali feel rather guilty.

'Why is this mission getting priority?' John asks Geoff. 'Is it just because a government minister is involved?'

'Not at all,' says Geoff. But he undermines this slightly by saying, 'But Isaac Templeton is an important man.'

'He's an awful man,' says John. 'Have you heard his views on prisons? Close the gates. All that stuff.'

'Finn works for him,' Ali reminds him. She has always tried not to indoctrinate Finn with her left-wing views but it's still a bit of a shock to find him working for the government. Finn says that this doesn't make him a Tory but, given that he spends his working life trying to advance the career of a Conservative minister, this argument seems specious, to say the least. The 'gates' remark rattles her a bit. *We call it going through the gate.*

John doesn't reply to this. He's the member of the team who best understands Ali's feelings for her only child. He has two beloved daughters of his own.

'We all know the risks,' says Geoff. 'But we can minimise them as much as we are able.' He looks worried, though, and takes an extra doughnut back into his office.

'You're bigger than most Victorian women,' says Dulcie at the London College of Fashion.

'Gee thanks,' says Ali. 'That's all I need today.'

'No, really,' Dulcie says earnestly. 'Humans are getting taller and heavier. Mostly due to better nutrition.'

Ali banishes the image in her head of a corpulent, jolly Victorian, taken, she realises, from the pages of Dickens. She remembers Elizabeth telling her, 'Whatever you do, don't trust Dickens.'

Dulcie continues, whilst measuring Ali's waist, 'Women were, on average, two inches shorter in the nineteenth century. Queen Victoria was four foot ten.'

Ali is five foot six and a size fourteen. She's not sure what she weighs but, possibly until this very second, had been quite satisfied with her dimensions.

'Hands and feet were smaller and narrower then too,' says Dulcie. 'What size shoe are you?'

'Six.'

'Average for women in 1850 was our equivalent of a four. We'll have to get your boots specially made.'

Dulcie seems to be taking the assignment very seriously. Maybe she thinks that Ali is going on a TV programme of the freak-show type: *Huge Woman with Giant Feet*.

Dulcie has provided Ali with a tube-like garment, floor-length with capped sleeves. Next she pins a white cotton petticoat round her waist. Ali finds it rather weird to have a stranger standing so close to her, although Dulcie's manner is professional and detached, almost like a doctor.

'You'll need a corset,' says Dulcie.

'Do I have to wear one?'

'The silhouette will be all wrong if you don't,' says Dulcie. 'Victorians thought that corsets were healthy. It was believed that women's delicate internal organs needed support.'

'Believed by men, I bet,' says Ali.

Dulcie laughs. 'Actually they're not uncomfortable to wear, more comfortable than most bras, in my opinion.'

'Do you dress up in these clothes often then?'

Dulcie is pinning a hem and doesn't answer for a moment but, when she straightens up, she says, with a slight blush, that she belongs to a Victorian re-enactment society.

'We go for the whole crinoline thing, but you said 1850 and the steel crinoline didn't come in until 1856.'

'Thank God.'

'Actually it's more comfortable to wear than loads of petticoats,' says Dulcie, who is beginning to add another layer of fabric, warmer and thicker this time. Flannel? 'And I love the swaying movement they create. You have to walk in quite a different way, like a dancer.'

Ali has never wanted to be a dancer, though she likes a rave as much as anyone who was a teenager in the nineties. Ballet lessons, of the type enjoyed by Poppy and Mia, Declan's daughters with his second wife, Nikki, were not on offer in 1970s Hastings.

'How many petticoats will I need?' she asks, watching with slight trepidation as Dulcie brings out a roll of material that looks like carpet underlay.

'Maybe as many as four or five,' says Dulcie. 'This one is made from linen mixed with horsehair, which will make it stand out more. Feel how springy it is.'

Ali touches the grey felty stuff. It feels abrasive, like a scouring pad.

'This fabric is called "crin au lin",' says Dulcie. 'It's where the name comes from.'

'What's next?' asks Ali.

'Corset cover and chest preserver,' says Dulcie, busily pinning.

'Blimey,' says Ali. She's beginning to feel rather trussed up. And her back is aching again. She looks at the headless figures placed around the room. Tailors' dummies, she thinks they're called. They look rather sinister, nipped in at the waist as if they, too, are wearing corsets.

'I've got a great dress for you though,' says Dulcie. 'Black silk.

Based on one Queen Victoria actually wore. I've got the original pattern. Fashion plates were becoming more common in the 1850s.'

Will Ali look like a fashion plate as she parades through the London streets? Will anyone even be able to see her? Jones thinks she will be more visible this time although Ali doesn't know how this will be achieved. Will she actually walk amongst real Victorian people, wearing a dress from a design once worn by Queen Victoria? It just doesn't seem possible.

'Clothes were becoming more colourful by the mid-century,' says Dulcie, 'but black is always a safe colour if you're . . . not a teenager. You can pretend to be a widow.'

'I often do,' says Ali.

It's five o'clock when Ali leaves the college. She's not far from Bow so she thinks she'll go straight home. There's a lot to do in the new house and she's worried that Terry, who's still not allowed out, will be feeling bored. Ali is waiting for a bus when her phone pings. It's Geoff. 'Ring me.' He never likes to text and doesn't even trust encrypted messages.

'Hi, Geoff. What's up?'

'Isaac Templeton's been on the phone. He wants you to go through the gate on Wednesday.'

'It's not up to him, though, is it? What does Jones say?'

'She says she's ready. But what about you?'

'I'm ready,' says Ali, raising her hand as the red single-decker bus edges towards her through the rush-hour traffic.

Chapter 7

'The Victorians were in crisis,' says Elizabeth. 'In 1835 a German man called David Strauss wrote a book called *The Life of Jesus*. It was actually translated into English by George Eliot in the 1840s. Strauss's main thesis was that Jesus probably existed but the gospels were written long after his death and so there was no evidence for any of the miracles, et cetera. It's hard to overemphasise the shock waves this created. The Victorians nearly lost their collective minds. You see it in all the literature of the time. If the gospels weren't gospel truth, what could they rely on? Nothing and no one.'

'Did they stop believing in God?' asks Ali. Being in Elizabeth's office makes her feel like a student again, with the freedom to ask stupid questions. This is her third session with Elizabeth. She doesn't know whether Elizabeth believes in the 1850 cold case but her ex-tutor certainly seems to enjoy telling Ali about the madness of the Victorians.

'Of course they didn't,' says Elizabeth. 'But belief in itself started to be the important thing, not evidence. Feeling rather than thinking. As Tennyson wrote in "In Memoriam . . ."' She clears her throat and assumes her quoting voice.

'If e'er when faith had fall'n asleep,
I heard a voice, "Believe no more"
And heard an ever-breaking shore
That tumbled in the Godless deep,

A warmth within the breast would melt
The freezing reason's colder part,
And like a man in wrath the heart
Stood up and answer'd, "I have felt."'

'The word "e'er" always makes me feel slightly sick,' says Ali. '"O'er" is the same.'

'You'll have to be less squeamish if you're going to be a Victorian,' says Elizabeth, glasses gleaming as the late-afternoon sunlight reflects on the windows of the building opposite. 'You'll have to launder your own sanitary napkins, you know. Best to use cold water and salt.'

'I'm past the menopause,' says Ali.

'Lucky you.' How old is Elizabeth? Ali had assumed that she was a lot older than her but maybe this isn't true. Time behaves oddly in academia. Put a gown on someone and surround them with panelled walls and books, and they immediately seem older.

'The Victorians believed in ghosts,' says Elizabeth. 'They were fascinated by mesmerism and somnambulism. They loved freak shows and stories about monkeys stealing children. Conjoined twins were displayed in fairs, as were men who supposedly looked like dogs or elephants. Have you heard of Spring-heeled Jack?'

'I don't think so.'

'He's a kind of devil figure, variously described as wearing a black cloak, having clawed hands and red eyes like hellfire.'

'I think I might have dated him.'

'Dated is such an Americanism. Although, from what you told me, if you dated him, you'd probably have married him. Anyway, there was a spate of sightings of Jack in the 1830s and '40s, mainly in London. He was said to be able to leap over carriages and houses. In some reports he's described as being ten feet tall.'

'Was high-jumping all he did?'

'No. He also attacked women. In 1837, a servant girl called Mary Stevens was walking to her parents' house in Battersea when a strange figure jumped out from a dark alley. According to Mary, he gripped her with claw-like hands and sexually assaulted her before leaping over a wall and making his escape, cackling with manic laughter. Then, in 1838, a woman called Jane Alsop answered the door of her father's house to a man claiming to be a police officer. He told her to bring a light because he'd caught Spring-heeled Jack in the lane outside. Jane went to fetch a candle and saw that the man at the door was wearing a black cloak. As soon as she handed him the candle, he threw off the cloak and revealed himself to be a devil, vomiting blue and white flames from his mouth. Jane screamed for help and her attacker fled.'

'She was lucky,' says Ali. She no longer feels like joking. She remembers Sarah Everard, another woman walking home in south London, this time in 2021. Sarah was abducted by a serving police officer and subsequently murdered. The case made Ali consider quitting the force altogether.

'There are other reports of Spring-heeled Jack attacking women.

Some of them report him wearing tight-fitting white oilskins and having metal hands.'

'Where are you getting all this stuff?'

'From the archives of the *Illustrated Police News*,' says Elizabeth. 'They're very interesting. Have you heard of the jumping ghost of Peckham?'

'You know I haven't.'

'There were several sightings in the Peckham area of a tall figure leaping out at women. Some witnesses say that he had horns and could run at superhuman speed. Like Jack, he could levitate.'

'All these people are variations of Satan, aren't they? Bogeymen, meant to frighten women into staying indoors.'

'Except that there are actual police reports of their assaults,' says Elizabeth. 'There has always been violence against women.'

There's a pause. Ali can hear a clock ticking somewhere. She remembers an estate agent once telling her that they play tapes of this sound in empty houses: 'It's like a heartbeat.'

Ali glances up at Elizabeth's bookshelves. As well as tomes on history, and modern paperbacks, there's a whole set of Charles Dickens, gold tooling on blue leather.

'Why did you tell me not to trust Dickens?' she asks.

'He makes things up,' says Elizabeth. 'Well, of course he does. He's a writer, a storyteller. You just can't trust Dickens for a view of what Victorian society was really like.' She gives Ali a sidelong glance. 'Actually, he was rather interested in time travel.'

'Was he?' This is definitely news to Ali.

'What's *A Christmas Carol* if it's not a time travel book? Dickens thought about the subject a lot. There's another short story called

The Haunted Man and the Ghost's Bargain. A strange little tale. It's about a chemist, Mr Redlaw, who's haunted by his own past. He's visited by a phantom and Redlaw begs it to tell him what would have happened if he'd made certain decisions differently.'

'A bit like the film *Sliding Doors.*'

'Dickens used a similar phrase. He called them the revolving years. The quote is something like, "They come back to me in the music, in the wind, in the dead stillness of the night, in the revolving years."'

And Ali has the strangest sensation, that she and Elizabeth are sitting still in the third-floor office while the whole of east London whirls around them like a merry-go-round.

It's getting dark as Ali leaves the campus. The lights are on in the library and the shadows are long across the Novo Cemetery. What would Elizabeth say if she knew that, tomorrow, Ali will be treading these same streets but in long skirts weighted with horse-hair? Ali hardly believes it herself but the event has its own entry in the unit's shared calendar: *2 p.m. Ali goes through the gate.*

Ali has completed almost all of her pre-assignment tasks. She has money and clothes. She also has UV spray to mark the ingress point, plus a rather more prosaic notebook and pencil. Tomorrow, Jones will collect her in her Fiat 500. Ali will leave her phone and house keys with Jones, then they will drive to Hawk Street and Ali will stand on the spot. At fourteen hundred hours exactly, Ali will disappear. It's happened before so she knows the feeling, a jolt as if she is being pulled forward by her navel, an unpleasant form of rebirth. The first time she wasn't sure if anything had happened, not until she and John had reached the end of the road and noticed they were in a pre-pandemic world. When Ali and Dina had seen the 1970s fashions around them, they looked at each other and mouthed, 'Wow.' Tomorrow, there will be no one to share the excitement. Ali will be alone in the nineteenth century.

Passing the Queens' Building, Ali is surprised to hear someone calling her name. Ed Crane is hurrying down the steps.

'Ali! What are you doing here? Have you come to see the collection again?'

'No. I just called in on my ex-tutor, Elizabeth Henderson.'

'I know Elizabeth. She pops in here quite often.'

They look at each other, somewhere between goodwill and shyness. Ed is on ground level now and Ali has to look up at him. She has a sudden urge to tell him everything; about time-travel, about Cain Templeton and his great-great-grandson, the man who'd visited the museum in search of a photo opportunity.

'Well,' says Ali at last, 'I'd better be off.'

'Yes,' says Ed. 'Take care now.'

It's the sort of thing anyone would say, thinks Ali as she walks to the Tube station, but Ed's words seem to have a special resonance today. Until the moment when Geoff told her about the unit's special project, Ali had not thought of herself as a particularly brave person. She had survived as a single mother, battling the benefits system, school secretaries and university admissions, but only because there was no alternative. The only sign of physical courage was an early enthusiasm for roller coasters. However, since the approach of the menopause, Ali has hated anything that whirls her round or disturbs her balance. She is dreading the vertigo that accompanied previous trips through the gate. Maybe she should take some seasickness pills, just in case.

Back at home, Ali makes herself risotto. Although she's only been to Italy once – Rome with Hugo – she's a fan of the food and culture. She's able to follow an Italian YouTube video, so maybe those Duolingo sessions are paying off, but she skips a few of the stock-adding stages, so her rice remains rather stodgy. Still, washed down with a glass of white wine, it's an acceptable supper. Terry watches her closely but he doesn't approve of Mediterranean food so he doesn't attempt to share. After washing up her plate and glass (she hasn't plumbed in the dishwasher yet), Ali goes upstairs to lay out her wardrobe for tomorrow.

Cotton chemise.

Knickers. Or, as Dulcie called them, 'drawers'. Knee-length bloomers that tie with ribbon at the waist. Dulcie said that the authentic Victorian garment would have been open between the legs. 'To make it easier to go to the lav.' But these have a neatly sewn gusset. Hopefully Ali will not have to visit a nineteenth-century lavatory, given that she will only be there for an hour on this trip. If it all works out, she'll go again for a longer period of time. That's the plan anyway.

Wool stockings. Apparently, these got more colourful from 1850 onwards but Ali's are conservative black. They are fastened by garters that go just above the knee and look like they will destroy her circulation for ever.

Corset, stiffened with whalebone at the front and tied at the back by a complicated pulley system. Despite Dulcie's words, it looks the opposite of comfortable. Ali thinks she might have to ask Jones to help her put it on tomorrow.

Two cotton petticoats.

One flannel petticoat.

Horsehair and linen petticoat.

Vest, camisole, chest preserver.

Black silk dress with concertina sleeves that narrow to tight bands.

Black wool shawl.

Poke bonnet.

Gloves of soft grey leather.

Fur muff. Even in her own head, Ali can't say the word without a childish giggle.

Once I've got all that on, she thinks, I'll need a lie down. How on earth did Victorian women get through the back-breaking work of their day? Well, with any luck she won't have to attempt any manual work during her brief sojourn in 1850.

Ali goes back downstairs, makes herself tea and begins the worst task: writing a letter to Finn 'just in case'.

'Darling Finn . . .' she writes. She usually calls him 'love' and thinks of 'darling' as too middle-class, but it seems right here. She stops and meets Terry's judgemental stare.

Why is Ali prepared to risk her life to prove that a Tory MP's ancestor was not a murderer? She knows that she's not doing it for Isaac. She's not even doing it to further the cause of human knowledge, something that brings a messianic gleam into Jones's eyes. She's doing it for the unit, to make Geoff proud of her and Dina say that she's an inspiration. Ali has never considered herself a people-pleaser. In fact, when she was younger, she often went out of her way to shock and offend. She succeeded so well that, by the time she took her GCSEs, her teachers had more or less given up on her. She stayed on to do A levels but was soon absorbed by her relationship with Declan. Her only ambition was to live with him and horrify both their parents. Well, she achieved that. Was this rebellion? It didn't feel like it at the time. But, deep down, Ali had always thought that she was cleverer than her exam results suggested. This was why, as a single mother working in a zero hours job, she had managed to get a first-class honours degree. And now she's embarking on an adventure from which she might never return, just so that her boss can look up from his morning doughnut and say, 'Well done, Alison.'

It's a sobering thought.

Chapter 8

Friday, 25 January 1850

The snow is the first shock. Ali had expected the cold. Elizabeth told her that there was a mini-ice age at the beginning of the nineteenth century and, even though that was over by 1850, winters would still be much colder than people today are used to. But Ali still isn't prepared for this glacial chill, the air thick with it, so that moving would be an effort even if you hadn't travelled one hundred and seventy-three years back in time. Last night, when laying out her wardrobe items, Ali had considered wearing ski socks inside her boots. As she gets older, she feels the cold more in her extremities. In the end she'd decided to remain authentic and now her feet have turned to ice in their woollen stockings.

But the snow presents another problem. Ali has to mark the ingress point with her special invisible ink. How can she see it when she is ankle-deep in slush? She looks around her. This is immediately difficult because of the poke bonnet that obscures her vision on both sides, like a horse wearing blinkers. She's glad of it though because her head is fairly warm, helped by the hair piled up in a bun. The street is quiet and the low light suggests a winter afternoon. The pavements are white but the road is grey, stained with horse shit and cut through with wheel tracks. A man in a top hat walks by on the other side of the street. The sight gives Ali a thrill of excitement. An *actual top hat*. Is she really in the world of Dickens and George Eliot? Can the man see her? He doesn't acknowledge her but his head is bowed against the wind and he's leaning heavily on a stick. Or is it just that Ali is below his notice? Her dress and jacket are respectable, Dulcie told her, but not fashionable enough to attract attention. Ali clasps her shawl more tightly around her shoulders. It's no substitute for her padded North Face anorak.

The swirling snow makes it hard to get her bearings. This, and the slight vertigo. Ali stands still, trying to control her breathing, difficult because the corset makes her chest feel like it's bound in iron bands. A horse and cart trundle past, spraying her with slush. Is this any way to treat a lady? thinks Ali. *Is* she a lady? Surreptitiously she kicks the snow away until there is a patch of stone, a paving slab that looks almost modern, beneath her feet. Ali takes out the small can from her fur muff (the only wardrobe item she likes; it keeps her gloved hands wonderfully warm) and sprays the area around her leather toes. Is this enough? 'Come back to the ingress point after an exact hour has passed,' Jones told her, 'and I'll get you home.' But is Ali's new timepiece – an unusual accessory for a woman, apparently – as accurate as Jones's iPhone 14? Ali and John had taken their phones the first time they went through the gate but, faced with the shock of time going backwards, technology had given up and both screens went blank. She will have to make sure she's back in this spot with at least five minutes to spare. Well, she can't stand here for ever. Slowly, she starts to walk forward, one hand pulling her shawl over her hat and face.

'Sorry, ma'am.' An errand boy in a peaked cap skips to avoid her. She is visible. She is in 1850 and she can see and be seen. What's more, the boy thinks she's respectable enough to be called 'ma'am'. His accent is pure cockney which reassures Ali that she's in London. She should be in Hawk Street, not far from Bethnal Green, the house owned by Cain Templeton, the place where the first of the murders occurred. Elizabeth had shown her a map of the street from the 1800s. It had looked reassuringly the same, the same curve of houses on one side of the street, although the other had gained several fast food restaurants and a block of flats. But, standing in the middle of the road, as Ali did a few minutes ago, you could imagine the Victorian skeleton. Ali looks around for a street sign – did they even have such things in 1850? – and sees a brass plaque on one of the houses. It reads 44 Hawk Street. Bravo, Jones.

Ali lifts up her skirts to climb the steps to the front door. The material is damp and heavier than she would have thought possible. Moving the four petticoats is like a workout at the gym. She should tell Finn. Except she can't.

Ali raises her hand to ply the griffin-shaped door knocker and, to her surprise, the door opens. Is this one of the almost supernatural happenings which, according to Jones, will accompany time travel? 'You'll experience a sense of knowing what to do and why,' Jones had said the first time. 'A godlike omnipotence. Think of it as advanced déjà vu. This is because everything *has* happened before.'

Ali is in a hallway, dark with panelling and smelling of beeswax and something sharper and more sinister. It's wonderful to be out of the wind but the temperature feels as cold as the street outside. A clock ticks somewhere in the background. The arrow of time, Jones would say. Ali starts to climb the stairs. She is not aware of any feeling of omnipotence. She just knows she has to go upwards. 'An attic studio in my great-great-grandfather's house,' Isaac had said. 'They say that's where it happened.'

On the first landing, Ali trips over her skirts and almost falls. 'Another one for the collection,' says a male voice. It sounds close but when Ali turns she can see only blackness. Has she gone blind? No, it's just the poke bonnet. By the time she makes a careful circle in her skirts, the stairwell is empty.

Slightly scared now, Ali continues to climb. The vertigo is getting worse and Ali remembers shooting skywards in Isaac Templeton's outdoor lift. Was it really only two and a half weeks ago? But that was a tower block and this is a Victorian town house. How many floors can it have? Ali plods upwards, occasionally finding herself walking on the bottom of her petticoats. Eventually she is standing before a door that looks different from the rest, scarred and paint-smeared with a dent in the lower panel as if someone has tried to kick it open. The smell is stronger here and, on the floor below, she can hear someone playing the piano, the scales going up and down in an uneasy chromatic rhythm.

Ali tries the handle and the door opens. At first all she sees is an attic, with a round window reflecting the white sky. Then, in careful order, she registers an easel, a chaise longue and a woman lying on the floor, a pool of blood slowly congealing about her head.

'Cover her face,' says a voice. 'Mine eyes dazzle. She died young.'
That does it. In an instant, these words snap Ali back to herself.

If there is one thing she hates, it's men who go around quoting. Hugo used to do it all the time.

'It might be more helpful to call a doctor,' she says.

'She's beyond the help of medicine,' says the man.

He's taller than Isaac Templeton, and a lot heavier, with a dark moustache and greying hair, but there's no denying the family resemblance. He's looking at her with an expression that would annoy her more than the quoting if it wasn't for the unmistakable fact that she is being observed by someone from 1850. And, however he is looking at her, it isn't the way a man looks at an apparition.

'Are you Cain Templeton?' she asks.

'Your servant.' He makes her an elegant bow. 'And you are?'

'Alison Dawson,' says Ali, before realising that she should have prefaced this with 'Mrs'. This is the first conversation she's ever had with someone beyond the gate. She thinks of the Charter: *Don't Interact.*

'But how charming,' murmurs Templeton.

'None of this is charming,' says Ali. 'What happened to her?' She gestures towards the woman. Templeton is right; it's too late. Ali has seen violent crime before, many times when she first joined the police, and this is no less shocking for having happened a hundred and twenty-two years before she was born.

'It looks as if someone hit her on the head with a heavy object,' says Templeton.

'Is that someone you?'

'Sorry to disappoint you,' says Templeton, sounding almost amused. 'But I'm innocent. Of this crime, anyway.'

'Do you know this woman?'

'You're correct, alas. She was no lady. Her name is Ettie Moran. She is – was – an artist's model.'

'Are you the artist?'

Again, he sounds amused. 'I am not. The occupant of this studio and – I assume – the perpetrator of this crime, is a man called Thomas Creek.'

'Do you know where he is?'

'No. And that is knowledge I would like to have. He hasn't paid his rent for several weeks. I came here to discuss the matter with him.'

It is said in the same light tone but Ali thinks she detects a note of menace all the same. She's not sure that she would like a discussion with Cain Templeton.

'Do you own this house?' she asks.

'I do. I'm somewhat of a collector of artists.'

The Collector. For the first time, Ali realises that the sound of piano scales has stopped and the house is in total silence.

Chapter 9

Finn

2023

Finn doesn't start to worry until Thursday. It's not as if he hears from Ali every day. 'I'm not going to text you to say goodnight,' she'd said when he first started university. 'I don't want to worry if you don't reply and I don't want you to have to stop having fun and think about your old mum.' Finn hadn't been on good terms with Ali at the time – she'd just married the ridiculous Lincoln – but he'd appreciated the thought, even if 'your old mum' sounded a bit self-pitying.

Finn gets on well with his mum now. Some days there will be quite a chain of texts including jokes, gifs and memes. Terry, her psychotic cat, is their big bond. If Finn feels that he needs to reach out, a cat meme will usually do it. On Wednesday he sends two, 'When a cat thinks it's a dog' and 'Your cat on holiday' with two white paws on a sun-lounger. There's no reply but Finn knows that sometimes Ali turns her phone off at work. When she first joined

CID, he used to worry about her. He'd been in his teens and going through his anxious phase. He kept thinking that she'd be shot by some desperate gunman or knifed by a drug dealer. Of course, he knew that Ali was thinking the same about him, a skinny schoolboy in east London. All the same, Finn had been pleased when she'd joined the cold case team. Nothing could happen to his mother if she was investigating crimes so old they were frozen in the ice age. And he likes the team. Geoff was really kind when Finn was thinking of applying for the civil service, spent lots of time going through the forms and kept on asking Ali about the application long after Finn had decided not to send it. Dina is funny and interesting. John is clearly the epitome of a good bloke. Even Bud is good for a sci-fi joke or two.

The first twinge of fear came when Ali still hadn't answered on Thursday afternoon. All Finn's messages, even a fairly desperate 'Love you mum', remained on 'delivered'. He was busy at work – they were preparing for Isaac's speech to the Prison Officers' Association – but checked his phone several times an hour. Nothing from the contact marked 'Mum' and personalised by a picture of Terry. Eventually even Isaac asked if something was wrong.

'No. I'm fine.' Finn always tries to keep his private life away from work. Isaac didn't even know about Cosima, although Chibu and Piers both did. In fact, it was Chibu who had introduced Cosima to Finn. They'd been at school together.

'Everything all right at home?' Isaac was doing the sincere thing that worked so well on TV.

'Yes. All good,' Finn reassured him.

By Thursday evening he's properly worried. He decides to go over to Bow after work. He cycles, which takes him a good hour but means that he's too busy trying to stay alive in the traffic to have time to think. Ali's new road is cobbled, picturesque but hard on the wheels. Finn dismounts and pushes his bike the last hundred metres. As soon as he sees the little terraced house, which seemed so welcoming last week, his heart sinks. There are two parcels by the front door. The exercise bike has gone though.

Finn puts his newly cut key in the lock. As soon as he does so, there's a terrible spine-chilling shriek. Finn can feel his heart pounding. 'Mum?' He steps into the house and is hit by the smell of cat pee. Then the shriek resolves itself into the angry shape of Terry. The cat rushes over to Finn and winds himself desperately round his feet. Finn picks him up and goes into the kitchen area. The litter tray is full but Terry's bowls are both empty. Really scared now, Finn mechanically fills one bowl with water and the other with Terry's special food. Terry noses Finn out of the way to begin eating. Finn puts the litter tray outside and looks through his phone. He doesn't have contact details for any of the team but he remembers that, years ago, he accepted a Facebook friend request from Dina. Finn hasn't been on social media as himself since he became a special advisor but he can still send Dina a message.

Worried about Mum. Can you ring me?

He adds his number and is more alarmed than ever when Dina rings almost immediately.

'Dina. Hi. Thanks for calling back. The thing is, I'm in Mum's house. The new house. And she obviously hasn't been here for a couple of days. Terry was starving.'

'I thought you had Terry,' says Dina. 'Otherwise I would have—'

'What? Has Mum gone somewhere for work?'

He knows from Dina's voice that something is wrong. She sounds wary and also scared. 'Yes, she's on an assignment for work.'

'But why . . .?'

'Look, I can't explain on the phone. Can you come to the office tomorrow? Nine o'clock.'

'OK,' says Finn. 'See you there.' He's reassured that Dina seems to know Ali's whereabouts but alarmed by her tone. He wanders into the sitting area. Ali's flowers are drooping and two of her 'Welcome to your new home' cards have fallen onto the floor. Finn picks them up and goes to put them back on the mantelpiece. Then he sees a folded piece of paper behind the clock with one word on it. *Finn.*

It's dated Tuesday and the page is full of Ali's characteristically loopy writing.

Darling Finn,

If by any chance I don't get back, can you look after Terry? My internet banking details are in a file marked RobberBarons. The password is your birthday.

And, just know this, I love you more than anything else in the world and I've been so proud to be your

Mum xxxxx

The past tense in the last line makes Finn feel quite sick. He rings Dina back.

'I've found a message from Mum. She wrote it in case she didn't get back.'

'We all do that,' says Dina. 'Try not to worry too much.' Her voice sounds more normal now and, despite himself, Finn feels slightly soothed. Even so, he has many questions.

'You all do that? What do you mean? Where are you all going? I thought you were the cold case team. Mum says you never leave the office.'

'Ali will be OK. I promise. Geoff will explain tomorrow.'

Finn sits on the sofa, staring into the empty fireplace. He jumps a mile when Terry takes a flying leap into his lap, but stroking the smooth, pale fur makes Finn feel calmer. He'll stay in Ali's house tonight, he decides, and in the morning he'll find out what's really going on in the unit. Terry nuzzles his face, which means he's hungry again. Finn gets up to feed the cat and himself. He wonders if there's any wine left.

Finn sleeps badly. He didn't like to take Ali's room and the spare room was still full of junk. There was a bed in there though and, eventually, Finn found a spare duvet in a box marked 'Stuff'. He slept on the mattress and was woken in the night by Terry joining him. He was glad of the company.

Finn wakes at six and stares at the ceiling which has a stain in the rough shape of Chile. He checks his phone. No messages. Finn gets up and has a shower in the bathroom which must be Ali's first redecorating priority. Because he cycled yesterday, he still has his work clothes in a backpack. Should he wear them for the trip to Ali's office or should he arrive in Lycra? He decides to wear his suit and travel by public transport. The bike can stay at Ali's. He's pretty sure that he'll be back here tonight.

Terry is lying on the top step, just to remind Finn of his existence. As Finn steps over him, Terry streaks downstairs to stand by his bowl. Finn feeds the cat and makes himself a herbal tea. He doesn't trust the milk. The bread is stale too, but it's OK toasted with Marmite. Standing in the sunny kitchen, eating and drinking, Finn feels his spirits rise a degree or two. He changed the cat litter last night and the house smells better. Ali's old-fashioned transistor radio is tuned to Radio 4.

'Justice Minister Isaac Templeton is to address the Prison Officers' Association today. Templeton is expected to praise the work of prison officers and promise reform of custody services . . .'

But not more money, thinks Finn, switching off the radio. It's odd to think that the speech, over which he and Chibu have laboured for weeks, is today. All the dog-whistle words 'service . . . community . . . law-abiding families . . .' the digs at Labour (no matter that they haven't been in power for thirteen years), the subtle apportioning of blame onto supposedly left-leaning organisations like the probation service . . . it all seems unimportant compared to the mysterious disappearance of Ali Dawson. Finn messages Chibu saying that he won't be in because his mother is ill. She messages back saying that she'll tell Isaac. Then, as an afterthought, she texts: 'Hope Ali is OK.' Finn smiles. Chibu is normally quite good at emotional stuff but today all her energy will be concentrated on Isaac. Today and every day.

Finn gives Terry extra biscuits to keep him going through the day, checks his phone again and steps out to join the commuting masses. He's wearing his anorak over his suit. It's his cycling one, so it isn't smart and has a reflective panel on the back, but it's too cold to go without. It's only ten minutes on the District Line from Ali's house to her work, one of the reasons why she chose it. Finn puts in his AirPods and tries to concentrate on the latest political podcast but Ali's voice keeps playing on a loop in his head. 'How come you sound so much posher than your mother?' Chibu once asked. Finn, like Ali, was state-educated but he supposes that the LSE and working for the government have worked their magic and given him one of those 'classless' BBC accents. Ali, though, is still distinctly estuary around the vowels. Finn loves her voice.

It'll be lovely in the spring.

You can tell Isaac that danger and me don't mix.

I love you more than anything else in the world.

Although he has often met the team in the pub or at Ali's, Finn has only been to the unit's headquarters once before. He was struck then by how featureless it was; he wouldn't have been able to pick it out from hundreds of similar office blocks. Today, though, the very anonymity of the place seems almost sinister. Who are the companies who have offices on the other floors? Finn peers at the list by the lifts. Quantum Mechanics, Niffenegger and Co, Wells, Pevensie Ltd. People must work in these businesses but today, as on Finn's previous visit, there's no sign of anyone else in the building. It's nearly nine o'clock, the time when workers arrive at work, but there are no suited figures carrying takeaway coffee, no footsteps on the higher floors. The lobby is silent apart from a hum so faint that Finn thinks it must be in his head.

One lift has a sign saying 'Out of Order' which makes Finn distrust both of them. He takes the stairs two at a time and, on the third floor, pushes open the door marked 'Department of Logistics'.

They are all there in the open-plan room. Dina, John, Bud and Geoff. They look at Finn as he enters in a way that, if he hadn't already been scared, would have terrified him. Dina has actual tears in her eyes. John comes over and gives him a hug.

'What's going on?' says Finn, extricating himself.

A woman appears in the doorway of an inner office. She's tall with short black hair, wearing jeans and a grey jumper.

'Come in, Finn,' she says. 'I will explain everything.'

Chapter 10

Finn makes his way towards the inner office, conscious of eyes following him. He doesn't realise, until the door shuts behind them, that Geoff has followed too. Geoff sits behind his desk and the woman takes her seat at one of the visitors' chairs. This configuration reminds Finn that Geoff is in charge.

The woman leans forward. 'Serafina Pellegrini. People here call me Jones.'

'Finn Kennedy.'

They shake hands. Her fingers feel thin and cold.

'Can I get you a drink, Finn?' says Geoff. 'Tea? Coffee?'

'No,' says Finn. 'You can tell me what's happened to my mum.' The words sound childish in his own ears. *Where's my mummy?*

Geoff leans back in his chair. Finn doesn't miss the fact that he looks at the woman – Serafina? Jones? – before he speaks. Finn has always thought of Geoff as harmless, slightly pompous maybe, but basically one of the good guys. Ali told him that Geoff used to be married to an artist called Bobby, who died. 'He lost his sparkle then,' Ali said. It was hard to imagine a sparkly Geoff but Finn had been prepared to give him the benefit of the doubt. But now Geoff's restrained, corporate manner seems to verge on the monstrous. Finn looks at the World's Best Boss mug on his desk. He knows this was a present from Ali.

'Ali is currently away on an assignment,' says Geoff. These are the words Dina used. Finn has been in politics long enough to spot the party line.

'Where is she?' he says.

Jones turns to face Finn. She has very dark eyes and an intense stare. Finn, though, has spent two years watching Isaac do the same thing in interviews. He hopes he's immune.

'Finn,' says Jones. Repeating the interviewer's name, spin doctoring 101. 'Finn. What I am about to tell you might seem impossible to believe but it's the truth. I swear to you. Geoff does too.'

Geoff is clearly uncomfortable with the vocabulary but he croaks, 'It's true. I promise.'

Finn says nothing, knowing the value of silence at such times.

Jones's voice is low and almost unsettlingly melodic. Finn knows what's she's doing, creating a sense of intimacy by speaking so softly that he has to lean forwards to catch her words, but he does it all the same. 'Some years ago,' she says, 'I discovered a way of moving in time. It's hard to explain but think of the difference between walking up the stairs, one by one, and taking the lift.'

Finn thinks of the out-of-order elevator downstairs. The names Quantum Mechanics, Niffenegger and Co, Wells, Pevensie Ltd start to make a horrible kind of sense. Audrey Niffenegger, *The Time Traveler's Wife*. H. G. Wells and his time machine. Wasn't there a TV programme called *Quantum Leap*? He's not sure about

Pevensie, although the name rings a faint bell that first sounded in his childhood. *Make your choice, adventurous Stranger. Strike the bell and bide the danger* . . .

Jones is still speaking, her slight Italian accent turning the words into a song.

'Think of falling through a wormhole, a very specific wormhole adapted exactly to the atoms in your body. Think of falling into water, the displaced water goes . . . where? Time passes faster in the mountains than it does at sea level. That is scientific fact. I thought, what if I could manipulate time? What if I could open the gate between one reality and another? I took my theory to the government, of course, and they gave me a team.' She makes a gesture which encompasses the glass-walled office and the equally characterless room beyond. She doesn't wait for Finn to reply, which is just as well.

'A team comprising exceptional police officers and one of my most gifted students, Buddhika Sirisema.'

Bud, thinks Finn. He never did seem like a police officer.

'These officers,' says Jones, 'were prepared to take the risk of reassembling their atoms. And, in 2020, we managed our first journey. Your mother, Finn, was one of the first people ever to travel in time. A pioneer.'

Finn says nothing. He feels exactly as he did when, aged nine and just about tall enough, he'd taken his first ride on the Waltzer on Brighton Pier. The feeling you get when your brightly coloured compartment is whirled round so quickly that the world turns into a scream and you realise that you've left your stomach back at the entry sign.

'Over the next few years, we honed the process,' Jones is saying.

'Now we can travel in time and space. We can occupy the space corporeally. And, a few weeks ago, we received our greatest challenge. A request to travel back to 1850. Your mother was prepared to make the journey.'

She stops. Finn feels the room spinning and, to anchor himself, tries to count objects: desk, possibly IKEA and at least ten years old, two metal filing cabinets, wall planner, framed print of a wood with light filtering between the trees. Objects on desk: laptop, phone in a black silicone case, framed photograph (he can only see the back), lined foolscap pad, World's Best Boss mug, glazed pot containing assorted pens and a silver letter-opener. Finn looks up to meet Geoff's rather anxious gaze. He wonders how long it has been since he's spoken.

He says, surprised to find that his voice still works, 'My mother travelled in time to 1850?'

'Yes,' says Geoff, sounding relieved that these words are out in the ether. 'She went on Wednesday.'

'And she's still not back?' Finn can hear his voice rising, the childish note back.

Desk, filing cabinet, wall planner.

'She didn't appear at the designated meeting place,' says Geoff.

'So she's lost?'

'Lost is not a word I'd use,' says Geoff. 'But we are not currently aware of her location.'

Finn lunges across the desk. As an assault, it's not a success, causing the pot and several pens to fall to the floor and Geoff stops his hand halfway. Finn sits back down, breathing heavily.

'You bastard,' he says. He can't remember the last time he swore.

Isaac hates bad language so he's got out of the habit. Ali swears like a trooper.

'Let's all calm down,' says Jones. Her low-pitched voice has a soothing effect on both men. She says, 'I know this is a terrible shock, Finn, but I'm confident we can retrieve Ali. We know where she is.'

'*Do we?*' Finn means this to be witheringly sarcastic, but the woman seems to take his remark at face value.

'Oh yes,' says Jones. 'Ali is in January 1850 in the vicinity of Hawk Street, London E2.'

'Great,' says Finn. 'What was I worrying about?'

Jones laughs, surprising Finn greatly.

'I can get her back, Finn.'

'How?' says Finn. He realises that, on some level, he actually believes what he's being told.

'The whole team is working day and night on this,' says Geoff.

'The whole team?' says Finn. 'Three people?' He doesn't believe in the crack team of exceptional officers if it includes Ali who can't even change her computer password without help.

'It's not three people,' says Jones. 'Every floor in this building is full of dedicated professionals working on this project.'

'So all those other companies. Niffenegger and Co . . .'

'It's just a private joke,' says Jones.

Four children called Pevensie, a snowy wood, a faun, a talking lion. Going through the wardrobe into a different world.

Jones says, her voice lower and huskier than ever, 'We can send someone to find Ali.'

'Does that mean sending them to 1850?'

'Yes.'

There's a silence in the room and Finn is aware of the hum again, a faint electric sound that seems to hover just on the edge of consciousness.

'Why 1850?' he says. He's not expecting this to be the question that makes Geoff and Jones exchange anxious looks. There's another humming silence. Then Geoff says, 'Our work is, of course, known to the government at the highest level.'

Finn has no idea why this is relevant. It doesn't seem the time for Geoff to show off about his powerful contacts. He waits.

'So,' says Geoff, 'when we received a request from Isaac Templeton, we felt that we had to give the matter serious consideration.'

Finn hears that name so often that, for a moment, it fails to register. He says, after a few seconds, 'Wait. What? Who?'

'You work for Isaac, don't you?' says Jones.

'I'm one of his special advisors,' says Finn. 'Geoff, what the hell has Isaac got to do with any of this?'

'Isaac asked us to investigate his great-great-grandfather, Cain Templeton, who was believed to have killed three women in the 1850s.'

'*Isaac* asked you to do this? Isaac knows about this? Isaac sent my mother on this . . . this suicide mission?'

'It's not a suicide mission,' says Jones. 'I promise you, I'll get her back.'

Finn ignores her. He looks at Geoff who says, in an almost apologetic tone, 'He asked for her specially.'

Chapter 11

In the Tube, Finn sits and stares straight ahead. He has his AirPods in but he isn't listening to music or a podcast. Looking at the map opposite with its familiar names – Monument, Cannon Street, Mansion House, Blackfriars – he doesn't believe it. He does not believe that Ali – his *mother* – is currently in 1850, walking around in clothes apparently especially made for her by the London College of Fashion. It's a lie, an extravagant hoax, a practical joke. He stares at his reflection as it slides in and out of stations, superimposed on brick walls and on advertisements for beer and employment agencies. Is it possible, he thinks suddenly, that he's actually dreaming? Finn takes a pen from his inside pocket and digs it into his hand. Immediately there's a discernible pain. The train is almost deserted (it's the endless sort with no carriage dividers) but a woman a few seats away looks at him curiously. Finn puts the pen away. There's a black Biro indentation on his palm. He's not dreaming.

But how can it be true? Poems on the Underground. This station has step-free access. Mind the gap. The regular rhythm and drone of

London. Finn thinks of Dina's tears, John's hug, of Geoff's office: desk, filing cabinets, wall planner, woodland print. This is the real world and these are real people. And they tell him that his mother has travelled in time.

Finn gets out at Westminster and walks to the Houses of Parliament. For the first time in his working life, he doesn't feel a glow of satisfaction as he is waved through security. He passes through the panelled halls and past the portraits of dead prime ministers. He sees some journalists he recognises, someone calls his name, but Finn keeps walking until he reaches the green-carpeted corridor where Isaac's office is situated. He's surprised to hear voices inside. He thought that Isaac would still be at the Prison Officers' Association. Then he realises that it's nearly midday. He spent far longer than he thought with Geoff and Jones. Maybe he has travelled in time? He laughs, an uneven, hysterical sound that sounds unhinged in his own ears, then pushes open the door.

'I thought you weren't coming in,' says Chibu.

'It went very well,' says Piers. 'They even laughed at your joke about porridge.'

'How's your mum?' says Isaac. He's doing the caring face that Finn knows well. It seems as insincere as any other politician's expression but, if Geoff and Jones are telling the truth, Isaac must know that Finn's mother is in real danger, that he put her there.

'Isaac?' says Finn. 'Can I talk to you in private?'

He agrees so quickly that Finn knows it must be true.

After the door has shut behind the clearly discomfited Chibu and Piers, Isaac looks at Finn with his 'compassionate Tory' expression, the one that works so well on daytime TV. It doesn't last long.

Finn doesn't know what's written on his own face but it makes Isaac retreat behind his desk in a way that reminds Finn of Geoff.

'I've just been to see Geoff Bastian,' says Finn. 'Serafina Pellegrini was there too. You probably know her as Jones.'

Isaac says nothing. He starts to fiddle with his signet ring but stops himself, clearly with an effort.

'My mother's missing,' says Finn. 'I think you know why.'

Isaac sits down and rubs his eyes. He says, 'It must sound un-believable to you. It did to me at first.'

'I believe that my mother is in danger,' says Finn. He's still standing, which makes him feel at an advantage. He's the same height as Isaac but the politician always seems taller somehow. Now Finn is actually looking down on his boss. Is the famous dark hair thinning a little?

'When I first heard about the team, what they can do,' says Isaac, 'I thought it must be a joke. I mean, I've learnt some crazy things since I've been in the cabinet . . . you learn all the secrets, it does your head in. But this . . . Did you really have no idea what Ali was doing in that place?'

Finn doesn't like Isaac's tone, which sounds as if Finn should have guessed that his mother was commuting, not to Whitechapel, but to the nineteenth century. He says, stiffly, 'Neither of us talk about our work.' Except that Ali does. She tells him about Dina's dating disasters and Bud's attempts to learn Russian. She tells him that Geoff is going to WeightWatchers and that John is in AA. But she never mentioned Jones, she never told Finn that she travels in time.

'Your mother is a remarkable woman,' says Isaac. This annoys Finn more than anything that has gone before. Isaac has no right to admire his mother, to talk about her in that proprietorial way.

Finn says, 'Thanks to you I might never see her again.'

Isaac flinches and puts his hand to his eyes again. 'Geoff Bastian says she's not in danger. He says they'll get her back.'

'So you spoke to Geoff and not to me?'

'I was told not to talk to you,' says Isaac, so quickly that Finn almost tells him, 'Don't sound defensive, wait a beat before replying.'

'Who told you?'

'Geoff. Serafina – Jones – was there. They said they could get Ali back. Jones sounded very confident.'

'I don't think they've got the faintest idea what to do,' says Finn.

'Geoff said they'd send someone after her. John Cole is very experienced, an ex DCI.'

'He's an alcoholic,' says Finn. He's fed up with keeping everyone's secrets.

'Is he?' says Isaac. 'I didn't know that.'

'There's a lot you don't know,' says Finn. He's never said anything like that to Isaac, though he's often wanted to, but Isaac just replies, almost humbly, 'You're right.'

This has the effect of cooling Finn's righteous anger. He sits down. 'Why did you do it, Isaac? Why did you ask my mum to go back to 1850? Geoff said it was because you were writing a book about your family but that can't be the only reason.'

Isaac's answer is to open one of the drawers in the grotesque desk he inherited from the former minister of justice. He takes out a cardboard folder and places it on the blotter in front of him.

'My ancestor, Cain Templeton, was a remarkable man,' he says. 'He was an amateur archaeologist, a collector, a patron of the arts.'

'Geoff said he was also accused of murdering three women,' says

Finn. He's in no mood for the past glories of Isaac's family. He saw enough of that in East Dean last weekend.

Isaac doesn't respond. He has his hands flat on the file. 'One of the most remarkable things about Cain,' he continues, 'is that he kept a diary. I've been working my way through it and I found this. Here's a transcript.'

He takes a sheet of A4 from the file and passes it to Finn. One paragraph is marked in the green pen Isaac uses for annotating his speeches.

I saw Alison again today. There is some mystery about her. I don't know what it is. She seems to have appeared from nowhere and her speech and mannerisms are like no woman I've ever met. Her looks too. She's not young and yet she glows with a strange vitality. I know she's a widow and today she mentioned that she had a son called Phin. She told me that Phin's father was called El Vis, which must be a foreign name.

Finn looks at Isaac and, for the second time that day, feels like committing physical violence. 'You knew,' he says. 'You knew that this would happen.'

Chapter 12

'It wasn't until I heard Ali's name that I remembered this passage,' says Isaac. 'Then I just couldn't resist asking for her to be the one to make the trip. I mean, it was meant. It had already happened.'

'If you think that absolves you,' says Finn. 'It doesn't.'

'But it happened,' says Isaac, putting the page back in the file. 'This is proof.'

Finn is back on the Waltzer again. Was this preordained? Is Ali meant to stay in 1850? Oh God, maybe she married Cain, maybe Isaac is her great-great-grandson? But no, Ali was born in Hastings in 1972. Finn has seen the photos in his nan and grandad's house. 'Ali was always trouble,' Nan says, not without admiration. Finn's mother exists and now she's in danger. Finn clings onto this and the merry-go-round slows.

'What are you going to do now?' says Finn. 'How are you going to get Ali back?'

Isaac spreads his hands. 'There's nothing I can do. Geoff and Jones said—'

'There's always something you can do,' says Finn. If nothing else, the last few years have taught him this.

'I've told Geoff he can have unlimited resources but, really, it's all down to Jones.'

Finn thinks of the tall woman with the hypnotic voice. He can imagine her captivating Isaac, but this is Finn's mother they're talking about.

Isaac says, 'Geoff talked about sending John Cole to rescue . . . retrieve . . . Ali. I know you said John has . . . has his problems but Geoff seems to have complete faith in him. He's worked with Ali before.'

Ali trusts John too. 'He's my work husband,' she sometimes says, 'not that I need another one.' John sent Finn a bottle of champagne when he got his job with Isaac.

Isaac looks at his watch. 'I'm sorry, Finn . . .'

Is Isaac really going to leave it there? But of course he is. It's Friday. The constituency calls. Two p.m. on Friday is almost over-time for an MP. Unless there are drinks available.

'You have to go,' says Finn.

'Miranda will be here any minute.'

Miranda is Isaac's wife. Although undeniably posh, she's not otherwise what you'd expect. She's a lawyer and always seems in a hurry. 'She looks like she's never brushed her hair,' says Chibu, 'and her clothes are always creased. I can't think why Isaac married her.' Finn can because Miranda, flyaway blonde hair and all, is extremely attractive.

'So that's it then,' says Finn. 'Goodbye and sorry about your mum.'

'Take some time off,' says Isaac. 'I promise, by next week it will be OK. Ali will be back with a tale to tell.'

He says this like he knows Ali better than Finn does. Finn is trying to think of a suitably crushing answer when Miranda bursts in.

'Darling,' she says to Isaac. 'I'm so sorry I'm late. Beastly solicitors. Oh, I'm sorry . . .' She makes a pantomime of noticing Finn. 'Hello, Finn. I'm so sorry to interrupt. It was lovely to see you last weekend.'

'Lovely to see you too.' Finn is quite surprised to find himself still capable of saying things like this.

'You must come down to East Dean again.'

'I'd love to.'

'We have a cricket match with the villagers in the summer.'

'Sounds great,' says Finn.

'Am I interrupting affairs of state?' says Miranda. 'Shall I wait outside?'

'No, it's fine,' says Finn. 'I think we've finished.'

On the green outside the Houses of Parliament, surrounded by tourists and watched benignly by Nelson Mandela, Finn taps 'Hawk Street E2' into his phone. He's shocked to see how close it is to Ali's office in Whitechapel. He just needs to retrace his route on the District Line. Will it help to see the place where Ali supposedly is, at this moment? Finn doesn't know but he has to do something, go somewhere. 'All travel is time travel.' Jones said that, only a few hours ago. Finn thinks it was only her voice that stopped him yelling at her. 'Stop saying stuff that sounds like it comes from an inspirational quote.' But Jones is a scientist and, if Isaac is to be believed (Finn looks back at the Victorian Gothic edifice behind him as if it adds weight to that belief), she has found a way of altering the laws of physics.

He doesn't know how he gets to the Tube station or onto a train. He sits in a zombie-like daze. In this way, of course, he fits in well. It's too early for the home-going commuters and the majority of travellers are in a liminal zone of their own, headphones on, lost in time.

At Whitechapel, Finn consults his phone and follows the blue dot towards Hawk Street. It's a typical London scene: cars and litter and fast-food restaurants. Finn forces himself to look up. On one side of the road is a row of handsome, four-storey houses. They are overshadowed by tower blocks but there's still a sort of grandeur about them. Finn approaches, negotiating a section of pavement that's apparently being mended, and looks up at the buildings. Geoff didn't mention the number of the house. Is Ali there, behind one of the windows? Finn has never considered himself psychic. He doesn't believe in star signs or ghosts. Cosima once told him that this was typical of an Aries and he couldn't tell if she was joking or not. He has no sense that his mother is inside any of the houses. He remembers, when he accompanied Ali on her cleaning jobs, the fear he felt when she went out of his sight, disappearing into one of the endless corporate corridors. It's the same now. A mixture of panic, agoraphobia and vertigo. He starts to count the English monarchs from William the Conqueror, a trick his father once taught him.

William Rufus, Henry Beauclerc, Stephen and Matilda—

'Watch out!' The man on the electric scooter gestures angrily, despite the fact that he is on the pavement illegally and Finn is standing still. But the everyday aggression brings Finn back to himself. There will be no electric scooters where Ali is. What will there be? Horse-drawn carriages and penny-farthings? Finn did History A level, but that was mostly the Corn Laws and the

Russian Revolution. He can't imagine actually being there, which is probably a fault in the English education system but not something that concerns him now.

Finn walks back towards the Tube station. He tries, from the depths of his sceptical soul, to send Ali a thought message. 'It's all right, Mum. We'll get you out of there.' A *Big Issue* seller tells him to cheer up because it might never happen.

Finn travels the few stops from Whitechapel to Bow Road. The trains are more crowded now, full of commuters leaving early on a Friday, so he doesn't try to get a seat but sways with the movement of the carriage. As he emerges into the light, he sees a Historic England sign next to the exit. 'Bow Railway Station was opened in 1850 by The East and West India Dock Company and Birmingham Junction Railway.' Finn stops, causing a pushchair to run into the back of his legs. 1850. Is this a coincidence or further evidence that, as Isaac said, everything has happened before? For a moment, the grimy station rearranges itself into Victorian vaults and towers. Finn shakes his head and heads for the Tesco Express. He has a feeling he'll need a bottle of wine tonight.

It's only twenty past three but the lights are already on in Ali's street. It's a friendly-looking terrace. 'These houses used to be cottages for workers at the match factory,' Ali told Finn when they moved her in. 'Do you remember me telling you about the matchgirls' strike?' Finn didn't but he knew that Ali would like being connected to genuine working-class history. He wonders when the strike was. If it was 1850, he thinks he'll lose it.

Terry is delighted to see Finn. He weaves around his legs and then jumps onto the kitchen worktop to talk to him in strange Siamese language. Finn feeds the cat and makes himself a cup of peppermint tea. Even if the world has turned on its head, he can't start drinking alcohol before six. Finn values self-discipline. His parents tried their best but they never quite seemed in control of their own lives, Ali marrying three times, Declan constantly changing jobs and imagining that the next one would make him rich. From the age of fourteen, by which time both his parents were on their second marriages, Finn decided to be his own mentor. He kept a revision diary in which he also noted what he ate and how much he exercised. This approach led him to excellent exam results and a mildly obsessive personality. Finn tries to remedy this by scheduling times when he can be impulsive. His final row with Cosima involved a surprise holiday booked for 2024.

Finn drinks his tea and tries to get the day's events into some sort of order. He imagines writing them in his diary. He realises that keeping a journal is something he has in common with Cain Templeton.

9am	*Meeting with Geoff and Jones. Learn that Ali is lost in 1850.*
12pm	*Meeting with Isaac. Learn that Cain Templeton mentioned Ali in his diary.*
2.30pm	*Visit Hawk Street.*
3.30pm	*Drink tea.*

Last night, Finn sat in this kitchen eating toast and worrying about Ali. Now he's beyond worried. He's in a state that veers between hysteria and despair. And he realises that he's hungry. It's been a long time since breakfast – more toast. He's bought ingredients for a healthy stir-fry tonight, but now Finn finds himself heading for the bread bin and the slightly stale loaf again. He's waiting for the toaster to ping when there's a knock on the door. Terry yowls and Finn takes his point. He too hopes that, by some miracle, it's Ali.

Finn knows, looking at the bulky shape through the glass, that it's not Ali, but he's surprised when the open door reveals Geoff Bastian, smiling nervously and holding a bottle of wine.

'Hi, Finn. Thought you might like some company.'

Chapter 13

Finn wakes on Saturday morning with a dry mouth and a heavy weight on his chest. Is this it? The heart attack at thirty? There's a sinister growling noise too. Is that actually coming from inside his body? But no, it's Terry lying on his chest, purring. For a second Finn stares into the cat's disconcertingly blue eyes, then Terry stretches out a paw to pat Finn's cheek lightly before melting away on business of his own. Finn lies back on the pillow – he still hasn't got round to finding covers for anything. The shape on the ceiling no longer looks like Chile. Now Finn can see a face with a pointed Elizabethan beard. Finn closes his eyes, wondering if he's going to be sick. How much did he and Geoff drink last night? Both bottles of red wine and some of Ali's holiday ouzo. It's no wonder he feels like death. Finn tries to regulate his drinking too. He hasn't been properly drunk since university.

He must have fallen back to sleep because, when he opens his eyes again, bright sunlight is filtering through the blinds. Finn gropes for his phone. It's nine thirty. There are texts from Chibu and Piers and several updates from the many news outlets he follows. Finn doesn't look at any of them. He gets up and goes into the bathroom. He has his emergency washing kit with him, so at least he's using his own toothbrush, but the razor and shaving gel have both seen better days. A shower helps with the hangover but it's horrible putting on yesterday's boxers, shirt and trousers. He'll have to go back to his flat and get some more clothes. He could take Terry with him – they are used to being room-mates, after all – but somehow Finn feels it's essential that he stays at Ali's house.

'We'll get her back,' Geoff said last night. 'I know it all seems like guesswork and magic but it's actually very precise physics which, admittedly, feels a bit like witchcraft. John is set to go through the gate on Monday.'

'Why Monday?' said Finn. His mood veered, throughout the evening, between antagonism, terror, optimism and appalling sentimentality. This was during the antagonistic stage.

'Jones needs another day or two to prepare things. Also John needs to get kitted out in Victorian clothes and learn about life in the nineteenth century.'

'Did Mum do that?' Finn asked.

'Of course,' said Geoff. 'She prepared very thoroughly.'

It was a strange evening, thinks Finn, searching under the bed for his socks. He doesn't really know Geoff but he got the feeling that, fuelled by pizza, wine and ouzo, they talked in a way that was unusual for both of them. Geoff told Finn how much he missed Bobby and that he'd give anything for just one more hour with him. Finn told Geoff that he disliked both his stepfathers but didn't feel that he had much in common with his father either. He also remembers Geoff waxing lyrical about Jones's brilliance. 'You're dazzled by her,' Finn told him. He could understand this reaction, even from his one meeting with the Italian physicist, but it didn't make him trust either of them exactly.

Finn draws the line at his socks. He goes into Ali's room to borrow some of hers. He has small feet for his height and thinks he can find some to fit. It's weird being in Ali's bedroom, her bed with its William Morris duvet, her clothes thrown carelessly on a chair (she must be missing the exercise bike), a Sally Rooney novel open face-down beside the bed. The giant vase is on the floor by the window. On the chest of drawers there are framed photographs of Terry and Finn. The one of Finn was taken on the balcony of his flat, his hair longer then, and he's grinning in what he considers to be an inane way. There's another photograph of Finn, aged five, on a carousel horse. Finn and Ali were living in a flat in Stratford, Finn had just started school and Ali was working as a cleaner. She used to take Finn to work with her in the holidays. He has a memory of riding around a vast sitting room on a Hoover but mostly it was waiting, sitting on stairs with a picture book and later doing homework at unfamiliar tables. Ali cleaned office blocks too, miles of grey carpets and sinister whining lifts. Maybe *that's* why Finn doesn't like elevators.

When Chibu heard that Finn's mother had been a cleaner, she said, 'Oh that's so brave, a single mum working to support her child. Isn't it wonderful how far she's come since?' Chibu saw cleaning as a degrading job and Ali's current work as an escape but Finn knows that Ali didn't see anything wrong with making a living that way. 'It's an honest profession,' she used to say. She didn't always say the same thing about being a police officer.

Tucked in the corner of Ali's make-up mirror there's another photo, a polaroid. It's the team at some sort of Christmas party. Ali and Dina are wearing paper hats and Bud has a fez-type thing that has fallen over one ear. Geoff is wearing a Christmas jumper. John, presumably thanks to AA, is the only one who looks sober. If you had to rely on one of the people in the photograph to rescue your mother, you would definitely choose John. But the picture, kept in a place where Ali would see it every day, reminds Finn how much Ali's workmates mean to her. They won't let her down, he thinks.

Finn finds a pair of Ali's ski socks and puts them on. The warmth is comforting because Finn hasn't worked out the central heating yet and the house is very cold. An admonitory wail from downstairs reminds Finn that it's time to feed Terry. And himself. He never got round to making his stir-fry last night. Finn and Geoff had ordered pizzas at midnight and the sight of the open boxes in the kitchen makes him feel slightly sick. Time for some more toast. He's eating it at the counter when there's a knock on the door. Once again, Finn's heart leaps. Is it Ali? He races Terry to the front door. This time there are two shapes behind the glass.

Finn opens the door.

'Finn Kennedy? I'm DS Mary O'Brien from East Sussex CID and this is DC Josh Franks. Can we come in?'

At first Finn thinks this must be about Ali. Presumably the Met know about the unit and their investigations. Then he thinks . . . East Sussex?

He stands aside to let the officers in. Both are in plain clothes and though Mary showed her warrant card Finn didn't take in any of the details. Mary is probably in her thirties, hair in a no-nonsense bob that nonetheless looks quite stylish. Josh looks younger than Finn, he has acne and a wispy goatee. Finn disregards him immediately.

Mary sits on the sofa and gestures for Finn to do the same. Josh stands by the door. Finn feels the first stirrings of a new anxiety.

'Do you know what this is about?' says Mary.

'No,' says Finn. He's not going to mention Ali until they do.

'You work for Isaac Templeton, don't you?'

'Yes.'

'I'm sorry to tell you,' says Mary, not sounding all that sorry, 'that Mr Templeton was murdered last night.'

Finn is back on the Waltzer. He only just makes it to the downstairs loo before being sick.

Chapter 14

Ali

1850

'I'm somewhat of a collector of artists.'

Ali thinks of the brain floating in formaldehyde, of Isaac's voice describing his ancestor, not without admiration, as a collector of women. She looks at the woman's body at her feet. Her hair is the colour often poetically called auburn, but now it's darkened with blood. One outstretched hand, wax white, seems to be clutching strands of darker hair. Ali wishes she could send this clue to the scene-of-crime team.

Ali says, 'Should somebody call the Peelers?'

She's proud of herself for remembering the nickname of the police force created by Sir Robert Peel. But is 'call' the right verb? To Ali it suggests a mobile phone but she supposes that, in 1850, you call the police by yelling their name out of the window.

Cain Templeton shows no inclination to do this. He says, 'What would be the use? The poor girl is dead.'

'Don't you want to find out who did it?' says Ali.

'I know,' says Templeton. 'She was killed by Thomas Creek.'

'Do you have any evidence for that?'

Templeton smiles, the corners of his moustache lifting. 'Evidence? What does a lady know about evidence?'

Is this another word she shouldn't have used? Well, too late now. Ali says, 'How do you know Thomas Creek killed this wo— this lady? What did you say her name was? Ettie?'

'Ethel Moran. Known as Ettie. I know Thomas Creek killed her because he's a man of low morals.'

If only policing was that easy, thinks Ali. Mind you, she had colleagues in the Met who would condemn someone on their perceived morals. Or on the colour of their skin.

'Did you know Miss Moran?' asks Ali. She remembers that she's here to gather evidence from Cain Templeton, not to set an enquiry in process. Ettie Moran has been dead for over a hundred years. Ali is not going to help matters by asking the police to examine her corpse. If they would even do such a thing.

'I met her a few times,' says Templeton carelessly. Too carelessly, in Ali's opinion. 'She was a pretty little thing.'

'How come you were here when she was killed?' asks Ali. 'Did you hear her cry out?'

Now Templeton is looking at her curiously. 'You ask a lot of questions,' he says. 'Can I ask one in return? Who are you?'

'I'm Alison Dawson. Mrs Dawson. I was . . .' she extemporises, 'looking for a room to rent.'

'How lucky, then,' says Templeton, 'that one has recently become vacant.'

'Ettie's room?'

'No. Creek's room. This room.'

Would Templeton even bother to clean the floor before letting the room? wonders Ali. She's not going to stay to find out. She picks up her skirts, preparatory to making her exit, when she hears something that chills her to the bone. The clock downstairs strikes once, twice, three times.

'Shit!' says Ali, forgetting everything she's been taught. 'Is it three o'clock?'

Cain Templeton laughs aloud. He really seems to find her delightful. 'That clock is always five minutes fast. Farewell, Alison.' This last is delivered to Ali's back as she heads for the stairs. She gallops down them in a distinctly un-Victorian way, holding her skirts almost waist high. She pushes the door open and skids across the icy pavement. The street is busier now with several carts rattling past and a street-seller shouting his wares, but Ali can see the spot where she cleared the snow. She runs towards it and, discreetly using her ultraviolet light, places her feet in exactly the right position. She checks her timepiece. Two minutes to three. She waits. Come on, Jones. Come on, angelic pilgrim. Ali waits as the street seller's cry resolves itself into 'Hot sheep's feet. Two for a penny.' She stands still as two women and a little boy push past her, apparently anxious to purchase this delicacy. She's still there when they return with their steaming bundles.

Time's arrow has missed its target.

She doesn't know how long she stands there. Carts trundle by and spray her skirts with muddy slush, urchins rush past on their way to the hot sheep's-feet man who is eventually replaced by a woman selling baked potatoes. Someone says, 'Look at her standing there,' and just one person asks if she needs help. 'Yes,' Ali wants to say to this kind-faced woman, 'I need to get back to 2023.' But instead she shakes her head and says, 'Thank you, but no.' At least she didn't use the word 'OK'. The act of speaking brings Ali back to herself. She realises that she is freezing and that she needs to go indoors. Since the only house she knows is Number 44 Hawk Street she retraces her steps, walking with difficulty on frozen feet towards the griffin door knocker.

At the entrance, she stops. Something is being carried down by two men, a cumbersome shape inadequately covered in a bed sheet. Ali can see strands of red hair and one bare foot. Ettie's body is placed into an open cart and the two men climb up in front. The driver flicks the horse's reins and the corpse is carried away, jolting over the cobbles. Ali looks up and sees Cain Templeton watching from the doorway.

'Mrs Dawson! You've decided to return.'

He must see something in her face because he descends the steps and takes her arm. 'But you're frozen. Come inside.'

Ali allows Templeton to lead her into the panelled hallway. Somewhere in the house, the piano is playing again. Templeton ushers her into a small parlour where there's a fire in the grate. Ali finds herself sitting beside it with a rug over her knees while Templeton asks an unseen servant to bring a pot of tea.

Ali is almost grateful for the numbness of the cold. Drinking the tea revives her and the thoughts come rushing back. She is stuck in 1850. Will she ever return to her own life? Will she ever see her son again? At the thought of Finn tears come to her eyes.

'My dear Mrs Dawson,' says Templeton, in a tone which, even in her distress, Ali recognises as overfamiliar. 'You are in some trouble, I know. Won't you tell me about it?'

'I was expecting to meet someone,' says Ali. Once again, she finds a strange comfort at the sound of her own voice. 'A relative. But he hasn't arrived.'

'It's Friday,' says Templeton. 'The streets will be crowded. Country people returning to their homes. Factory workers drinking in taverns. Maybe your relative has been delayed.'

For a moment, Ali stares at him. Friday? When she left 2023, it was Wednesday. But, of course, 25 January 1850 would fall on a different day. It had not occurred to her that Jones's calculations would not coincide with the calendar.

Templeton is looking at her. His expression seems benign but she senses something else in him. A watchfulness, perhaps, that makes her wary.

'Is it possible to stay here for tonight?' she asks, adding, 'I have money.' Helpfully provided by the Royal Mint.

'But of course,' says Templeton. 'I will ask the maid to clean the room. Don't worry, there will be no trace of its former occupant.'

'Thomas Creek?'

Templeton strokes his moustache, which makes him look like a Bond villain, an idea that comforts Ali in its relative modernity.

'Creek is a dangerous man. I know that he possesses a firearm. If you see him, do not approach him.'

'What if he decides to come back to his room?'

'He wouldn't dare return to this house.'

This is not very reassuring. Ali doesn't relish the idea of a possible armed killer bursting into her room in the middle of the night. She's also not very comfortable about being in debt to Cain Templeton. But what else can she do? She knows no one else in Victorian London. She doesn't know what will happen to her if

Jones doesn't retrieve her. 'It's impossible for it to go wrong,' Jones had told her, only that morning, 'because it has already happened.' Ali must get back to her own time in order to be born in 1972 and give birth to Finn in 1992. But what if she doesn't? What if this is a new reality in which Finn doesn't exist? The thought makes her gasp aloud. Some of her tea spills into the saucer.

'Mrs Dawson?'

'I'm sorry. I feel a little faint.'

'Very natural,' says Templeton. 'I will see about getting your room prepared.'

He leaves the room and Ali is left with the piano music and the sound of the clock striking four.

Chapter 15

Ali wakes to a knocking sound. Even in her befuddled state, she thinks this is odd. She realises that she's very cold and reaches down to pull up her duvet. Instead of Egyptian cotton she touches alien material, thin and scratchy. That sensation brings everything back. Ali sits bolt upright. Hard winter sun is shining through a round, uncurtained window. Ali leans forward and sees a snowy street, cut through with one set of cart tracks. A man is walking from house to house carrying a long stick which he is using to tap on upstairs windows. That explains the knock, which must have been on the window below hers. A Victorian wake-up call. What time is it? Ridiculously Ali reaches for her phone. But it's not there. What about her? Is she really there?

There's ice on the inside of the glass. Ali went to sleep in her clothes, partly because she couldn't work out how to undo her corset, but she's still freezing. She wraps the blanket round herself and looks around the room. It's an attic with a sloping roof under which a few items of furniture hunker. A monstrous-looking wardrobe looms over her but there's the chaise longue that she remembers from yesterday, next to an empty easel. Ali also notices a dressing table that looks like a new addition. It has a jug and a bowl on it as well as a mirror on a stand. Suddenly it seems imperative for Ali to see her own reflection. When she puts her feet on the floorboards, they shrink from the cold. She took off her stockings last night because she couldn't bear the garters for another minute. There's a small rug nearby so she pulls it towards her and exposes a dark stain on the wood. Whoever cleaned the room hasn't been able to eradicate Ettie's blood entirely. Ali pushes the rug back and stumbles over to the mirror. There she is, brown hair loose about her shoulders, anxious face, tiny scab where her nose piercing used to be. Remembering how comforting she'd found her own voice last night, Ali says, 'I'm alive.' Her breath clouds around her.

She's alive but she's lost in 1850. She's also cold and dying to use the loo. This last becomes her most urgent preoccupation. For a moment she wonders where the bathroom is located. Then she remembers. There's no bathroom. She has a chamber pot under her bed. She hears Elizabeth's voice: 'There would be a privy in the garden. Waste would simply drop on the earth below. Quite hygienic if there's enough composting material. Or pigs nearby.' Shuddering, Ali gets out the chamber pot and pulls down her voluminous underpants. She almost wishes that she had the authentic Victorian open-gusset version – there's no doubt they would have made peeing in a pot easier. When she's dressed again she feels grubbier than ever. She goes to the jug to wash and finds that it's empty. Of course, she should have brought water up with her last night. Presumably, rich people have servants to do this for them but, although there is a maid in the house, Ali is pretty sure that the woman won't wait on her.

Last night, after telling the maid, Clara, to prepare Ali's room, Cain Templeton departed. Seeing him leave the house was terrible. He was the only person Ali knew in this new world and he was a link to Isaac and so to Finn. But Ali couldn't ask him to stay. She guessed that Clara already had her suspicions about their relationship. After all, Ali had turned up out of nowhere with no luggage and no male protector. She wonders if Templeton is in the habit of taking in stray women. *Another one for the collection.* But Clara served Ali some watery stew which she'd eaten in the kitchen, a room which was warm enough to be almost cosy. While she was eating, another lodger called Mrs Rokeby appeared, clasping a baby to her bosom. She didn't take much notice of Ali but, listening to her conversation with Clara, Ali learnt that her husband, Len, was the one who played the piano. Ali asked Clara who else was living at Number 44. Clara replied that she did not have the time to sit around gossiping but she relented enough to say that the two other rooms were taken by artists, neither of whom paid their rent regularly.

'Mr Templeton is too kind for his own good.'

'Does Mr Templeton live here too?'

'No.' Clara sounds quite shocked. 'He's got a house in Kensington. A lovely place it is. I used to work there.'

Ali wonders idly what all these London houses would be worth in 2023. It was a profoundly capitalist thought and she's ashamed of it. All the same, she has a brief fantasy about buying a house in 1850s Pimlico and returning home to present the keys to Finn.

'What about Thomas Creek?' she says. 'Has he left?'

'Vanished,' says Clara. 'And good riddance. I never want to see his wicked face again.' But, apart from this remark and the shiver that went with it, it seemed to Ali that Ettie's death had not left much of a mark on the household, apart from a single stain on the floorboards. Mrs Rokeby hadn't even mentioned her; she was pre-occupied by the need to find 'cow's milk' for her baby. Ali thought of the body carried away on the jolting cart. If nothing else, she thought, she would find out who had killed Ettie.

But this morning, detection does not figure highly in Ali's prior-ities. She makes a mental list of these. She needs some food – maybe Clara will provide breakfast, especially if Ali gives her one of her carefully stored coins – and then she will go back to the ingress point. She must keep trying until Jones gets her back. Maybe the gate will work at three p.m. today. This last idea takes over. Of course, Ali tells herself, that's the answer. She will be standing on the spot from two thirty onwards. It has to work this time. It must.

Ali feels better having made this decision. She decides to go downstairs, empty the chamber pot in the privy, wash herself and procure some breakfast. Ali sits on the bed to put on her stockings and boots. If she stays here any longer she'll have to find some more clothes and learn how to undo the corset, but she won't be here after three o'clock today, she tells herself firmly. She won't.

Thank goodness the pot has a lid but, even so, it sloshes horribly as Ali makes her way down the stairs. The piano is playing again but she doesn't see any of the house's residents. The clock in the hallway says it's seven thirty. Ali notices for the first time that the numbers are accompanied by little scenes – twelve o'clock seems to show imps pushing a man into hell. Ali takes the door that she remem-bers leading into the kitchen. She can hear someone – presumably

Clara – moving about and smells baking bread. Her stomach rumbles. There's a brick-lined passage that leads beyond the kitchen to the back door. It's bitterly cold outside and snow lies thickly on the garden, but a line of footsteps marks the way to a wooden shed which must be the privy. The only other stain on the white is a dark pile of embers, still smoking slightly. Someone must have burnt something last night. Ali wonders what.

The shed is next to what must be a hen house. Sounds of squawking can be heard within but Ali supposes it's too cold to let the birds out. 'Consider yourselves lucky,' she tells them. 'Battery farming is on its way.' She opens the privy door. Inside there's a lavatory with a wooden seat and a slop pail containing water with which to flush down the waste. Ali holds her breath and does the deed. She can't face washing at the outside tap but, back in the house, she finds a room with a sink, several copper tubs and a mangle. Ali washes her face and hands with green soap that smells sharp and acidic. She feels much fresher afterwards.

There's a line of chamber pots by the back door so she leaves hers there. Then she ventures into the kitchen. Clara is at the stove and Mrs Rokeby is sitting at the table, feeding her baby from a bottle. Clara says, without looking round, 'There's bread on the table and tea in the pot. If you want beer, it's extra.'

Ali cuts herself a slice of bread and spreads it with butter, which is wrapped in a damp linen cloth. To her surprise, Clara also hands her a bowl of porridge.

'Thank you,' says Ali.

'It's a penny,' says Clara.

'Can I give it to you later?' says Ali. Her money is upstairs, wrapped in the fur muff, along with the spray and the ultraviolet light. One thing hasn't changed since Victorian times; women's dresses don't have pockets.

Clara grunts as if this confirms her worst fears but she doesn't take the food away. The porridge tastes smoky but the heat is wonderful. Clara is cooking at an iron range which looks a bit like the industrial version of a trendy Aga. Ali can see the fire burning in the grate and imagines that Clara was up at the crack of dawn to get it going. The furnace makes the kitchen by far the warmest, and cosiest, place in the house. There's a large wooden table and a dresser with blue and white china arranged on it. Ropes are looped across the ceiling and from these hang herbs, a cooked ham and a selection of cloths and aprons. It resembles a spread in one of the magazines Dina likes, *Farmhouse Chic* or something similar, but the reality is different somehow. Maybe it's the smell: coal and bread and the rather pungent scent of the swaddled baby.

The food makes Ali feel better. She longs for strong coffee but the tea is dark brown and seems to soothe the caffeine craving. She asks the baby's name and is told that he's Leonard, after his father. It seems a strange name to give a baby but Ali supposes that Mrs Rokeby – Marianne – would think Finn a positively heathen moniker.

'Are you an artist's model?' Marianne asks Ali, looking her in the eyes for the first time.

Ali laughs. The sound surprises her and makes Clara look round from the range. 'No,' she says. 'Who'd paint me? I'm a widow,' she adds, remembering Dulcie's words, 'and I've come to London to visit my family. I'm from Hastings originally.'

'You speak funnily,' says Marianne, who is younger than Ali first thought, maybe only in her twenties. 'Is that a Hastings accent?'

'Yes,' says Ali.

'How do you know Mr Templeton?' asks Clara.

'He was a friend of my late husband's,' says Ali, lowering her eyes modestly. She thinks it's the most respectable thing to say and trusts that Clara will be too much in awe of her employer to question him.

'I was an artist's model once,' says Marianne. 'Everyone wanted to paint me. Then I met Len.' She sighs.

'Is he an artist?' says Ali. 'No,' she remembers, 'he's a musician.'

'He's a beautiful piano player,' says Marianne, 'but he can only get the music halls these days. He'll be playing late tonight.'

Ali is surprised to hear that Music Hall existed in 1850, she thought of it as a turn-of-the-century thing. She asks where Len is playing at the moment and is told he's 'at the Canterbury', which doesn't make her any the wiser. He'll be playing late, she realises, because it's Saturday in this new world.

Ali is about to ask more when there's a noise from the hallway, slammed doors and raised voices.

'That'll be Mr Tremain,' says Clara, opening the door of the range to stoke the fire.

'Oh dear,' says Marianne.

Ali knows she should investigate but she doesn't want to leave the kitchen. A few seconds later, though, the door opens and a man appears – he's bearded and romantic-looking, very Hoxton.

'I'm leaving this house today,' he says. 'I won't be insulted like this.'

'I'm sure,' says Clara. 'Porridge?'

'Thank you.' The man sits down at the table, notices Ali for the first time and stands up again.

'Frederick Tremain.' He makes her a slight bow. 'Usually just known as Tremain.'

Ali is always slightly suspicious of men who are called by their surname only. She thinks that Tremain, dashingly handsome in shirtsleeves and waistcoat, looks the type.

'Mrs Dawson,' says Ali, though this still sounds wrong. 'I'm staying here for a few days.' She really hopes this isn't true and that, at three o'clock, she will say goodbye to Clara, Marianne, Baby Leonard and the whole lot of them.

'What was the shouting about?' says Clara, placing a bowl in front of the newcomer.

'Arthur was accusing me of not caring about Ettie's death. That poor innocent.' He manages to look sorrowful and eat a large mouthful of porridge at the same time.

'Arthur's upset,' says Marianne. 'Ettie was his muse.'

'Muses are ten a penny,' says Tremain. He laughs rather brutally and Marianne looks away.

'Who do you think killed Ettie?' asks Ali. 'It's just . . . I arrived as it happened . . . I saw her . . .'

'I would have fainted,' says Marianne, implying that this was the correct response.

'I've seen death before,' says Ali. 'Being a widow,' she adds.

'Thomas Creek killed Ettie,' says Tremain. 'We all know that.'

In Ali's experience, if everyone knows who the killer is, they are usually right. But, of course, in this new world she has no experience of murder or murderers.

'Arthur was very insulting to me,' says Tremain. 'And then Mr Templeton appeared and started talking vulgar commerce.'

'You mean he was asking you to pay your rent,' says Clara. Tremain ignores this and Ali takes the opportunity to stand up and thank Clara for breakfast. She offers to wash up her cutlery but

Clara waves this aside. Ali leaves the kitchen and enters the hall to
find Cain Templeton deep in conversation with a fair-headed man.
They stop talking when they see her.

'Mrs Dawson,' says Templeton. 'I trust you slept well.'

'I did,' says Ali, conscious of her untidy hair and shiny face. The
green soap feels like it has scrubbed away a layer of skin.

'This is Arthur Moses,' says Templeton, 'another of our happy
band.'

Arthur makes an inarticulate noise.

'What are your plans for the day, Mrs Dawson?' Templeton asks,
with rather more than polite interest.

'I'm going to visit my husband's family,' says Ali, thinking it best
to carry on with her cover story.

'Where are they from?' asks Templeton.

'Bow,' says Ali.

Templeton and Moses exchange looks. Ali wonders what Bow
was like in 1850; even in the 1990s people were wary of the East
End. It's as trendy as hell now, of course. What would the two men
say if Ali told them that the Olympics was staged there?

'I wish you a pleasant day,' says Templeton.

It's a dismissal but Ali doesn't go. 'I owe you some money,' she
says, 'for the room.'

'You see, Moses?' says Templeton. 'There is still honesty in the
world. There's no hurry for you to pay your debt, Mrs Dawson.'

Ali doesn't like the word debt but she thanks him and makes her
way up the stairs – so many of them! – to her room. There she
collects her fur muff, wraps the shawl round her shoulders and sets
out again, not before nipping into the kitchen to pay Clara. The
piano is playing as she descends the staircase, but the two men are

gone. The clock says that it's nine o'clock, the number represented by a carriage driven by a skeleton in a top hat.

The snowy street is now full of horse-drawn vehicles, some grand two-storey affairs, some carts drawn by a single horse. The pavements are crowded too, street sellers joined by hurrying pedestrians, dawdling children and at least three loose dogs. With a panic Ali thinks that she won't find the ingress point, but she stood there so long yesterday that the spot is engrained on her mind. By the lamp post with the barrels on the other side of the street. Ali reaches the position and starts scuffing away the snow. She starts to ease the UV light out of its hiding place.

'Hoy!' It's the man she saw yesterday selling sheep's feet. Now he has a basket full of oranges. They are so bright in the monochrome world that Ali blinks at them.

'I saw you yesterday,' says the man. He has a scarred face and an eyepatch that gives him a rather piratical appearance. 'You stood on this self-same spot for nigh on an hour.'

'Really?' says Ali, trying to sound quelling.

'Yes. Before you there was a man. He stood where you are and then he vanished. Just like that.'

'He vanished?'

The man stares at her as if he hasn't said the word first. Then he bawls, 'Oranges! All the oranges in the world!' And, before Ali can question him further, he is lost in the crowd.

Chapter 16

Ali is back by the lamp post at two thirty. Her timepiece seems to have stopped but the clock in the hall showed the smaller hand halfway between two (a graveyard) and three (a man with a scythe). The sky is already darkening with the promise of more snow in the air. Ali finds her spot and kicks away the slush. The UV torch concealed in her sleeve shows the outlines of her footsteps. The sight of them makes Ali's heart race. They are proof that she arrived here yesterday, that she travelled in time. And, if she travelled backwards, she can travel forwards. She thinks of the first time, frantically trying to find the right paving stone in 2020 London. But then she had only travelled backwards by a week. Finn was still there, in his Pimlico flat, just about to go into lockdown. The worst that could happen would be some uncomfortable déjà vu. 1976 had been more frightening but that trip had gone like clockwork. She and Dina had arrived at the ingress point and, at the exact hour, Ali had felt the cold, lurching sensation that always accompanies the gate opening.

But, in 1976, Ali had had company. She remembered thinking:

if I'm stuck here, in a world where I am also four years old, at least I'll have Dina with me. But now she is completely alone. She stands stock-still, shivering. The wind has picked up and snow swirls around her. She waits, expecting the lurch and the pull backwards. Soon she'll be back in 2023, she'll see buses and *Big Issue* sellers. She can go back to her new, cosy house, feed Terry and call Finn. He won't even know that she's gone. She closes her eyes. She can sense the future, she can smell it: fried food and vanilla vape. She opens her eyes. The Victorian lamp post is still there and, in the distance, a street seller is shouting about 'mussels, a penny a quart'. It might not be three o'clock yet but, as soon as she thinks this, a clock strikes somewhere nearby. *You shall not go, says the great bell of Bow.* Ali waits, nerves tingling. She realises that tears are running down her cheeks. But she stays at her post until the bell strikes the quarter hour.

Slowly, stiffly, Ali moves forwards. There doesn't seem much point to anything but she seems to still be alive so she has to do something. Will she start to fade as the days go by? Jones was irritatingly vague on this point. 'You should be solid,' she told Ali, just before she sent her into 1850 with nothing but an ultraviolet light and a handful of coins. 'Will I stay solid?' Ali had asked. 'I think so,' said Jones, 'for a while, at least.'

How long is 'a while'? thinks Ali. As units of time go, it's not very satisfactory. She thinks of the letter she left behind the clock. When will Finn see it? At least he will know how much she loves him. But . . . She stops in the middle of the street and is nearly run over by a coal wagon. If she stays here will Finn ever be born? Perhaps there's a 2023 in which neither of them exists. She steps backwards onto the pavement and doubles over with sudden nausea.

'Drunk,' says someone, in a tone of deep disapproval. Once again, most people just ignore her. Eventually, Ali straightens up. Even if she no longer really exists, she might as well keep on walking. She is very cold, especially above the waist. Her legs are protected by the multiple skirts, but Ali's chest bones seem to have turned to ice. Is this a normal 'outside on a January day' feeling or is it a sign that she is shortly to vanish altogether? The word makes her think of the street seller.

Before you there was a man. He stood where you are and then he vanished. Just like that.

Clara had said the same thing about Thomas Creek. He had vanished and she never wanted to see his wicked face again. Is it possible that Creek made his way to the gate before Ali? Jones has always explained – as much as she explains anything – that she is making a space in time that fits one particular person. Ali left 2023 and she should have been able to return by the same route. 'It can't go wrong,' Jones had promised her, as they zipped through the traffic in her little space-age car. But it had gone wrong. Jones is not infallible. That's almost the most shocking thing of all. Could Thomas Creek, a Victorian man – possibly also a murderer – have found the ingress point, almost certainly by chance, and passed through it? Is he, even now, wandering along the Old Kent Road in a top hat?

She's walking as she thinks, feeling some sensation returning to her feet. She has no real idea where she's going but, along the way, she will look for the sheep's-feet man. It's unlikely that she will find him in this bewildering world, full of unfamiliar sounds and smells, but she has to do something. And detection might be all she has left.

★

She walks for miles. It seems like years ago when, back at Queen Mary's, Elizabeth had shown her a map of nineteenth-century London. Then, the streets had seemed to form grids around church-yards and open areas like Shoreditch. Ali had been able to trace a route from Hawk Street to the Mile End Road. The areas had religious names like St Matthew and St Leonard and, in later maps, the roads were bisected by the Great Eastern Railway. But, on the ground, trudging along in the boots which seem to have sprung a leak, Ali can see none of this order. She passes terraced houses and cobbled yards, which get progressively shabbier as she walks. Even-tually she finds herself in a road lined with stalls displaying fruit, vegetables, hunks of meat and whole fish, pungent and glassy-eyed. The crowd seems more ethnically mixed here: she sees embroidered clothes that look vaguely Middle Eastern and hears other languages spoken – Yiddish, Dutch and French. Nowhere can she see the man with a pirate patch.

Ali spots a woman selling clothes from a barrow and, on the top, is a short, fur-lined cloak with a hood. Ali asks how much, relieved that her voice still works, and is told it's a shilling. 'Free from the pox,' says the woman, encouragingly. Ali wonders if she is susceptible to diseases like smallpox, which have been eradicated in modern Britain. She buys the cloak anyway, wondering if she should have haggled. She will have to start preserving her money if she's going to be stuck here for much longer. Ali fights down this thought. Jones will get her out. She must.

Almost in defiance, Ali buys a chemise, a nightshirt and some stockings from another barrow. She really needs more bloomers but she can't see anywhere that sells them. She does find a rather gorgeous pharmacy and buys a pot of dentifrice, which she thinks must be toothpaste, and a small cake of soap. It smells like the tea-tree oil she bought when Finn had headlice. No toothbrush, she will just have to use her finger.

By now it's getting dark and the taverns are starting to open. Their lighted windows look very cosy but Ali can see that they are frequented only by men. On a street corner there's a trestle table with mugs, a large milk jug and what looks like a tea urn. The sign says, 'Coffee Penny a Mug'. Ali buys a mug's worth. It tastes odd, like chicory, but it's still warm. Ali thanks the woman and hands the mug back. She wonders if they are washed between customers.

Snow is falling again and Ali is glad of the cloak. She might be lost in time, maybe even in a liminal zone between life and death, but at least she's not freezing now. She walks on with her face down and hood up. Someone pushes past her and she wonders how safe women were in Victorian streets. Not very, is her guess. *A strange figure jumped out from a dark alley . . . he gripped her with claw-like hands and sexually assaulted her before leaping over a wall and making his escape, cackling with manic laughter.* Is Ali about to be accosted by Spring-heeled Jack or the jumping ghost of Peckham? She hurries on. The numbness is starting to go and, in its place, is panic. Where is Hawk Street? It's not as if she can look at her phone and she doesn't even have one of Elizabeth's maps. Should she ask someone? She chooses a respectable-looking woman pushing a pram. 'Don't know, love,' is the unwelcome answer, 'I'm not from round here.' Ali looks down at the pram, preparing to coo, and sees that it's full of coal. 'Gotta keep warm,' says the woman, sounding defensive. Ali wonders if the coal is stolen.

She makes a few more random turns. The streets seem rowdier now and there's music coming from some of the pubs. Is that what

Len is doing now? Playing for drinkers in a tavern somewhere? Ali feels almost homesick for Number 44, which just shows how strange the mind can be.

'Mrs Dawson? Alison?'

The sound of her name makes Ali stop dead. She pushes back her hood and sees Cain Templeton smiling down at her.

'What are you doing here?' she says.

Templeton sounds surprised. 'This is my house,' he says.

Ali turns and sees that she's by the steps to the front door of 44 Hawk Street. Is this an example of Jones's promised God-like powers? Has some mysterious déjà vu brought her through the alien streets to her own temporary front door?

'Been doing some shopping, I see,' says Templeton. He nods at her packages, which are wrapped in brown paper. His tone makes it sound as if she's laden with carrier bags from Harrods or M&S, depending on your social register.

'I got lost,' says Ali.

'Well, now you're home,' says Templeton with a warmth that seems both reassuring and slightly sinister. He gives her his arm and they walk up the steps to the front door. Templeton opens it with his key, which reminds Ali that she doesn't have one.

'Would you take some tea with me?' says Templeton, gesturing towards the drawing room.

'Thank you,' says Ali. The alternative would be sitting in her room and driving herself mad. At least this way she can pretend to be investigating. And tea sounds wonderful. She can still taste the coffee but not in a good way.

Clara brings tea and a sandy-looking layer cake. Ali wonders if this is a genuine Victoria sponge. It certainly looks different from the ones produced on *Bake Off*. She peels off some of her outer layers, cloak, shawl and hat, and wonders if this is an indelicate thing to do in front of a man. Templeton doesn't seem to notice and Clara hangs the wet garments on the stand by the fire. Ali is glad that she gave her some money earlier.

Ali pours the tea clumsily, spilling some on the lace table-cloth. Cain sits opposite and regards her with what looks like amusement. He's a rather unsettling presence. Ali is aware of the physicality beneath the foppish Victorian clothes. Isaac had looked like a mannequin, too handsome to be real, but Cain seems all too corporeal.

'Did you find your family?' asks Templeton. For a moment, this question strikes Ali to the heart. Finn is her family and she has lost him. Well, she supposes her parents and brother are family too but, fond as she is of them, only Finn really matters.

'Yes,' she says at last. 'It was . . .' What's the best word? 'Pleasant to see them.'

'Pleasant?' Templeton laughs. 'That bad?'

It's such a genuine laugh that Ali smiles too. 'Families can be difficult,' she says.

'They certainly can.' Ali thinks Templeton is still smiling but it's hard to tell with the moustache. 'Do you have children, Mrs Dawson?'

'A son, Finn.'

'Interesting name. Is he named for his father?'

'No, his father's name was Elvis.' The old joke comforts Ali but she thinks that Templeton gives her a rather sharp look.

'What about you?' Ali asks him. 'Do you have children?'

'Five,' says Templeton.

According to the family tree Isaac showed Ali, Cain Templeton had two children: Ephraim, who was Isaac's great-grandfather, and a daughter called Imogen. Did the others die in childhood? Or did history simply not record them? Ali hopes it's the latter.

Beyond vouchsafing that his children live in Sussex with their mother, Templeton does not seem interested in talking about his progeny. 'Let's talk about you,' he says. 'You interest me.'

'I can't think why,' says Ali. And she can't think of any reason why Templeton should be interested in her, a middle-aged widow in drab clothes. Unless he has spotted that there is something odd about her, something that makes her worth collecting. It's an unpleasant thought.

Templeton is giving her that look again, leaning back in his chair with long legs crossed. 'Are you making a long stay in London?' he asks.

'Just a few more days.' Ali crosses her fingers.

'The room is yours for as long as you want it,' says Templeton.

'Are you sure the previous occupant won't be coming back?'

'Thomas Creek? No, we won't see him again in this world.'

Ali's skin prickles. 'What do you mean?'

'Creek killed Ettie and then someone killed him. It's the simplest explanation.'

Is it? thinks Ali. She can think of several other explanations for Creek's disappearance. Including him disappearing into a wormhole linked to 2023.

Ali has her back to the door but she knows from Templeton's face that someone has entered. The quizzical amusement has been wiped away, to be replaced by something altogether less benign.

'Did you want me, Arthur?'

Ali twists round – quite difficult in a corset – and sees Arthur Moses standing there.

'Ettie's . . . Miss Moran's parents are here.'

Templeton sighs. 'I had better see them. Excuse me, Mrs Dawson.'

He leaves the room. Ali hopes that Arthur will follow him but, after a few seconds, the fair-haired man takes Templeton's seat. And a piece of cake.

'I say,' he says, thickly through crumbs, 'you know not to trust Templeton, don't you?'

'I hardly know Mr Templeton,' says Ali.

'He's not safe,' says Arthur. 'Not for a respectable woman like you.'

Is that what I am? thinks Ali. She's inclined not to take Arthur too seriously. He has a sort of chaotic but lightweight energy. On the other hand, she knows very well that some men are not safe around women, respectable or not.

'What do you mean?' she asks. 'He seems very kind. After all, he let me stay here.'

'If he lets you stay here,' says Arthur, 'it means he has a use for you. I mean, Tremain and I are artists. Len too. Templeton likes to collect artists.'

That word again.

'When I arrived here,' she said, 'someone said "another one for the collection". Was that you?'

Arthur looks over at the door but the voices seem to be moving away. Ali wonders if Templeton is showing Ettie's parents up to her bedroom, the place where their daughter was murdered. But, no, she hears the front door open and shut. Where is Templeton taking the bereaved couple? Ali doesn't know but she, like Arthur, relaxes a little.

'No,' says Arthur. 'It sounds like the sort of remark Thomas Creek might make.'

'Won't you tell me more about Mr Creek?' says Ali. 'I'm slightly nervous that he might come back to his room.'

Arthur pours tea. 'He won't come back.'

'How can you be sure?'

Is it because he's escaped to 2023?

'He killed Ettie and then he ran away. That's what Mr Templeton thinks too. He burned Creek's paintings in the garden.'

That explains the smouldering pile of ashes but not much more.

Ali shivers. She's overdoing the terrified woman act but her fear is not entirely faked. There is something chilling about the matter-of-fact way the other tenants talk about Thomas Creek, as if it's normal to share a house with a man who batters a woman to death.

'What if he comes back and kills me?' she says.

Arthur cuts another piece of cake and doesn't answer.

Chapter 17

Next morning Ali awakes before the tap on the window. The church bells are ringing, which reminds her that it's Sunday. The light coming through the round window is blue and otherworldly. Ali knows without looking that snow is still on the ground. She's not as cold as she was the night before, though, because Clara gave her a hot brick to put in her bed. She managed to take her corset off last night, though she thinks she broke a lace or two, and get into her new nightgown. It was surprisingly warm, although the voluminous material got wrapped around her legs in the night. Perhaps because of this, she slept fitfully, constantly waking up in a confused panic thinking of Finn, Jones, Templeton and Thomas Creek prowling through the streets of twentieth-century London.

Ali sits up, the panic taking over. Again, she reaches for her phone. She has always prided herself on not being addicted to her phone in the way Dina and Bud are. But, right now, she would give anything for the sight of the plastic case with its picture of Terry (a present from Finn). She hadn't realised how much time she spent looking at the screen, playing Words with Friends, looking up obscure facts on Google, chatting on her various WhatsApp groups. She's not on Facebook or any other social media platforms, partly because of her work, but it seems she's as addicted as any teenager. In this new world there are huge swathes of time when she has nothing to do, sitting in her room every evening or even just waiting around for Clara to bring her meals. What did Victorian women do with their time? She hears Elizabeth's voice. *You have to be able to make a posset, sew a seam and recite the Lord's Prayer. Can you do any of those things?* Whatever your views on praying and sewing, they certainly fill in the time.

Last night, Ali took a book from the shelf in the drawing room. *The Pickwick Papers* by Charles Dickens. She chose it because of her conversation with Elizabeth and because the blue binding reminded her of the books in her office. True, Elizabeth had told her not to trust Dickens, but she had also said that he was interested in time travel. Maybe Ali would be able to pick up some tips, although she was doubtful of her ability to understand the Victorian writer. Ali has always felt insecure about her reading. She took English Literature A level but only got a D and doesn't think she finished either of the set books, *Jane Eyre* or *The Great Gatsby*. She's tried to catch up since. She has her book club and reads a lot of contemporary fiction. But the classics have always intimidated her. She read a lot of heavy history tomes for her degree but has always felt wary of nineteenth-century literature. There are too many people called Chuzzlewit and Pumblechook, too many deathbed scenes, too many words. But, last night, sitting in her room with an oil lamp beside her, she was amazed how easy *The Pickwick Papers* was to read. Far easier than some recent Booker prize winners. She actually laughed aloud at the exploits of

Samuel Pickwick, Nathaniel Winkle and Augustus Snodgrass. The long sentences soothed her and calmed her breathing. She had to stop reading when her eyes became too tired in the poor light but she fell asleep with the syntax running through her head.

But now she's awake and the dread is back. She stretches out her hand for her shawl, wishing with all her heart that she was touching Terry's soft fur. She misses him as much as she misses her phone, almost as much as she misses Finn. But, in some strange way, the cat still seems to be with her. She keeps imagining that she can see him: a quick movement on the stairs, pale sunlight on the eiderdown, a pacing shadow following her through the streets.

Ali picks up her shawl, which was draped on the bed and has fallen to the floor, swings her feet onto the chilly floorboards and pads across the room, taking care not to dislodge the rug. Last night she brought up a jug of water to wash with and now there's a thin layer of ice on it. Shivering, Ali uses the chamber pot, far easier in a nightdress, and then washes her underarms, hands and face. The freezing water and tea-tree soap makes her skin sting but it's the most thorough wake-up call Ali has ever had. It reminded her of those people who insist on telling you their cold-water swimming routines. When Ali grew up in Hastings, 'wild swimming' was just called 'swimming' and no one made a fuss about it.

Before going to bed, Ali washed her drawers in soap and water and hung them in front of a fire, kindly kindled by Clara. They are still slightly damp and they smell a bit smoky, but at least they're clean. How do people procure new underwear? Maybe women are meant to sew the more intimate items themselves. *Can you sew a seam?* Ali can't face her corset so she leaves it off. She has so many layers to put on that she doesn't think anyone will notice.

It already feels like a routine: empty chamber pot in privy, wash hands in laundry, go to kitchen for breakfast. She's earlier than yesterday but Clara is already up, stoking the range. Marianne is at the table, holding her baby, and with her is a man who can only be Len, the pianist. Ali had imagined this personage to be another romantic-looking type with dark hair and long, artistic fingers. Instead, Leonard Rokeby the Elder is a heavy-set individual with short, distinctly ginger, hair. He looks like a rugby player at a fancy-dress party.

Len stands up when Ali enters, a courtesy that she quite likes, and mutters something about being pleased to meet her. Ali says how much she enjoys his music.

'I like playing the new composers,' says Len. 'It's Schumann's song cycles at the moment.'

All over again, Ali registers the shock of being in a world where Schumann is a new and possibly avant-garde composer. She knows next to nothing about classical music but the noises coming from the piano seemed to her entirely traditional and therefore soothing. She'd thought she was listening to Classic FM when it was, in fact, more like Radio One.

'Marianne said that you play at music halls,' says Ali.

Len gives his wife a reproachful look. 'They are not places for ladies,' he says repressively. 'Today I'll be playing the organ at St Barnabas's. A much more congenial venue. And I get paid,' he adds, in a different tone, 'a shilling a service.'

'Praise be to God,' says Clara.

Sunday. Ali's third day in 1850 and she's still solid enough to eat porridge, tickle a baby's chin and chat about music. How long will this last? What's happening in 2023? Has Finn read her letter yet? Is Jones planning her rescue? Ali feels light-headed at the thought.

'Are you unwell, Mrs Dawson?' says Len.

'I'm OK,' says Ali. 'Fine,' she amends.

'I told you she talked funny,' says Marianne.

Back in her room, Ali makes a plan for the day. She's glad she thought to bring a notebook and pencil because she saw no stationery items on any of the market stalls yesterday. It seems there's no Victorian equivalent of Ryman's or Paperchase. Ali has extravagant handwriting, but she tries to make it as neat as possible because the pages are very small.

'To do,' she writes. Immediately she gets the same sense of relief achieved by reading a page of Dickens, as if something clenched inside her has loosened. Dina laughs at her 'to do' lists but, when you're not sure if you even exist anymore, an itinerary is essential.

She has decided that she will investigate Ettie's death and, if possible, the disappearance of Thomas Creek. Yesterday, after assuring Ali of her safety, Arthur seemed to lose his nerve and, after another slice of cake, made his excuses and left. But Ali had the feeling that there was more that he could tell her.

Back in his penthouse apartment, Isaac Templeton had told her that his ancestor was suspected of killing Ettie Moran and two other unnamed women. Ali wonders when this suspicion first raised its head. At this moment, two days after her death, no one suspects kindly landlord Cain Templeton of murdering Ettie. All the suspicion focuses on Thomas Creek. But he has mysteriously vanished . . .

Ali writes 'Ettie Moran' in tiny capitals.

Then she adds: 'Frederick Tremain, Arthur Moses, Marianne Rokeby, Leonard Rokeby, Clara'. She will try to talk to all these people, starting with the members of the household. At two thirty she'll go back to the ingress point, just in case. Ali tucks the note-book under her pillow, rearranges her shawl so that it looks less like a noose, squares her shoulders and leaves the attic room.

She still doesn't understand the layout of 44 Hawk Street. From the outside it looks plain and box-like, three storeys high with sash windows placed symmetrically and Ali's round window like an eye in the roof. But, inside, there are steps that lead up and then down again with no discernible purpose, a tiny door set into the upstairs wainscotting, rooms leading into one another. Ali thinks of Bud with his *Doctor Who* mug. The Tardis is famously bigger on the inside than the outside. The same can't be true of this house but, all the same, she'd like to see a floor plan.

Frederick Tremain's room is on the first floor. Ali learnt that much from Arthur Moses, who is next door. To her surprise, the artist seems almost pleased to see her. He ushers her inside. It's a large space with two sash windows, a couch covered with rumpled bedclothes and a fireplace with clothes draped over the fender. An empty wine bottle rolls across the floor as Tremain pushes a pile of books to one side.

'Excuse the squalor,' he says, sounding proud if anything. 'But the room does possess splendid north light.'

All around the room, paintings stand on easels or are casually propped against the walls. They are all of women, some young and some old, but all painted with extraordinary vitality and char-acter. Ali stops before a golden-haired beauty, seated at a piano. You know immediately that she can't play it but wishes she could. The woman's thoughts are elsewhere, her eyes fixed on something out of the frame, one hand resting on a book in her lap, the other tentatively touching her face.

'Marianne,' says Tremain. 'In her prime.'

'That's Marianne? Mrs Rokeby?'

'Yes,' says Tremain. 'She was a good model. Shame, really . . .'

His voice dies away. What's a shame? That she married Len? That she had a baby? That she's no longer the beauty in the frame? Meg once told Ali, quite matter-of-factly, that her husband told her that she had 'coarsened' after having two children, *his* two children. Ali would have divorced him. Which says it all really. Ali thinks of Tremain saying, with what now sounds like calculated cruelty, 'Muses are ten a penny'.

'Have you got any pictures of Ettie?' she asks.

'Yes.' Tremain pulls out a canvas from behind the divan. It shows a red-haired woman in a garden. Unlike Marianne, she is completely naked.

'I drew her as Eve,' says Tremain. 'Before the fall.'

No Adam, Ali notes. There's something sad about Ettie's face, half-hidden by her long hair. She looks as if she knows she's being exploited.

Not looking at Tremain, Ali asks, 'Were you in the house when Ettie was killed?'

Tremain pauses before replying and she thinks he backs away slightly because a floorboard creaks. 'Yes,' he says. 'I was talking to Clara in the kitchen. Trying to get her to sit for me, actually. I've been commissioned to do a tavern scene. I wanted someone to play an old drunkard.'

Ali hopes that he worded his request slightly differently.

'Who else was in the house?' she asks.

'Why do you want to know?' asks Tremain. 'This isn't a subject for a lady.'

Ali turns to look at him and is relieved to see a smile on his face. All the same, she has to be careful. She realises that she has slipped into her police officer voice.

'Ettie had just been killed when I arrived here,' says Ali. 'It's been preying on my mind.' She tries to look soulful.

Tremain sits heavily on the couch and runs a hand through his long, dark hair. Ali excuses him of deliberately trying to look romantic. He just can't help it. In fact, Tremain sounds genuinely troubled when he says, 'Arthur was here. I know Len was because I remember the piano playing. Ettie was sitting for Thomas, up in the attic. The room where you are now.'

Ali thinks of the room, the round window, the hulking wardrobe. She's had no feeling of Ettie's spirit hovering but then, as successive husbands have told her, she has very little sensibility. Besides, she's had other things on her mind.

Tremain continues, almost talking to himself now. 'I heard footsteps running downstairs. Then, seconds later, Mr Templeton came in. I know his step. I came out of the kitchen and saw a woman going upstairs. That must have been you.'

'Was it you who said, "Another one for the collection"?'

'No, that wasn't me.'

'Who could it have been?'

'Creek perhaps. It's his sort of humour.'

Arthur thought it was Creek too. But the words didn't sound like a joke. She says, 'You didn't go upstairs to investigate? When you heard the footsteps?'

'No. People are always coming and going in this house. I went back into the kitchen. The next thing I knew, Arthur was banging on the door saying that Ettie had been killed.'

'Who do you think killed her?'

Another hair ruffle. 'Why, Thomas Creek, of course. He was obsessed with her. Painted her all the time.'

'What sort of a painter was he?'

Tremain looks contemptuous. 'Creek was all show, bright colours and female flesh. He couldn't draw hands or feet. Of course, portraiture wasn't how he made his money. That was something else entirely.'

'What?' Ali's mind boggles.

'Dead babies,' says Tremain.

'What?'

'When children die, which they do, of course – my mother lost three – families want their likenesses drawn. That's what Creek did. He drew dead babies.'

'How horrible.' But even as she says this, Ali knows she's wrong. Elizabeth told her about the high rate of infant mortality in Victorian England. If you lost a baby, wouldn't you want an image to remember them?

'It's not an art form that appeals to me,' says Tremain. 'Sometimes families want their dead children propped up next to their living siblings . . . but it's not for me to judge. These days, many photographers specialise in taking images of the dead. It's cheaper, of course, but a portrait can add a hint of colour to the cheeks, an illusion of life. Creek was expert at this. I will say that Creek was not a man I would trust around grieving women. I think he abused their trust.'

Creek sounds a real charmer, thinks Ali. She asks Tremain why he thinks Creek killed Ettie.

'Simple,' says Tremain, his voice harder than before. 'Ettie wouldn't become his mistress. She was a good girl, a country girl. Creek must have strangled her out of sheer frustration.'

Ali has her own thoughts about men who kill women out of supposed sexual frustration. Also, about men who define women as good girls or bad girls.

'Who told you she'd been strangled?'

'Someone said. Maybe Arthur?'

'Ettie was hit over the head with a heavy object.'

Tremain gapes at her, looking slightly less Byronic. 'How do you know?'

'I saw her. There was a lot of blood.'

'How terrible,' says Tremain faintly. 'I have a horror of blood. My father was a surgeon. Not a very respectable profession but there it is.'

All the surgeons Ali has met seem to think that they are the very apex of society. It's interesting to see Tremain quite embarrassed by his link to the medical profession.

'My family don't approve of me being an artist,' says Tremain, 'but it's my calling. And I'm starting to get commissions. I'd like to draw you one day, Mrs Dawson. I could do a sketch now.'

'No thank you,' says Ali.

She can't be sure that Tremain isn't still looking for someone to portray a senior citizen with a drink problem.

Arthur's room is tidier and his pictures, insipid watercolours, definitely less impressive. Ali remembers Marianne saying that Ettie had been Arthur's muse. She squints at the blurry pictures, trying to see if any of them show the red-headed woman. She wonders now if Marianne was Tremain's muse.

'You must be very sad about Ettie,' she starts.

Arthur blinks as if this is a trick question. 'Yes,' he says at last. 'She was a pretty little thing. A good model too.'

'I saw her . . .' Ali wonders how to put this delicately, 'when she was no more. I'll never forget it.' This is true.

'Mr Templeton asked me to help carry her . . . her body . . . downstairs,' says Arthur with a shudder. 'It was awful seeing her, the blood on her face and in her hair . . .' He turns away, apparently genuinely overcome.

After a respectful pause, Ali says, 'So you were in the house when she died, when she was killed?'

'I was in this room,' says Arthur. 'Painting. I had an idea for a woodland scene. Pastoral, you know. I was lost in my work.'

Is it possible to be so lost in painting trees that you don't notice a murder upstairs? For some reason, Ali thinks of the framed print in Geoff's office, a forest glade with light slanting through branches. For a moment she feels so homesick for Eel Street that she can hardly speak.

Luckily Arthur continues, which might mean that he too thinks his evidence sounds flimsy. Although he doesn't know it's evidence, of course. 'I heard a noise, like something falling, but I thought it was just an easel crashing over or something. Creek flails around when he's working. Besides, he's often drunk. Things get knocked over a lot. Then there were footsteps on the stairs, doors slamming. I heard the clock striking three. It's always a bit fast. Then Mr Templeton knocked on my door. "I need your help," he said. He didn't tell me about Ettie or say he was sorry. I had to discover her for myself.' Another shudder.

'That must have been horrible,' says Ali.

'It really was,' says Arthur. 'We carried her downstairs and then the men from the morgue came with their cart. They took her away. Her parents came yesterday. That must have been where Mr Templeton took them.'

The word 'morgue' has a gruesome, penny-dreadful sound. *The Murders in the Rue Morgue*. Has that been written yet?

'You said yesterday that you thought Thomas Creek killed Ettie.'

'Yes, that's the only explanation.'

'Is it? When I saw Ettie lying dead on the floor there was only one other person in the room. Cain Templeton. You told me yesterday that he wasn't safe. Could he have killed Ettie?'

'No!' Arthur sounds outraged. He stands up and takes a quick turn around the room. 'It was Thomas Creek. He must have forced himself on Ettie and she resisted. She was an innocent girl.'

'Marianne said that Ettie was your muse.'

Arthur sits down again and rubs his eyes. 'I liked painting her, that's all. She was beautiful.'

'Why did you tell me to beware of Mr Templeton?'

'There are rumours around him. Nothing I could relate to a lady. I just wanted you to be on your guard.'

'Are the rumours about a club called The Collectors?'

Arthur gapes at her. 'How can you know about The Collectors?'

'I've heard rumours too.' What would Arthur say if he knew they had lasted until the twenty-first century?

'I don't know much,' says Arthur. 'But a friend of mine has attended some of their meetings. You have to be high-born to join.'

'What's your friend's name?'

'Burbage. The Honourable Francis Burbage.'

Ali suspects anyone who uses an inherited title and she's not about to make an exception for the unknown Mr Burbage.

'Do you know any of the other Collectors?' she asks.

She sees Arthur's eyes widen in horror and, after a few seconds, Ali realises that he's looking at something behind her back. She turns, easier without the corset. Cain Templeton is standing in the doorway.

'How charming,' he says. 'I like it when my tenants become friends.'

Arthur has stood up. He mutters something about rent.

'No matter.' Templeton raises a hand. 'The end of the day will suffice. Mrs Dawson, could I have a few minutes' conversation with you?'

They go out onto the landing. Schumann's latest hit ripples around them.

'Mrs Dawson,' says Templeton. 'Will you do me the honour of dining with me tonight?'

Chapter 18

The invitation is to Templeton's house in Kensington. He sends his carriage for Ali, which makes her feel like she's being abducted or carried off to the underworld in one of those spectral horse-drawn vehicles that appear so often in ghost stories. Of course, all those Victorian tropes – The Woman in Black, The Woman in White, The Woman Who Raises Her Veil to Reveal the Hideous Crone Underneath – weren't yet clichés in 1850. To Ali's modern mind, there are BBC2 costume dramas around every corner: black horses, swirling cloaks, fog reflected in wavering lamplight.

Ali could also be going into real danger, not just the fictional sort. She has been warned, after all, that Cain Templeton is not 'safe'. But Ali finds it hard to feel scared, or to experience anything much. She feels numb, disassociated from reality. Or is it just that she's frozen with despair? At three she went to stand at the ingress point amidst the falling snow. All that happened was that a man sidled up and asked, with a leer, if she was 'doing business'. Was her appearance becoming less respectable, Ali asked herself as she trudged wearily back to the house, or was any woman propositioned if they stood still long enough? Ali's faith in Jones is growing dimmer by the day. In fact, they are all growing dimmer, all the people in her life: Jones, Geoff, Dina, John, Bud, Meg. Ali even struggles sometimes to remember Finn's face. In 2023, when she can't sleep, she scrolls through photos of Finn on her phone. Now, she has to imagine the brown hair, curly in childhood now cropped short, the blue eyes and long eyelashes, the dark stubble that always surprises her, the reminder that her boy is now a grown man. Maybe that's why artists like Tremain are always in work. And why photography is now the latest craze. People need likenesses.

When Ali looked at herself in the mirror before setting out, she saw a worried-looking woman with lank hair pulled back into an unsuccessful bun. Her face, bare of make-up, looked every day of its fifty years but also, strangely, looked very much like her mum, Cheryl. She's never thought of herself as resembling her mother but it is oddly reassuring. Ali spent most of her teenage years arguing with Cheryl and, even now, their relationship is one of continual misunderstanding only slightly leavened by affection. But there's something curiously comforting about seeing Cheryl's face staring out at her.

The carriage arrived as the clock was striking seven, a black cat with yellow eyes. Templeton's coachman helped Ali inside, which was good because the step was very high and she still found her skirts cumbersome. She was tempted to leave off some petticoats that morning but it's too cold for shedding layers. She's aware that she doesn't present a very glamorous image in her short cloak and creased black dress, now slightly dusty and stained about the hem, but she hopes that she at least looks clean. She managed a complete wash with the tea-tree soap that morning. Her hair remains dirty, though, and rather greasy, but she has forced it into a more severe bun. If Cain comes close enough to smell her – a curiously disturbing thought – she hopes he won't be revolted.

The ride through the night-time streets is mesmerising, even for someone insulated by despair. The carriage jolts over cobbles and the sound of the horses' hooves is hypnotic. There's a full moon – impossible to travel without it, Ali supposes – and its light turns the snow almost purple in places. The lamplight is buttery and golden, making the dark houses look like advent calendars. Ali presses her face to the window and thinks: I'm here, this is me. She must have said it aloud, because her breath mists the glass.

Eventually the carriage pulls up outside a house that is positively blazing with light. There are lamps on either side of the front door and in most of the windows. The coachman helps Ali down and the door is opened by a maid in a black dress and white apron. Ali had been worried about seeing Cain Templeton on her own – she was pretty sure this was scandalous behaviour, especially because Cain's wife and children were 'at the country house' – but, of course, she'll be chaperoned by his staff. She wonders what job Clara did when she worked here.

'I don't have a butler in London,' Templeton tells her, as if this were a tremendous hardship. 'But Dorothy looks after me. And I have a cook and a housemaid, of course.'

Of course.

They are in a large room, much grander than anywhere at Number 44, with dark red wallpaper and a white marble fireplace in which what looks like half a tree is burning. The unaccustomed heat, and the red walls, make Ali think of Hell Hall in *The One*

Hundred and One Dalmatians, one of her favourite books as a child. It hasn't been written yet, she realises.

Templeton pours them both a drink from a decanter on a tray. Ali supposes she should be wary of unknown liquids, but she takes a sip and it's clearly sweet sherry.

'And now,' says Templeton, 'I have something to show you.'

This is very much Victorian Villain behaviour, but Ali is intrigued so she follows him out of the room. They cross the hall, which, like Number 44, is tiled in black and white, and into another darkly damasked chamber, this one of deepest green. Templeton lights an oil lamp and Ali sees the shimmer of myriad reflections. The room is full of cabinets, wooden chests with many shelves, glass boxes, some of them reaching as high as the ceiling. With a thrill of déjà vu, Ali recognises the Roman skull and the mummified cat from the collection at Queen Mary's.

But Templeton is leading the way towards a box on a pedestal, a bit like a goldfish bowl. Ali peers at the object within, which looks rather like a large peach stone, or a prehistoric sea creature, pitted and fossil-like. She has seen it before, of course.

'Do you have any idea what this is, Mrs Dawson?'

Did Victorian women know what a human brain looked like? Ali thinks it's safest to answer no.

'It's the mind of a murderer,' says Templeton.

'A murderer's brain! How did you get it?' Then, slightly too late, 'How horrible.'

'A man called Percival Green, the *Reverend* Percival Green,' he adds with a melodramatic verbal flourish. 'He killed five prostitutes over the space of six months. He claimed to be saving them from themselves, or for himself, as the case proved. He was hanged in 1845.'

'Why is it here?' says Ali. 'Why is any of this here?'

'I like to collect objects,' says Templeton. 'I have the skull of a murdered Roman woman, a piece of hangman's rope and a cursed mummy from an Egyptian tomb.'

'Someone once described you to me as a magpie,' says Ali.

'Who said that?' says Templeton.

'It doesn't matter,' says Ali. Ed Crane had been referring to a magpie's love of glitter, but don't the birds also enjoy feeding on carrion? 'You seem interested in death.' She allows herself to look directly into Templeton's face, almost for the first time. His eyes are very dark and, for once, the amused expression has vanished. They stare at each other for what feels like a full minute. Ali has the ridiculous feeling that Templeton is about to kiss her. A kind of horrified delight surges through her. She realises that she is leaning forward.

'Dinner is served, sir.'

Ali hadn't seen the door open, but Templeton obviously had. He smooths his cravat. The first nervous gesture Ali has ever seen him make.

'We will be in presently, Dorothy.'

Dorothy must have retreated because Templeton says, in his normal voice, 'I'm interested in crime. And solving it. You know that there are men whose job it is to understand the minds of murderers? Detectives, they're called.'

Would it blow his mind to discover that the future holds women detectives?

'I've heard that you belong to a secret society called The Collectors,' says Ali, keeping her eyes fixed on Templeton's face.

She means to catch him off guard but, to her surprise, he smiles, moustache lifting. 'Who told you about The Collectors? Was it Arthur Moses?' says Templeton. 'He talks too much, that boy.'

Ali says nothing. Templeton takes a turn around the room, touching a glass box here, adjusting the angle of a jade elephant there.

'The Collectors is just a group of gentlemen who are interested in unusual things. Objects like those in this room.'

'A murdered woman, the brain of a man who killed women.'

Templeton stops in front of her. 'As I say, I'm interested in criminality.'

'The first time I saw you, there was a dead woman at your feet.'

'I didn't kill her,' says Templeton.

'I've heard it said that, in order to be one of The Collectors, you need to have killed a woman.'

Templeton's face darkens. 'Who told you that?'

'I can't reveal my sources,' says Ali.

'You are an unusual woman,' says Templeton.

'I'm really very ordinary,' says Ali.

Templeton turns away to adjust the bowl containing Percival Green's brain. 'A woman died in this house,' he says. 'Her name was Jane Campion. She was my mistress. Living under my protection. I hope I haven't shocked you. But I feel you are a woman of the world.'

It must be the shawl. Ali nods, indicating her unshockability.

'Jane died of opium poisoning. It was a tragedy but not a murder. But I fear that it was with Jane's death that the rumours started.' Ali is not sure if she believes him. This is why she has travelled to 1850, to clear Cain Templeton's name, but she realises that the first time she heard about the sinister society with its innocuous name, she had thought him guilty.

'Tell me more about The Collectors,' she says.

Templeton laughs and the dark look vanishes. 'For that conversation, I need food. Shall we eat?'

The meal seems to take for ever. Dorothy brings in course after course: soup, fish, roasted pigeon, milk pudding. Ali eats heartily, glad she's left off her corset. Templeton picks at his food, though he does gnaw a pigeon leg to the bone. He also drinks several glasses of red wine. Ali is careful to stop at one. Over the last few days, she's been surprised to experience a craving for alcohol. She doesn't drink that much usually, barring parties and book club nights, but now she finds herself fantasising about the lighted windows of public houses, Tremain's bottle rolling across the floor, the advertisements for blue gin that appear in the windows of shops. Last night Clara had offered her a drink from a black bottle she kept concealed in the pantry. Ali had no idea what was in it, but she'd been very tempted to find out. If she could get drunk enough, she could forget everything, even the fact that she's lost in another century. For this reason alone, she must stay sober.

'I'll say it again,' says Templeton, regarding her over the rim of his glass. 'You're a very unusual woman, Mrs Dawson.'

'And I'll say again that I'm not,' says Ali, taking a spoonful of milk pudding.

'But you are. You turn up at my house out of the blue, simply dressed but clearly possessing money. You walk the streets on your own, you eat like a trencherwoman, you ask questions about murder. Are all women in Hastings like you?'

'Yes,' says Ali. 'It's full of gluttonous hags with a morbid taste for death.'

ELLY GRIFFITHS

Templeton laughs. 'You see what I mean. Tell me, Mrs Dawson, what happened to your husband?'

'Do you suspect me of murdering him?'

'I'm curious, that's all.'

Ali can't resist saying, 'Actually, I've had three husbands.'

Templeton's eyebrows raise. 'Three? You've been very unlucky to lose three husbands.'

'Haven't I just?'

'Tell me about them.'

'Well,' Ali thinks fast. 'My first husband was a lot older than me.' She thinks this is necessary to explain his tragic death. Besides, Declan is a good ten months older than her; Ali was one of the youngest in her year. 'He's the father of my son. My second husband was a teacher and my third was a . . . cowboy.'

'A cowboy?' Templeton's tone implies that, even if he doesn't believe her, he's enjoying the story.

'Yes,' says Ali. 'It's a dangerous life.' She sighs, implying that Lincoln was killed by a stampede or extreme rodeo-riding.

'Have you been to the Wild West then?'

'Yes,' says Ali. Well, she's seen the Badlands in Canada, which is almost the same.

'Remarkable,' says Templeton. 'And you have just one son? What did you say his name was? Phineas?'

'Finn. Yes.'

'Where is he now?'

'In Hastings.' The town is beginning to sound like a euphemism for heaven.

'I have a house in Sussex,' says Templeton. 'East Dean.'

Ali hears Finn's voice, which always surprises her with how deep

141

and patrician it is. *A big Gothic mansion on the cliffs. Apparently it's a popular spot for suicides.*

'Do you spend much time there?'

'I have a studio there but I prefer the city. Fedora – my wife – likes the country though. Which is convenient.'

What does he mean? Is this the beginning of a pass? Templeton's eyes gleam in the candlelight but Ali still can't believe he'd be interested in her, not with this hairstyle.

'Can we talk about The Collectors now?' says Ali, leaning back as Dorothy takes away her pudding plate.

'What do you want to know?'

'How do you become a member? Where do you meet? Do you have to be wealthy? Do you have to be a man?'

There's a silence, broken only by the clock ticking in the hallway. 'It's a club for people – men – who collect unusual objects,' Templeton says at last. 'Historical artefacts. Curiosities.'

Ali thinks of Ed Crane saying, 'It's quite a curiosity' and of Isaac wanting the university to display the exhibits. What would Cain Templeton think of his great-great-grandson? Ali suspects he'd be delighted with him. Isaac is a powerful man and he plots his inevitable political rise from East Dean.

'Objects can have strange powers,' says Templeton. 'Don't you think? One has heard of cursed mirrors, of books that will kill you if read in a certain light. I suppose it's natural that one invests inanimate things with life. If a man sits in a chair all his life, will that seat not retain something of him?'

There's a witticism to be made here but Ali suspects that Victorian women don't make bum jokes.

'I don't agree,' she says. 'Things are just things.' Even as she says this, she thinks of the room at Queen Mary's, the skulls and the baleful jewellery. There was something otherworldly about these objects, if only because they existed in such an atmosphere of secrecy.

'Have you no treasures? Something that you keep for sentimental reasons only?'

Ali has moved so many times that she hasn't been able to keep many mementos but she still has the first scan of Finn and his wristband from hospital. 'Boy of Ali Kennedy.' These are in an old tobacco tin of her grandfather's. Perhaps Templeton has a point.

'I have a few keepsakes,' she concedes. 'And I collect glass and china in different colours.'

'So you do understand,' says Templeton. 'Why is it that a child's shoe or a father's watch can move us to tears? There is emotion contained within inanimate objects.'

What would Templeton think of *The Repair Shop*, the TV programme where people bring prized possessions to be restored by experts? There are enough tears in each episode to float the *QE2*. But nothing in these sentences would be intelligible to Cain Templeton.

'I've been to Egypt,' he continues, 'and entered the tombs of the pharaohs. Their treasures are just lying there, waiting to be taken. In the room across the hallway, I have a mummified cat. You know that ancient Egyptians worshipped cats?'

Ali does know this and, as far as she is concerned, it's a mark in their favour. She notes that Templeton thinks that Ancient Egyptian artefacts are just 'waiting to be taken'. She longs to tell him about the fate of the people who discovered – and plundered – Tutankhamun's tomb.

'You've travelled a lot,' she says. How long would it take to get to Egypt without the benefit of planes? The longest trip Ali has taken was to Canada, to meet Lincoln's family. The experience put her off air travel for life.

'I'm lucky enough to have both money and an enquiring mind,' says Templeton. 'Come, it's getting late. The moon is high. I should send for the coachman.'

Chapter 19

For some reason, maybe the wine and sherry, or maybe all the
food, Ali has the worst night so far: sleepless, panic-filled, pacing
the attic trying to remember how to breathe. When she eventually falls asleep, she dreams of murdered women, bodies floating
in formaldehyde, a hangman's hands. She wakes to find a different
light filling the room, the sun slanting through the round window.
More snow has fallen and the street is full of people. It's Monday
morning in Hawk Street.

Ali gets up slowly. A new week in 1850. How long before she
vanishes altogether? But, when she passes the looking glass, she's
still there: greasy hair, pink nose and all. She thinks of Templeton
talking about cursed mirrors. 'Who's the fairest of them all?' The
answer is very definitely not Ali Dawson. Somehow she dresses
and makes her way downstairs. Len is playing scales, up and down,
up and down. The Italian for stairs is *scale*. Ali thinks of one of
Jones's favourite sayings: 'Time travel is like using a lift rather than
taking the stairs.' But Ali has been scared of lifts ever since she and

Finn were trapped in one years ago, in an office block that Ali was cleaning. She wonders if Finn remembers. Please, Jones, let me see my boy again.

Marianne is in the kitchen, feeding the baby. She tells Ali, rather disapprovingly, that it's nearly nine o'clock.

'I overslept,' says Ali.

'You look peaky,' says Marianne. 'Ask Clara for a tonic. It has laudanum in it.'

Laudanum, Ali knows, is another word for opium. She thinks of Jane Campion, dying of an overdose.

'I don't want to take laudanum,' she says.

'It's harmless,' says Marianne. 'Clara gave me some gripe water for Baby Leonard. That has laudanum in it.'

'Don't give it to the baby,' says Ali, too sharply.

Marianne clutches Leonard to her breast, as if Ali has threatened him. Clara enters through the door that leads into the scullery and the garden. She's carrying a trug with eggs in it.

'Good morning, Mrs Dawson. Would you like some tea?'

'Yes, please.' Caffeine is a drug that Ali won't refuse. She still longs for proper coffee.

Clara puts a cup in front of her. 'It's another shilling for the week,' she tells her.

'I'll get you the money,' says Ali. Her stock of coins is growing smaller. What will she do when she's destitute? Pose as an old drunkard for Tremain? Throw herself on Cain Templeton's dubious mercy?

Clara has turned back to the stove, but she hears the door open and says, without turning round, 'You owe me money too, Mr Moses.'

'All in good time, Clara.' Arthur assumes a lofty tone. He sits opposite Ali and smiles, rather lasciviously.

'How was your evening with Mr Templeton?'

Ali stares him down. 'Very pleasant.'

'You never went to his house on your own?' says Marianne.

Clara puts porridge in front of Ali. 'Evil to him who thinks evil,' she says.

Isn't that on the royal coat of arms? thinks Ali. *Honi soit qui mal y pense*. Something like that anyway. She's grateful for Clara's unexpectedly high-flown support.

'I hope you didn't mention my name,' says Arthur.

Ali makes a non-committal sound that Arthur obviously interprets as 'no'.

'Speaking of your previous conversation,' he says. 'Francis Burbage is coming here today. I could introduce you.'

'What time is he coming?'

'Three o'clock.'

'I've got something to do at three. I'll be with you at ten past.'

She hopes that she won't be.

But she is. At three o'clock Ali stands in the street and nothing happens, not even a proposition. The road is, for once, almost empty. She hasn't seen the sheep-feet man, the one with the eyepatch, since he told her about the vanishing pedestrian. Was it Thomas Creek? Did he take her portal and, if so, can Jones make her another one? A dog, a tight-skinned mongrel that Ali has seen before, sniffs around her skirts. Ali moves away before he can lift his leg on her. Dog wee added to horse hair wouldn't be the best combination. She really should get some more clothes.

Ali makes her way back to the house. She still hasn't got a key but the door never seems to be locked. She climbs the stairs to Arthur's room. She can hear voices inside and knocks boldly.

Ali dislikes Francis Burbage immediately. He has wet lips and straggly hair. He kisses her hand, which is an unpleasant experience in itself.

'Mrs Dawson. What a pleasure to meet you. Arthur here has been telling me all about you.'

'That's interesting,' says Ali. 'What has he told you?' Burbage seems disinclined to answer this. Arthur says, rather hurriedly, 'I've been telling Mrs Dawson about The Collectors.'

'You don't know about The Collectors,' says Burbage, rather sharply. 'You have to be a gentleman to join.'

Arthur looks abashed and, almost for the first time, Ali feels sorry for him.

'I had dinner with Cain Templeton last night,' she says, hardly caring any more if she shocks them. 'And he told me that it's a club for people who collect interesting objects.'

Ali gets out her notebook. Both men look at it as if mesmerised (mesmerism, according to Elizabeth, being another Victorian obsession).

'I went to one meeting,' says Burbage, 'and it's true that the conversation was about furniture and other such prosaic matters but I've heard there are other, more secret, meetings. At the Hangman's Club in Limehouse.'

'Why do you think you were invited to that one meeting?' asks Ali. She expects Burbage to boast about being a gentleman again but, instead, a sly look comes over his face.

'Because of these,' he says and takes out a sheaf of what look like postcards.

'What are they?'

'*Photographs.*' He makes the word sound extremely salacious. Ali remembers Elizabeth saying that photography grew in popularity in the 1850s and '60s. Studios producing daguerreotypes, photographic images projected onto silver-plated copper, sprang up on every London street. Tremain mentioned photographs of dead children. Ali is sure that there were other, seedier, uses.

Sure enough.

'I can't show some of these to a lady,' says Burbage, licking already wet lips. 'But look at this one.' Ali leans over and sees a woman lying prone on a bed, her hand touching the floor. She could be asleep if it weren't for the dark stains on the white sheet that doesn't quite cover her body. There's a half-opened window behind her. Ali was briefly a cleaner in a hospice (the happiest place she ever worked) and she remembers one of the nurses leaving a window open so that the dead person's spirit could fly out. Is that the intention here?

'Photographs of murdered women,' she says. 'Is that why you were invited to a meeting of The Collectors?' She feels as she does when faced with a female corpse at the start of a book or film. Stop using women's bodies in this way, she wants to say, and tell me who the killer is.

'I thought that might be the case,' says Burbage. 'But they just wanted me to photograph some old chairs.'

'Who posed for this picture?' says Ali. She hopes they paid her, at least.

'An artist's model called Jane Campion,' says Burbage. 'She was very beautiful. I believe she's dead now.'

Ali thinks about the image all afternoon. Jane's beauty had shone out from the black and white photograph, its edges furry from handling. Her hair must have been blonde and she had full lips and long eyelashes lowered over shut lids. Ali thinks of Ettie's auburn hair becoming redder with blood. These two women earned their livings by posing for men with easels and cameras. And now they're both dead. Jane might have died from a drug overdose but someone got her hooked in the first place. Ettie had been bludgeoned to death. Tremain and Arthur are insistent that Thomas Creek killed Ettie. This might well be true but the fact remains that Ali saw Cain Templeton standing over her dead body. *Cover her face*. And Jane Campion died in his house, under his 'protection'. Ali knows what she, as a police officer, should make of that connection.

Burbage's account of The Collectors' meeting was almost laughably banal. They talked about furniture, he was asked to photograph some chairs. But that doesn't account for the frisson that always accompanies the mention of the group. What happens at the other meetings, the ones that take place at the Hangman's Club? Ali thinks of the first time she entered 44 Hawk Street. *Another one for the collection*. Admittedly, Ali's introduction to the household was hardly conventional but isn't it true that there's something odd about the house? The memento mori clock, the strange layout, the sense of people coming and going without being seen, the footsteps on the stairs, the murder in the top room.

Ali thinks of the moment when she almost kissed Cain Templeton. The moment when his eyes became unfocused and he moved towards her. She knows that she moved towards him too. What would have happened if Dorothy hadn't come in? Would they have kissed? Would this have led to something more? Would they have gone upstairs to Templeton's bedroom which, she is willing to bet, contains a double bed? Ali hasn't had proper physical contact with a man in years. She divorced Lincoln in 2015, the same year she joined the cold case team. Since then there was one date with Simon, a teacher friend of Meg's, which ended in a kiss on a cheek and a sudden realisation, by Ali, that she needed to rush home and watch *Strictly Come Dancing*. Is she attracted to Cain? How can she be when, in Ali's world, he's been dead for over a hundred years? Is that even Ali's world any more? She lies on the bed, pulls the blanket over her, and closes her eyes.

She wakes to the clock striking six. Supper time. Ali is ravenous, as she always is these days. At least it shows that she's still alive. She gets up, tidies her hair as best she can, rearranges her shawl and starts to descend the stairs, trying not to look too eager. *You eat like a trencherwoman.*

There are four of them round the table: Tremain, Marianne, Arthur and Ali. She supposes that Len is playing at the Canterbury. Baby Leonard is asleep in his crib by the range. Clara doesn't eat with them and Ali wonders if this is through choice or class prejudice. But she has produced a stew, which, though tasteless by Taj Mahal standards, is warm and filling. Ali feels comforted, despite everything.

Tremain produces a bottle of claret and pours them all a glass.

'I sold a painting. Thanks be to God.'

'Which one?' asks Arthur, dipping bread into his gravy. 'Jochebed and Amram?'

'No. The Slave Girl of Naaman.' Tremain glances at Marianne and then looks away. Ali wonders if she posed for the picture.

Ali takes a sip of wine. It's rough and strong and makes everything feel just slightly better. Once again, she warns herself to stop at one glass.

'I saw Burbage leaving here today,' says Tremain. 'What did he want?'

'Just a friendly visit,' says Arthur. Blushing is very obvious on his fair skin.

'Buying some more of his postcards, were you?' asks Tremain.

'He's an artist,' says Arthur. 'Photography is an art form.'

'I don't like the idea of it myself,' says Marianne. She glances at her baby and Ali wonders if she's thinking of the dead infant industry.

'Have you ever posed for a photograph, Mrs Dawson?' asks Marianne.

Ali hesitates. Would she be expected to have had a wedding portrait with the mythical Mr Dawson? Or at least one of them. In the end she takes advantage of her exotic birthplace and says that such sophistication has yet to reach Hastings. The others nod as if this is what they would have suspected.

As Ali goes up to bed later, carrying a candle, she thinks that Number 44 must be rather like living in halls of residence. She never experienced this herself; she was a mother with a child when she was at university, but she has often thought that it must be the perfect living arrangement, sharing a house with like-minded people yet each possessing your own space. Finn has often told her that the reality is rather different but Ali wonders if she has travelled to 1850 in order to live out this particular fantasy, which seems a bit extreme.

In her bedroom, shivering under the covers, Ali wonders, for the first time really, if she will be in the nineteenth century for ever. If so, she'll have to find some sort of job and discover what opportunities exist for a woman of fifty. Maybe she can specialise in modelling elderly crones for photographs or portraits. She lies still in the darkness, listening to the house breathing. Life goes on, she thinks, until one day it doesn't.

Chapter 20

Ali wakes thinking: this is the beginning of my new life. It's a hollow feeling but there's a certain comfort in reaching rock bottom. She has no idea how long she will continue to exist in 1850. Jones only said that she would be solid 'for a while' and Ali is beginning to realise that a lot of Jones's theories are only guesswork. How can she know the truth, sitting in her office at Imperial College or striding through the desks in Pevensie? Jones doesn't know what it's like to wake up in a Victorian bed, to see pale Victorian sky out of the window, to know that you have to put on layers of uncomfortable clothes, go downstairs and talk to people who have been dead for over a hundred years.

But Ali has to do just this. She decides that, after breakfast, she will walk to Eel Street. It's near Spitalfields Market – still a thriving place – so she thinks she must have been very near the site that first day when she walked and walked. She remembers hearing (from John? Geoff?) that the street name came from the days when the market used to sell fish, before the new centre was built at Billingsgate. So Ali sets out, in her fur cape, stepping over slush that, in places, is mixed horribly with horse shit and other refuse she prefers not to identify.

Once again, it's hard to make sense of the Victorian streets. Ali tries to follow the line of the train track leading to Liverpool Street but that proves impossible and she has to take several diversions. She passes Brick Lane, which has stalls selling clothing and bric-a-brac. Should she buy some more underwear? She can't quite face it. She sees several Orthodox Jews, their clothing almost the same as it is today, and hears Yiddish and Spanish spoken. She thinks of the Novo Cemetery at QMUL. Maybe some of the people shopping today are buried there? It makes Ali feel kindly towards them although, when she smiles in a comradely way at a woman selling lengths of silk, she's asked what she's grinning about. Londoners haven't changed that much then.

Spitalfields is also busy although Ali can't see any stalls selling fish. Leaving the main market, she heads down a side street. The houses are very close together and washing criss-crosses the upper storeys. Is this Eel Street? At the end of the road, Ali sees a familiar landmark, the beautiful spire of Christ Church. She can see this from the window of the Department of Logistics. Now, though, the church looks onto open land, a rural oasis in the middle of the city. There are even sheep grazing on the marshy grass. This must be where Eel Street was built later. No wonder they have damp problems.

Ali retraces her steps towards Spitalfields. At the bottom of the street there's a pub called the Bag O'Nails. Ali knows immediately that it's not a place where a woman, or anyone claiming to be respectable, can enter. Although it's barely ten o'clock, the place is already doing a roaring trade. Ali sidles past and almost falls over a man sitting on the kerb outside, smoking a clay pipe.

'Sorry,' she says, startled into her twenty-first century voice.

The man leers at her and she sees that one eye is covered by a patch.

'Excuse me,' she says. 'Were you selling sheep's feet near Hawk Street last week?'

'Might've been,' says the man, without taking the pipe out of his mouth.

'Do you remember talking to me? You told me that you'd seen a man disappear.'

The man stares at her out of one rheumy eye. 'Buy me a drink and I'll tell ye.'

'You mean,' says Ali, 'go in there?'

The man laughs, showing a mouth almost empty of teeth. 'Ye can't go in there. It's for the high mobsmen. Dippers and snidesmen. Give us a penny.'

Ali only understands one part of this utterance but she supposes it's the important part. She gives the man a penny and he gets up with surprising agility. She wonders if he'll emerge again but, a few minutes later, there he is, clasping a pewter tankard.

'Thank 'ee,' he says.

'You're welcome,' says Ali, wondering if this is nineteenth-century parlance. 'Now tell me about the man.'

'Nowt much to tell. He was a toff, dressed all in black. Wearing a cloak, like an opera cloak. I saw him in the street, right where you'd been standing. While I was looking, he just vanished. Like a candle flame going out.'

It's a surprisingly poetic image.

'He disappeared?'

'Like the earth opened up for him,' says the man. 'I thought he must be a demon or summat.'

Ali thinks of Spring-heeled Jack. *He threw off the cloak and revealed himself to be a devil.*

'Maybe he was,' she says. 'Can you remember anything else?'

'He were carrying a pistol,' says her new friend. 'Looked dangerous.'

Ali is back at the ingress point by three o'clock. At one point during the day, she wondered whether she would bother to keep her self-appointed deadline. It's obviously not going to work. Or maybe it did work, for Thomas Creek, and he has now taken Ali's place in the twenty-first century. But she can't quite bring herself to miss the magic hour. Three o'clock. The end of the school day, Finn running towards her carrying artwork thick with poster paint or trailing a muddy PE kit. Older children drifting home through the suburban streets, laughing and arguing, pushing each other into hedges. In the office, three o'clock is when someone usually suggests tea or a chocolate run to the nearest Tesco Express. It's a gentle time of day, picnics on the lawn and ice creams on the beach. Although isn't it also the time when Jesus died on the cross? Ali remembers once accompanying Declan's mother to the Good Friday service, the statues shrouded by purple cloth, the priest prostrating himself on the altar.

Ali stands on the spot by the lamp post for almost half an hour, judging by the church bells, so many more of them than in 2023. It's a real effort to move away. She feels as if she has taken root, becoming part of the pavement. According to the sheep's-feet man, the earth opened up for Thomas Creek. If only it would do the same for her. A line from a song comes into her head, the one that Dina was singing the day Geoff first told her about the gate into the nineteenth century. *Enjoy yourself, it's later than you think.* In every sense, it's later than Ali thinks. She supposes, in a theoretic sense, that she enjoyed dinner with Cain Templeton and eating with the other lodgers last night. But it's like an echo of remembered emotion. Her real self is in the future, with Finn, Dina, Geoff, Meg and all the other people who make up the complicated tapestry of her life.

Wearily, she climbs the steps to Number 44 and pushes at the ever-open door. The time, according to the clock, is a quarter to four, the headless horseman. As Ali stands in the hall, she sees a shape scurry past, almost at ground level, before disappearing into the shadows.

She ventures into the kitchen. Clara is at the table, smoking a pipe rather like the one enjoyed by the sheep's-feet man earlier. The black bottle is on the table.

'Sorry to disturb you,' says Ali. 'I just wondered, have you got a cat?'

To her surprise, Clara rubs her eyes. 'My Ginger died at Christmas. I miss him. He was a devil with the mice too.'

'I've got a cat at home,' says Ali. 'I miss him too. It's funny, but I thought I saw a cat in the hall just now. Something darted past me.'

'Probably a mouse,' says Clara. 'Will you be in for your supper? I'm making tripe.'

'I'll be here,' says Ali, without much enthusiasm. She gave Clara a shilling yesterday, which is probably why she is getting menu updates. In this case, she'd really rather not know.

Ali is the only one dining that night so Clara sits at the table with her. The men are out 'carousing', according to Clara. 'As soon as Mr Tremain gets money, he spends it.' Marianne isn't feeling well and is eating in her room.

'How long have you worked here?' asks Ali.

'I was brought up at East Dean,' says Clara, assuming that Ali knows where this is, which of course she does. 'My father was the gardener, my mother was a maid there. Lady Rosemary, that was Mr Templeton's mother, brought me to the London house to train as a lady's maid. I got married to Jim, who was training to be a valet. Then he died of consumption and I lost the baby I was carrying. Oh well,' she finishes, without a shred of self-pity. 'You have to keep on, don't you?'

Ali struggles to think of a response. Clara clearly doesn't want sympathy but Ali wants to say something that shows that she values her.

'You're a very important person in this house,' says Ali. 'You're the housekeeper.'

'Housekeeper!' says Clara. 'I can't read or write. I'm a maid of all work really.' But there's a faint note of pride in her voice. She offers Ali more tripe which she feels she has to accept, despite the fact that it tastes like gristle in white sauce.

'I used to be a maid,' says Ali, thinking that Clara might not understand the concept of a cleaner who wasn't in the service of a family.

'I could tell that you weren't really a lady,' says Clara. But it's said in a comradely tone and accompanied by an offer to share in the contents of the black bottle. Once again, Ali declines.

'Is Mr Templeton a good person to work for?' she asks.

'He's a good master,' says Clara. Then, after a pause, 'I know people say things about him because he surrounds himself with artists and, well . . .' She looks at Ali. 'Unfortunates. But that's because he's a kind man at heart. He lets Mr Tremain stay here and hardly pay anything because he thinks he's a genius. Arthur gets away with it too. Goodness knows why. Only the Rokebys pay their rent. And you.'

'I hope Mrs Rokeby's illness is nothing serious,' says Ali.

Clara laughs harshly. 'I'd say she was in the family way again.'

'Really? But the baby is so little.'

'That's the way things are for women. It's why I never married again.'

'Very sensible,' says Ali. She wonders how the Rokebys will cope living with two children in one room. She hopes that Len becomes a famous pianist. If she gets home – when she gets home – she'll look him up.

'Have you ever heard of a woman called Jane Campion?' she asks Clara.

'No,' says Clara. 'I don't bother my head with things that don't concern me.'

It's a definite reproof. Clara clears the plates away and the clock strikes eight. The prospect of a long evening stretches ahead. Ali asks Clara what she does to fill in the time. Clara looks surprised at the question. 'I sew until the light goes, then I go to my bed.'

'I wish I could sew,' says Ali.

For the first time, Clara looks at her with complete amazement. 'You can't sew? Didn't your mother teach you?'

'She died when I was five,' invents Ali. *Sorry, Cheryl.*

'I was sewing at three,' says Clara. 'At five I could stitch a sampler.'

'I was a bad pupil,' says Ali. *You have to be able to make a posset, sew a seam and recite the Lord's Prayer. Can you do any of those things?*

'How do you mend your clothes then?'

'With difficulty.'

'I'll teach you, if you like,' says Clara.

'Thank you,' says Ali. Maybe she can get a job as a seamstress. Or, at least, make herself some new drawers.

Perhaps it's the walking or the promise of learning something new, but Ali sleeps well that night. She wakes at the usual time, washes her face, dresses, uses the chamber pot and carries it downstairs.

Marianne is waiting for her in the hall.

'There's a man asking for you,' she says. 'He's in the kitchen.'

'A man?'

'Yes. He talks strange. Just like you do.'

Chapter 21

Finn

2023

'Are you all right, Mr Kennedy?'

It's the younger detective, Josh something, on the other side of the door.

Finn flushes the loo, washes his face in cold water and emerges. The DC is standing in the kitchen area, looking uncertain. Mary O'Brien is sitting in an armchair by the fire, as if she is going to remain there for ever. Terry is purring treacherously round her legs.

'I'm sorry,' says Finn, wishing he could brush his teeth. 'Too much to drink last night.'

'Speaking of last night,' says O'Brien, not getting up, 'can you tell us where you were between midnight and three a.m.?'

'Is that when he . . .' Finn can feel the roller-coaster sensation coming back. 'I'm sorry, but you said that Isaac was *dead*? What happened?'

The detective looks at him for a long, considering moment.

'We'd like you to come to the local police station to answer some questions, Mr Kennedy.'

'To the police station? Why?'

'Just for an interview. You're not under arrest.'

Something about the way she says it makes Finn ask, 'Do I need a lawyer?'

'I don't know,' she says. 'Do you need a lawyer?'

Richard the Lionheart, John Lackland, Henry the Third, Edward the First.

'Excuse me,' says Finn. 'I'm going to put some shoes on.' He runs upstairs. He goes into the bathroom and brushes his teeth. His face in the cracked mirror looks wild, eyes red-rimmed and staring, chin pink and still bristly from his unsuccessful shave. He opens the cabinet and searches for aspirin, Nurofen, anything. Ali's not much of a one for medication but eventually he finds a blister pack with two ibuprofen and swallows them with a cupped handful of water. Then he goes into Ali's spare room and picks up his phone. Fifteen missed calls from Chibu. He rings back, keeping his voice low. At the same time, he pulls on his trainers.

'Have you heard?' says Chibu. 'Christ. I can't believe it. Piers rang me this morning. He saw Isaac's name trending on Twitter.'

'The police are here now,' says Finn.

'The police? Why?'

'I can't explain. Look, your brother is a solicitor, isn't he?'

'Yes.'

'Can you text me his number?'

'OK.' Chibu's voice is full of questions but, to her credit, she doesn't ask them. She sounds genuinely upset. Finn knows that, of the three of them, she was the closest to Isaac. And now he's dead. Finn clicks on the number for Adedayo Akinyemi.

'Call me Ade,' says the solicitor, who is tall and good-looking, dressed in what is obviously designer leisurewear. Finn realises all over again that it's Saturday. The rest of the world is going to the gym, taking children to the park, doing the weekly shop. But he is in a room at a police station, a building that seems to have given up hope sometime in the sixties, talking to his lawyer about murder.

'I would advise you to give a no-comment interview,' says Ade.

'But won't that make me sound guilty?'

'Are you guilty?' Finn thinks that Ade deliberately avoids eye contact, opening his laptop.

'No!'

'A no-comment interview lets us see what they have,' says Ade. 'And they must have something otherwise they wouldn't have brought you in.'

'They said I wasn't under arrest.'

'No, and this isn't an interview under caution. But you must be a person of interest. They've come all the way from Sussex. They've tracked you down to your mum's house. They brought you in here.' Ade looks more closely at Finn. 'You look like shit,' he says. 'Are you OK?'

'Hangover,' says Finn. His skull feels paper-thin and he wonders if he's going to be sick again.

'Here.' Ade reaches into his laptop bag and pulls out a cellophane pack containing three digestive biscuits. 'First rule of life,' he says. 'Always take the hotel biscuits. I'll see if I can get you a cup of tea.'

He leaves the room and comes back, a few minutes later, with two Styrofoam cups, one containing weak tea and one water. Finn sips the water. The biscuit has had a miraculous effect, as if it's a wonder drug. He no longer feels like curling up into a ball and dying.

'Big night last night?' says Ade.

'I had some drinks with a friend.' Finn pauses, not sure how to describe Geoff. 'With my mum's colleague.' *We discussed whether we could rescue her from 1850.*

'What time did your friend leave?'

'About midnight, I think.'

'That's potentially a useful alibi.'

'He's a police officer too. Quite an important one.' This thought makes Finn feel slightly better. He takes a bite of the second biscuit. Maybe Geoff will rescue him? Even if he can't disclose the truth about Ali, surely he won't let her son be wrongly accused of murder?

'Do you know when it happened?' he asks Ade. 'When Isaac was killed? How he died? I don't know anything. I was too scared to look at my phone on the way here.' It had been terrifying, driving through the quiet streets in the unmarked car, Josh at the wheel, Mary beside him, neither of them giving anything away. Once Josh turned the radio on. *Sounds of the Sixties.* Mary turned it off after a few bars of 'Hey Jude'.

'It said on the news that he was found dead at his country house,' says Ade. 'No more details. I rang Sis and she didn't know any more. She's been trying to contact Isaac's wife but she's not picking up her phone. Understandably enough.'

It's funny to think of Chibu being 'Sis' to someone. Finn thinks of Miranda Templeton, chaotic and glamorous, whirling into Isaac's office. *Am I interrupting affairs of state?* Miranda is a lawyer too, he remembers, though a barrister not a solicitor.

'Well, let's see what they have to say.' Ade stands up. He gives Finn the ghost of a smile, suddenly looking like Chibu at her most approachable. 'Cheer up. I've been in tighter corners than this.'

But I haven't, thinks Finn. And Ade doesn't even know about his time-travelling mother.

'Interview with Finn Kennedy,' says Mary O'Brien, speaking into her body cam. 'Present DS Mary O'Brien, DC Josh Franks and Mr Kennedy's solicitor, Adedayo Akinyemi.'

He may not be under arrest, thinks Finn, but it certainly feels like it.

'Mr Kennedy,' says Mary, 'can you tell me where you were between midnight last night and three a.m. this morning?'

Finn clears his throat. 'No comment.'

Mary sighs, leaning back in her chair. 'Are you really going to do this? All we want is a nice civilised chat. Where were you last night?'

Finn looks at Ade, who gives an almost imperceptible shake of the head.

'No comment.'

Finn is amazed that he's allowed to walk out. He expected to be arrested at any moment, to be stopped by one of the uniformed officers at the door of the custody suite. But, after the interview, Mary had just sighed again, looked at the ceiling and said, 'You're free to go.' Now Finn and Ade are standing on the steps outside the police station. It's a cold bright day. Finn shivers. He's still wearing his suit but with no coat. Ade is wearing a padded jacket that looks discreetly expensive.

'They must have an eyewitness account of a man at the scene,' Ade says. 'Someone matching your description. Maybe even CCTV. They asked a lot of questions about the house in Sussex.'

It was so excruciating to keep saying 'no comment' that Finn almost stopped listening to the questions.

'How can that be possible?' he says.

'It can't be a good enough image to charge you,' says Ade. 'They were hoping to scare you into confessing.'

'I wasn't there,' says Finn. It feels very important to keep reminding Ade of this.

'No, of course not,' says Ade, almost absent-mindedly. 'Well, keep in touch. Where are you going now? I'd give you a lift but I came on my bike.'

I'm a cyclist too, Finn wants to tell him. In another life, they could be friends.

'I'd better go back to my flat,' he says. 'I'm staying at my mum's house to look after her cat but I need some fresh clothes.'

The flat feels strange, as if Finn has been away years rather than days. Letters on the mat, the *Guardian* open on the table, a half-drunk cup of coffee with mould beginning to sprout, work shirts on a hanger waiting to be ironed. Automatically, Finn switches on the retro radio, a moving-in present from Chibu and Piers.

'Justice Minister Isaac Templeton was found dead at his Sussex home in the early hours of this morning. Police haven't revealed any more details. Templeton, aged forty-five, was widely seen as a rising star of the Conservative Party. The Prime Minister said that he was devastated by the news . . .'

How can Isaac be dead? Murdered? More than anything, Finn wants to ring his mum and tell her about it. 'Don't worry, love,' she'd say, as she'd said about many childhood problems that had seemed insoluble at the time, 'I'll sort it out.' Finn realises that he's crying and, furious with himself, he heads to the bathroom for another shower.

When he's washed and dressed in jeans and a jumper, Finn feels better. He makes himself toast – it seems like all he's eaten for days but the thought of yesterday's pizza makes him feel sick again – and sits at the table to eat it. He picks up his phone, it's on silent but it seems to be bursting with the sheer number of messages it contains. Amongst them are five missed calls from his father. Finishing the toast, Finn clicks on 'Dad'.

'How are you, son?' says Declan. 'I couldn't believe it when I saw the news.'

'It was a shock,' Finn agrees.

He often wonders if Declan calls him 'son' to remind himself of their relationship. They get on fairly well but it's a struggle to pretend that they have anything in common. Declan still lives in Hastings where he shares a comfortable semi-detached house with Nikki, a care worker, and Poppy and Mia. After trying several careers Declan now seems to make a living as a web designer although Finn suspects it's Nikki's regular pay cheques that keep the family afloat. Finn is fond of his stepmother and half-sisters, and he supposes he loves his dad, but after a day or two in their company he's longing to get back to London.

'Do you know what happened to him? Isaac?'

Declan is a confirmed socialist – one of the few beliefs he shares with Ali – and Finn knows that he struggles with the idea of his son working for a Tory. Well, there's one Tory fewer today.

'The police say he was killed last night. I don't know any more.' He doesn't want to tell Declan that his son is currently one of the main suspects. Enough time for him to worry about that later.

'How are you?' says Declan, and the genuine concern in his voice touches Finn. 'It must have been horrible for you to find out that he . . .' His voice dies away.

'I'm OK,' says Finn. 'I've been with friends.' It's a stretch but Ade is, at least, the brother of a friend.

'And you've got Ali,' says Declan, with the familiar half-laugh that he reserves for her.

'Yes, I've got Ali.'

'Well, I'm here for you too, son.'

'Thank you. But I'm fine.'

There's a pause. Finn hears voices in the background.

'Do you have to go?' He knows that Saturdays are busy because the girls seem to do every activity under the sun. Ali takes the mickey out of them sometimes – 'What is it today? Synchronised finger painting?' – but Finn thinks it's rather sweet.

'Sorry. It's my turn to take Poppy to ballet.'

'Give her my love. Nikki and Mia too.'

'I will. Bye, son.'

Finn ends the call and looks down at the half-finished crossword on the table in front of him. 'Be careful! The time is not right (5,3)'. *Watch out.* He starts to fill in the answer when the doorbell buzzes. Finn freezes. Is it DS O'Brien, come to arrest him? Is it – Oh my God, could it be? – Ali? He runs to the answerphone.

'Finn. It's Chibu.'

He presses the button and, seconds later, his colleague enters the flat, for the first time since the moving-in party thrown, rather half-heartedly, by Finn and Cosima.

To his surprise, Chibu hugs him fiercely. 'It's so awful,' she says.

'I know.'

'The police have questioned Piers too.'

Finn is ashamed of how relieved he is to hear this. Ade must be right and the police only have a vague image of a man in the vicinity of Isaac's house. They must be interviewing every male of his acquaintance.

'Thank you for Ade's number,' he says. 'He was brilliant.'

'Yeah,' says Chibu, 'he's the best. Did he give you some hotel biscuits?'

'He did. I think they may have saved my life.'

'Piers asked me for Ade's details too, but you were first.'

'Piers must have other contacts. Isn't his dad a High Court judge?'

'Yes,' says Chibu. 'What happened at the police station?'

Finn tells her about the no-comment interview.

'Didn't that make you seem guilty?' says Chibu.

'Ade said it was standard practice,' says Finn. 'But, yes, it made me feel very shady. And it was so embarrassing just saying the same words over again. I kept wanting to apologise.'

'You are a great apologiser.'

'Am I?' It feels like a criticism but now is not the time. 'Do you know what happened?' he says. 'To Isaac, I mean.'

Chibu is pacing the kitchen area, picking things up and putting them down again. 'No,' she says, 'just what I've seen online.

Someone on Twitter said that he was shot but I haven't seen that anywhere else.'

'Shot? Oh my God.'

'He was at East Dean with Miranda and the children. I've tried to get hold of her but she's not answering. Is this the coffee you use? Illy is nicer.'

'Let's go there,' says Finn.

'Where?' Chibu is still looking at his blender.

'To East Dean. We can't just sit here doing nothing. Let's go to Sussex and see if we can talk to Miranda, anyone.'

'My car's outside,' says Chibu.

Chapter 22

In any other circumstances, it would be a pleasant drive, a nice Saturday day trip. Chibu's car, an electric BMW iX, purrs through the London suburbs. Finn looks at her as she drives, eyes straight ahead, subtly expensive watch catching the light. She's wearing leggings and a hoodie that remind him of Ade's leisurewear. What sort of upbringing did the siblings have? He knows that their parents emigrated from Nigeria in the eighties. Chibu went to a private girls' school and read PPE at Oxford. Ade had exuded the same air of upper-class confidence.

Finn looks at his phone. The words 'Isaac Templeton' appear again and again, in news updates, in messages from concerned and frankly curious friends.

'What did Ali say?' asks Chibu.

'What?'

'When you told her? What did Ali say?' Along with almost all of Finn's friends over the years, Chibu adores Ali. She thinks she's funny and feisty and the salt of the earth. All the things posh people say about women who are unapologetically working class.

'I didn't tell her,' says Finn. 'She's away. On a work assignment.'

'I thought she was ill.'

Finn can hardly remember the excuse he gave, so long ago, for not attending the speech to the prison officers. He knows that Chibu has turned to look at him because the BMW wobbles a little before correcting itself.

'She was ill but now she's away on an investigation.'

'I thought Ali worked on cold cases.' Chibu especially likes the fact that Ali is a police officer. 'A real person doing a real job,' as she once described her.

'It seems that her job's more hush-hush than I thought,' says Finn, hearing the note of bitterness creeping into his voice. 'In fact, it seems like there's a lot I don't know.' As he says this, his phone buzzes. Unknown number. Finn taps 'Accept'.

'Finn. It's Geoff Bastian.'

'Geoff! Any news?' He means about Ali and Geoff seems to understand this.

'John's all set to go through the gate on Monday. There were a few complications, but Jones is confident that she's sorted everything out. Look, Finn. I've just spoken to Sussex CID. Told them I was with you last night.'

'Thank you.' Finn feels himself deflating with relief. 'Did you speak to DS O'Brien? Is she the one in charge?'

'It's a bit tricky,' says Geoff. 'Sussex Police are officially in charge because that's where Isaac died. But they'll be liaising with Parliamentary and Diplomatic Protection because Isaac was a high-profile MP. They'll also be talking to the Met, because Isaac has a London address too.'

'They interviewed me at a station in east London. It was grim.'

'How are you feeling today?' says Geoff. 'I feel very rough. Must have been the ouzo.'

'I've been better,' says Finn. 'Geoff, do you know what happened to Isaac? I can't get much from the news.'

'Police report says that he was shot at the family home in Sussex. May have been an intruder. Apparently, CCTV has caught a few shots of a man in the grounds. I'll try to get hold of them.'

That was what Ade suspected. Finn hopes that the Templetons had many security cameras and that one of them got a perfect picture of the gunman.

'Of course,' Geoff is saying, 'Templeton was a cabinet minister. There are wider implications. The killer could have been a disaffected constituent or even a hired hitman. You can't be justice minister without upsetting some criminals.'

Finn thinks of the speech to the prison officers, the section about 'remorse not being enough' and prison needing to hurt. He hopes with all his heart that Isaac's killer was an outsider, an ex-offender with a grudge, a deranged stalker.

'Anyway,' says Geoff. 'I'll keep my eye on things, but I don't think DS O'Brien will contact you again. From what I've heard, she's a tough cookie, but she's fair.'

'Thank you,' says Finn again. 'Thanks so much.' It's hard to remember that, only yesterday, he'd attempted to punch Geoff in the face.

'That was Geoff.' He turns to Chibu. 'Ali's boss.' He tells Chibu about the CCTV and the possible intruder.

'But who would want to kill Isaac?' she says. 'Everyone loved him.'

That's the problem with being a spad. Much though you might

complain privately about your minister, you live in a world where everything revolves around him or her. But there are plenty of people out there who don't like Isaac Templeton, simply because he's a Tory. Ali is probably one of them.

Piers rings when they are on the Brighton Road. He sounds irritable.

'Why isn't Chibu picking up?'

'She's driving. We're on our way to East Dean.'

'To Isaac's place? Why?'

'Just to see what we can find out.'

'Why didn't you wait for me?'

'We weren't sure when you'd be free,' says Finn, trying to sound soothing. The truth is that he never considered inviting Piers on the trip. Piers is Isaac's parliamentary assistant, which is subtly different from being a political advisor. Besides, Chibu is almost a friend. Piers isn't.

'You were interviewed by the police too, weren't you?' says Piers.

'Yes. It was bloody terrifying.'

Piers gives a reluctant snort of laughter. 'Did you give a no-comment interview?'

'Yes. Did you?'

'Yes. My dad sent along this hot-shot solicitor. I thought it made me look as guilty as hell.'

'I had Ade. Chibu's brother.'

'Yeah. You got there first. What did he think? My solicitor, Lucy, thought they were fishing in the dark.'

'He thought they had something but nothing concrete. I spoke to Geoff, my mum's boss, and he thought they had a CCTV image of a man.'

'I forgot your mum was a policewoman. Can she help?'

Ali hates the word 'policewoman'.

'She's away,' says Finn.

'Well, let me know if you discover anything,' says Piers. 'I'm not keen on going to jail. I know too much about it after working for Isaac.'

'I thought anyone who'd been to an English public school would feel right at home in prison.'

'The food might be better,' says Piers. 'But no exeat weekends. Ciao for now.'

From Brighton they take the coast road to Seaford and then move inland. They cross a river whose meandering loops Finn remembers being used, in his geography textbook, as an example of late-stage oxbow lakes. Today, the valley is full of families going for walks with their dogs. Finn has always wanted a dog.

The countryside becomes more and more like a Sunday afternoon cosy crime series: thatched cottages, village churches, duckponds, pubs with names like 'The Smugglers' Retreat'. Eventually, Chibu takes a turning towards the sea and they are driving across grey fields spotted with sheep. The cliffs appear suddenly, stark and dangerous, and there, perilously close to the edge, is a large red-brick building that looks somehow institutional, a school, maybe, or an exclusive clinic. East Dean.

Chibu stops the car about a hundred metres away from the main entrance. They can see that the gates are guarded by a uniformed police officer but, on the other side of the road, there are several cars that probably belong to reporters.

'Isn't there another way in?' says Chibu. 'Last Sunday, with Isaac, didn't he take us through the gardens?'

'Yes,' says Finn. 'Let's drive on a bit.'

The house is surrounded by a high wall that curves round, with the sea on one side. A turn inland and there's the second gate, much less impressive than the wrought-iron version at the front but still firmly locked. Chibu parks and Finn gets out. The air is salty and refreshing, seagulls calling high above. Finn spots an entryphone in the wall and, more in hope than anything, presses the button.

'Hello?'

Finn is so shocked that it's a second before he finds his voice. 'Is Miranda there?'

'Who's asking?'

'It's Finn Kennedy and Chibu Akinyemi. Isaac's special advisors.'

To his utter surprise, the gates start to open.

Chapter 23

The electric car rolls past lawns and low, flint walls. Everything is grey and brown this January day, but it's pretty impressive all the same: the greenhouses and stables, the trees, slightly stunted by the wind but still forming a respectable orchard. The house itself, with its towers and battlements, looms on the right and, standing by the archway that leads to the kitchen garden, is Miranda Templeton.

Chibu stops the car and gets out. She almost runs up to Miranda and embraces her. Finn follows more slowly. Miranda hesitates for a second and then hugs him too.

'I'm so sorry,' says Finn.

'I still can't believe it,' says Miranda. She is wearing jeans and a thick, blue roll-neck sweater, the sleeves pulled down over her hands in a way that makes her look young and vulnerable. 'Look, the house is a crime scene so we can't go in. I've been hiding out in the summer house. Jacinta and the kids are with my mum and dad. They live nearby. Shall we walk?'

They go through the archway and walk between the herbs, some still flourishing, others looking withered and dead. Finn knows that the path leads to the deck with a hot tub and steps to the heated pool. Last weekend Finn had swum there while Chibu and Piers sat in steamer chairs, fully dressed in coats and hats, yelling encouragement and insults.

They sit in the chairs now, looking towards the pool, which is covered in a blue tarpaulin.

'Isaac used to swim every morning,' says Miranda. 'Fifty lengths. The mad fool.'

'What happened?' says Chibu. 'If you can bear to tell us?'

Finn is impressed with her for asking the question. Is it his imagination or does Miranda glance at him and then look quickly away before saying, 'It's all a bit of a blur. I went to bed early last night. Isaac was in the great hall, reading by the fire.'

Finn knows the hall well. It's a huge mock-Gothic space, created when the house was remodelled in the nineteenth century. Two storeys high, with a minstrels' gallery running round three sides, its panelled walls are crowded with swords, axes and blunderbusses. 'A collection of things to kill people with,' Piers had remarked.

'I woke up at two a.m.,' says Miranda. 'Isaac hadn't come to bed. I heard a noise, a door opening, footsteps – maybe that was what woke me – so I got up. I was halfway along the gallery when I heard Isaac say, "What are you doing here?" Then there was a gunshot. By the time I got down the stairs, he was dead.'

She's crying now but makes no attempt to stop the tears. They slide, unchecked, into her polo-neck.

'I had my phone with me,' she continues. 'I was using the torch. I called an ambulance. It seemed to take ages to come. I was crying and trying to do CPR. I must have woken Jacinta because she came and helped me. Jessie and Tom were still asleep, thank God.' Jacinta is the children's nanny. 'The paramedics told me Isaac was dead but I knew that already. The police came soon afterwards.'

'What do the police say?' asks Chibu, who is patting Miranda's back in an ineffectual way.

'They say he knew his attacker,' says Miranda.

Once again, she doesn't look at Finn.

They don't stay long. Miranda says that she's going to her parents' house for a few days. 'It'll be good for the kids to be away from here,' she says, wiping her eyes with her sleeve. 'This is a lot for them to take in. They adored their dad.'

'They'll never get over it,' says Chibu, as they drive out through the gates. 'The kids. They'll never get over it.'

'I suppose they'll have counselling,' says Finn.

'Counselling's not going to fix it,' says Chibu. 'My mum died when I was twenty-one, supposedly an adult, supposedly able to cope, but I went to pieces completely. Even with the best counselling money could buy.'

Finn doesn't know what to say. This certainly adds something to his picture of Chibu's family background. He wants to tell her that his mother is missing, that he feels that her loss is something that he, even at the age of thirty, is unable to face. Instead, he just says, 'I'm sorry.'

Chibu stops the car and gets out. In front of them are a few metres of green turf and then a sheer drop to where the waves are pounding against the cliffs, the chalk forming jagged white teeth in the grey water. Chibu walks forward and then stops. Finn gets out of the car and stands beside her. The air is full of salt and the sound of the sea. Finn thinks of Isaac telling them, almost casually, that this was a popular spot for suicides. There's a bench in front of them. Does it commemorate someone who lost their life? It seems a tactless location, if so.

'I'm sorry,' says Chibu. 'It just got to me, that's all. Thinking of Jessica and Tom.'

Finn has met Isaac's children a few times. They were at the house last weekend but immersed in their own activities, eating their meals with Jacinta. Finn has only a vague recollection of a tall dark girl and a stocky blond boy. It's almost impossible to imagine how they're feeling today.

'Don't apologise,' he says. 'It's awful.'

'We'll just have to do everything we can to help.' Chibu turns to Finn with a slightly manic gleam in her wet, brown eyes. 'Right, Finn?'

'Right.' Finn hopes they can get back in the car soon. It's cold and he's feeling nervous about standing so near the cliff edge.

Piers rings when they are crawling along the Lewes Road on their way back to London. Finn puts him on speaker phone.

'What was it like?' he says. He's eating, a telephone habit that always annoys Finn. Piers rang *them*. Why not wait until he's finished his snack?

'Sad,' says Chibu, braking smoothly as the traffic comes to yet another standstill. 'Sad and strange.'

'Did you see Miranda?' Chomp, chomp. Probably an apple.

'Yes,' says Finn. 'She came out to talk to us. I thought that was nice of her.'

'She was devastated,' says Chibu. 'It broke my heart.'

'You've never been a fan of Miranda before,' says Piers.

Chibu ignores this. 'I keep thinking about Jessica and Tom. So awful to lose a parent like that.'

'Did Miranda say anything?' says Piers. 'About what happened?'

Finn answers because he can see a tear rolling down Chibu's cheek. 'Miranda was woken up at two a.m. last night. No, this morning.' Can it really still be the same day? 'Isaac wasn't with her. She left him reading in the great hall. She went to find him, heard him say, "What are you doing here?", then a gunshot. When she got to the hall, he was already dead.'

'Jesus,' says Piers. '"What are you doing here?" That means . . .'

'It was someone he recognised. Yes.'

'Jesus,' says Piers again and takes a meditative crunch. 'What do the police say?'

'No signs of a break-in. They think the intruder probably had a key.'

'Doesn't Isaac have a security detail?'

'He sent them home, apparently. Miranda says he was worried about them being outside on such a cold night.'

'Doesn't sound like Isaac. Mr "being cold is for snowflakes, watch me take a dip in a freezing pool".'

'Piers,' says Chibu. 'Have some respect.' The traffic is moving again. It's only three p.m. but already getting dark. The lights of Brighton twinkle in the distance.

'So someone with a key, someone Isaac knew. Suspicion's going to point to you and me, mate.'

'We're not the only people Isaac knew.' Finn doesn't feel like playing this game. 'And I don't have a key. Do you?'

'No.'

'Let's hope they find some real evidence soon,' says Finn. 'DNA or something like that.' He realises that he has a childlike faith in forensics. He's watched too many episodes of *Silent Witness*.

'Let's hope so. Do you have an alibi?'

'I was drinking with Geoff, my mum's boss.'

'Not bad,' says Piers. 'I was with a girl.'

'Now that can't be true,' says Finn.

'Stop it, you two,' says Chibu. 'This isn't a game.' The traffic suddenly clears and she takes the turning for the motorway, hands clenched on the wheel.

Chibu drops Finn outside Ali's house. He thinks she wants to come in but he doesn't invite her. By now, his only wish is to be alone. He agrees to meet Chibu the next day. They promised Miranda that they would cope with all the messages from constituents and Isaac's fellow MPs. Finn kisses Chibu on the cheek, picks up his bag and makes his way to the now-familiar front door.

He still half expects to see Ali but there's only Terry, purring and doing his more conversational miaowing. Finn feeds the cat and pours wine. Hair of the dog, he tells himself. The glass, one of Ali's junk shop finds, a strange object with a curly blue stem, brings his mother back in all her vivid contrariness. So many of his childhood memories involve trailing behind Ali while she rifled through boxes marked 'nearly new' or 'seconds'. 'So much nicer than having a matching set,' she'd declare. Finn resolved that, when he was a grown-up, everything in his house would match. He's kept to that vow but now he feels that his life would be richer for some mismatched glassware.

Ali's flowers are almost dead now, their petals scattered over the floor. Finn sits in an armchair and switches on the TV. Isaac's face fills the screen: making an impassioned speech in the house, on walkabout at a factory, hands behind his back like King Charles, laughing with carefully selected voters, standing with Miranda and their children at the gates of East Dean. Finn realises that he is crying again. He didn't love Isaac, or even like him much really, but he does miss him.

Chapter 24

Finn is woken by someone yelling in his face. He flails a bit and touches fur. The yell becomes a squawk. Finn opens his eyes and sees Terry sitting on the end of the bed, looking positively disgusted with him. Finn reaches for his phone. Nine o'clock. He went to bed before the ten o'clock news so must have slept for almost twelve hours. It's years since he's slept that long and he feels oddly exhausted by the feat. He pads downstairs to feed Terry. The house is very cold. He really ought to try and work out the heating. There must be a boiler somewhere. He doubts if Ali has anything as high-tech as an app.

Ali. Tomorrow he'll see her again. He has to believe that. However nightmarish yesterday's events – the knock on the door to tell him Isaac was dead, the police interview, the trip to East Dean – they did at least partly distract him from the fact that his mother was missing and that everything he knew about time, space and reality was, in fact, a lie. Finn puts the kettle on and picks up his phone. He scrolls past all the Isaac messages to 'contacts', where he saved Geoff's number yesterday. He worries, for a minute, that he shouldn't be calling on a Sunday morning but then dismisses this. Geoff was the one who sent Ali on this mission. He deserves to be interrupted in the middle of prayer or golf, or whatever semi-retired DCIs do at the weekend.

'Finn. Hello.'

'Hello, Geoff. I just wanted to check that everything was all right for tomorrow.'

Geoff hesitates for a second before replying and Finn's heart sinks but then he says, sounding as calm and professional as ever, 'Yes, we're all set. John's going to go through the gate early. Eight o'clock.'

Finn imagines John, heavy-set and serious, looking like a geography teacher on holiday. He's standing in a busy London street and then . . . what?

'What happens?' says Finn. 'Will everyone see him disappear?'

'Jones says that it's so quick, less than a millionth of a second, that people don't notice. It's just a flicker. Less than a flicker.'

Finn thinks he'd notice if someone just flickered and disappeared, but he supposes Jones knows best. He *has* to believe this.

'Try not to worry,' says Geoff. 'Ali will be back with you by mid-morning tomorrow.'

It's too wonderful to believe.

'How are you?' says Geoff. 'Have the police been in touch again?'

'No,' says Finn. 'Chibu and I went to see Isaac's wife Miranda yesterday.'

'How is she?'

'She seemed in shock.' Finn wonders whether to tell Geoff about 'What are you doing here?' but then decides that the fewer people who know, the better. 'We said that we'd go into the office today to try to answer some of the messages.'

'Take care,' says Geoff. 'It will be emotional.' He says this like it's a dangerous concept. Which, perhaps, it is.

Just walking along the corridor is an ordeal. It seems that everyone – security guards, cleaners – wants to offer condolences and softly spoken memories of Isaac. Helen Graham, the Labour MP who has the office next door, takes Finn's hand and says, 'He was a Tory bastard but you couldn't help liking him.'

'He was very likeable,' says Finn, trying to edge past.

'It won't be the same around here without Fizz Fridays.'

One of Isaac's more endearing habits was opening a bottle of champagne at the end of the week and inventing an excuse to share it: the nights are drawing in, Mercury's in retrograde, Andy Murray's won a match. Isaac got on very well with Helen, despite their political differences. Piers used to say that their arguments, fuelled by much flirtation and playful banter, made him feel sick.

Finn finally makes his escape and opens the door of Isaac's office. Chibu is already there, going through emails.

'I've come up with a form of words,' she says, not looking up. 'I'll send you a batch of emails. Thank God it's Sunday and there are no actual letters.'

Because he was a cabinet minister, Isaac's post is opened by security. There's always a lot of it, constituents' complaints mixed with declarations of love and hate. Finn dreads to think what tomorrow's postbag will bring.

He looks at Chibu's suggested reply. 'On behalf of Isaac's parliamentary team, I'd like to thank you for your sympathy at this difficult time. I will make sure that your message is passed on to his family.' It's a little stilted, he thinks, but OK.

'Anything nasty?'

'A few saying he deserved to die. One person admitting to killing him. I've passed that one on to the police.'

'Let me see.'

Chibu turns her laptop towards him. 'I killed the Tory Scum,' Finn reads. 'I went to his house and stabbed him in front of his wife and kid's.'

'Stabbed,' says Finn, 'not shot.'

'I don't think they really did it,' says Chibu, with a touch of asperity, 'but I thought I should report it.'

Chibu is the type who'd been a prefect at school, thinks Finn, reporting rule-breakers 'for their own good'. All the same, 'bulldog@bulldog.com' doesn't seem a very pleasant person. Terrible grammar too.

Finn opens his laptop and starts on the emails. Paste and send, paste and send. Piers arrives at midday. He's seems very hyper and, Finn thinks, possibly a little drunk.

'Bloody reporters camped outside,' he says. 'Did you see them?'

'They're just doing their job,' says Chibu. Sometimes her reasonable voice works with Piers, at other times it makes things worse.

'They're parasites,' says Piers. He walks around the office and sits at Isaac's desk. It feels almost shocking. This hideous piece of furniture, with its carved legs and unnecessary scrollwork, seems to belong to Isaac alone. Chibu and Finn have deliberately kept to the conference table.

'Where's Isaac's computer?' says Piers.

'The police took it,' says Chibu.

'He didn't use the desktop though,' says Piers. 'Only his laptop.'

'I expect they took that too.'

Piers picks up a silver-framed photograph which Finn knows contains a tasteful picture of Miranda, Jessica and Tom.

'Do you know what I'm thinking?' he says.

'Put that photo down,' says Chibu.

Piers ignores her. 'Do you want to know who I think killed Isaac?'

'Piers . . .' says Chibu.

'Chillax,' says Piers. 'I'm only saying what everyone is thinking. Who doesn't need a key to get into a house? Someone who's already there. And, statistically, who's the most likely murderer? The spouse. That's you, Miranda,' he says, chattily, to the figure in the photograph.

Finn is glad when the emails are done. After his revelation, Piers curled up on Isaac's uncomfortable leather sofa and went to sleep. Now Finn shakes him, none too gently.

'We're off.'

'Let's have a drink. Not here. A pub.'

'You've had enough,' says Chibu, picking up her bag.

'I wouldn't say no to a quick half,' says Finn. He only has about twenty hours to go before Ali is back. It's childish, he knows, but he keeps thinking that everything will be OK when his mum gets here.

They walk down the wide stairs, past busts of former prime ministers. Poor Isaac. He'll never join their ranks now.

They leave by a side exit to avoid the journalists. It's dark outside and raining hard. Chibu puts up her umbrella. Headlights shimmer and the sounds of Westminster echo around them: the shouts of the anti-Brexit campaigner permanently camped on the green, the multilingual chatter of tourists, a police siren getting closer.

'Look who's here,' says Piers.

Finn rubs water out of his eyes and sees Mary O'Brien and Josh Franks approaching. Josh has his hood up but Mary's hair is plastered against her face. Her expression, one of quiet triumph, is the scariest thing Finn has ever seen.

'Finn Kennedy,' she says, 'I'm arresting you for the murder of Isaac Templeton.'

Chapter 25

Ali

1850

Ali almost drops the dreaded container.

'What?' she says.

'There's a man in the kitchen,' says Marianne. 'He's asking for you.'

Ali puts the chamber pot down and rushes past Marianne into the kitchen. There, watched with suspicion by Clara and frank curiosity by Len, is John Cole. John, dressed in Victorian black and holding a top hat in his hand. Looking, in fact, rather like an undertaker. John regarding her with relief, anxiety and something else that she can't quite name.

'John,' she says.

'Cousin Alison,' says John. 'I have an urgent message from the family.'

'In Hastings?' Ali has to suppress a smile. John sounds so careful, so out of place. Is that how she was in the beginning, uncertain even of speaking to these people? Now that she's leaving them, Ali feels a rush of camaraderie, almost affection, for Clara, Len and Marianne. And, please God, she *is* leaving them. She sways, suddenly dizzy. Marianne takes her arm and manoeuvres her into a chair.

'Is it bad news?' she says to John. 'Death travels fast, my mother used to say.'

'Not bad exactly.' John looks more uncomfortable than ever. 'Is there somewhere we can . . . um . . . converse in private?'

Ali grins up at him. 'Let's go into the parlour.'

In the dark little room, which is cold without the fire, Ali turns to John and hugs him.

'I can't believe you're here! It's like a dream. A miracle. How did Jones manage it?'

John says, 'Ali—'

'How long have we got? I've got so much to tell you. I had dinner with Cain Templeton. I saw the collection—'

'Ali—'

'Isn't it strange being here? Can you believe it?'

Suddenly the thrill of exploration, which energised Ali on her first trips through the gate but has been notably absent this time, is back. She's almost sorry to leave 44 Hawk Street. It will be strange to wear trousers again, to have a hot bath, to watch television. Maybe she'll read *The Pickwick Papers* instead. But – oh! – she will see Finn again. And Terry too. She takes a quick turn around the room, unable to keep still. Then she realises that John is talking to her.

'Ali. I've got to explain. The gate is only open for an hour.'

'I'll go and get my things. Not that there's much.' Could she take Pickwick with her? 'How is Jones managing to transport us both? I thought it was one set of footprints, one transfer of atoms.'

'Yes,' says John. 'That's right.'

Ali stops her excited pacing and looks at him. 'What do you mean?'

'Look, Ali.' John grasps her hand. 'You must listen. It's one in and one out. That's the rule. You have to use my gate.'

'But you'll be left here.'

'Yes,' says John. He squeezes her hand tighter. 'It's OK, Ali. Jones is confident that she can get me back. She just has to figure it out. I'm in a much better position than you were because I know what's going on. I'm prepared. I've even brought a bag.' He smiles.

For the first time Ali notices the carpet bag at John's feet.

'No,' she says. 'I can't go back and leave you here.'

'You have to,' says John.

'No,' says Ali.

'Ali,' says John. 'You have to. Isaac Templeton was murdered on Saturday morning.'

'What?' Ali thinks of the handsome man in the hall-of-mirrors apartment. He can't be dead. He's not the type.

'Isaac Templeton was murdered,' repeats John. 'That's why you've got to go back.'

Now Ali says nothing. Her Victorian body is cold with twenty-first-century fear.

'You have to go back because Finn has been charged with Isaac's murder.'

The new ingress point used by John is only a few yards from the front steps. At ten to nine − one hand on the grandfather clock pointing to a tower, the other nearly at the skeleton carriage − Ali is standing on John's footprints, clutching *The Pickwick Papers*. She's left her notebook for John, together with all her money and some gabbled instructions: 'Fill the water jug at night, empty the chamber pot in the privy, pay Clara for food, don't eat the sheep's feet . . .'

'I can't leave you here,' she says suddenly.

'It's OK.'

'Don't say OK,' says Ali. 'It's too modern. All right is all right, I think.'

'It's all right,' says John, smiling. 'Geoff and Jones will find a way to get me back. I'm quite looking forward to being a Victorian for a few days.'

From inside Number 44, Ali can hear the clock preparing to strike. There's always a slight wheeze before the hour.

'It's kept five minutes fast,' she tells John. 'Oh, it's Wednesday here. Don't forget that. Len plays the piano at the music hall on a Saturday and the organ in church on a Sunday.'

'He sounds an interesting character.'

'I don't know him very well. Be wary of the others. Arthur's friend Francis Burbage too. I think they were all involved with Ettie. Marianne said that Ettie was Arthur's muse. Mind you, I think Marianne was Tremain's muse. He's certainly got enough portraits of her.'

'I'll see what I can find out,' says John. 'Keep still,' he warns, as Ali wobbles slightly on the spot. Snow is falling again but Ali feels as if her blood is boiling. Maybe she's having a hot flush. John, on the other hand, is shivering in his long black coat.

'Ask Clara for a hot brick for your bed,' says Ali.

'I will.'

'What's the time?'

John takes out a handsome fob watch. Ali hopes it survives better than hers did. 'One minute to go. Stand completely still.'

'It won't work,' says Ali, in a sudden panic.

'It will.'

Carts trundle past. A dog barks. Ali looks up at John standing on the steps in the snow. He raises a hand. Ali closes her eyes.

Chapter 26

2023

'Good morning.'

Ali opens her eyes. She sees a flash of red and hears an incredible rushing noise. She moves forwards and her arm is taken in a firm hold.

'*Calmati*,' says Jones.

Ali looks at her, taking in the short hair, jeans and padded jacket. The street is full of people, not one of whom have noticed a woman materialise in front of them. A bus has stopped at the lights. That was the red. The noise was simply London traffic. A bewildering array of words: McDonald's, Nando's, No Entry, Ultra-low emission zone.

'Oh my God.' Ali lurches into Jones's arms. 'I'm back. I can't believe it.'

'It's OK,' says Jones, just as John did a few minutes ago. 'Now let's get you in the car.'

The vertigo is stronger than ever. The pavement swoops like a magic carpet under Ali's feet. She looks back at Number 44. It's almost unchanged, cleaner and shinier if anything, with blinds at the windows that give it a closed, secretive look. But John is no longer standing on the steps and the front door is now pale blue and adorned with buzzers and entry phones. The griffin is still there though.

'Come on, Ali.' Jones steers her towards an electric Fiat 500 which is parked a few metres away. Typically, Jones has used the time to charge the battery. Ali gets into the passenger seat, manoeuvring her long skirts with difficulty, while Jones unplugs the charging lead and stows it in the boot. Then she types quickly on her phone, using her thumbs like a teenager.

'Just letting Geoff know you're here. *Andiamo.*' The car moves soundlessly away. Ali realises that she's crying.

'It's OK, Ali,' says Jones after a few minutes. 'You're safe.'

'Sorry.' Ali wipes her eyes on her shawl. 'It's just a bit overwhelming.'

Jones gives her a sideways glance. 'How was it?' she says. 'Were you solid? Could you walk and talk?'

Ali thinks of eating porridge in the kitchen, of drinking wine with Templeton, of the moment when she almost kissed him.

'I was solid,' she says. 'I could walk, talk, eat and piss. I was freezing cold most of the time.'

'My God,' says Jones. Her voice is soft with awe. Ali knows that despite everything, she is delighted.

'It was amazing,' says Ali, 'but right now I want to hear about Finn. John said he'd been arrested.'

'That's right,' says Jones. 'I'm taking you back to your house now but then you can go to see him. Geoff says he's still in the custody cells.'

Custody cells. The words, once so familiar, seem monstrous when applied to Finn, her high-flying, pure-minded son.

'I don't understand,' she says.

Jones, negotiating traffic with a one-handed style which must owe a lot to her Neapolitan birth, says, 'Isaac was found dead at his country house. He'd been shot. Finn was questioned, as were a couple of other people. Geoff thinks the police must have something. A blurred image on CCTV or something. Then Finn was arrested. We don't know any more.'

'Finn's innocent,' says Ali. She hardly knows how to move one foot in front of the other but her mothering instinct is as strong as ever. She is ready to fight for her child. 'He would never do anything like that.'

'Of course he is,' says Jones. Ali is grateful. In her time as a police officer she has heard many parents say that their child could never have committed the crimes of which they are so manifestly guilty. But this is different, she tells herself. This is *Finn*.

'I met Finn, you know,' says Jones. 'He came into the office. He was worried about you. Geoff told him about you going through the gate.'

This is almost as shocking as the murder.

'What did Finn do?'

'He tried to hit Geoff.'

'No!' Ali has never known Finn roused to violence, not even in the playground. He is a negotiator, a conciliator. Declan once said that he should have been called Matt, short for diplomat.

'He was angry for your sake,' says Jones. 'He loves you.'

Ali tries to speak but can't. After a few moments, Jones says, 'Finn's got a good lawyer. Geoff's on the case too. Now that you're here, I'm sure we can fix things.'

Finn has a good lawyer. Finn has been accused of murder. Ali has come back from the dead.

'I want to see him now,' she says.

Jones gives her a sideways glance. 'I'd advise getting changed first.'

Chapter 27

Jones parks outside Ali's house. It's still too new to feel like home but maybe nowhere feels that way now. Ali struggles to open the car door until Jones presses the button for her.

'Are you coming in?' says Ali. Now that she's here she knows that she wants to shower. There's a musty smell in the Fiat and Ali fears it's coming from her.

'It's OK.' Jones waves her phone. 'I'll catch up on my messages and wait for you to change. Here. You'll need this.' She hands a house key to Ali.

Ali gets out of the car and, holding up her skirts with one hand, approaches her front door. Two of her neighbours are standing in the street, looking at a car which has been clamped by the police. They both stare at Ali.

'Fancy dress,' she says feebly.

She opens the door. The house is quiet. Too quiet.

'Terry?' she calls.

Complete silence. Ali looks around her newly furnished sitting room, which now seems strangely bland and colourless. Cold, too. Her 'new home' flowers are still on the mantelpiece and, as she watches, a petal falls soundlessly to the floor. Panicked now, Ali runs upstairs, with difficulty because of the bloody dress. Terry is lying asleep on her bed. He looks up when she comes in, then turns his head away, apparently deeply offended.

'My baby.' Ali picks him up. She's crying properly now. Terry emits a faint squeak of protest. Ali continues to cuddle him, breathing in the scent of cat litter and tuna.

Eventually she puts Terry down and he stalks out of the room.

Feverishly, Ali pulls off her jacket. She must have left the shawl in the car. She pulls the creased silk dress over her head and kicks the petticoats out of the way. One, two, three, four. Buttons snap as she rips off her chemise and the hated drawers. Naked, she runs into the shower and turns on the hot water.

Despite everything, the sensation is so blissful that she cries out. Water streams over her hair and down her back. She rubs shampoo and conditioner into her scalp, imagining the Victorian grease and dirt gurgling down into the drain. She thinks of standing, shivering, in the attic bedroom, running a flannel over her body. How could she ever have thought this bathroom shabby and old-fashioned? It's the height of luxury. Ali closes her eyes and gives herself up to sensation.

Terry calls, piteously, from the landing.

'Coming!' She needs to get to both her boys but, first, she has to clean her teeth. Her electric toothbrush is like an exquisite torture device. She presses the bristles against her gums until they bleed. Then she rinses her mouth and grimaces at herself in the mirror. She's appalled by her grey complexion. How *could* Templeton have almost kissed her? Ali rubs moisturiser into her face and contemplates mascara before deciding that she hasn't got time.

In the bedroom she dresses quickly. Her cotton knickers make her want to cry. Her lambswool jumper seems ridiculously warm and practical. And the joy of wearing jeans again! She strides around the room before putting on socks and trainers. Then she runs downstairs and fills Terry's bowls. There are still some biscuits left. Someone – Finn? – must have fed him not that long ago. Terry makes it clear that the old food must be completely removed before he can contemplate the new.

Ali gives Terry some extra biscuits, finds her purse in the cake tin where she left it, grabs her North Face anorak and leaves the house.

'You smell better,' says Jones.

'Have you got my phone?' counters Ali.

'Yes. Sorry.' Jones reaches into the glove compartment.

Ali keys in her passcode. The texts from Finn make her want to cry all over again. The cat memes, then the increasingly worried messages.

How are you doing?

How are the cold cases? Heating up?

What's the difference between a politician and a snail? One's slimy and leaves a trail, the other's a garden pest.

Are you OK? You haven't been answering my hilarious texts.

Love you mum.

Ali types. 'Love you too. On my way to see you xxxxx.' She knows that Finn won't be able to have his phone but it makes her feel better to write the words.

Jones, driving carefully over the cobbles, says, 'How was life without a smartphone?'

'Hell,' says Ali. Then she thinks of reading *The Pickwick Papers* by the light of an oil lamp. The leather-bound book is on the dashboard in front of her, looking out of place next to the space-age digital displays. 'Restful sometimes,' she says at last.

'Finn's at Marylebone custody suite,' says Jones. 'Geoff is meeting us there.'

'Can you drive faster?' says Ali.

'I can only stretch the laws of physics so far,' says Jones.

Geoff is waiting for them in the lobby. He hugs Ali, the first time they have ever had physical contact. His paunch feels oddly hard, as if he's pregnant.

'Thank God you're back.'

'Yes,' says Ali. 'I've got lots to tell you. But I need to see Finn first.'

'Of course. I've asked if you can have a private room.'

'How long are they holding him here?'

'The case is up before the magistrate today. His solicitor – bright chap – says he'll ask for bail when it gets to the Crown Court but he's not hopeful.'

'Jesus, Geoff. What happened? What can they have on him?'

'Apparently they have his DNA at the scene. I'm trying to find out more. They must have a case, or the CPS wouldn't be acting so quickly.'

'But how . . .' Ali stops because they are inside the building now, all grey corridors and flickering overhead lights. Geoff talks to the desk sergeant and Ali is shown into a small room containing two chairs and, oddly, a large stuffed elephant. Doors opening and shutting, voices in the corridor and then – oh God! – her son is there, her beautiful boy. Ali runs to Finn and wraps her arms round him. He smells reassuringly the same, although there is already a faint prison tinge, a whiff of disinfection and incarceration.

When she releases him, they both have tears in their eyes.

'Bloody hell, Mum,' says Finn. 'I couldn't believe it when Geoff said you were back. They told me that John was going to get you but I didn't dare hope . . .'

'It's OK,' says Ali. 'Everything's going to be OK.'

'I'm glad you think so,' says Finn, 'because it feels like I'm in a bit of a fix.'

His shaky attempt at his usual ironical tone breaks Ali's heart. But she makes herself reply in her calmest Mum-knows-best voice.

'I'm going to talk to Geoff and we'll sort this. I'm a police officer, remember.'

'I'm not sure what you are.'

Finn sounds bitter. Ali doesn't blame him but there's no time for any of that. She gently pushes Finn towards a chair and sits opposite. She keeps hold of his hand. It's wonderful to be able to touch him. Even better than cuddling Terry.

'Tell me everything,' she says.

'There's not much to tell. The police came to my door – *your* door, I was looking after Terry – they told me Isaac was dead and more or less ordered me to come in for questioning. I rang Chibu and asked for her brother's number. He's a solicitor.'

'Good thinking.'

'God knows how I thought of it. I was all over the place. I hadn't got over finding out about you. Jesus – *time travel!*'

Instinctively, Ali glances at the door. There's no CCTV in the room – it's mainly used by solicitors and their clients – but you can never be too careful. She knows that police stations are the leakiest places on earth.

'When Geoff and Jones told me, I thought I was going mad. I tried to hit Geoff.'

'I heard.'

Finn gives her a reluctant grin. 'Jones scared me most but, oddly enough, it was her I believed. Then, when Isaac told me that he'd seen your name in his great-great-grandfather's journal—'

'*What?*'

'Didn't you know? Cain Templeton wrote about you in his diary. That's why Isaac asked for you specifically. I could have killed him.'

'Bloody hell, Finn. Don't say that.'

'No. Sorry. Anyway, I went back to your place after seeing Isaac. Later on, Geoff came round and we had a drink. The next morning the police were at the door saying Isaac had been murdered.'

'And they interviewed you under caution?'

'Not at first. Ade, the solicitor, told me to give a no-comment interview. They'd called Piers in too so I thought they might just be interviewing anyone who knew Isaac. Then Chibu and I drove down to Sussex.'

'Why?'

'I don't know. It just felt wrong to do nothing. Isaac was killed at East Dean, the Sussex house. I suppose it felt like we should go there. Anyway, we saw Miranda. She was still in shock, I think, but she told us that, before he was shot, Isaac said something like "What are you doing here?" The police thought that meant he knew his killer. Then, the next day, they arrested me.'

'Do you know why?'

'They said my DNA was found at the scene. But that's impossible.'

'Is it? Weren't you there the weekend before?'

'Yes.'

'So your DNA could be all over everything.' Ali jumps up; she wants to see the magistrate, the high court judge, and tell them to let her son go *now*. 'It could be anywhere. If Isaac was wearing clothes that he'd worn around you. Anywhere.'

'He lent me a sweatshirt after I swam in his pool.'

'Exactly.' Ali sits down again. She tries to collect her thoughts, to think more like a police officer and less like a mother. 'It's all wrong, them arresting you so quickly. What about the wife? Miranda? It's usually the spouse.'

'Miranda wouldn't kill Isaac. She adored him.'

'All the more reason.'

Finn laughs. The sound is so out-of-place in the dingy room that Ali almost expects the toy elephant to prick up its ears.

'I've missed hearing you say stuff like that.'

'I've missed you. You don't know how much.'

'More than Terry?'

'The little bastard hardly looked up when I came in.'

Finn laughs again. Ali grips his hand. 'Look, love. We will sort this out. I'll get the team on to it. If it means finding out who did kill Isaac, then we'll do it.'

'Thank you for believing it wasn't me.'

Ali ruffles his hair. She wishes he still had his curls. 'You can't even kill spiders.'

'I like spiders,' says Finn. Ali remembers a rather revolting insect phase. Although spiders aren't really insects, are they?

'They seem interested in the gun,' says Finn. 'The one used to kill Isaac. I think it was an old one, from his collection. They asked me lots of questions about bullets. Of course, I didn't know any of the answers. I've never fired a gun. I wouldn't even do clay pigeon shooting on that ghastly team-building day a few years ago.'

'Isaac was killed by an antique gun,' says Ali.

'Apparently so.'

Ali looks at the stuffed elephant and sees the man with the eye-patch, drinking his beer outside the Bag O'Nails. *He was carrying a pistol. Looked dangerous.*

'What is it?' says Finn. That's the trouble, they know each other too well.

'Nothing,' says Ali. 'Don't worry. I'll get you out of here.' She sees a uniformed shape in the glass of the door. The interview is nearly over. She reaches out to give Finn one last kiss.

'Mum,' he says, 'there's something else I've got to tell you. Dad is here.'

'What?'

'Well, I had to call someone last night. And I didn't know where you were.'

Finn sounds defensive and Ali doesn't blame him. But she'd rather face a Victorian chamber pot than her ex-husband.

Chapter 28

Declan is staying at the Premier Inn across the road. Ali texts him and he's waiting for her in the restaurant area. Ali is surprised to find that she's hungry. It's midday. When did she last eat? It must have been the tripe in the kitchen with Clara.

She takes the laminated menu from between the salt and pepper pots.

'How can you think about food at a time like this?' says Declan.

Ali is seized by a desire to annoy Declan. It's such a familiar emotion that it feels almost comforting.

'I think I'll have a burger,' she says.

'For Christ's sake, Ali.'

His voice breaks and she feels guilty. Declan looks terrible. He's tall and lean, like Finn, but now his face looks almost skull-like. And he's got much greyer since she saw him last.

'What are we going to do?' he says.

'I'll talk to Geoff and the team,' says Ali. 'We'll investigate. We know Finn didn't do it. That means that the real culprit is still out there. We'll find them.'

Declan's face spasms and he puts his hand over his eyes. Ali real-ises that he had been afraid that Finn was guilty.

'He didn't do it, Dec,' she says, touching his cheek.

'I know that,' says Declan, angrily. 'Of course I know that.' He rubs his eyes and says, going back on the attack, 'Where were you yesterday? Finn said you were on some sort of secret mission.'

'Yes,' says Ali. 'And the point about secret missions is that you don't tell anyone about them.'

'Secret missions, cabinet ministers,' says Declan. 'It's all very sus-picious. Do you think the Russians are behind this? The Chinese? Some secret right-wing think tank?'

Declan, Ali remembers, has always liked a conspiracy theory. When they were at school, he almost convinced her that the moon landings didn't happen. She can see him now, skinny and dark-haired, his blazer studded with badges proclaiming his political and musical allegiances. The memory makes her less caustic than she could have been.

'It's possible,' she says. 'Anything's possible. Isaac Templeton was a powerful man. He probably had plenty of enemies.'

'I never met him,' says Declan, 'but I didn't like him. He seemed a smarmy bastard to me.'

'He was.' *Ah, the Creator.*

'What can they have on Finn? It's a stitch-up. Police corruption.'

'It's a bit of a departure for them to frame a white middle-class man,' says Ali.

'There's something dodgy about it, Ali. Finn wouldn't hurt a fly. Remember how upset he got when Nemo died?'

Nemo was a goldfish. He was won at a fair and lived a short life with Declan and Ali in their Hastings council flat. There is no one else on earth who remembers Nemo. Finn himself probably doesn't remember him. Ali suddenly feels very close to Declan.

'There's definitely something dodgy about it all,' she says. 'But we'll get to the bottom of it. I know people now. I can find things out. We can save our boy, Dec.'

Declan reaches across the table and clasps her hand. They stay like that until a waitress interrupts them. Ali asks for a burger with extra fries.

After lunch with Declan – he had a salad but ate most of her chips – Ali gets an Uber to the Cold Case Unit. The meal has made her feel better but less alert. She needs her wits about her but it's difficult when every traffic light comes as a shock and she flinches whenever they overtake a bus. Her driver is the chatty sort but she can't respond to his stream-of-consciousness about sport. She'll probably lose her five-star rating.

Eel Street looks reassuringly the same: blank windows, featureless lobby, one lift out of order. Ali almost runs up the stairs. She pushes open the door of the Department of Logistics. Dina, Bud and Geoff are all there. They look oddly still, as if they haven't moved since Ali was last in the office. Then Dina runs up to Ali and gives her a fierce hug.

'Oh, Ali.'

'Yeah,' says Ali. 'It's been a wild few days.'

She hopes she won't have to hug Bud and Geoff too, but Geoff seems to think that they've done enough of the emotional stuff. He contents himself with a wave and Bud does the same. Ali looks over at John's desk and away again.

'He wanted to do it,' says Dina gently.

'Dina offered too,' says Geoff. 'And Bud.'

'Bud?'

'Don't sound so surprised,' says Bud. 'I'm human too.'

'Are you sure?' It feels good to tease him again, to catch Dina's eye and see Geoff torn between wanting to join in and not knowing how.

'John felt,' says Geoff, 'and I have to say I agreed with him, that it would be easier for him to assimilate into nineteenth-century society.'

'Yes,' says Dina, 'it turns out it's easier for a white middle-aged man to blend in than it is for a black woman. Yay for the patriarchy.'

'He did look quite at home,' says Ali. 'And rather like an undertaker.'

'I still can't believe that you've actually been there,' says Dina. 'That you wore a big dress and rode in a horse and carriage.'

'I did both those things,' says Ali. She sits down at her desk. The lumbar-support chair seems to sigh with satisfaction at having her back. The view of the office block opposite, with its garish underwater mural, is exquisitely comforting. If she cranes her neck, she'll be able to see the spire of Christ Church. This building, which feels as if it has squatted on the site for ever, was once a field where sheep grazed. Ali shuts her eyes.

'Are you OK, Ali?' Dina's voice seems to come from a long way away.

'I'm fine. It just takes a bit of . . . adjustment.'

Her to-do list is still there.

1. *Final briefing from Elizabeth*
2. *Get money for trip*
3. *Write letter for Finn*
4. *Go through the gate*

Ali scores a line through the lot.

'Would you like a coffee?' says Bud. Ali says yes to give him something to do.

'We really should have a debrief,' says Geoff. 'Jones will be in soon.'

'We've never seen so much of Jones,' says Dina. 'It's been strange. As if Santa Claus came to live with you.'

'I'll tell you everything,' says Ali, 'but can we talk about Finn first? I really need to help him.'

'Of course,' says Geoff. 'We'll make it Operation Exonerate Finn. You and Dina can work on the case.'

'What about your 1966 case?' Ali turns to Dina. 'Finding out whether Martin Grantly killed that boy.'

'No one is going through the gate until John is back,' says Geoff. 'If we want the unit to survive, we can't afford to take any more risks.'

'Have you told the prime minister what happened?' says Ali, thinking of Declan and his conspiracy theories. 'About me getting stuck in 1850?'

'That information is on a need-to-know basis,' says Geoff, sounding more like his old, pedantic self.

'And Number Ten didn't need to know?'

'No.'

'Do you think,' says Ali, 'there could be any link between the gate being opened and Isaac's murder?'

'What do you mean?' asks Bud, appearing at the door of the kitchen with two mugs in his hands.

'Jones says that it's one gate for one person. That's why . . .' Ali looks over at John's desk, clear apart from his Moleskine notebook, pen lying beside it, and his West Ham water bottle, its claret and blue colours reassuringly garish. 'That's why John's there and I'm here. I think the reason I couldn't get back the first time might be because someone else took my gate.'

'You think someone came back from the nineteenth century and killed Isaac Templeton?' Geoff is there first.

'Thomas Creek, the man most people think killed Ettie Moran, disappeared. He just vanished. Someone in the street said they saw it happen. Finn just told me that Isaac was killed with an antique gun.'

'But Jones would have seen him,' protests Dina. 'She was there, in the street, waiting for you.'

'Actually . . .' Geoff sounds embarrassed. 'It was me. I was the one waiting for Ali. Jones had a lecture to give.'

'Didn't you see anything?' asks Dina.

'I may have been distracted . . . er, for a moment or so. There was a traffic warden, you see.'

Dina gives a shout of laughter. 'So, you missed a murderer escaping from 1850 because you were parked on a double yellow line.'

'I'd bought a ticket,' says Geoff, sounding shocked that anyone could think otherwise. 'But it had fallen off the dashboard. By the time I'd explained to the warden, who was rather obstructive, the moment had passed.'

'That could only have taken a couple of minutes,' says Dina.

'That's all it takes,' says Ali.

'If this is true . . .' Geoff rubs the top of his head as if he'd like to run his hands through the missing hair, 'we'll be shut down for sure.'

'It's just a hypothesis,' says Ali. 'I haven't ruled out a simpler explanation. Isaac being killed by his wife, for example. We only have her word for it that Isaac said, "It was you," or whatever it was, to an intruder.'

'She said that he said, "What are you doing here?"' says Geoff.

'I wonder,' says Ali, 'if it was "What are *you* doing here?" or "What are you doing *here*?" That makes a difference.'

'I don't know,' says Geoff. 'The briefing notes didn't include the emphasis.'

'Was he surprised to see the person or just surprised to see them in his house?'

'But if it was your Victorian villain,' says Dina, 'wouldn't it be more like "Who the hell are you and why are you dressed like that?"'

'Unless Isaac knew him,' says Ali, thinking of the diary. If Isaac had read his great-great-grandfather's journal, would it have included a description of Thomas Creek?

Geoff clears his throat obviously thinking this is too ridiculous to consider. 'I think we should also explore the possibility of a disgruntled constituent or political enemy.'

'Should be plenty of those,' says Ali. She feels invigorated at the thought of an investigation, of working with Dina, of working out a plan of action. She opens her pad at a new page.

TO DO

Find out who killed Isaac Templeton.

At two-thirty pm Ade Akinyemi rings to say that Finn's case has come up before the magistrates' court and he's been remanded in custody. A date has been set for his Crown Court appearance. 'I'll ask for bail then,' says Ade. 'The mags can't grant bail on a murder charge but,

I'll be honest with you, it's very unlikely to be granted by the Crown either. Not unless there are extremely unusual circumstances.' Like the murderer being a time traveller, thinks Ali. She hopes she hasn't said it aloud – it's becoming rather hard to tell the difference between thought and reality – but Ade doesn't react so presumably she's safe. Ali forms a positive impression of Finn's solicitor. She'd been worried when she'd heard that he was Chibu's brother. She's only met Chibu a couple of times but she seemed a little vapid, a little too excited at the thought of meeting an actual working-class person. But Ade is businesslike without seeming callous. He tells Ali that Finn is being held at HMP Thameside. It will be Ali's first call tomorrow.

Jones turns up just as Ali is putting the phone down. She's carrying *The Pickwick Papers*. 'You left this in my car. Did you get him to sign it?'

'Who?' Ali is feeling a little thick-headed by now. She didn't sleep well last night and the bed where she didn't sleep was in 1850. Part of her just wants to go home and pull her duvet over her head.

'Charles Dickens,' says Jones. 'Shall we?' She indicates Geoff's office.

Ali exchanges a look with Dina. It helps a lot.

Jones takes her normal chair, turns to Ali and says, 'Tell us everything.'

So Ali does. She tells them about finding Cain Templeton standing over the dead woman, about waiting on the ingress point while the sheep's-feet man shouted his wares in the background, about the possibility of Thomas Creek using her gate, the cold and feeling of dread, about the inhabitants of 44 Hawk Street, about having dinner at Templeton's house, about the moment when John materialised in the kitchen.

'I tried to tell him everything I could,' says Ali. 'There wasn't much time.'

'There never is,' says Jones. 'But I'm delighted at how things turned out. You mean to say that nobody noticed anything odd about you?'

'I wouldn't say that,' says Ali. 'They thought I talked strangely. I told them it was a Hastings accent. Luckily none of them had ever been to Hastings. Templeton definitely knew there was something unusual about me, but he couldn't work out what it was.' She hopes she isn't blushing.

'I'll write a report,' says Jones. 'They can't ignore me now. Perhaps there'll be real funding for the project at last.'

'Steady on,' says Geoff, which seems a very English reaction to the Italian physicist. 'We can't tell the PM anything about this last trip. He'll say it's too dangerous. An operative getting stuck in the nineteenth century. A possible malfunction with the gate.'

'That's true,' says Jones. 'We can't tell them any of that. But we did it. We really did it.'

'We did,' says Geoff. 'You did. Ali did.'

Ali wants to puncture the mood of self-satisfaction. 'What about John?' she says. 'How are you going to get him back?'

'I'll work something out,' says Jones. 'I'm working on an AI version of John including his DNA and fingerprints. I think that might work.'

But you're not sure, thinks Ali. She imagines John standing in the street, opposite the beer barrels, with the urchins and the dogs capering around him. Will he go to the spot every day, as she did? Will he, too, start to despair? Will he, too, start to feel that he belongs there, in the pungent 1850s, and not in sterile 2023?

'I can't believe he did that for me,' she says.

'He wanted to,' says Geoff.

'He was prepared,' says Jones. 'He knows he will be there for some time. He's going to carry out several experiments for me.' Ali wishes she wouldn't sound quite so excited.

By four o'clock, Ali is drooping.

'Go home,' says Dina. 'Whatever the time travel equivalent of jet lag is, you've got it.'

Ali stands up and sways so violently that she has to grab onto her desk to stay upright. The underwater mural on the building opposite pulsates unpleasantly. Did the whale just wink at her?

'I'm calling you an Uber,' says Dina. 'And, tomorrow, we'll start work on Finn's case.'

'That sounds good,' says Ali. 'Thank you, Dina.'

The car, a blue Toyota, is outside. Ali means to confirm her address in Bow but finds herself saying, 'Can you take me to Hawk Street, E2?' She doesn't know what she's doing or why she's doing it. Is this the godlike feeling Jones once described? It's more like she's receiving instructions from some remote control centre. Luckily this driver isn't a talker. It's rush hour and their progress is slow but Ali is content to be part of the snarling entity that is London: black cabs, red buses, sirens, Deliveroo bikes, commuters weaving between cars because they can't wait for one more second at the zebra crossing. When they arrive at Number 44, there are lights in most of the windows. Ali thanks the driver (who is being paid on Dina's account) and lurches onto the pavement. Then she climbs the steps and contemplates the griffin door knocker. She thinks it must be only for show, visitors are clearly expected to ring one of the many bells. She tries the number of what must be one of the top flats. To her surprise, the door is buzzed open without any need for an explanation. Perhaps they're waiting for a Deliveroo order.

The hall looks much lighter than she remembers. This is because the wood panelling has been painted a rather unsuccessful magnolia. There are the same black and white tiles, though, and, looking up, she sees the elaborate cornices and the ceiling rose. Attached to this last is a modern-looking chandelier. Wires snake out of the walls in a way that would have amazed, and disturbed, the original inhabitants. The half-moon table looks familiar although, instead of a single vase, it's now piled high with post, some of which has fallen on the floor. Is that . . .? Oh God, it's the clock, the grandfather clock. It seems to have stopped at midday – or midnight – but Ali follows the numbers around the dial: the iron gate, the yawning grave, the man with a scythe, the headless horseman, the sinister children, the owl, the cat, the witch, the carriage, the tower, the white lady, hell itself. She notices, for the first time, that there's a door in the clock and a little golden key. On impulse, she reaches out to turn it.

She stops because someone is descending the stairs. It's a young woman wearing headphones. She doesn't acknowledge Ali, or even seem to notice her, but Ali doesn't think she can remain lurking in the hallway. She starts to climb the stairs.

Was it only this morning that she was here, walking down, carrying a full chamber pot? Now she bounds upwards in her jeans and trainers. Past Tremain's studio, Arthur Moses' room, the Rokebys' quarters. On the first landing a cat appears, looks at Ali in horror, and streaks past her. It's a fluffy orange creature, not like Terry's sleek teal, but it reminds Ali of the feeling she had, back in 1850, of being accompanied by a cat, a feline companion, always just out of sight. Maybe this one is the descendent of Clara's beloved Ginger?

Ali climbs the last flight and stops by her old room. What will she find inside? She knocks on the door. It's opened by a man who is probably in his mid-twenties, the sort of person who smiles even though he's not sure who the visitor is.

'Hi,' says Ali. 'I know this sounds mad, but I used to live here. I wondered if I could . . .'

'Have a look inside?' says the man. 'Of course. I warn you, it's pretty untidy. There are three of us here.'

The attic space has been expanded to form a flat. There must have been rooms on either side of Ali's because there's now a galley kitchen, a shower room and three small bedrooms, all with sloping ceilings. The man, who introduces himself as Asif, says that the flatmates are all medical students. 'It's not the biggest place but it's convenient for Barts.' St Bartholomew's Hospital would have been around in 1850. Ali remembers reading that there's been a place of healing on the site since the twelfth century. What would Cain Templeton think of these new lodgers? Ali remembers Tremain saying that being a surgeon wasn't a respectable occupation. Maybe Templeton would have preferred his artists, even if they never paid their rent.

The sitting room is Ali's bedroom. Is John here now, at this very moment but also one hundred and seventy-three years ago? The thought is dizzying, so much so that Ali fears she might faint.

'Are you all right?' asks Asif.

'Yes. Fine,' says Ali. He's still watching her with concern, so she turns to look out of the round window. From this height, the curved street looks remarkably unchanged.

'When I lived here before,' she says, 'a man tapped on the window to wake me up.' She wonders now if someone in the house had paid for this personal wake-up call.

'Really?' says Asif politely, but he's clearly worrying that he's let a mad woman in. Ali thanks him and makes her way downstairs. Halfway down, she stops. Someone is playing the piano. Ali doesn't know much about classical music but it sounds very much like the sort of tune Len Rokeby used to play. Ali presses her ear to the nearest door. Should she knock? Who will she find there? The great-grandson of the baby she once saw being bottle-fed in the kitchen? No, it's probably just Radio 3. She continues her descent.

Ali walks back to Bow. It takes her over an hour but she thinks she needs the time to get reacquainted with the twenty-first century. She still has the feeling that she is walking different streets, lower and darker, crowded with horse-drawn carriages rather than taxis and buses. This makes things rather dangerous at zebra crossings. Once or twice she has the strong sensation that she is being followed. It's rather like her sightings of cats at Hawk Street, a glimpse of something moving just out of eyeshot, a shadow that somehow keeps pace with her as she navigates the rush-hour crowds.

It's dark by the time she reaches her cul-de-sac. It has old-fashioned lamp posts which, combined with the cobbles, create a misty B-movie atmosphere. As she fumbles for her house key, she sees the shadow again, a dark fluttering, almost like the movement of a bird's wing. But when she turns there's nothing there, just a misshapen tree in her neighbour's garden. Inside, she switches on every light she can. Terry watches closely but he's in one of his aloof moods and won't let her pet him. Ali looks in her fridge.

There are some vegetables, which she assumes were put there by Finn, and half a bottle of white. There's also a slice of pizza, which she eats. Did Finn send out for pizza? It seems unlikely. Ali pours herself a glass of wine, remembering the craving for alcohol that had surprised her in 1850. She doesn't feel that now. She has to keep her wits about her, for Finn's sake.

Ali makes a stir-fry with the vegetables and sits at the kitchen table to eat it. She has brought her laptop from the office and angles it towards her now, thinking she'll read something on the Kindle app. Instead she finds herself typing the name 'Cain Templeton'. She did this before she travelled to 1850 and, once again, only the Templeton Collection comes up. She tries Frederick Tremain and is surprised when the screen is filled with images, tiny jewel-like pictures of women. It seems that an authentic Tremain now goes for several thousand pounds at auction. 'This artist has been enjoying a renaissance in recent years,' says a rather breathless article. 'He is admired for his glorious flesh tones and for the shimmering beauty of his brushstrokes.' There's even a portrait of Tremain himself, brooding and romantic. Ali wonders who painted it. There are no results for Arthur Moses, Leonard Rokeby, Ettie Moran or Jane Campion.

On impulse, Ali types 'Reverend Percival Green'. This is the most rewarding search yet. Page after page of lurid details accompanied by engravings and sketches of a depraved-looking man in a dog collar. She learns that the Reverend Green posed as a friend of 'fallen women'. He lured them into his Whitechapel vicarage, murdered them and kept their hair as souvenirs. He's thought to be the inspiration for the Reverend Green in Cluedo. Ali remembers the sponge-like object in formaldehyde and shudders. Cain's voice, taking on the slightly prurient tone of some true crime documentaries, 'He killed five prostitutes over the space of six months. He claimed to be saving them from themselves, or for himself, as the case proved. He was hanged in 1845.' *I've seen his brain*, she thinks.

The scrolling is making her feel quite sick. She's lost the art of looking at screens. Ali closes the laptop and moves to the sofa. Despite everything, it feels wonderful to sit on comfortable cushions and pull a blanket over her knees. It's a luxurious chenille affair, a present from Meg. Ali had almost forgotten what it was like to feel completely warm. She switches on the television and, after a few minutes, Terry relents enough to come and sit on her lap, kneading the soft material briskly. Ali lets the light and sound wash over her, not really watching. She finishes the wine. Perhaps she had a craving after all. She's watching a programme about renovating camper vans when a news flash appears on her phone.

Man charged in Isaac Templeton case.

Finn hasn't been named, but he will be tomorrow. Ali hesitates before clicking on the link. She missed her phone so much when she was away but, now that she's reunited with it, she feels almost scared of the powerful little box. Also, she knows that, over the next few days, everyone in her life will be messaging her, wanting to know about Finn. Now there are only a few notifications. Two texts from Declan and one from Dina. A WhatsApp from her book group. And a message from a number she has saved only as Ed.

Could you give me a ring? Something rather strange has turned up. It's to do with the Templeton Collection.

Chapter 29

Thameside Prison is one of the new ones, owned and run by a private company. It's painted in pastel colours, which is meant to produce a calming effect on inmates but has left Ali with an enduring hatred for pale pink. She's been here several times before, to interview suspects or escort prisoners, but she's never been in the position of waiting with the other relatives: the exhausted wives and girlfriends, some poignantly dressed in their best clothes, the angry parents demanding justice, the silent children. After ten minutes, she is infected with the despair emanating from the waiting area. She starts to think that she will never see Finn again and that she will never rescue him from this primrose and mauve monstrosity. When her name is called, she hardly recognises it. She gets up, smiling apologetically at the woman next to her, who was there when she arrived and looks as if she will be in the bolted-down plastic chair for ever. Ali checks her belongings into a locker, walks through the airport-style scanner and follows the guard along a corridor. It smells, like all prisons, of urine unsuccessfully masked by disinfectant. They pass through three doors which must be unlocked and locked again behind them. Each key turn makes Ali's heart clench.

Finn is waiting in the visitor centre. Because he's on remand, he's allowed to wear his own clothes and Ali is able to hug him. After a few seconds, though, the guard tells them to sit down.

'How are you?' says Ali, ridiculously.

'I've been better. I told Piers that prison's like boarding school. It's your fault for sending me to a comprehensive.'

'I'm going to talk to Piers today, and Chibu too.'

'Are you being a detective?' says Finn.

'I am a detective,' says Ali, 'and I'm investigating. Geoff has said that I can have Dina to help me.'

'Geoff's a good bloke. You know, he came round when you were . . . away. We shared two bottles of wine and a pizza.'

'I can't imagine Geoff unwinding that much.'

'I think he felt sorry for me.'

'Geoff's going to find out exactly what the police think they have on you. What's this DS O'Brien like?'

'Youngish. Scary. I think she thought it was me from the beginning.'

'Looks to me like they arrested you because they wanted to have a result. The Met must be under pressure from Isaac's family. From the PM too. The government won't want this case to hang around in the media for weeks.'

'Isaac's family. You mean Miranda?'

'Well, she is a high-powered lawyer. I want to see her too. She's my number one suspect.'

'Miranda?'

'It's usually the spouse. And we've only got her word for a lot of it. Isaac recognising the intruder, for example. The killer could have been Miranda's accomplice – she could have let them in.'

She doesn't tell Finn about her Thomas Creek theory. She doesn't want him to think that she's cracking up.

'Have you told Nan and Grandad about me?' says Finn.

It's painful to hear Finn use the childish names. He loves his grandparents, on both sides, and they all adore him.

'Yes,' says Ali. 'They send their love. They know you didn't do it.' Cheryl had burst into tears on the phone. Declan said his mother had to take a Valium.

'Dad's had to go back to Hastings,' she says. 'But he'll be up to see you next week. If we haven't got you out by then.' Remand prisoners are allowed one visit a week. Ali has pulled strings to get this meeting and she will pull them again and again until Finn is released.

'Do you really think you will get me out?' Finn looks at her with such faith that Ali nearly breaks down.

'Of *course* I will,' she says. 'Trust me.'

Ali's first visit is to Ade Akinyemi. The solicitor's offices are in an anonymous building near King's Cross but Ali can tell by the carpeting and the silent lift that it's a prestigious firm. Ade himself, in a dark suit and blindingly white shirt, looks the image of a corporate lawyer.

'It all depends what the police actually have on Finn,' he says. 'The CCTV was inconclusive. And, if there's DNA at the scene, it could have been from Finn's previous visits.'

'That's what I said,' says Ali. 'Finn worked really closely with

Isaac. They've spent a lot of time together. Well, you know that from your sister.'

'Yes,' says Ade. 'It's a close relationship, isn't it? Political advisors and their minister. Chibs talks about Isaac partly like he's a child with learning difficulties and partly like he's her husband.' He pauses before saying, 'I think the police are working on a theory that Finn and Isaac were lovers.'

'Really?' Finn always accuses Ali of being disappointed that he's not gay and, when he was growing up, she certainly tried to have open conversations with him about sexuality. Too open, Finn said. He preferred Declan's jokey 'got yourself a girlfriend yet?' approach. As far as Ali knows, Finn has only had relationships with women, but she wouldn't be the first mother not to know the details of her child's private life. Could it be true about Finn and Isaac?

'Why do they think that?' she says.

'It's motivation, I suppose,' says Ade. 'A lover's quarrel. But there's no evidence and, unsurprisingly, Isaac's wife vehemently denies that he was gay or bisexual.'

'What do you think of the wife?' says Ali. 'She doesn't have an alibi.'

'Not that we know of,' says Ade. 'But the police seem to have ruled her out.'

'I wonder why?' says Ali.

She expects Ade to acknowledge the irony in her tone, but he seems to take the question at face value. 'I don't know why,' he says, 'but I'll try to find out.'

Chibu has agreed to meet Ali at a café near Victoria Station. 'It's handy for the House,' she says, obviously meaning the House of

Commons. Has Chibu still got a job? wonders Ali. Has Piers, who was Isaac's parliamentary assistant?

Chibu wells up as soon as she sees Ali. She gives her a hug, too, which seems a little intimate considering that they have only met twice before.

'I'm so sorry,' sniffs Chibu. 'Finn's so sweet, you know?'

I do know, Ali wants to say. And she wonders what Chibu is sorry about. Is she sorry that Finn has been arrested or that an innocent man is in prison?

'Finn didn't kill Isaac,' Ali begins briskly, sitting at a table with a flat white that looks as if it's largely milk. Chibu is drinking green tea. She's wearing a soft grey jumper over black leggings and looks, despite the tears, as smooth and sleek as an athlete, hair braided and pulled into a ponytail.

'Oh, I know.' Chibu wipes her eyes. 'Finn would never hurt anyone. He's a pacifist. We've talked about it a lot. I believe in a just war, you know?'

Ali assumes this is a rhetorical question. It's news to her – welcome news – that Finn is a pacifist.

'As you know,' Ali continues, 'I'm a police officer and I'm making it my job to find out who did kill Isaac. So I need your help.'

'Mine?' Now Chibu sounds distinctly nervous.

'You knew Isaac as well as anyone. Can you think of anyone who would have wanted to kill him?'

'No,' says Chibu, eyes brimming. 'Everyone loved Isaac.'

'Really? Because I only searched on the internet for half an hour today and I saw him described as a racist, a misogynist and a privileged wanker.'

'He wasn't a racist,' says Chibu, which rather begs the question about the other accusations.

'Did anyone ever threaten Isaac? I thought MPs got death threats all the time.'

'There were some . . . unpleasant . . . emails. I've forwarded them all to the police.'

'Anything that struck you as a credible threat?'

'Not really. It was mainly just people who hate Conservatives. I mean, I'm not a Tory myself. At Oxford I was a member of the Liberal Democrats.'

God, thinks Ali, a university education is wasted on some people.

'Why did you work with Isaac then?'

'I was a civil servant in the Home Office. I used to see him at meetings and I liked him. Admired him too. I thought that he would be prime minister one day. So, when he offered me a job, I accepted it.'

'Finn always said Isaac wanted to be prime minister.'

'Well, most politicians do, I suppose.'

'What about Piers?' says Ali. 'Did he admire Isaac too?'

There's a tiny hesitation. Chibu takes a sip of tea before replying. 'Piers isn't the type to admire people. He's very cynical, you know? I think he got the job with Isaac because his dad knew Isaac's. But he was good at what he did. Finn always said there was no one like Piers for making bad news sound like good.'

'How nice,' says Ali. She wonders whether Isaac's father is still alive. He hasn't been mentioned in any of the press coverage. Presumably, given that Isaac is occupying the family mansion, his father is dead. But he could just be living in a smaller house somewhere, or in a nursing home. If so, does he know that Isaac was investigating his great-great-grandfather? She remembers Cain talking about his five children. Ephraim, perhaps one of the only two surviving, would have been Isaac's father's grandfather.

'How well do you know Isaac's wife, Miranda?' she says.

'Not that well, but she was always nice to us when we went to East Dean. She didn't resent us for being around. Even when we sat up talking for ages in the great hall. Miranda must have been dying for us to shut up so that she could get some time with Isaac. When I think of Miranda and the children now, I feel like crying.'

Ali hopes that Chibu doesn't act on this feeling. 'The great hall,' she says. 'That was where Isaac died, wasn't it?'

'Yes,' says Chibu. 'It's so horrible.'

'You were at East Dean the weekend before Isaac died, weren't you?'

'Yes. Just for a day and a night.'

'Did you see anything that might seem suspicious, in retrospect?'

'Not really. We brainstormed with Isaac in his office, then we had lunch. In the afternoon we did more work, then we went for a walk. Finn had a swim. After supper, we stayed drinking and talking in the hall. We didn't see anyone except Miranda and the kids. Oh, and Jacinta. The nanny.'

'Does the nanny live in?' Ali makes a note of the name.

'Oh yes,' says Chibu, sounding surprised. 'Of course, they're usually at the London house but, with the hours Miranda and Isaac work, they need a full-time nanny.'

Of course they do, thinks Ali. She could have done with one herself whilst working as a cleaner, looking after a child and trying to get a degree.

Annoyingly, Chibu has been thinking along the same lines. 'I really admire you, Ali,' she says. 'You did it all yourself. Finn's a credit to you. He really is.'

'Thank you,' says Ali. 'And thanks to your brother for taking on Finn's case.'

'Ade's the best,' says Chibu.

'I've just been to see him,' says Ali. 'He told me that the police think Finn and Isaac were having an affair.'

She wanted to spring this on Chibu to see her reaction. She's not disappointed. Chibu's eyes grow wide and she actually gasps.

'Finn and Isaac. Never! Finn isn't gay. Nor was Isaac. Definitely not. And he'd never do that to me. To Miranda.'

It's a tiny mistake, instantly corrected, but Ali catches it. She thinks of Ade saying that Chibu talked about Isaac as if he were her child or her husband. She knows which relationship was uppermost in that moment.

Ali isn't meeting Piers until five. She needs to get back to the office but thinks she'll make a quick detour to see Ed Crane first. He asked her to phone him but Ali thinks that she'd rather see the curator in person. It's an easy trip on the District Line from Victoria to Mile End and she feels the need to talk about something other than Finn, just for an hour or so.

QMUL looks at its best in the winter sunshine but it doesn't lift Ali's spirits as it usually does. She sees the students scurrying across Library Square with their laptops and takeaway coffee and resents them for having their liberty while Finn is locked up in a pale pink cell. She climbs the steps to the Queens' Building and thinks about standing there on her graduation day with Finn next to her, a thin thirteen-year-old with curly hair and a large camera. This last had belonged to Ali's father, who'd had the happy idea of asking Finn to be the official photographer. Ali has an abiding memory of Finn squinting through the lens and trying to corral the grown-ups for group shots. She doesn't think it's a coincidence that Hugo was cropped out of most of them.

Ali asks for Ed Crane and is told that he's in the storeroom doing some repairs.

'Visitors aren't usually allowed up there,' says the receptionist doubtfully.

'It's OK,' says Ali. 'I've been there before.' She shows her warrant card, which shocks the woman into pointing out the stairs.

'The lift's broken, I'm afraid.' Ali starts the long climb upwards. She's not as out of breath this time and wonders if her trip to the past, and all the walking she did there, has made her fitter. *Time travel is like using a lift rather than taking the stairs.*

She pushes open the door to the attic room and the first things she sees are Ed's long, thin legs. He's standing on a step ladder, apparently fixing a broken light fitting.

'Hello,' says Ali.

Ed starts and almost falls off.

'Ali! Thank you for coming in. Let me just finish here.' He screws in a bulb and the light flickers and then dies. 'Oh well. I tried. All the electrics in this building are shot.' He climbs down but still seems several feet above her.

'Your text was very mysterious,' says Ali. 'You said you had something to show me.'

'Yes,' says Ed. 'It's very strange. Quite a coincidence. I was cataloguing the Templeton Collection yesterday. We've got an inventory coming and I wanted to check that everything was listed.

There's this writing slope. Do you know what that is? A sort of portable desk. Well, why don't I just show you?'

Ed folds up the ladder and leans it against the wall before leading the way through the cabinets to the locked door and then to an antique-looking desk. Ali hardly noticed it on her first visit, she was too preoccupied with skulls and pickled brains. On the desk is a wooden box with a sloping lid, bound in green leather and tooled in gold. Ed lifts this up. Inside, there's a space divided into compartments.

'You'd keep your wax, seals and pens and ink in here,' says Ed. 'But look at this.'

He takes out one of the compartments and presses the wood behind it. The entire mechanism springs forward, revealing a hidden area.

'Secret drawers were quite common in Victorian writing cases,' says Ed, 'but this one was hard to spot. I only came across it by accident. Look what I found inside.'

He lifts out a sheet of paper. There are several lines written in flowing black letters, but Ali only takes in the first word: *Alisoun.*

Chapter 30

Alisoun. It's been an annoyance all Ali's life that her father, apparently under the influence of several pints taken to 'wet the baby's head', spelt her name like this on her birth certificate. It doesn't alter the pronunciation but it always seems like an affectation, or a mistake, to Ali. She usually ignores it and goes for the more conventional 'Alison', but the name appears in its original form on her passport, on all three of her marriage certificates and on her degree diploma.

'That's how my name is spelt,' she says to Ed. 'Officially anyway.'

'I know,' he says. 'I looked you up in the student register.'

Ali decides to ignore this for the moment. 'What's in the envelope?' she says.

'A letter,' says Ed. He takes out a single sheet of paper and lays it on the green leather slope. Ali moves closer to read it, aware that this also brings her very close to Ed.

Alisoun , my time-travelling angel. I don't know when I will ever see you again but I must trust that fate will bring us together. I carved our names on a tree today. Cain and Alisoun. Maybe one day you'll see it. There will never be anyone like you, in my past, present or future. No one like you in heaven or earth. If you're an angel, I'm a devil and my hell is being away from you. I hope that one day I will see your face again . . .

There the writing stops.

'It's a love letter,' says Ed, 'and it looks to be from Cain Templeton to someone called Alisoun. Isn't that a coincidence?'

'Is it real?' says Ali. Her voice sounds as if it is coming from a very long way away.

'It could be,' says Ed. 'It's quite possible that no one has ever found the secret compartment before. But I looked Cain Templeton up in the catalogue to the collection and couldn't see anyone called Alisoun in his biography. His wife was called Fedora.'

Ali thinks of Cain talking about his wife preferring their Sussex house. Is that where the tree is? The one with their names on it? She realises that she hasn't spoken for some minutes and that Ed is looking at her rather quizzically.

'It's certainly a curiosity,' she says. 'Can I take a copy?'

'Of course. There's a photocopier in the office.'

They leave the room. Ed switches off the light and locks the door. The sound of the key turning reminds Ali of Thameside. Weren't prison warders once called turnkeys? She shivers.

'Are you cold?' says Ed. 'The heating doesn't work either, I'm afraid.'

Now Ali comes to think of it, she *is* cold, even in her coat. Ed is obviously used to the temperature. He's wearing just a flannel shirt and jeans.

They descend the stairs and, on the ground floor, Ed leads the way to an untidy office full of packing cases and broken pieces of statuary. He photocopies the letter, puts it into a brown envelope and hands it, rather ceremoniously, to Ali.

'I hope you can solve the mystery,' he says.

'I'll try,' says Ali.

Ali walks back through the campus in a daze. *Alisoun . . . my time-travelling angel . . . There will never be anyone like you, in my past, present or future . . .* Can this letter have been intended for her? Because, if so, it suggests she will go back to the nineteenth century and clearly have some sort of affair with Cain Templeton. It's a frightening thought, yet, through it all, Ali is almost ashamed to feel a thrill of excitement. She has been married three times but never has anyone called her an angel and said that there is no one like her in heaven or earth. *My time-travelling angel.* This must mean her, surely, and, if so, Cain knew that she could time travel, that she was a visitor from the future. *There will never be anyone like you, in my past, present or future.*

'Ali!'

Ali starts and looks up, almost surprised to see modern buildings around her. She's actually on the edge of the Novo Cemetery, the tombstones flat and grey with no spring flowers to soften them. Elizabeth is approaching from the library side, her arms full of books. Ali thinks quickly. Part of her wants to tell her old tutor everything: that she put her advice into practice and actually became a Victorian woman for five days. But she knows that, once those words are out, they cannot be retracted. Either Elizabeth will believe her, and become part of the secret, or she will think Ali has gone mad.

'Were you coming to see me?' asks Elizabeth. She looks so much herself, square and self-sufficient in a padded coat and sensible shoes, that Ali feels a rush of affection for her.

'No,' says Ali. 'Though I'm delighted to see you, of course. I've just been to see Ed at the museum.'

'He's an interesting chap, isn't he?'

'Yes, he is.' Ali makes a quick decision. 'Can I show you something? Have you got a minute?'

'Yes. Let's have a coffee.'

They go to the Ground Café, a student hangout in the shadow of Clement Attlee. Young people are lounging around, eating, talking and laughing, but Ali no longer resents them. She feels detached, as she did in 1850, as if their world is no longer hers. Elizabeth finds a table and Ali buys them both flat whites. The joy of twenty-first century coffee hasn't worn off.

'So, what have you got to show me?' says Elizabeth.

'This.' Ali gets the photocopy out of her backpack. 'It's a letter. Ed Crane found it inside a Victorian writing slope.'

'I love those things. I've got one at home. You know desks with a slope were sometimes called Dickens desks?'

'I didn't know, but I've been reading *The Pickwick Papers*.'

'Really? I love that book. Very picaresque.'

Ali isn't going to ask what this means. 'Read the letter,' she says.

Elizabeth looks down at the paper. 'Alisoun,' she says. 'That's how you spell your name.'

'Well remembered.'

Elizabeth reads on, wearing the expression with which she perused Ali's student essays. Then she looks up at Ali and down at the paper again.

'This is very strange,' she says. 'Has it really been in the desk all that time?'

'Ed says so. It was in a secret compartment.'

'The Victorians did love their secrets, bless them.'

She gives Ali one of her searching looks and, once again, Ali feels a compulsion to tell Elizabeth everything: about Hawk Street, The Collectors and about the gate itself.

Then she looks down at her phone and sees an alert flash up.

Suspect named in Isaac Templeton murder.

'I'm sorry,' she says to Elizabeth. 'Something urgent's come up. I have to go.'

Dina is in the kitchen watering Tom, the spider plant, who has been looking rather forlorn lately.

'I've got us some sandwiches,' she says.

'Thanks,' says Ali. She switches the kettle on and switches it off again.

Dina says, 'Finn was named on the midday news.'

'I know,' says Ali. 'I saw it on my phone.' Dina is watching her anxiously so Ali forces herself to say, 'It had to happen sooner or later, I suppose. Let's get on with trying to find the real killer.'

'Exactly.' Dina looks relieved at her reaction.

They go into the open-plan area where Bud is frowning at his laptop as if to emphasise how difficult and complicated his work is.

'I got you a sandwich too,' Dina tells him. 'Cheese and pickle. I got us tuna because it's good for the brain.'

'I'll take that as a compliment,' says Bud.

'I made a list,' says Dina to Ali. 'I'm Watson to your Holmes.'

Ali reads while eating her sandwich, which tastes like plastic but in a good way.

OTHER SUSPECTS
Miranda Templeton
Chibu Akinyemi
Piers Fletcher–Hogg
Political enemies
Possible girlfriend
Persons unknown

'I think the police have been very lax about "persons unknown",' says Ali. 'They don't seem to have chased up any threats sent to Isaac. Chibu admitted he'd had them. She said all politicians do and I suppose she's right.'

'Geoff says he's trying to get you an interview with the officer in charge of the case,' says Dina. 'DS Mary O'Brien. She's reluctant apparently.'

'I'm not surprised,' says Ali. 'This investigation feels very dodgy. I wouldn't be surprised if they were being leant on. There must be a lot of pressure to get a quick result.'

She looks at the list again. Dina's writing is rather round and childish, quite unlike Cain Templeton's flowing script. *My darling Alisoun.*

'You can add Jacinta the nanny,' says Ali. 'In fact, she might count as "possible girlfriend" too. Chibu too. By the way, the police theory is that Finn and Isaac were having an affair.'

Dina looks up. 'That's not true, is it?'

'Not as far as I know but I suppose I can't be sure.'

'Finn's not gay,' says Bud, who is. 'I'd be able to tell.'

'But Isaac could have been having an affair with someone,' says Dina. 'He was very good-looking.'

'You don't have to be good-looking to have an affair,' says Ali. 'You just need to be deceitful. I did wonder about Chibu. She definitely had a crush on Isaac.'

'Let's ask Piers when we see him,' says Dina. 'OK if I come with you?'

'Please do,' says Ali. 'I have a feeling that Piers might prove a slippery customer.'

Piers Fletcher-Hogg is not so much slippery as sozzled. He asked to meet Ali in a bar near the House of Commons. It's clear that he's been there for most of the afternoon. Piers is tall and blond and might be called handsome were it not for a slight sloppiness about his features and a rather wet lower lip. Ali thinks that he reminds her of someone and realises, with a shock of time travel, that it's Francis Burbage.

'I've been drinking libations,' he informs them. 'A ritual drink for the dead. I studied Classics, y'know.'

Never a good sign, thinks Ali. She asks Piers if he'd like another drink, though he's clearly had enough. He suggests they buy a bottle of wine. Ali gets him a glass of red and water for her and Dina.

'You two are no fun,' he says.

'We're on duty,' says Ali. 'Thank you for meeting us.'

'You're Finn's mother, aren't you?'

Ali has met Piers the same number of times she has met Chibu;

twice, at House of Commons events. But Chibu seems to think they are best friends and Piers hardly recognises her. Maybe it's because her hair isn't red anymore.

'Yes, I'm Finn's mother,' she says, 'and I'm also a police officer.'

'Ooh!' Piers gives a theatrical shudder. 'I'd better be careful.'

'We're trying to find out who killed Isaac,' says Dina, 'since obviously Finn didn't.'

'You don't look like a police officer,' says Piers. 'Not because you're black. You just don't seem the type.'

'I'm not a police officer,' says Dina. 'I'm a CFI.' It stands for Computer Forensics Investigator. Dina is probably counting on this silencing Piers. And it does.

'So,' says Ali. 'Do you have any idea who killed Isaac?'

'Yes,' says Piers immediately. Ali and Dina look at each other in surprise. 'It was Miranda, of course. It's always the wife.'

Although this is very much what Ali herself has been saying, it sounds wrong coming from Piers, partly because he has difficulty pronouncing the name Miranda.

'Why do you say that?' she asks.

'I don't know. Maybe Isaac was playing away.'

'Do you have any idea who he could have been having an affair with?' says Ali. 'The police think it could have been Finn.'

This takes a second to register. 'Finn! That's a good one. Isaac wasn't gay. He was a womaner . . . a womaniser. A Lothario.' The word is said with relish – and some spittle.

'Do you have any names for us?'

'Yes. Helen Graham. She's a Labour MP. Pretty sure she was screwing Isaac. Oh, and Chibu, of course.'

'Chibu was sleeping with Isaac?'

'Oh yes,' says Piers. 'I thought everyone knew.'

Ali gets the Tube home, stopping for some food shopping on the way. She's thankful that she doesn't have any phone reception on the Underground but, when she's back in her house, having fed Terry and made herself a cup of tea, she looks at her mobile. Finn's name is everywhere. Everyone she knows seems to have sent messages of support, concern and downright nosiness. There's even an email from Hugo.

Dear Ali

I was so shocked to hear about Finn. I always knew him as a sweet boy, a little shy but basically a good lad. Do message me if you need any support.

All best,

Hugo.

Breathe, Ali tells herself. That Hugo, who only knew Finn for three years, and was cordially hated by him for all of them, should presume to call her son 'basically a good lad'. That he, the least reliable man in the universe, should offer support. It's almost laughable. She doesn't laugh though. She shouts, 'Fuck off, Hugo!' and throws the phone across the room. Terry takes refuge on her highest bookshelf.

Ali retrieves her phone and deletes the email. She can't help contrasting the missive from her ex-husband with the letter from Cain Templeton. *There will never be anyone like you, in my past, present or future. No one like you in heaven or earth* . . . Ali's old DI used to say, 'Sometimes the strangest thing is the true thing.' It seems impossible – fantastical – that Ali could have had an affair with Cain. But, in a weird way, it's the only explanation that makes any sense.

Several times that afternoon, Ali was tempted to tell Dina about the Alisoun letter. Dina, at least, would understand the context, would accept that the missive might be proof that Ali will return to the nineteenth century one day. But today, with Dina, was all about solving Isaac's murder and proving Finn's innocence. Ali's time-travelling love life would have to wait.

Ali makes herself some pasta with a pre-prepared sauce. It's not very nice and she knows that 'Nonna Luisa', whom she follows on YouTube, would not approve. But she has to eat something. When she's finished, it's still only eight o'clock. Far too early to go to bed. Ali sits in her chair with her blanket over her legs and her cat beside her (he's not sitting on her lap because he's still offended about the phone-throwing incident). How can she fill the time? *I sew until the light goes, then I go to my bed*, Clara had said. It's a shame, in a way, that Ali never had a chance to learn needlework from Clara. She doesn't want to watch TV. Even her old comfort shows – *The Office, Brooklyn Nine-Nine* – have lost their power to soothe. Ali checks her phone. Meg: 'Do you want to talk? Thinking of you xxx' Declan: 'Hows it going its hell here.' There's even a text from Ali's brother, Richard. He's only two years older but they have never been close. Richard seemed to navigate childhood and school without feeling the need to rebel in the way that Ali did. He married his teenage girlfriend, Faye, and they have two children and three grandchildren. Richard still lives in Hastings. He used to be a postman but was made redundant and is now a delivery driver. Richard and Ali have little in common but she is rather moved by his message which reads simply: 'It's shit. Finn is innocent. You'll get him off.' 'I will', she replies, adding two kisses.

There's also a message from Geoff telling her that DS O'Brien will meet her tomorrow at nine o'clock.

Ali sighs and takes *The Pickwick Papers* down from its shelf. She has reached one of the stand-alone stories which pop up within the main narrative. Ali usually reads these with impatience, wanting to go back to Snodgrass and Co. But this one, 'The Bagman's Story', piques her interest with these words.

Tom gazed at the chair; and, suddenly as he looked at it, a most extraordinary change seemed to come over it. The carving of the back gradually assumed the lineaments and expression of an old shrivelled human face; the damask cushion became an antique, flapped waistcoat; the round knobs grew into a couple of feet, encased in red cloth slippers; and the old chair looked like a very ugly old man, of the previous century, with his arms a-kimbo. Tom sat up in bed, and rubbed his eyes to dispel the illusion. No. The chair was an ugly old gentleman; and what was more, he was winking at Tom Smart.

Ali thinks of Cain Templeton saying, 'Objects can have strange powers . . . If a man sits in a chair all his life, will that seat not retain something of him?' The chair/elderly gentleman in the story eventually guides the narrator towards a hidden letter. Ali thinks of Elizabeth saying that Dickens was obsessed with time travel. Ali reads on, safe in her own chair.

Chapter 31

DS O'Brien agrees to meet Ali at Bow Street station. Ali assumes that she's spending a lot of time in London and wonders whether this case, involving a high-profile victim and liaison with the Diplomatic Protection unit, will be slightly intimidating for the Sussex CID officer. But as soon as she meets the DS, she dismisses this idea. Mary O'Brien does not seem the intimidated type. In any other circumstances Ali might have rather liked her. She's businesslike to the point of brusqueness but there's a hint of humour in her, a suggestion that she doesn't take herself too seriously. Ali also admires her cheek-length bob and finds herself wishing that her own hair wasn't so nineteenth-century and dull. Today it's pulled back into a ponytail which doesn't exactly scream high-flying police professional. Or time-travelling angel.

Today, though, there's no chance of bonding over hairstyles or even the travails of being a woman officer. DS O'Brien clearly resents having to talk to Ali and Ali doesn't blame her.

'It's very irregular,' she says. 'You shouldn't be involved in the investigation at all, given your personal involvement.'

Her sidekick, a man called Josh who looks about twelve, nods in the background.

'I'm not involved,' says Ali. 'But given that you've arrested my son on very little evidence, you can forgive me for having some questions.'

O'Brien tilts her chin up. 'There's plenty of evidence.'

'All of it circumstantial. The CCTV was inconclusive.'

'CCTV showed a man of Finn's description running away from the scene.'

'From what I've heard, the cameras just caught the vague shape of a man. You'll never get a positive identification from that.'

Geoff has said he'll try to get the footage. Ali ploughs on. 'You don't have a murder weapon, as far as I know.'

'We have a bullet.'

'Fired from an antique gun, I believe,' says Ali. 'Do you have the gun?'

'There's a collection of firearms at the house,' says O'Brien.

'But are any of them missing?'

The silence tells Ali all she needs to know. The gun that killed Isaac is still at large. Is it in Thomas Creek's hands?

'What actual evidence do you have against Finn?' she says. 'This looks to me as if you're under pressure to get a result. Who's leaning on you?'

'Finn's DNA is at the scene.'

'His DNA was on the victim's lips,' Josh chips in. Mary O'Brien swings round but the damage is done.

'On Isaac's lips?' asks Ali.

'Forensic evidence is confidential until the trial.' O'Brien looks directly at Ali. 'I'm sorry. This must be hard for you to hear. But we're satisfied that Finn killed Isaac Templeton.'

'On Isaac's lips?' says Dina. 'How can that be?'

'I don't know,' says Ali. 'DS O'Brien clearly thinks they snogged before Finn shot him.'

'Even if they did kiss,' says Dina, 'there's nothing to prove Finn killed him. Is there anything else that links Finn to the scene? Fibres? Fingerprints?'

'I haven't seen the SOCO report but I think they would have mentioned it if Finn's fingerprints were all over the scene. Mind you, Finn, Chibu and Piers were all at East Dean only the weekend before. Chibu says they sat up late, talking in the great hall. I'd be amazed if Finn's prints *weren't* there.'

'They probably have a housekeeper who dusts the place within an inch of its life.'

'You'd be surprised. Posh people don't mind dirt. I learnt that when I was a cleaner.'

'Do you think Piers was right about Chibu having an affair with Isaac? Does that give her a motive?'

'Potentially it does. I've asked Chibu if she'll meet me again. I've also asked to meet Miranda Templeton. No answer from her, which isn't a surprise, I suppose.'

'What about Jacinta, the nanny?'

'I'm seeing her this afternoon. She has to be finished at three to pick up the kids from school.'

'How old are they?'

'Ten and eight.'

'Poor little things. Seems a bit harsh that they're back at school when they only lost their father a few days ago.'

'Maybe Miranda thought they should stick to their routine. Norland Nanny and all.'

'Norland Nannies. Are they the ones with the uniform?'

'And the hats? Yes. At least she'll be easy to spot.'

Ali frowns at her screen, where she's been looking at Google Earth images of East Dean. It's a strange location for a large house, so near the cliff edge, but maybe coastal erosion has eaten away at the land over the years. What was it like when Cain Templeton lived there? Did Ali ever go there with him? If so, surely she'd have some memory of the place? 'Déjà vu,' Jones keeps telling them, 'is a form of time travel.'

'Ali!' Geoff calls from his office, not getting out of his chair, a habit that drives the team mad. 'I've got something to show you.'

'Promises, promises.' Ali gets up. After a second's hesitation, Dina follows.

Geoff turns his laptop towards them, narrowly missing the World's Best Boss mug. 'DC Franks just sent this through. It's the CCTV footage from East Dean. Here's the first image.'

The grainy video shows a man running between trees. He has an odd, spidery gait and is dressed all in black including a long garment that flies out behind him.

'That's not Finn,' says Ali. 'Look what he's wearing.'

'What *is* that?' says Dina.

'I think it's an opera cloak,' says Ali. 'Someone told me that's what Thomas Creek wore.'

'Could this be Creek?' asks Geoff.

'Well, it's not Finn,' says Ali. 'That's not the way he runs.' Finn has an easy, loping style of moving. Declan used to run like that, in the days when he was the star of the school football team. Declan had encouraged Finn to play football and tried not to be disappointed when his son gave up all team sports. But Finn still retains a natural athleticism that Ali envies.

'Here's the other picture.'

This is a screenshot. The man is almost facing the camera, but the picture is so blurred that it's hard to make out individual features: pale face, dark hair, shadows that look like the branches of trees.

'Has he got shoulder-length hair?' says Dina. 'Or is that a hood?'

'It's not Finn,' says Ali.

'No,' agrees Dina. 'This man looks kind of scary.'

He's a kind of devil figure, variously described as wearing a black cloak, having clawed hands and red eyes like hellfire.

Ali meets Jacinta in a café near the prep school attended by Jessica and Tom Templeton.

'They wanted to go back to school,' she says. 'To be with their friends. The child psychiatrist said it was a good idea.'

Jacinta has a faint Irish accent, which is a surprise. From her name, Ali had thought the nanny might be Spanish. She's older than Ali expected too, maybe about thirty, although the beige uniform and brown bowler hat would put years on anyone. She's the only person in the café dressed that way, although she tells Ali that half of the women are nannies.

'That's the good thing about the uniform,' she says. 'You can tell who's the nanny and who's the mother.'

'Is that important?'

'Of course it is. You need boundaries.'

'Do you have boundaries with Miranda? Mrs Templeton?'

'Yes. We're not friends. She's my employer.'

Ali stores this away. She's feeling slightly guilty because she contacted Jacinta as DS Dawson, not disclosing her link with Finn or the fact that she isn't one of the investigating officers. It's worth it if it clears Finn's name, she tells herself.

'And what was your relationship with Isaac Templeton?'

'The same. He's my employer. Was. Jesus, I can't believe he's dead. Sorry,' she adds, presumably for taking the Lord's name in vain.

'Did you see a lot of Isaac?'

'Well, he worked long hours but I saw him at the weekends. We usually went down to East Dean because that's his constituency. Isaac tried to make time for the kids. He was a good dad.' She wipes her eyes. 'Sorry,' she says again.

'We're interested in any threats made to Isaac,' says Ali. 'Anyone hanging around the house. Did you ever see anything like that?'

'Not really,' says Jacinta. 'We always had security, in Chelsea and East Dean. And no one could get into the grounds at East Dean.'

Except someone did, thinks Ali, remembering the dark figure running between the trees. And Finn told her that Isaac had given his security guard the night off on the day he died.

'What are you asking?' says Jacinta. 'I thought the advisor had been charged. Piers. No, Finn.'

'Why did you say Piers first?'

'He just seemed . . . not more likely, but . . . I just couldn't believe it of Finn.'

Ali warms to the woman. 'Why not?'

'He was always so nice. So decent, you know? Piers and Chibu treated me like a servant. Finn talked to me like a human being.'

He's been well brought-up, Ali wants to tell Jacinta. Instead she says, 'Tell me about the night Isaac died. If it's not too difficult for you.'

'I told the other policewoman,' says Jacinta.

'I know,' says Ali, 'but if you wouldn't mind telling me again . . .'

'It was about two a.m. I heard shouting so I got up. It was coming from the great hall. I thought it might just be a row but then I heard a gunshot and Miranda screaming. I should probably have called the police there and then, but you don't think clearly, do you? I ran out of my room and down the stairs. When I got to the hall Isaac was lying on the floor. There was blood on his chest. Miranda was leaning over him and crying. I learnt first aid at Norland so I sort of pushed her out of the way and took Isaac's pulse. He wasn't breathing.'

'Did you try mouth-to-mouth? Did Mrs Templeton?'

'No. I knew it was no good, you see. I knew he was dead. I called the ambulance. Miranda was still hysterical. The paramedics said I did all the right things,' she added, rather defensively.

'Sounds like you did brilliantly,' says Ali. 'I've done the training too, but it must be very different in reality.'

'Completely different,' says Jacinta. 'It was so spooky. The screams echoing round the hall. Isaac just lying there.'

'Were the Templetons a happy couple?' asks Ali.

'Yes,' says Jacinta immediately. 'Why do you ask?'

'You mentioned rows . . .'

'All couples have rows,' says Jacinta. 'Miranda and Isaac loved each other. I'm sure of it.'

'We've heard rumours of affairs,' says Ali, trying to keep her voice casual.

'I never listen to those sort of rumours,' says Jacinta. Which proves, of course, that they exist.

It hasn't been an entirely wasted day, thinks Ali, walking home past the old Bryant & May factory, once the scene of the match girls' strike, now a smart housing development called Bow Quarter. She has found out about the DNA – which is a mystery that must be solved – she's seen the CCTV, and she has learnt that rumours of Isaac's affairs have reached the ears of the nanny. In that case, Miranda must have heard them too. Was this the reason why Miranda and Isaac had rows? Could it be the cause of a fight that ended in Isaac's death?

For all her progress, though, Ali feels depressed. Finn is in prison. Her fastidious son is even now slopping out, possibly in the company of a murderer or drug dealer. It's fine for Ali to say, as she did earlier to Dina, that Finn is used to insalubrious company, working for the Conservative Party, but the reality, Finn behind bars, is very different.

She feels odd too. The vertigo is back, making each step a frightening experience, as if the ground is turning liquid beneath her feet. 'We don't really know what to expect,' said Jones, who had popped into the office at lunchtime, 'no one has ever been away for so long.' Once again, concern was imperfectly masked by a rather gleeful interest. The 'Alisoun' letter seems to have given Ali a kind of mental vertigo. She thinks about it and her mind swoops away, twisting and turning into some very dark alleyways. 'Samuel Pickwick,' Ali says to herself, as a kind of mantra. 'Augustus Snodgrass, Sam Weller.'

She turns the corner into her street. It's starting to feel like home: the sulphurous light, the motorbike chained up outside her neighbour's house, the clamped car, the ginger cat that patrols the front gardens. Maybe, when she finally lets Terry out, they will be friends. Ali fumbles for her key and then stops. There's a figure moving past the fence at the end of the terrace. It's visible through the wooden slats, illuminated by the old-fashioned streetlamps. A man in a cloak that flies up behind him like black wings.

Chapter 32

John

John takes a deep breath and pushes open the door of the house. It's as he imagined it from poring over old pictures of Hawk Street and the surrounding area. In fact, he's surprised how normal it feels to be there. Successive therapists have told him that he has too much imagination so it's a surprise to find himself quite sanguine about going back in time and posing as a Victorian. Well, perhaps sanguine isn't the right word (what does it mean anyway? Something to do with blood?) but John feels able to cope with the situation. 'You might have to stay a few days,' Jones told him, 'but I'll rescue you. I make you a solemn promise.' As a police officer, John knows the value of promises. No lies, no threats, no promises: that's the first rule of the police interview, a rule that is broken in almost every TV drama. John knows that Jones wouldn't give him an assurance that she wasn't sure she could deliver. Now he just has to play his part.

Inside the panelled hall, John considers his options. Ali has given him breathless descriptions of all the inhabitants. Tremain: handsome, talented, dissolute. Arthur: weak, gossipy, link to The Collectors. Clara: stoic, kind, source of food and information. Marianne: muse, mother, possible link to Tremain. Of course, the person who really interests John is Cain Templeton. Where is the landlord today?

John pauses to look at the grandfather clock. The little scenes are actually beautifully painted on what looks like ivory. It's now five past nine, one hand pointing at an ornate gate, the other at a carriage drawn by four black horses, a top-hatted skeleton gleefully holding the reins.

'It's a curiosity, isn't it?'

John turns and makes a quick calculation. The man addressing him is blond and, judging from previous conversations with Ali, John doesn't think she would consider him handsome. This must be Arthur Moses then.

'I've never seen a clock like it,' says John. 'Let me introduce myself. I'm John Cole.' Would a bow be appropriate? He bows slightly.

'Arthur Moses.' A bow back, which reassures John. 'Mrs Rokeby told me that you're a relative of Mrs Dawson's. Has she been called away suddenly?' Ah, there's the gossip. Always useful in a murder enquiry.

'I'm afraid so,' says John. 'She's had to return to Hastings. I'm hoping to stay here in her place. Do you know how I can contact Mr Templeton?'

'He's usually here on a Wednesday,' says Arthur. 'Looking for his rent money. You know what landlords are like.'

He tries a conspiratorial grin, which John returns, although he can't quite see what's wrong with a landlord collecting rent.

'Should I see Clara about meals and so on?' asks John. He thinks Arthur will like being asked for his advice and, sure enough, the man draws himself up and his smile takes on a condescending shape.

'Let me escort you,' he says. 'Clara's a simple soul but she won't rob you.'

Escorting simply means opening the door to the kitchen passage. Clara is in what seems to be the laundry. There are several copper tubs placed around the room and Clara is stirring the items in one of them, using what looks like a three-legged stool. It's obviously hard work because her face is pink and her hair is escaping from its cap. She says, without looking up, 'Don't you know better than to interrupt me on washday, Mr Moses?'

'I thought washday was Monday,' says Arthur.

'It usually is,' says Clara, swirling vigorously.

'And now you've got the new wringer and mangle it should be easy,' says Arthur.

'Do you want a go then?'

It's a long time since John studied Latin but he remembers 'questions which expect the answer no'. This is clearly one of them.

'I don't wish to interrupt you, Mrs . . . er . . . Clara,' he says. 'I just want to pay you for a week's board and lodging.'

'I don't know about board and lodging,' says Clara. 'You pay me a shilling a week for food. Or you don't, in Mr Moses's case.'

Arthur mutters something. John reaches for his wallet and takes out a shiny silver coin with Queen Victoria's head on it. Clara and Arthur both stare as if they've never seen money before.

Clara says, 'What's happened to Mrs Dawson?'

'She had to return to Hastings,' says John.

Clara pushes wet hair out of her eyes. 'She never said goodbye.'

John is surprised by her tone, which sounds genuinely hurt. He knows that Ali has the ability to make friends in unusual places, but he hadn't expected 1850 to be one of them.

'She asked me to pass on her regrets,' he says, 'and best wishes.'

'Did she mention me?' asks Arthur.

'No,' says John.

John places the coin on the wooden board by the mangle. 'I bid you good day,' he says to Clara. He hopes he's getting the language right. To his own ears, he sounds like a Radio 4 afternoon play.

Arthur follows him out into the passage. 'There'll be no midday meal if Clara's doing the laundry,' he says. 'Would you care to visit the tavern later?'

John hasn't been inside a pub for ten years, but he finds himself accepting the invitation.

John used to love drinking. He started when he was a young policeman, beers after work and whisky at weekends. His social life revolved around the pub until he met Moira, a nurse in charge of a ward containing a man injured in the course of a bank robbery. Her fierce protection of this obvious villain won John's heart. During their courtship and the early days of their marriage he managed to hide his dependence on alcohol. John thinks Moira first realised when Hattie was a baby and he'd return to the house in suspiciously ebullient mood, telling his 'two ladies' how much he loved them. There were darker moments too, mornings when he'd wake up covered in bruises but not remember how he'd acquired them; frightening lapses of memory, a fall in the street which lost him a tooth. Moira gave him an ultimatum: stop drinking or she'd leave, taking the baby with her. After a brief spell in rehab, John stopped long enough for Emily to be born but then there was a promotion and a high-profile murder case. John caught a serial killer and was lauded in the press but by now he was a full-blown alcoholic. Moira kept her promise and took the girls to her parents in Scotland. John attempted suicide and doesn't know to this day whether he meant to die or not. He does remember lying in the bath, his blood flowing painlessly into the water, and thinking: this is it, no more decisions to be made. He was saved by an irate downstairs neighbour who found water seeping into his ceiling. A spell in a psychiatric hospital followed, then more rehab punctuated by several relapses. Moira came back and this, combined with a job offer from Geoff Bastian, pulled John back from the brink.

But he knows he's never very far from the precipice. This is why he hasn't drunk a drop of alcohol since the day Moira and the girls moved back in. Hattie and Emily are at university now. John and Moira live in an atmosphere of tranquillity that John could never have imagined but he knows that his peace is hard won and that he owes a lot of it to the cold case team. Ali, in particular, has been a constant support. Although spouses are not meant to know, John has told Moira about the time travel. *No secrets* was one of the conditions of their reunion. And Moira understands why John had to be the one to rescue Ali.

And now, a few hours into the mission, there's the first temptation. The pub is the cosiest place he has seen in 1850, perhaps ever. There's a roaring fire, a stone-flagged floor and wooden benches around the walls. There's no bar but, as John watches, a hatch in the wall opens and a pewter tankard is handed to the drinker. Arthur leads the way into a back room where a handsome, bearded man is frowning into his beer glass.

'This is Frederick Tremain,' says Arthur. 'What do you want to drink, John? We don't have to pay until the end of the week.'

John has been thinking about how to word this. 'I don't . . .' He pauses.

But, to his surprise, the men both nod. 'Band of Hope?' asks Tremain.

'Temperance Union?' suggests Arthur.

Of course, there was a Victorian teetotalism movement. John thanks God for his Presbyterian ancestors and says, 'I'm afraid I did drink once but . . .'

'Signed the pledge?' says Arthur. 'Well, you won't mind getting me a pint of Old Tom, will you? The beer here has henbane in it.'

'It doesn't,' says Tremain. 'Not like the stuff at the White Hart. That nearly poisoned me once. Indian berry.'

John goes to the hatch and asks for Old Tom, not knowing what it is. He pays a penny and is given a glass of what looks like gin. He'd like to ask for a non-alcoholic drink for himself but guesses that the establishment doesn't stretch to elderflower or tomato juice. He's been warned not to drink the water.

He takes the glass to the table and sits with his new friends. Both regard him curiously.

'So, you're a relative of Mrs Dawson's?' says Tremain.

'Cousin,' says John. This was the story they concocted in the minutes before Ali disappeared.

'I found her a very interesting woman,' says Tremain. 'I wanted her to sit for me.'

John can't imagine this. He finds Ali attractive but he can't quite see her posing for a portrait.

'She was interested in The Collectors,' says Arthur, taking a swig of gin. Ali was right about him; he does enjoy secrets. 'I introduced her to Burbage. He went to one of their meetings.'

'I wouldn't trust anything Burbage says,' says Tremain.

'Who are The Collectors?' asks John. He wonders why Ali didn't include this Burbage in her handover notes.

'It's a secret society,' says Arthur. 'Mr Templeton is a member. They meet at the Hangman's Club. The rumour is, to join you need to have killed someone.'

'You need to have killed a woman,' elaborates Tremain.

'Is that really true?' asks John. He thinks that his role might be that of slightly naive country gentleman.

Tremain shrugs. 'I don't know. The ways of the quality are a mystery to me.'

'Your family has money,' says Arthur.

'My father's just a surgeon, a sawbones,' says Tremain. 'Besides, he cast me off without a penny when I became a painter. I'm a labourer now.'

John has met people like this before, middle-class intellectuals determined to prove their working-class credentials. His parents had been lower middle-class and proud of it. He says, 'I'm wondering if I should stay in Mr Templeton's house after all.'

'Oh, it's a decent lodging,' says Arthur. 'And Clara's generous with the vittles.'

'Except that a woman was killed there last week,' says Tremain. 'In Mrs Dawson's room. I suppose that's your room now, John.'

'How terrible,' says John. 'How did she die?' Should he cross himself? No, he's decided that he's a non-conformist.

'Murdered by a man called Thomas Creek,' says Arthur, not without relish.

'Who's Thomas Creek?' asks John. He knows Ali mentioned the name but it's always valuable to hear from character witnesses.

'He's an artist of sorts,' replies Tremain. 'He lodged in the house and Ettie, the victim, was one of his models. He was painting her, and she must have refused his advances. He killed her.'

'How?' asks John. Means before motive.

'I heard that she was hit with a heavy object,' says Arthur. 'Maybe the barrel of a gun. Creek kept pistols. I helped carry her downstairs. There was so much blood. It quite turned my stomach.'

'That was the day Mrs Dawson arrived,' says Tremain, with a sideways look at John. 'Like a harbinger of death.'

'That doesn't sound like Cousin Alison,' says John. 'What happened to Thomas Creek? Is he in custody?' He hesitates, wondering if that's the right word.

'He's nowhere,' says Arthur. 'He's disappeared. Mr Templeton burned his canvases in the garden.'

Disappeared. Ali had thought someone else had taken her gate. Could it be the villainous Thomas Creek?

'I hope he doesn't return while I'm sleeping in his room,' says John.

'Mrs Dawson wasn't scared of that,' says Tremain.

'Cousin Alison is a brave woman,' says John.

'She interests me,' says Tremain again. 'I feel she's a woman with secrets.'

You can say that again, thinks John. He offers both men another drink, thinking that he'd give anything for a can of Diet Coke.

They return to the house at three o'clock, having stopped to buy pies from what looked like someone's front room. John climbs the stairs to Ali's room, wondering if it's really his now. He stands at the round window and looks down into the street. There's snow on the ground but it's been turned into dirty slush by carriage wheels and plodding horses. He's noticed a pervading smell of horse shit in the air which reminds him of the city farm where he used to take the girls. It's cold but his long wool coat is warm and, as for the top hat, it provides such a vacuum of comfort that John is tempted to bring the fashion back with him. Does he honestly believe that he'll get back to 2023? If anyone can do it, Jones can.

John remembers when he first met Serafina Pellegrini. Geoff had sent him to her office at Imperial College, London. John trekked along subterranean corridors marked 'Hazchem Do Not Enter' until he found a door with more eccentric decorations: the Ferrari prancing horse and a hammer and sickle above the initials PCI. John learnt later that this stood for Partito Comunista Italiano, an organisation Jones admires for what seem to be aesthetic reasons. She's far too wary to join any political party. John had been hypnotised by her that day, listening to the softly accented voice talking Einstein, Galileo and Clausius. But he had assumed that her theories about creating a space through which atoms could travel were just theories, wonderful fantastical ideas that might form the basis of Professor Pellegrini's next slim volume of theoretical physics for dummies, her photograph on the back cover bigger than the synopsis. But when he'd described the visit to Geoff, his new boss had replied, 'She's going to do it. *We're* going to do it.'

Five years later, John and Ali had stood on a London street, eerily silent because of lockdown. They had placed their feet in the position directed by Jones, as John now called her. 'How will we know if it works?' said Ali. But, even as she said those words, John felt himself jolting forwards, an unalarming but definite movement, like going over a speedbump. He'd looked around him and seen maskless pedestrians, open shops and the general weekday bustle of city life. They had travelled in time. Over the last week, John has spent a lot of time with Jones while she briefed him on this new adventure, having apparently done a lot of research on Victorian life, especially the monetary side. 'I will get you back,' she told him. 'You know that I can do impossible things.' He has to believe in her.

But he knows that there is a chance that he could be stuck in this strange world for ever, that he will never see Moira or his daughters ever again. It's a kind of death, he thinks, looking at the grey sky above the chimney pots, and he's prepared for that. But he squares his shoulders in the unaccustomed suit and hopes for the best.

Chapter 33

John's day starts, as Ali promised, with a tap on the window below. He climbs out of bed, aware that his nightshirt has ridden up under his arms. The thought of Moira seeing him in such a garment makes him laugh and then gulp with unhappiness. He can't afford to think about Moira and the girls. Last night he allowed himself just one look at their photographs which are hidden in a special compartment in his wallet. The Victorians had cameras, he knows, but he still thinks they'd be taken aback by these vibrant images: Moira on the ramparts of Edinburgh Castle, Hattie and Emily on their last family holiday, smiling into the Greek sun. Jones will get you back, he tells himself, like a mantra. Ali told him that, during her exile in 1850, she went and stood on the ingress point every day. But John has no such marker. Ali has taken his gate. He doesn't know when or how he'll be able to return. Jones will get you back.

John uses the chamber pot and puts the lid on. Then he starts the process of getting dressed. He's lucky because, by and large, Victorian men's clothing is both comfortable and practical. The long-sleeved woollen vest and long johns ('*What* are they called?' he hears Moira asking) are slightly itchy but very warm. Trousers come next, high-waisted and rather tight over the long johns, flaring slightly from the ankle. Then there's a shirt which seems huge, coming down to his knees before he tucks it in. Then a detachable collar which is very stiff. His neck already feels sore from wearing it yesterday. Then cuffs and cufflinks. He's using the pair that Moira gave him for their silver wedding anniversary. Next is the waistcoat and finally the long jacket. It seems a lot of clothes to wear for emptying a chamber pot, but he gathers that it's shocking for a man to be seen in his shirtsleeves.

John descends the stairs, finds the corridor to the garden and the privy. He empties the pot, then returns to the house to wash in the room where Clara did the laundry yesterday. He places the pot in the corridor with the others. He supposes it's important to recognise your own design. His is rather ornate, holly and ivy and a scroll saying. 'Bide a wee'. Who says Victorians don't have a sense of humour?

He wonders whether he should take a stroll before breakfast. Jones has given him a variety of tasks to do, one of which is to draw a map of the surrounding area. John goes into the hall to collect his hat and coat and sees a man on his knees, apparently mending the grandfather clock. At John's approach, the man stands up and John realises that this isn't a workman. In fact, it can only be Cain Templeton. The landlord is a heavy-set individual with dark hair and moustache. He's wearing a coat that has a kind of caped effect round the shoulders and this, combined with his belligerent stance, makes him seem very broad and rather intimidating. A hard obstacle to get around, John would have said in his rugby-playing days.

'Mr Cain Templeton?' says John.

'Yes. Who might you be?'

'My name is John Cole. I'm a relative of Mrs Dawson's. I was wondering if I could take over her room for a few days. I'm afraid I took the liberty of doing so last night.'

'Has Mrs Dawson left?' It's said almost angrily but there's a hint, just a hint, of Clara's hurt feelings when she complained that Ali hadn't said goodbye.

'She's been called away unexpectedly,' says John. 'Her son isn't well.' He hopes this isn't ill-wishing Finn but the truth is that Finn *is* the cause of Ali's departure. He wonders what's happening to Finn, of whom he's very fond. Well, if anyone can save him, Ali can.

'Phineas?' says Templeton.

'Finn. Yes.' John is surprised that Templeton knows – and has remembered – Finn's name.

Templeton gives John a hard stare under heavy brows. Then he says, 'I've no objection to your taking the room. Rent is six shillings a week. Mrs Dawson was prompt with hers.'

'I will be too,' promises John. According to Jones, he has a year's worth of money in the leather wallet.

The time on the grandfather clock is half past seven, one hand on a cat, the other on an owl. In fact, the two creatures look rather similar. Templeton eyes it with disfavour. 'Bally thing is always five minutes fast. I'm always trying to remedy it, but I never succeed.' He locks the front of the clock and, with his back to John, says, 'You say you're related to Mrs Dawson?'

'I'm her cousin.'

Templeton turns to face him. 'Will you dine with me this evening?' he asks. 'I've got some questions for you.'

John says that he'd be honoured. He tries a bow but, judging by Templeton's expression, this is a mistake.

They eat in the small room Clara calls the parlour. None of the other lodgers are invited. Clara tells John that they usually have their evening meal in the kitchen. 'I do for myself,' she adds, 'although Mrs Dawson kept me company once.' John is beginning to understand that Ali formed a friendship with the woman whose status in the house is still unclear to him. He's slightly taken aback, though, when Clara tells him that she was going to give Ali sewing lessons. 'She never had a chance to learn, what with her mother dying so young.' As far as John knows, Ali's parents are both still living. He wonders how many more biographical traps lie ahead of him, Ali's supposed cousin.

John wonders what to wear for his tête-à-tête. He has brought just the one suit with him, but he has a quantity of shirts and waistcoats. 'Men were starting to wear black in the cities,' said Ali's friend Dulcie, over lunch at the London College of Fashion. 'The industrial middle classes were taking over and black was the most practical colour for them, as well as being sober and respectable. When Prince Albert died in 1861, England went into mourning and never came out again.' But Prince Albert is alive and well in 1850 and clothes aren't yet monochrome. John considers a red and gold waistcoat before going back to black. He thinks that the John Cole who has taken the pledge would be above such frivolity. Formal clothing has, in fact, changed very little. John could easily attend a modern wedding in his nineteenth-century attire. Thank God he doesn't have to wear a corset, like Ali. Although Dulcie told him that men sometimes did so. 'There's a cigarette card of Disraeli in 1826 when he's definitely wearing one, plus red trousers and an orange waistcoat.'

It feels wrong to wear a jacket and stiff-collared shirt for an evening at home but when he enters the parlour John sees that Templeton is dressed in similar style, dark frock coat covering all but a hint of white shirt and tartan waistcoat.

A table has been laid with a white tablecloth, silver cutlery and a candelabra. The combination seems oddly romantic, like dinner for two on Valentine's Day, but John supposes that candles are essential in Victorian homes. Electric lighting existed in the nineteenth century. Jones had been sure to emphasise the roles of Italian physicists Luigi Galvani and Alessandro Volta in harnessing the power of the charged particle. But, according to the books, domestic homes didn't possess electricity until the turn of the century. John is doomed to an evening of looking at the interesting shadows on Cain Templeton's face.

Templeton offers John a glass of sherry which he declines, citing the temperance excuse.

'I wouldn't have taken you for a Band of Hoper,' says Templeton. 'Mrs Dawson enjoys a glass of claret.'

This John can believe.

'I'll ask Clara to bring in some lemonade,' says Templeton. 'I'm not an admirer of these new effervescent drinks – made popular by the temperance movement, I believe – but I bought some to take home for the children.'

John is relieved. He's been thirsty all day. He had tea with breakfast but there seemed to be no way of procuring another drink. He could hardly ask Clara to put the kettle on the range just for him. Unrefrigerated, unpasteurised milk was not appealing but he supposed that it might come to that. He was starting to fantasise about his West Ham water bottle, an object of derision to his workmates.

But Templeton's mention of 'home' is interesting. John asks where this place is.

'East Dean in Sussex,' says Templeton. 'The house has been in my family for generations but I'm making some real changes to the place.'

John hears, as clearly as if there's a radio in the room: *Conservative MP Isaac Templeton found dead at his Sussex home*. It feels wrong that he knows of the death of someone in Templeton's family, even if it's a relative his host has never met.

Clara brings in a joint of lamb with potatoes and cabbage. There's no other sign of greenery but John supposes vegetables were hard to come by in the winter months. Even if Templeton had them delivered from his country estate, what would be growing in January? At Templeton's request, Clara goes out and returns with a glass bottle, stoppered by a marble. Drinking the sour lemonade is John's best sensory experience so far.

It doesn't take Templeton long to get back to the subject of Ali.

'I understand that Mrs Dawson is a widow. She's lost three husbands, I believe.'

'That's right,' says John. The only husband he met was Lincoln, who was still hanging round when Ali joined the unit. He remembers a good-looking man whose only topic of conversation was his biceps. He's quite happy to kill him off.

'Tell me about Mrs Dawson. You must know her well.'

John thinks quickly. He's usually good at cover stories but he's not sure what Ali has already told Templeton. The man's manner seems to suggest that they had an almost intimate connection. Ali mentioned a dinner. What was discussed?

'She's a very independent woman,' he says at last, 'but devoted to her son. And to her friends.'

'She's clearly had some sort of education,' says Templeton.

'She educated herself,' says John.

'What sort of family are you from?' asks Templeton.

John answers carefully. Class is complicated enough in modern-day England, he has no idea of the social indicators in 1850. But he's sure of one thing; he could never pass for an aristocrat.

'My father was a cabinetmaker,' he says. This is true. 'As was Alison's.' He thinks this is safest. Presumably their fathers were brothers. It could be a family business.

'Really?' Templeton looks absolutely fascinated by this news. He regards John for a long minute, stroking his moustache.

'Did you follow in your father's footsteps?' he asks.

'I'm afraid I had no aptitude for it.' This is also true.

'Pity.' Templeton takes a long drink of wine before returning to what seems to be his favourite topic.

'Mrs Dawson asked me all sorts of questions,' says Templeton, smiling in a reminiscent way. 'She was interested in a club that I belong to. She'd heard rumours about it and wanted to know the truth. I've never met a woman who asks so many questions.'

'She has an enquiring mind,' says John.

Templeton laughs. 'I used the very same words to Mrs Dawson. We had dinner at my Kensington house. I hope I haven't shocked you?'

'I have faith in Mrs Dawson's character.'

'A loyal cousin,' says Templeton. They have finished most of the meat and all the potatoes. John has been ravenously hungry all the time he's been in 1850. It must be the cold. Templeton pours himself a glass of red wine.

'Tell me,' he says, 'is there more to this than meets the eye? Mrs Dawson appears from nowhere. Then she disappears and you appear. Both of you seem . . . strange.'

'In what way?' asks John.

'I can't quite describe it,' says Templeton. 'You have an odd manner of speaking.'

'We're from Hastings,' says John.

'Remember, I have a house in Sussex,' says Templeton, 'and none of the village people speak like you.'

The phrase 'village people' inserts an unwelcome earworm of Y.M.C.A. John says, 'Hastings is different.' He's never been to the place.

'Mrs Dawson appeared just when a woman was murdered in this house,' says Templeton.

'I heard about that,' says John. 'It sounds horrible.' He hopes this is the right word.

'It was very sad,' says Templeton. 'A poor innocent country girl murdered by a devil. Mrs Dawson asked many questions about Ettie and about another lady of my acquaintance, alas sadly no more. But she seemed chiefly interested in The Collectors.'

'Who are The Collectors?' asks John.

Templeton leans back and surveys him for a moment before replying, 'There's a meeting tonight. Will you accompany me?'

The two men gather their top hats and overcoats and, dressed almost identically, step out into the street. They walk to the end of the road and, at the junction, Templeton raises a hand. Almost immediately, a small carriage pulled by a grey horse draws up beside them. The chassis is low-slung with high wheels. Inside there's just enough space for two people to sit side by side with the driver raised above them. Is this a hansom cab? It's certainly some sort of vehicle for hire. Templeton gives an address to the driver and climbs in. John follows him.

The horse's white hindquarters seem very near but the passengers are protected from dirt and flying pebbles by a curved fender and a leather flap over their knees. It feels oddly like being on a fairground ride.

John wonders why Templeton has invited him, a perfect stranger, to this supposedly secret society. Arthur and the others implied that membership was very select. He asks where they are going.

'Limehouse,' answers Templeton. His sidelong glance suggests that he expects this location to be rather shocking. John *is* shocked but for a different reason. He grew up in nearby Poplar and remembers the docklands before they became fashionable. 'I knew Canary Wharf when it was still a wharf,' he likes to tell his uninterested family.

Thinking of his origins makes John say, 'I've heard that The Collectors is a club for the aristocracy. As I told you, I'm the son of a working man.'

'There's no shame in that,' says Templeton.

'I'm not ashamed,' says John.

'You said your father was a cabinetmaker,' says Templeton. 'I'm very interested in furniture.'

This is a surprise. John has suspected Templeton of murder but not of being a Victorian antiques dealer.

'Our lifespan is short,' says Templeton, 'but furniture goes on for hundreds of years. I can sit at a Tudor table, eat with Regency cutlery. It's a way of travelling to the past.'

'I suppose it is,' says John, slightly disconcerted by this turn of phrase.

The horse is now picking its way through streets that are getting narrower and more noisome. Occasionally John catches glimpses of water, dark and oily. There are fewer streetlights here and the cabbie is forced to hold his lantern high and to shout instructions to the horse. John is rather charmed that its name is Sulky. Eventually they stop ('Whoa, Sulky!') in front of a tall building with lighted windows. It has a rather grand portico, with pillars and marble steps, quite unlike the warehouses that surround it. Templeton pays the driver through a hatch in the roof and says to John, 'Don't be worried. There's no cholera here these days.'

It's not exactly reassuring.

Chapter 34

The doors seem to open automatically but John sees that they are being manoeuvred by two footmen. Given its setting, the opulence of the building takes him by surprise.

'It used to be a church,' Templeton tells him, 'built by Hawksmoor in the reign of good Queen Anne. Of course, this area wasn't so densely populated then. I believe the idea was that sea captains could worship here.'

The room they enter is a mixture of the ecclesiastical and the sybaritic. Tall stained-glass windows cast multicoloured light on sofas, chairs and reading lamps. A stone pulpit is partly hidden by swathed velvet curtains and there is unmistakably a bar amongst the choir stalls.

A liveried servant offers John a drink and he asks for lemonade. He's glad that the man accepts this request without a flicker. Templeton orders brandy.

There is a group of men seated around the fireplace. This last surprises John. Was it here when the building was a church? He supposes the congregation had to keep warm somehow. A grey-haired gentleman with a slight air of the Ancient Mariner rises to greet them.

'Cain, welcome.'

'Amos. This is John. First names only here,' Templeton explains.

John tries one of his bows. He's introduced, in quick succession, to Robert, Charles, Edward, Francis and Giuseppe. This last excuses his suspiciously foreign name by explaining that he's the son of Italian immigrants, 'glass-makers'. John stores this up to tell Jones when — if — he sees her again.

'There too many emigrés in these parts,' says Amos. 'Lascars, Africans, Chinese. You hardly hear an English voice these days.'

It's rather depressing to think that Amos would fit comfortably into a certain section of twenty-first-century British society.

'Foreigners bring new ideas and new crafts,' says Giuseppe.

'They bring disease and opium,' says Amos.

'I have a friend from Africa,' says John, hoping that Dina and her Ghanaian parents will forgive him. 'She's a very clever woman.'

'Truly, Hastings is a surprising place,' says Templeton.

John's lemonade arrives and he sits in a leather chair to drink it. He realises that the other men are having a whispered confabulation about him. 'Not a member,' says someone (Edward?). 'Cannot break protocol' (Amos). 'Setting a dangerous precedent' (Robert?). 'Could be to our advantage' (Giuseppe). Templeton leans over to John. 'This is where we usually read through the minutes of our last meeting and set the agenda for the next. I'm happy for you to stay but some of our other members are uncomfortable . . .'

'I understand,' says John. 'Perhaps I could wait elsewhere?'

'If you would be so kind. It will only take half an hour. George here will accompany you to the library.'

A footman appears. John has the depressing feeling that Templeton calls them all George.

The man leads John through a hall that looks like it was intended for public events and into a small room that might once have been the vestry. Now the walls are lined with books. After George has left, John examines the titles. *The Art of Wood Carving. Wanstead Sofas. A Guide to Cast-Iron Umbrella Stands. Oak Cabinets and Their Uses.* Is this really a club for gentlemen who are enthusiastic about furniture? John feels as if he's been sent to find Jack the Ripper only to discover that he's a member of a knitting circle. Hattie likes to knit. It seems to be becoming popular with young people. Moira wouldn't be able to sit still that long.

Thinking of his wife and children makes John bolder. He's taken this job which runs the grotesque risk of never seeing them again. The least he can do is some investigating. He prowls the room. There's nothing of interest on the shelves, unless you count bound copies of something called *Design in Everyday Homes*, which John doesn't. The small Gothic window looks out onto a dark courtyard. The stone fireplace is empty apart from a single pine cone. Frustrated, John leans against a wall. It moves.

Is this left-over vertigo from the gate? No. The section of bookcase is moving inwards to reveal a corridor. John looks around the room. George placed a candelabra on one of the low tables. John takes a lighted candle, props the false door open with a footstool, and ventures into the darkness.

The corridor is only a few metres long. There's a door at the end and, from behind it, the murmur of voices. Slowly, John turns the handle and pushes. A sliver of light is revealed. John is looking into the main church, where The Collectors are having their meeting. No one seems to be speaking though. The men are all gathered around a single chair. Is this thrilling item in line for the furniture of the week award? Nevertheless, there's something compelling about the scene. Maybe it's the shadows of the men in their dark suits or the high ceiling from which painted angels gaze down. It's also the silence, which has an expectant quality. None of the club members speaks or moves until one of them – John thinks it's Giuseppe – steps forward and sits in the chair.

There's a moment of charged stillness and then the man disappears completely.

Chapter 35

There's no hansom cab home. When they emerge from the building, a carriage with two horses is waiting.

'Mine,' says Templeton. 'Can I convey you back to Hawk Street, John?'

John accepts the offer. He wants to talk to Templeton about what he saw from the hidden door without admitting that he was spying. When George came to collect him, John was sitting innocently in an armchair, reading a book about ivory inlay. George led him back into the church where the collectors were drinking brandy and talking about Venetian glass. John did a quick headcount and nobody seemed to be missing. Giuseppe was in the centre of the group, holding forth on glassmaking, gesturing in an Italianate way although his voice remained scrupulously English. The conversation then became general. John was asked about Hastings, which he answered by describing Southend. Edward asked if John was interested in antique furniture. John replied that his father had been a cabinetmaker, which created the sort of interest that Ted Cole, a modest man, would have found hard to understand. There was no invitation to join the club, but John felt that he was being examined in some way and not being found entirely wanting.

The carriage is luxurious inside, quite unlike the bumper car motion of the cab. The seats are covered with purple velvet and this, combined with the curtains and general draperies and flounces, makes the interior feel a curiously intimate place, like being in a four-poster bed. There's no light inside but the coachman has oil lamps beside him. Templeton's face slides in and out of the shadows.

'Was it a successful meeting?' asks John.

'Successful . . .' Templeton seems to consider the word. 'You could say so, yes. We are contemplating buying a glass that was believed to be owned by one of the Borgias. When you consider that the Borgias were master poisoners, it's an interesting piece.'

There's something almost gloating about the way he says 'master poisoners'.

'So you're not just interested in old furniture then?' says John.

Templeton laughs, showing a gleam of white teeth, surely unusually good for a Victorian.

'Our objects have to have a certain provenance. In my private collection I have a murderer's brain, for example.'

'A murderer's brain?'

'Yes, belonging to a man called Percival Green who killed five women.'

'How did you get hold of his brain?'

'I know the hangman,' says Templeton. The word seems, appropriately enough, to hang in the air. 'The place where we met tonight is sometimes called the Hangman's Club because the hangmen used to go to the church to pray before performing executions.'

'Were they praying for forgiveness?' asks John.

'That or the strength to carry out their duty.'

John is vehemently opposed to the death penalty. He's seen enough innocent people convicted in his time. If hanging had still been operative in the UK, he, too, would have blood on his hands.

'Have you studied phrenology, John?' asks Templeton.

The word takes John by surprise. It conjures up an ornamental head that Moira keeps on a table in the hall. Luckily Templeton supplies the answer. 'Phrenology is the study of the skull,' he says. 'It began, I believe, with a German scientist called Franz Josef Gall. He studied the skulls of men convicted of terrible crimes and came to notice that there were similarities. As I understand it, the brain is a muscle so that, each time we exercise that muscle, a corresponding mass appears on our cranium. Each bump, each indenture, signifies something. A growth in a certain area can indicate mirthfulness, integrity or destructive qualities. What do you think, John? Are our secrets written on our heads?'

'I don't think so,' says John. 'I think the answer lies in the heart, not the head.'

'You are a romantic, then,' says Templeton. 'What about the physiognomy? The face? Surely that is the true mirror of character. Mrs Dawson, for example, has a high forehead and fine, dark eyes. She has a nobility in her formation.'

Ali certainly made an impression on Templeton. John doesn't think he's ever noticed her forehead but maybe he was distracted by the red hair.

'You have a different aspect,' says Templeton, 'despite being her cousin.'

'Less noble?' suggests John.

'More closed,' says Templeton. 'Mrs Dawson is easier to read. Her face, as the Bard says, is as a book where men may read strange matters.'

'I don't think that you can read a character from a person's features,' says John. 'I, too, have encountered villainous individuals and some of them have the sweetest, nicest faces imaginable.'

He thinks of a woman he encountered at the beginning of his police career. She had the bluest, most candid eyes John had ever seen. And yet she lied to him over the course of two days, while officers searched the countryside for a five-year-old child who was buried in her garden.

'Hastings must be a more dangerous place than I thought,' says Templeton.

'I've moved around a lot,' says John.

The carriage has reached the wider streets and the horses pick up their pace, harness jingling. John must ask about The Collectors while he has the chance.

'Can I ask why you invited me tonight?' he says.

'You said that your father was a cabinetmaker. I thought you might be interested in our collection.'

'But some of the proceedings were clearly secret. That's why I had to leave the room.'

Another carriage passes them, its lamps briefly illuminate Templeton's dark coat and white collar. His face is in darkness.

'There are many rumours about The Collectors,' he says at last.

'I've heard some of them,' says John.

To his surprise, Templeton laughs. 'Already? That must have been Moses and Tremain. They are both very credulous. Arthur is as gossipy as an old woman. Tremain is cleverer but he drinks too much. He's a fine artist though. That's why I let him stay.'

'You collect artists as well as furniture,' says John.

'In a way,' says Templeton. 'I have no artistic talent myself, but I admire it in others.' He sounds rather sad when he says this. The carriage rattles over cobbles. John holds on to a tasselled cord which is obviously there for this purpose.

After a few seconds of silence, Templeton says, 'The Collectors do not collect women. Or kill them, as I believe the rumour is, but we are engaged in great and mysterious work.'

This is it, thinks John. A clock strikes, somewhere in the distance. Midnight.

'I've long thought,' says Templeton, 'that certain objects possess special significance. Hence the club. Hence the collection. Well, tonight, we witnessed something extraordinary.'

John waits.

'We have a chair that has a long and interesting history. In fact it's one of four that are believed to possess magical powers. Have you heard of a man called Thomas Creek?'

John thinks quickly. It was Arthur who first brought up the subject of Thomas Creek, and given his earlier assessment, John thinks Cain will have expected this.

'Arthur Moses mentioned him,' he says. 'I gather this Creek was responsible for the death of the woman you mentioned at dinner.'

Cain sighs. 'Yes, it was a terrible thing. That poor innocent girl. I regret ever letting Creek stay in my house. I burned every one of his paintings. I wanted no trace of him to be left.' He adds, in a slightly less portentous voice, 'Of course, they weren't very good.'

John says, 'According to Moses and Tremain, Creek has disappeared.'

Cain pauses for so long that John is worried that they'll reach

Hawk Street without an answer. The horses start to trot and the carriage sways on its chassis.

Eventually, Cain says, 'Creek was one of The Collectors. Not my choice to admit him, but he comes from a respectable family. Creek claimed that he sat in one of the chairs and found himself in an entirely different room, one filled with strange objects and strange light. I have to say that I didn't believe him but, tonight, it happened again . . .'

'What happened?'

'Giuseppe volunteered to sit in the chair. He's a brave man. And, if you can believe this, just for a second he vanished. Ceased to be.'

John thinks that amazement is called for. 'How on earth could that happen?'

'I have no idea,' says Templeton. 'Giuseppe was back within seconds but, for that time, he ceased to be in our realm, our dimension. He said that he had only a brief impression of the other realm but it was definitely a different room, very light with strange shadows. He felt slightly unwell, as if he'd been on a boat.'

Tell me about it, thinks John. He only saw Giuseppe disappear, not return, because he heard a noise outside and thought that he should leave the secret passage. When he was readmitted to the group, they were chatting animatedly about Venetian glass.

'That's extraordinary,' says John. 'What is known about this set of chairs? You said something about magical powers?'

'I'm a rational man,' says Cain. 'I don't believe in magic. And yet I've seen it happen. The chairs were made by a carpenter on my estate. He was a strange creature and ended a somewhat dissolute life by murdering his wife and doing away with himself. That caused local people to say that the chairs were cursed. But many people have, of course, sat in them without experiencing anything out of the ordinary. I don't know why the magic happened tonight. Maybe it was because we were all there, together. *For where two or three are gathered together in my name* . . . Maybe it was our collective power that made the impossible happen. I don't know. I only know that I saw it.'

So did I, thinks John. Since knowing Jones, his tolerance for the impossible has grown. Is what she does magic? Maybe it is. He's not so sure about Templeton quoting the Bible though. There was something distinctly unholy about what he just witnessed. A whiff of sulphur and brimstone.

'What are you going to do now?' he asks.

'Experiment further,' says Templeton. His tone, which has been cautious, now becomes almost manic. 'We are on the edge of great discoveries. This is the age of discovery, is it not? New lands, new treasures.'

Wasn't the age of discovery earlier? thinks John. *In fourteen hundred and ninety-two, Columbus sailed the ocean blue.* He wants to tell Templeton that the lands were already there, and that their treasures do not belong to the Europeans who have suddenly discovered transatlantic voyage.

He realises that the carriage has stopped.

'Here I must leave you,' says Templeton. 'I hope we meet again. Will you be in contact with Mrs Dawson?'

'Yes,' says John, crossing his fingers.

'Do convey my respects. I have a feeling that she and I will also meet again.'

John climbs down from the carriage and watches as its dark shape merges with the night.

★

The ivory clock face gleams as John opens the front door. Clara has left an oil lamp burning but it's too dark to see the time. John thinks it's about a quarter past midnight. There are candles on the half-moon table beside the lamp. John lights one and begins his journey up the stairs. The house is still but not silent, the old timbers are creaking and John can hear a skittering sound behind the walls that might well be mice – or rats. The night's events keep pace with his steps: the carriage ride through the dark streets, the Hangman's Club, the man in the chair, Templeton's voice when he talked about rationality.

I don't believe in magic. And yet I've seen it happen.

Did Giuseppe travel in time? Did Creek before him? If so, the laws of physics are more flexible than even Jones suspects.

Deep in thought, John pushes open his bedroom door. The flickering candlelight reveals a man sitting on his bed.

Chapter 36

John's first thought is Thomas Creek. The man who murdered Ettie has come back to his old quarters. What will he do to the stranger who has taken his place? John holds his candle higher. It reveals a man who is probably in his thirties, with a narrow face and darting eyes. A weak face, he thinks, but not an evil one. But, then again, John doesn't believe in physiognomy.

'Who are you?' he says.

'My name's Burbage,' answers the man. 'Francis Burbage.'

'I'm John Cole. What are you doing in my room?'

The man stands up. 'I wanted to talk to you. About The Collectors.'

'Who are you?' says John again. 'Do you live in this house?'

He remembers Arthur mentioning Burbage. Did he say that he was one of The Collectors?

'No,' says Burbage, 'but I'm a friend of Arthur's. I was visiting him this evening and he told me you were visiting the Hangman's Club with Cain Templeton.'

John doesn't ask how Arthur knew this. Arthur's the type who always knows. He'd make a good police informer.

'Did you go to a meeting?' says Burbage. 'Did you see the chair?'

'What do you mean?' To give himself time to think, John takes off his coat and puts his top hat on the dressing table.

'Creek – Thomas Creek – told me that The Collectors have a chair that can make people disappear.'

'And you believe that?' John tries Sceptical Interrogating Officer 101.

'Well, Creek has disappeared, hasn't he?'

'I don't know,' says John. 'I never met Mr Creek. Now, if you'll excuse me, I want to get to bed.'

'Did Templeton mention me?' asks Burbage.

'No,' says John truthfully.

'He wants to kill me,' says Burbage. His face is now in shadow but John can hear the panic in his voice. It's genuine, he's sure of it.

'Why would Mr Templeton want to kill you?'

'He knows I've been talking about Jane.'

'Who's Jane?' asks John. But he thinks he knows. He remembers the name from Ali's notes. Jane Campion, the woman supposedly killed by Templeton but maybe the victim of an accidental laudanum overdose.

'Templeton killed her,' says Burbage, standing up. 'He's killed others. Maybe he killed your cousin, Mrs Dawson. She disappeared too, didn't she?'

'Mrs Dawson isn't dead,' says John.

'Don't trust Templeton,' says Burbage. 'Don't let him make you into a Collector.'

'I won't,' says John. 'Let's continue this conversation in the morning.'

'I won't be here in the morning,' says Burbage. But he moves towards the door. His last words to John are almost tender. 'Just be careful,' he says.

Burbage isn't there in the morning. Clara is alone in the kitchen. John asks after the other members of the household and is told that Marianne is indisposed and Tremain and Arthur are 'probably sleeping it off'. Clara puts porridge in front of him and a cup of tea. John drinks thirstily.

'I met a man called Francis Burbage last night,' he says. 'Does he live here?'

'Him,' says Clara with a snort. 'Mr Templeton wouldn't have him in the house.'

'Why not?'

'He's a leech, a hanger-on. And he takes *photographs*.' This last is said in extremely disapproving tones.

'What sort of photographs?' asks John, though he thinks he can guess.

'I couldn't tell you,' says Clara repressively.

John decides to spend the day completing his map for Jones. He notes down shops, inns and houses of ill repute. He tests his resistance to steak and kidney pudding, jam sponge and something called a clanger. He avoids a man wanting to save his soul and a small boy offering to shine his shoes for a penny. He wonders what Moira is doing. She's newly retired and full of enthusiasm for Pilates, pottery and catching up with friends. Will she be doing any of these things today or will she be consumed with worry over him? John thinks not. Moira is not one to let her emotions take over – 'wallowing', she calls it.

John returns to the house at five. Clara makes him a cup of tea and tells him that the evening meal is at six. Last night John and Templeton had eaten at eight, but he gathers that late dining is a luxury only afforded to the gentry because of the cost of candles. Tremain and Arthur turn up for supper and it's quite a convivial evening. Tremain has just fetched a bottle of brandy from his room when another man bursts in. He's red-haired and hatless, clutching his side as if he has a stitch. It's a few seconds before John recognises Len, Marianne's husband.

'What is it?' says Tremain. 'You look as if the hounds of hell were after you.'

'It's Burbage,' says Len. 'He's been murdered.'

Chapter 37

John accompanies Arthur, Tremain and Len to the tavern where they drank on the first day. At the back of the inn there's a narrow lane with high walls on either side. The innkeeper, an ex-pugilist known as Big Jim, is holding a lantern over a huddled shape.

'Potboy found him like this,' he says. 'Poor little tyke. He vomited his supper up.'

Evidence of this is a few yards away. It adds to the ghastliness of the scene: the lamplight, the blood pooling in the gutter, the shouts of laughter emanating from the pub.

'Did you recognise the dead man right away?' asks John.

Jim gives him a curious look but answers, 'Aye. Everyone knows Burbage.'

'Everyone who sells alcohol,' says Tremain, which seems an unkind remark given the circumstances.

'How was he killed?' asks John. He must remember not to ask too many questions. It seems all too natural to want to lead the investigation. Preserve life, secure the scene, identification of victim, identification of evidence, identification of suspects.

'Throat slit,' says Jim.

'Good God,' says Arthur, sounding very shaken. 'Who would do such a thing?'

Someone who knew Burbage well enough to lure him to this spot, thinks John. Someone who is proficient at using a knife, one that was probably sharpened to a murderous point. From what he can see, Burbage was killed with a single thrust to the throat.

'It's the high mob,' says Jim. 'They're powerful in this area. Burbage must have come up against them.'

'Have you called the Peelers?' asks John.

'No point,' says Jim. 'We know who done it. I've sent the boy for the undertakers.'

'Did Burbage have any family?' Tremain addresses Arthur.

'There's a mother, I think. She lives in the country. Dear God, this is awful. I only saw him last night.'

'Did he seem worried about anything?' John can't help himself.

'He seemed most interested in you,' says Arthur. 'And your meeting with Mr Templeton.'

There's a silence. Len says, 'Arthur, do you know Burbage's lodgings? We should inform them. Jim, can you watch over . . . over the body . . . until the mortuary men come?'

'I will,' says Jim, adding, 'There are stray dogs round here.'

It's not until they are out of sight of the tavern that John realises the implications of this remark.

The inn is situated in the centre of a knot of streets, some set across with posts to deter carts and horses. The roads get narrower and narrower, until they are just passages, dark and foul-smelling. The men walk in a line, Len leading and Tremain bringing up the rear. They don't see another human being but John has the feeling that they are surrounded by people on all sides. Once he hears a voice raised in song, something about 'Ratcliff Highway', but it stops suddenly as if the singer were physically prevented from continuing.

'Did Burbage live here?' he asks. 'I thought he was wealthy.'

'He was high-born,' says Arthur, speaking through a handkerchief which he is holding over his mouth and nose, 'but had fallen low of late.'

Len has a torch, just a lighted stick really, and he holds it high for them to see their way. They pass under a footbridge, the light hellish against the brickwork, and into a wider thoroughfare. The terraced houses look squalid and uninhabitable, several of them boarded up. There are no streetlights. Len holds the burning brand higher.

'Is this the place, Arthur?' he asks.

They have stopped in front of a house that looks rather more respectable than its neighbours. The windows are dirty but they have curtains up, the steps have been swept fairly recently. Len knocks on the door and it's opened a few minutes later by a woman wearing a purple dress that looks as if it was once fairly smart. 'Forgive the intrusion,' says Len, 'but does Francis Burbage reside here?'

'He does when it suits him,' says the woman. 'What's it to you?'

'I'm sorry to tell you,' says Len, 'that an accident has befallen Mr Burbage.'

'An accident?' says the woman. 'What do you mean?' She spots Arthur, who seems to be trying to hide behind the taller Tremain.

'Arthur! What's going on?'

'Francis has been killed,' says Arthur. 'It's terrible, Mrs B. Terrible.'

Mrs B puts one hand on the doorpost, as if to steady herself, but her voice is quite level when she says, 'Well, he always did keep bad company.' John wonders if Mrs B is Burbage's wife or just the landlady. Either way she doesn't seem devastated by his death.

'Do you have an address for his mother?' asks Len. 'We'd like to write to her.'

'He left a letter for her in the hall,' says Mrs B. 'He was going to put it in the penny post.' She is gone for only a few seconds before coming back with an envelope, which she hands to Len. John wonders inconsequentially if the stamp is a Penny Black. He went through a stamp-collecting phase as a child.

'Thank you,' says Len. 'And our condolences.'

'The Lord giveth,' says Mrs B, 'and the Lord taketh away.'

There seems to be no answer to this.

By mutual consent, they repair to a tavern in a more respectable part of town. Never has John wanted a drink more but he's strengthened by the presence of Len, who has apparently taken the pledge. Len procures coffee for them both which doesn't taste like anything John has ever drunk before. But at least it's warm.

Arthur and Tremain drink brandy. 'To Burbage,' says Arthur, draining his glass.

'I never liked the man,' says Tremain, following suit, 'but no one deserves to die like that.'

'Jim said he was killed by the high mob,' says John. 'Who are they?'

Arthur looks superior. 'You can tell you come from Hastings, John. The mobsmen are in charge in these parts. They take money in return for keeping order. Some of the poor people worship them but they're hard men. They'll kill you if you cross them. That must have been what Burbage did. God rest his soul.'

As with Thomas Creek, thinks John, the most convenient culprit gets the blame. For his part, he can't forget some of Burbage's last words to him.

Don't trust Templeton.

Chapter 38

Ali

Ali watches as the cloaked figure merges into the shadows behind the house. Then she almost runs to her front door, unlocks it, goes inside and puts on the double lock and chain. She turns on the lights to reveal Terry sitting on the sofa, engaged in clawing her velour blanket. Ali realises that she's breathing heavily. Has she just seen Thomas Creek? How did he find her house? Was he the shadow who followed her from Hawk Street on the day of her return? Is Creek now coming after her, having killed Isaac? Breathe, Ali tells herself. She tries Finn's trick of counting monarchs but gets stuck on Stephen and Matilda. She goes into the kitchen and makes herself a cup of tea. The traditional English solution to any kind of crisis. As she waits for the kettle to boil, Ali feels a moment's pang for Clara and her range. She wishes she could have said goodbye before she left.

Does she really think that Thomas Creek has escaped from 1850 and has tracked her down? Ali remembers the feeling of going through the gate: the vertigo, the sense of unreality. It had been all she could do to walk the few metres to 44 Hawk Street. Surely Creek would be even more discombobulated? What would he think when he found himself in a modern street with horseless carriages whizzing past? He wouldn't even have money in any usable currency.

Ali drinks her tea on the sofa with Terry. She needs to investigate the Creek angle without endangering Finn. The last thing he needs is his mother, his strongest supporter, coming across as a madwoman. Nevertheless, Ali determines to speak to DS O'Brien tomorrow. The detective told her that she'd be in London for a few days. Ali wonders what she's investigating. Surely the police have – in their misguided opinion – caught their man? Maybe O'Brien, too, is discovering that there's more to this case than meets the eye?

Ali is too keyed up to eat. She watches an episode of *The Office* with Terry on her lap, then she double-checks that all her doors are locked and goes to bed.

Mary O'Brien is not delighted to see Ali again.

'DS Dawson, I saw you the first time out of professional courtesy and as a favour to DCI Bastian. Any further interference in this case is quite unacceptable.'

Ali notes the use of her rank. DS O'Brien is reminding her that they are both police officers and should behave professionally. Bollocks to that, thinks Ali. Her son's liberty is at stake.

'I want to talk to you about the gun,' she says.

'I'm not at liberty to discuss evidence. You know that.'

'I understand the bullet was fired from an antique gun. Have you traced the bullet? Do you know the bore and calibre?'

Mary O'Brien gives her a flat-eyed stare. It's quite effective. Being a woman in the force means building up a range of intimidation techniques. O'Brien is good, she doesn't fidget or break eye contact. Ali tries another tactic.

'I think I'm being followed,' she says.

This, at least, gets a response. 'What?'

'Last night I saw a man outside my house. Look, I know this sounds crazy, but he was dressed in old-fashioned clothes. All in black, with a cloak. Like a Victorian. I think he's got something to do with the case.'

'You think you're being followed by a man dressed up like a Victorian?'

'He looks like the man on the CCTV footage.'

DS O'Brien says nothing.

'I know you think you've got the case closed,' says Ali. 'The chief super is happy and you might even get a promotion. Congrats, by the way. It's great seeing a woman officer doing so well. But the thing is, I think it's more complicated than that. I think you know that I've been involved with a secret assignment?'

'I'd heard something like that.'

'Well, I can't say any more, but this assignment is linked to the Templeton case. I think you should look into this man. The one who wears old-fashioned clothes and carries an old-fashioned gun.'

O'Brien gives her the stare for a few seconds and then, to Ali's surprise, moves her laptop so that Ali can see the screen.

'We got something else from the CCTV,' she says. 'I didn't share this one with DCI Bastian.'

Intrigued, Ali leans forward. With a few clicks O'Brien brings up an image of a man with shoulder-length dark hair. He's wearing a long black coat and round his shoulders is a cloak that reaches almost to the floor.

'We call him The Vampire,' she says.

Ali can see why. It's not just the clothes, it's the pure malevolence on the long, pale face. If this is Thomas Creek, Ali can see why Clara called him wicked.

'We ran the image through our database. No matches. And the description doesn't correspond to anyone with previous in the area.'

'I bet it doesn't,' says Ali.

The detective allows herself a flicker of a smile. 'He does look like something from the *Hammer House of Horror*, doesn't he?'

'He really does.'

'Does this look like the man who you saw last night?'

'Yes,' says Ali.

O'Brien gives her an exasperated glance, which Ali recognises. It's the look of an officer who thinks they've solved a case but now finds some inconvenient loose ends. Ali thinks that Mary O'Brien is a good enough cop to let this worry her. She presses home her advantage. 'There are other anomalies too. The Templetons have problems in their marriage. The nanny told me.'

She's gone too far. The laptop is turned back.

'DS Dawson, if you've been interviewing people involved with this case, that's a serious breach of protocol. We've made an arrest and the CPS are happy that we've got enough evidence against your son. His manner was very suspicious when we questioned him, his DNA is at the scene. We think that Isaac and Finn were in a relationship. Maybe Isaac tried to end it and Finn killed him.'

'With an antique gun and a lead bullet?'

'The case is closed,' says Mary O'Brien. 'Finn's DNA was found at the scene. The man on the CCTV does not form part of our investigation. Now, if you'll excuse me, I've got a lot of work to do.'

Outside Bow Street police station, Ali considers her next move. Despite its abrupt ending, she thinks that her meeting with DS O'Brien reaped some rewards. She now knows that a man who might well be Thomas Creek was seen in the vicinity of East Dean on the night that Isaac was killed. She also thinks that, despite her protestations, Mary has some doubts about Finn's guilt. Ali can work on these. She wishes she could see Finn now but she's only been able to get a visiting pass for Friday. Hang on in there, she tells her son, Mum's going to sort this out.

Ali's phone buzzes. Unknown number. She's not one to ignore the unknown so she slides to answer.

'Is that Alison Dawson?' asks a female voice.

'Ali. Yes.'

'Finn's mother?'

'Yes.'

'I'm Helen Graham. I'm a Labour MP. The reason I'm calling is because my office is next to Isaac's . . .'

She pauses. Now Ali is definitely interested. 'Yes?' she prompts.

'Isaac said something to me the day before he died. It might be nothing but I've been going over it in my head. I wanted to talk to you because . . . I know Finn and I'm convinced he didn't do it. Look, is it possible to talk face to face?'

'Yes,' says Ali. 'I'll be with you in half an hour.'

She's already walking towards the Tube.

*

Since Finn started working for Isaac, Ali has been to the House of Commons a few times. Finn took her on a tour as soon as he got the job and Ali felt overawed and out of place, which was surely the intention of the architects and designers. The mock-Gothic, the statuary, even the tattiness of the private areas, seemed to say: you have no place here with your estuary vowels, comprehensive education and scruffy trainers. But Finn, who was also state-educated, seemed immediately at home, bandying terms like 'strangers' bar' and 'members' lobby'. Ali felt proud that she had raised her son not to be intimidated by power and prestige. But it didn't stop her feeling intimidated herself.

Helen Graham meets her in the lobby, beyond the checkpoints and airport-like security. She's tall with shoulder-length blonde hair, wearing a Hillary-esque trouser suit in lime green. Ali googled her on the way and saw her variously described as 'stunning', 'stylish' and 'statuesque' but, really, she's just an averagely attractive woman who likes bright colours.

'Ali. Hi. Thank you for coming.' Helen has a soft Yorkshire accent.

'Thank you for contacting me,' says Ali.

'I've been agonising over it,' says Helen. 'But it was such an odd conversation. And I thought, seeing as you're a police officer as well as Finn's mother . . .'

'You did the right thing,' Ali assures her. She will decide later whether to share the information with DS O'Brien.

'Shall we go to my office?' says Helen. 'We should be safe. Chibu isn't in today.'

Safe is an interesting word, thinks Ali.

'Does Chibu come in a lot?' she asks.

'Most days,' says Helen. 'She has a key.'

That doesn't really explain why Chibu is still coming to work when her boss is dead. Ali follows Helen upstairs, through doors and along endless corridors, the green carpet becoming progressively more threadbare. Eventually, they reach Helen's office. Ali has never ventured this far into the building. So this is where Finn spends so much of his time.

'Isaac's office is a lot bigger and smarter than mine,' says Helen. 'But then he's a minister. Was. Jesus. I can't get used to it.'

'I know what you mean,' says Ali, although, in a way, it feels like Isaac has been dead, and Finn in prison, for ever.

Helen's office is certainly small. There's only just enough room for a desk and two chairs. The mullioned windows give a claustrophobic, imprisoned feel.

Helen offers coffee. 'I've got a kettle,' she says, as if this is an unheard-of luxury.

'Thank you,' says Ali. She's desperate for caffeine and, although the instant coffee, served in a portcullis mug, is undoubtedly horrible, it provides the necessary kick.

Helen takes a sip and grimaces. 'It's not very nice.'

'It's fine,' says Ali. 'What was it you wanted to tell me?'

Helen takes another sip but Ali thinks this is just to gain some time. Eventually she says, 'Isaac and I were quite friendly, despite being ostensibly on different sides. I mean, he's centre right and I'm centre left so . . .'

'My son's right and I'm left,' says Ali, 'but we still get on.'

'Exactly.' Helen smiles, which makes her look almost as attractive as the papers suggest.

'On the Friday before . . . before it happened,' she says. 'I was

299

here, in my office, at about midday. We'd had a vote in the house. I put my head round Isaac's door to say hello. He was with Chibu and Piers. I knew he'd been giving a talk to the Prison Officers' Association and I assumed they were having a debrief. I asked if anyone was up for a drink later. We often had drinks on Fridays. Fizz Fridays, Isaac called them. Isaac said he had to leave early because Miranda, his wife, was collecting him and they were going down to his constituency in East Dean. I went back to my office, but the door was still open and I saw Finn going past. There was nothing odd in that, of course, but, a few minutes later, Chibu and Piers left. As they walked down the corridor, I heard Chibu saying something about Finn being rude. Then, a few minutes later, I heard raised voices. That was very unusual. Finn is always so soft-spoken and polite.'

'He's been well brought-up,' says Ali. 'Did you hear what they were saying?' She thinks that Helen, with her conveniently open door, would have had a good try.

'I definitely heard Finn saying, "You knew," in an accusatory voice. Then I heard Miranda arrive. Finn left and, about five minutes later, Isaac knocked on my door. I thought he'd just come to say goodbye but he seemed odd. Agitated. And this is what I wanted to tell you. He said, "I just wanted you to know that I'm going to see the PM on Monday. If you hear anything about me, anything crazy, anything involving the nineteenth century, don't think I'm going mad. I promise you I'm not." Then he said goodbye and left.'

'Anything involving the nineteenth century?' says Ali. 'What do you think he meant by that?'

'I've no idea,' says Helen. 'But Isaac was killed the next day. I couldn't see how the conversation could be relevant, but I thought

I should tell someone. My conscience has been troubling me. At the very least it shows Isaac's mind was disturbed.'

'Yes,' says Ali. She's trying to decide whether Helen's evidence is useful or not. On the one hand, it might show that Isaac was behaving oddly, on the other hand, there's the supposed argument, which might be seen as a motive for Finn. *You knew.* Had Finn been confronting his boss about his connection to Ali's mission? That must have come as a terrible shock.

Helen breaks the silence. 'I should also tell you that Isaac and I had a . . . well, affair is too strong a word. We had a fling, if that doesn't sound too juvenile. We both got a bit carried away . . . in Isaac's office. On his leather sofa. It was after one of the Fizz Fridays. There was nothing to it. We were both married. But I suppose that's why I didn't come forward sooner.'

Ali looks at the pleasant face opposite her. Was the so-called fling the reason why Helen didn't come forward or a motive for murder?

Chapter 39

'Hot news,' Dina greets Ali as she enters the office. 'I've got hold of Isaac's telephone records.'

'How on earth did you manage that? No, don't tell me.'

Ali knows that Dina, through her work in computer forensics, has a network of contacts, some not exactly on the right side of the law.

'It involved a minimum of hacking,' says Dina.

It's a long time since Ali has seen her colleague looking so cheerful. She knows that the last few months have not been easy for Dina. She took the break-up with Liam hard, despite him being a gaslighting misogynist who wore golfing jumpers. Dina's parents are very keen for her to meet a new man and settle down. She is only thirty-five but her parents think, and frequently say, that she should be married with children by now. Ali thinks of Dina as a mere child. Young enough to get away with 'hot news' anyway.

Ali slides into her comfortable chair. John's desk, like a riderless charger, faces her reproachfully. Geoff's office is also empty. Dina says that he's gone to a meeting at the Met. 'You know how he likes an agenda.'

'Find anything interesting?' she asks Dina.

'Yes,' says Dina. 'On the day that he died, Isaac called Jones twenty-four times.'

'Twenty-four times? Did she answer?'

'It looks like she did once.'

'Let's talk to her,' says Ali. 'Is she here?' Since John's departure, Jones has been at the unit almost every day. As Dina said, it's disconcerting, as if a mythical figure had come to live with you.

'She's in Pevensie,' says Dina.

'Let's go,' says Ali, standing up. 'Did Isaac call anyone else?'

'One of his advisors. Not Finn. Chibu.'

'Interesting,' says Ali. 'Maybe Piers was right about them having an affair. And I learnt something else today.' She tells Dina about Helen Graham.

'On the sofa in his office,' says Dina. 'How tacky.'

'It's leather so it was probably very tacky,' says Ali. She thought at the time that it was odd of Helen to specify the material.

'Apparently Isaac also told Helen that she might hear some news concerning him and the nineteenth century.'

'So he could have been planning to go public about you going through the gate?' says Dina. 'Why? And would anyone have believed him?'

'Probably not,' says Ali. 'But I'm wondering who would want to silence Isaac. It could be someone very high up indeed.'

'Careful,' says Dina, 'you're starting to sound like Declan.' She's never met Ali's first husband but she knows all about him.

'Sometimes conspiracy theories are right,' says Ali.

★

Pevensie is on the floor below the Department of Logistics. It's where they work on AI, algorithms and all the things that make Ali remember GCSE maths. For this reason, she seldom ventures onto this level. She prefers Wells, where they are supposedly working on an actual, physical time machine. Dina is a frequent visitor though and she opens the door with a cheerful, 'What's up, geeks?'

The second floor is a cavernous open space, as dreary as the storey above, with stained carpet tiles and fluorescent lights, several of them flickering. A few desks are clustered in the centre, as if for safety. Sure enough, Jones is sitting at one of these, peering at a desktop computer.

'What are you doing?' asks Ali. Jones shuts down the screen. Ali has never seen her appear anything other than elegant but today she looks rumpled, almost dishevelled. Her short hair is standing up in a crest and her jumper is on inside out. Ali can see the Missoni label.

'I'm making a replica of John,' says Jones.

Ali and Dina look at each other.

'A replica?' says Dina. 'You mean, like a hologram?'

'At first I thought in those terms,' says Jones, 'but there needs to be a physical presence to create the footprints. The question is what to do with the . . .' She searches for the word and Ali thinks this isn't because of language difficulties but the problem of finding something Ali will understand. 'Digital model,' she comes up with at last. 'Even if John can pass through the space that we have created, what do we do with the model afterwards? If we leave it in 1850, there's a chance that it could change physics for ever.'

'I thought we couldn't alter the past.'

'That was when I thought we could only visit the past as

holograms ourselves. Wave fronts, interference patterns. But you were a living, breathing person there. That changes everything.'

'Could a time traveller kill someone?' asks Ali.

'Do you mean the person who might have come through your gate?' says Jones. 'Geoff told me your theory about that. It's possible, I suppose. But, even supposing this man was capable of murder, he would have been mentally confused, disorientated. Remember how you felt, and you knew what was happening. You were prepared.'

'I didn't feel very prepared,' says Ali. Once again, she imagines Thomas Creek suddenly finding himself in a street full of red buses and No Entry signs. Even if he survived that, how could he find his way to East Dean in Sussex? If he found a railway station, what would he make of the noise, the confusion, the electronic signs, the Tannoy announcements, the locomotives themselves? There were trains in the 1850s but nothing like the modern-day monsters. In Creek's shoes, Ali would be too terrified to move.

'Jones,' she says, 'Isaac called you twenty-four times on the day that he died.'

Is it her imagination or does the already watchful figure become even more attentive? With her long neck and dark eyes, Jones suddenly resembles a gazelle that has seen a lion on the horizon.

'Don't remind me,' she says, her voice light. 'What a nuisance.'

'Did you answer him?' asks Ali.

Again, a slight hesitation, before Jones says, 'Just once, I think.'

'What did he say?'

'He was babbling on about telling the PM that you were lost in the nineteenth century.'

'Do you think he would have?'

'Of course not,' says Jones. 'He would have looked like a complete madman.'

'But the PM knows about our work. He would have believed Isaac.'

'The PM knows in theory,' says Jones, pronouncing the last word like the Italian *teoria*.

'But he knows we went to 1976,' says Dina.

'Again, I'm not sure that Geoff explained that you were actually *there*. Indistinct but there.'

'But Isaac asked for me particularly,' says Ali. 'He believed that I could go to 1850 and clear his ancestor's name.'

'None of us really believed you could do it until you did it,' says Jones. Which wasn't what she had said at the time.

Ali and Dina spend the afternoon going through the evidence. Ali hopes that Mary O'Brien too will have received Isaac's phone records. Surely that will make her think that there's more to the politician's murder than a lovers' tiff. Will DS O'Brien interview Jones? Ali would love to see it.

At five o'clock Dina goes off to meet a man she has contacted through a dating site. 'He says he likes scuba diving,' she says. 'Hope that's not code for anything kinky.' Ali switches off her computer and packs up. Geoff still isn't back and the office feels too quiet with no one there. Is Jones still on the floor below? Ali pauses on the stairs but there's no sound from Pevensie. She continues on her way. She has decided to visit the Brick Lane Bookshop. As a remand prisoner, Finn is allowed to receive books but they have to be new paperbacks. Ali finds large bookshops intimidating, bombarding her with passive-aggressive invitations to read 'the book that everyone is talking about', or a classic that everyone but her has read before. She hopes that a smaller store will be friendlier, plus she likes to support local, independent businesses.

As Ali follows her phone's satnav, she realises that she is walking the same route that she took to Spitalfields in 1850, but in reverse. Her first thought is that the area has changed beyond recognition. Now the streets are full of coffee shops and vintage boutiques, there are tables on the pavements and pedestrian spaces with bright murals. Ali remembers the Victorian stalls, little more than barrows, piled high with silk and cotton, then the only patches of colour amongst the grey. Now it's a kaleidoscope of brightness, partly because of a preponderance of flower shops, filling the air with a green, stalky scent that reminds Ali of one – maybe all – of her weddings. Most of these establishments have teenagers outside them, taking selfies. The whole place is, as Dina would say, with only a small side serving of irony, Instagrammable.

Not for the first time in the last week, Ali experiences an almost out-of-body sensation as she walks past the banks of flowers and the sari stalls. Is she really here at all? Finn told her about stabbing himself with a pen to prove he wasn't dreaming. Several times Ali has had to pinch herself or dash her face with cold water just to be sure that she's alive and not a ghost, as she was when she first visited the past. 'I could walk, talk, eat and piss,' she told Jones when emphasising her physical presence in 1850, but those things alone are not enough to make a person properly present. Sometimes she feels that she was more herself when dressed in voluminous petticoats and eating tripe with Clara than she is now, wearing jeans and trainers and paying three pounds for a small-batch coffee.

The bookshop seems to want to evoke those earlier times. The name and number are in an old-fashioned typeface and the window itself, multipaned and enticing, looks like an illustration from *The Old Curiosity Shop*.

Don't trust Dickens.

Ali spends a pleasant half hour amongst the neatly curated shelves. Eventually she settles on *The Secret History*, one of Finn's favourite books, a P. G. Wodehouse anthology to cheer him up and a biography of Clement Attlee, in an attempt to win him over to the Labour cause. She takes her purchases to the till where she is served by a nice young woman who reminds her of Finn's university friends.

Ali asks how long the bookshop has been there.

'Since 1978,' says the assistant. 'Imagine.'

'Imagine,' says Ali.

Chapter 40

Ali thinks that Finn looks very slightly better. The shell-shocked expression has gone and the look he gives her when she enters the visiting area, part-affectionate, part-quizzical, is so familiar that it makes Ali's heart ache.

'I had a visitor yesterday,' he tells her.

'Really? Who?' As far as she knows, only Declan has permission to visit.

'DS O'Brien. And the other one. DC Franks.'

Ali's heart beats faster. Does this mean that O'Brien is having doubts about Finn's conviction? She must have come to see him as soon as she received the phone records.

'What did they want?' she asks.

'To ask me about Jones. Apparently, Isaac called her twenty-four times on the day he died.'

'I know. Dina got hold of his records too.'

'Has she been hacking again?'

'She says the hacking was minimal. What did the police ask about Jones?'

'Just whether I knew her. I said that you worked with her some-times.'

That must have made O'Brien think.

'Did they ask anything else?'

'They talked about the gun again. Did I collect firearms? Was I interested in antique weapons? I mean – as if!'

This is encouraging. It must mean O'Brien thinks there is still some investigating to do.

'I've found something out too,' says Ali. 'I got a call from Helen Graham yesterday.'

'From Helen? What did she want?'

'She wanted to tell me about an odd conversation she'd had with Isaac the day before he died. Did you know that she'd had a fling with Isaac?'

Finn pulls a face. 'Yes. Isaac once made a really crass remark about the sofa in his office. I said it was looking a bit the worse for wear. He said, "It's probably because I shagged Helen on it."'

'Charming. Did you tell O'Brien?'

'No. She didn't ask about Isaac's colleagues and Helen's married . . .'

'Finn, this is no time to be chivalrous. O'Brien's case is that you had an affair with Isaac.'

'Ade told me. It isn't true, you know.'

'They say your DNA was on his lips.'

'On his lips?' Ali is sure that Finn's confusion is genuine. 'I've never kissed Isaac on the lips. Or anywhere else. He's . . . he was . . . a definite handshake guy.'

'If Isaac had a one-night stand with Helen, it suggests that Isaac wasn't gay. Though he could have been bi, of course.'

'He wasn't gay,' says Finn. 'Nor am I. Sorry to disappoint you.'

'I'll live with it,' says Ali. 'What about Chibu? She seems to have had a thing for Isaac. He called her too. On the day before he died.'

Finn frowns. Ali knows the look. Finn is competitive, not about sport but about the game of life. He doesn't like the fact that his boss called his colleague and not him.

'Could Chibu and Isaac have been having an affair?' asks Ali.

'I think she might have had a crush on him,' says Finn. 'She was always saying how good-looking he was, how she didn't under-stand why he married Miranda when he could have had anyone. But I don't think there was anything going on between Isaac and Chibu. We would have been able to tell, me and Piers. We worked so closely together.' The frown again.

'Piers thinks Isaac was sleeping with Chibu. Helen too. A Lothario, he called him.'

'Piers said that? He must have been pissed.'

'He was but that doesn't mean he was lying.'

'Piers is good at lying,' says Finn.

'Chibu said something very similar,' says Ali. 'Anyway, Helen said that she overheard you arguing with Isaac on the day before he died. That isn't so helpful. But she also said that Isaac told her he was going to see the PM and not to think he was crazy if she heard something about him and the nineteenth century.'

Finn's eyes are wide, making him look very young.

'Oh my God. He was going to tell the PM about 1850.'

'Maybe,' says Ali. 'It's very frustrating that we can't tell the police the whole truth.'

'Yeah, that'd definitely make me look believable,' says Finn. 'Murder suspect says his mother is a time traveller.'

Ali laughs, a sound that is obviously so rare in the visitors' room that the warders look round suspiciously. 'Well, maybe not the whole truth,' she says. 'I've got this wild idea that someone went through the gate before me. That's why I couldn't get back. I think it's a man called Thomas Creek. DS O'Brien showed me CCTV footage of a man seen in the grounds of East Dean on the day Isaac died. He was dressed in Victorian clothes. The police have nicknamed him The Vampire. I think it could have been Creek.'

'And do you think he could have killed Isaac?'

'It's crazy, I know,' says Ali. 'But when I heard that Isaac was killed with an antique weapon, I thought it could have been Creek.'

'God.' Finn slumps in his chair. 'I'm done for. The police will never catch this Creek. I mean, he doesn't really exist, does he?'

'We don't have to prove who did it,' says Ali. 'Just that you didn't. These anomalies — the calls to Jones, the conversation with Helen Graham — they all point to there being a different story here. I thought at the time that O'Brien rushed things, arrested you without sufficient evidence. She was probably under lots of pressure to get a result. But she's got enough conscience to follow up these lines of enquiry.'

'I think she goes by the rules,' says Finn. 'But she's only a DS. She doesn't have that much power. I suppose the question is how far the authorities will go to suppress the Jones story. The whole time-travel thing. Maybe they're happy to sacrifice me.'

'Maybe,' says Ali, thinking this is all too likely. 'But we don't have to tell them everything. As you say, that would just make us look like fantasists. All we have to do is plant doubt, suggest alternative scenarios. There are lots of potential suspects who could have killed Isaac. Miranda, Piers, Chibu, Jacinta, a disgruntled constituent . . .'

'An escapee from the nineteenth century . . .'

'Probably best to leave him off the list for now. The important thing is to get you out of here. Terry misses you.'

'That I don't believe,' says Finn. But he sits up straighter and looks, for a moment, almost cheerful.

After leaving Thameside, grim and pastel-hued under the grey February sky, Ali takes the Tube to Mile End and Eel Street. She reaches the lobby just in time to see Bud sprinting up the stairs in front of her, takeaway coffee in one hand. Ali doesn't call out to him but, when Bud makes an unexpected turn towards the Pevensie office, she follows.

Somehow, Ali is not surprised to see Jones at the desk where she was yesterday. Bud goes to join her and Ali trails him, soundless in her trainers. How she loves twenty-first century footwear.

'Hello,' she says.

Bud starts guiltily but Jones says, 'Hi, Ali,' almost as if she is expected.

'I've just been to see Finn,' say Ali.

'How is he?' asks Bud. He has taken off his jacket to reveal a T-shirt saying, 'I may be wrong but it's very unlikely'.

'Not too bad, considering,' says Ali. She looks at Jones. 'The police have been to see him. They asked about you.'

Once again, Jones shows no surprise. 'They called on me last night. DS O'Brien. An intelligent woman, I thought. And a man.'

Clearly DC Franks is less memorable.

'They came to your flat?'

According to Geoff, who has only been there once, Jones has a flat in Islington. The sitting room, Geoff related with something like awe, is painted completely black.

'Yes,' says Jones. 'Somewhat of an intrusion. They wanted to ask about the phone calls from Isaac Templeton.'

'What did you tell them?'

'Just that Isaac wanted to talk to me about some government research. I said we'd met when he was in the ministry of science, innovation and technology. Which is true.'

Jones seems almost surprised by this last fact.

'Did they believe you? That he'd rung all those times just to talk about government research?'

Jones shrugs. 'They might have thought he was obsessed with me. Who knows?'

Bud stifles a snort, but Ali knows that he's obsessed with Jones in his own way, despite being gay. Geoff is too.

'By the way,' says Jones, 'I told them that Finn didn't kill Isaac.'

'Thank you,' says Ali.

'I know he didn't,' says Jones. 'Now, if you'll excuse us, Ali . . .'

She turns back to Bud. Ali is left looking at the underwater mural on the building opposite. The octopus waves a pink tentacle. Dina has often noted that there seem to be ten of them.

In the Department of Logistics, the open plan area is empty. Ali wonders where Dina is but she's pleased to have the place to herself. At her desk, she writes:

TO DO

Interview Chibu again. If she had affair with Isaac she has motive.
Ring O'Brien – does she know any more about CCTV man?
Go to Sussex?

Ali looks across at John's work station. Is John, even now, chatting with Clara in the kitchen or listening to Len play the piano? What does he think of Cain Templeton? Does Ali go back to the

1850s and have an affair with Cain? The strangest thing is that she almost believes it is possible.

Another, even stranger, thought strikes her. Ali thinks of talking to Isaac in his Battersea eyrie. He'd told her then that his ancestor had been accused of killing three women. Ali had assumed that the first was Jane Campion and the second was Ettie Moran (the only woman whose name Isaac knew). But what if the third was her, Alisoun Dawson? What if Cain Templeton was known to have consorted with her? Maybe she'd lived with him 'under his protection' and then mysteriously vanished? Is she part of the Templeton legend?

Ali doesn't notice the incoming call until her phone has almost buzzed its way off her desk. Another unknown number.

'Hello,' says Ali.

'Is that Alison Dawson?'

'Yes.'

'This is Miranda Templeton.'

Ali would have thought that she lost the power to be surprised the day she first moved her atoms in space but, at this, she almost gasps. Why on earth is Isaac's wife ringing her, the mother of his supposed murderer?

'This might sound a bit odd,' says Miranda. She has an upper-class voice but it doesn't set Ali's teeth on edge the way some do. She knows she's an inverted snob but what can you do? Perhaps Miranda's voice is less triggering because it's slightly hoarse with an undercurrent of humour that's still there, despite the subject matter.

'I've just found a letter from Isaac,' says Miranda. 'And it mentions you. There's a drawing too.'

'A drawing?'

'Yes. Look, this would be much easier face to face. Is there any way you could come to East Dean? It's only a couple of hours in the car.'

But Ali doesn't have a car.

'I'll come,' she says. 'But I'll have to get the train and I'm not sure of the times.'

'OK,' says Miranda. And Ali can tell that she doesn't really care about the proletariat who rely on public transport. 'Let me know when you're at the station. I'll come and meet you. I'll be on this number.'

She rings off and Ali is left staring at the space in front of her. It's a few seconds before she realises that it's now full of Geoff.

'Hello, Ali.' He's wearing a Barbour jacket, which doesn't succeed in making him look like a country gentleman. He's essentially urban: blue chinos, pale blue jumper, lace-up brogues.

'Geoff,' says Ali. 'Have you got your car?'

'Yes, as a matter of fact. I had some files I wanted to bring from the house.'

'Could you drive me to East Dean in Sussex?'

'Why on earth would you want to go there?'

'Miranda Templeton just rang. She wants to talk to me.'

'What about?'

'She says she's found a letter. From Isaac. It says something about me.'

'What?'

'She says she wants to tell me face to face. Please, Geoff. It would take me hours on the train.'

'Very well,' says Geoff. 'But let's have a sandwich first. I don't want to drive on an empty stomach.'

Chapter 41

Ali suggests that they eat their sandwiches in the car but Geoff obviously finds this shocking. They have lunch at their respective desks, Ali looking across to Geoff and willing him to hurry. He's brought crisps too. Ali can hear him crunching, agonisingly loudly and agonisingly slowly. Finn would hate it. He doesn't like eating sounds, especially over the phone. But, then again, Finn is probably, even at this minute, dining off a plastic plate in the company of several hundred hardened criminals. Ali has to rescue him.

When Geoff has finished the crisps and folded the packet into a tiny square, Jones appears. She goes into Geoff's office and closes the door, which Ali thinks is rude. She looks at the clock on the wall. Nearly one. If they don't set off soon, it'll be dark by the time they get to East Dean.

Finally, Jones emerges. She stops at Ali's desk.

'Geoff says he's driving you to Sussex.'

'Yes. Miranda Templeton rang. She wants to talk to me.'

'Why?'

'I don't know but it has to be face to face, apparently.'

Jones looks at her for a moment, her big brown eyes surprisingly sympathetic. Then she says, 'Good luck,' and strides out of the room. Geoff appears, wearing his jacket.

'Ready?' he says, as if *she's* been keeping *him* waiting.

Ali grabs her anorak.

Geoff's car is one of those Jeep-like things. Like the Barbour, it's a town indulgence pretending to be a rural necessity. There are box files on the back seat, and behind them is a cage once used for transporting Geoff and Bobby's dog, Hamish. But Hamish is no more. The only time Ali has ever seen Geoff cry – even during Bobby's illness – was when he told Ali last year that he'd had to have Hamish put to sleep. Ali wonders how he can stand to keep the travelling cage in the car. If anything happened to Terry, Ali would give all his belongings away, including the luxurious bed he has never once slept in. But she can't bear to follow that train of thought.

Geoff is an unexpectedly dashing driver, revving up at the lights and overtaking on the inside. But he's not quite as terrifying as Jones and Ali is able to relax. She's relieved that Geoff doesn't seem to want to talk.

They hit traffic on the M25. It's three o'clock and raining hard by the time that they have left the motorway and are driving through country villages and sodden brown fields. When they see the sea, it's the same iron-grey as the sky. Signs point to Birling Gap, Eastbourne and Hastings. Ali remembers going to Eastbourne as a child. It was meant to be posher than Hastings so her parents used to wear their best clothes and take them to a hotel for lunch. Ali's memories are of white tablecloths and blue skies, of running on the beach with Richard once the endless meal was over. It's hard to imagine anyone frolicking on the sand today.

Ali told Finn that East Dean sounded like a Victorian melodrama. She was thinking of *East Lynne*, she realises, a nineteenth-century novel about a woman who abandons her husband and children and comes to a tragic end. Ali saw the old black-and-white film one Sunday afternoon. When she sees the Templeton mansion, dark against the lowering clouds, she thinks it's just the sort of place for a tragic ending. The towers and crenellations also remind her of the grimmer Eastbourne hotels. It certainly doesn't look like a cosy family home. Ali remembers Cain saying that he liked the town but his wife preferred the country, which was 'convenient'.

Geoff stops in front of massive wrought-iron gates. He presses the intercom, waits for a reply and then comes back to the car. The Barbour doesn't have a hood and his bald head glistens with rain.

'No one is answering.'

'Miranda must be in,' says Ali. '*She* rang *me*.'

She rings Miranda's mobile number, but it goes straight to voice-mail. She texts, 'I'm outside' but it remains on 'delivered'.

'I know the passcode,' says Geoff.

Ali gapes at Geoff's back as he keys in the number. She longs to be able to tell John about this new breaking and entering side to their boss.

They drive through the grounds. The gardens have the windswept look of land so near the sea, but there are trees here and there, even what looks like an orchard behind a low wall. Does one of the trees have the names Cain and Alisoun etched on its bark? Geoff edges the car between outhouses bigger than Ali's house. Outmansions. Did Cain say something about a studio? Maybe that's still standing.

'Let's have a look round,' she says to Geoff.

'All right. I've got an umbrella in the boot.'

It's a huge golfing number in red and white. You might as well carry a flag saying, 'I am here'. Ali pulls up her hood and strides ahead. They are parked in front of the stables, a low flint-fronted building with blue eaves. Ali wasn't expecting to see a horse there – she imagined the place had been turned into a spa or something – so she's surprised when a shaggy head pops out and surveys her through its fringe (or whatever the horsy term is). Of course, Jessica and Tom probably have ponies.

'Hi,' says Ali to the horse, who turns away when he sees that she's not carrying any food. Ali continues along the gravel path, followed by the figure with the giant umbrella. Behind the stables there's a barn, black and somehow menacing, facing a building that's a similar size but with high windows on three sides. Surely this must be the studio, possessing the northern light that Tremain had talked about.

Ali walks over the grass, muddy from all the rain, towards the studio. There's a heap of soil next to it, possibly manure or fertilizer (Ali is vague about gardening but there's a pungent, farmish smell). Amongst the dark earth, Ali spots a blue glitter. She leans down and picks it up. It's a narrow piece of glass, rounded like a stem. Ali thinks of her beloved mismatched glass in the cabinet at home.

'I'll take it,' says Geoff. 'A dog might cut its paw.' He takes a poo bag out of his pocket and places the shard inside. Ali thinks it's touching that he still has the bags with him. She doesn't think the Templeton family have a pet but she was wrong about the horse so maybe there's a golden retriever running around somewhere.

Ali pushes at the double doors. She's surprised to find that they open easily. There's a cavernous space inside which contains only stacked chairs and a long trestle table. Presumably the Templetons use this area for entertaining. Geoff says, from the doorway where he is still sheltered by the umbrella, 'I'm going to go up to the house.'

'I'll have a look round here,' says Ali. 'Message me if Miranda's home.'

'Will do,' says Geoff, but he sounds worried. He's lost the spirit of daring with which he unlocked the gates.

Ali watches the red and white dome bobbing along the path. Then she turns back to the room. She has spotted a spiral staircase in the corner and it suddenly feels imperative that she should climb it. Time travel might be like taking the lift but, so far throughout this adventure, she has climbed steps. Three flights to her room in Hawk Street, three flights to the Department of Logistics, three flights to the museum at QMUL. Ali knows that she needs to proceed upwards. It's almost dark outside now and she can't find a light switch so she uses her phone torch. What would she have done in 1850? Carried a candle like a nursery-rhyme character? *Here comes a candle to light you to bed. Here comes a chopper to chop off your head.* Ali climbs the stairs.

She finds herself in an attic space, empty apart from a sofa that looks oddly familiar. Ali goes to one of the three round windows. From this vantage point she can see the umbrella making its way to the house but, as she watches, she sees another shape, a black shadow walking through the stunted trees on the other side of the drive. Ali catches her breath. Could it be Thomas Creek? But this person is wearing a distinctly modern padded jacket. It's this garment that Ali recognises, even before she takes in the short dark hair and long slim legs. Jones. What is Jones doing in Sussex when she's meant to be constructing holograms in London? And Ali remembers what Jones said about Finn.

I know it's not him.

At the time Ali had found this heart-warming. Jones believes in Finn, she had thought. If such a brilliant scientist was on their side, there was still hope. But what if Jones knew Finn hadn't murdered Isaac because she was the person who had? Isaac called Jones multiple times on the day that he died. He would have told her that he was going to see the PM, that he was going to tell him about the failure of the 1850 experiment. Would Jones kill to protect her work? Ali thinks she knows the answer.

Ali runs down the twisty steps. It's almost dark outside now. The rain is much heavier and the wind is stronger. What should she do? All she can think of is to get to the house. Maybe Miranda will be there now and surely Geoff will head for shelter soon.

Ali bows her head as she battles along the path towards the red-brick mansion. In the shelter of its eaves she stops and looks around. There's no sign of her boss anywhere. Even the bloody Where's Wally umbrella has vanished. There's only slanting grey sleet and, beyond that, the hazy shapes of skeletal winter trees. Ali climbs the steps up to the front door. She has no thought now beyond getting inside and keeping dry. She assumes that Geoff is in the building somewhere. How can she tell him her suspicions about Jones? Geoff adores her, it's a standing joke amongst the team. But Geoff, of all people, knows that Jones is ruthless. He's been involved with the time-travel project from the beginning. He must have seen Jones sweep enemies beneath her chariot wheels before. Ali thinks he will believe that she's capable of murder.

Ali raises her hand to knock and then lowers it again. This house has the same griffin door-knocker as 44 Hawk Street. Something makes her try the handle instead and the door opens silently. She's in a huge, panelled hall. Lights are glowing on either side of a medieval-looking stone fireplace but there is no other sign of life.

'Miranda?' Once again Ali's voice sounds strange in her own ears. 'Geoff?'

She steps forward. She realises that she must be in the great hall, where Isaac died. It's an impressive space, with its tall windows and sweeping staircase, but not a friendly one. A wall to her left is devoted to guns and swords. There's also a stag's head on a plinth and a cabinet full of what look like stuffed birds. Lots of death on display, thinks Ali. A clock ticks somewhere, reminding her of Hawk Street. *It's like a heartbeat.*

There's a single chair placed in front of the fireplace. At the sight of it, Ali realises how tired she is and thinks that she'll take a seat, just for a second, and get her breath back. She takes a step forward and then an arm is around her neck and steel pressed to her throat.

'Oh no you don't.'

It's a deep voice, upper-class but rough at the edges. Ali knows she's heard it before. She tries to twist away but the arm holds her tight. Her assailant smells of sweat, soil and something else, something that reminds her of Tremain's room and the women staring out from the portraits. Turpentine.

She brings her elbow back hard into the man's midriff and manages to extricate herself from his grip. He chokes and doubles over. Ali catches a glimpse of cloak and knows that she is struggling with Thomas Creek. He grasps at the chair. Ali staggers away. She knows she's not safe yet. She can still see the knife in the man's hand. And maybe he still has his gun.

What happens next is almost the strangest thing Ali has seen so far. Creek is holding the chair back and breathing hard. Then, he lowers himself into the seat. He looks directly at Ali and smiles. It's a particularly horrible smile. Then there's a sort of shimmer in the atmosphere, an electrical charge like the moments before a thunder storm. The lights flicker and Creek is no longer there. Ali remembers Jones telling her that, when you go through the gate, the movement is so fast that the human eye cannot comprehend it. 'The air parts for you,' she said. Ali stares at the place where, only a few seconds earlier, Creek had sat, grinning up at her. She hears someone calling her name and sees Geoff, standing halfway up the stairs.

'Did you see that?' she asks.

'Was it . . . was it Thomas Creek? The man you thought came through the gate before you?'

'Yes. And now he seems to have gone back. I don't know how. There's much more to this than Jones ever told us . . .'

'I'm beginning to realise I know nothing,' says an Italian-accented voice.

Jones is striding towards them, hair plastered to her head, dark eyes blazing. And Ali remembers that this could be the woman who killed Isaac Templeton in this very room. She backs away until she is standing next to Geoff at the foot of the staircase.

'Ali,' says Jones, her voice steady. 'Move away from him.'

And Ali understands.

Chapter 42

'It was you,' says Ali. 'You set Finn up. You went to my house and got him drunk. Then you came here and killed Isaac. You took Finn's wine glass because it had his DNA. You must have pressed it to Isaac's lips. That was a piece of one of my own glasses that I found in the compost heap.'

'I don't know how it got there,' says Geoff, sounding peevish. 'I thought I put the glass in the recycling. It must have been the garden waste bin.'

'Ali,' says Jones, just behind her. 'Move away.'

Ali understands that Jones thinks she's in danger but, even now, she can't connect that word with her boss, her exasperating but essentially good-hearted boss.

'Why did you do it?' says Ali.

'I couldn't let Isaac ruin all our work. Our groundbreaking work. Jones told me that he rang her, threatening to tell the PM. I had to silence him.'

'I should never have told you about that phone call,' says Jones. 'I never suspected . . .'

'When did you suspect?' asks Ali.

'I started to put the pieces together,' says Jones. 'But when DS O'Brien questioned me, I realised that there was only one other person who knew about the calls from Isaac, who knew that he was going to tell the PM. Then, when Geoff said that he was driving you here, I was scared for you.'

'Where are Miranda and her family?' says Ali suddenly. 'What's happened to them?' She has a vision of the mother and children tied up in a loft somewhere. Or worse.

'I rang them and told them to leave the house,' says Jones. 'I pretended to be the police.'

'Why didn't you call the police?' says Ali. 'The real police. DS O'Brien.'

'I thought we could keep it between ourselves,' says Jones.

Ali looks at Geoff. 'How could you do it?' she says. 'I can almost understand you killing Isaac, but you set Finn up. I thought you were my friend.' She realises that she's crying.

Geoff makes a move towards her. Ali thinks he's going to touch her arm, to say sorry, but instead, he darts past her, moving faster than Ali has ever seen him, running across the hall to a door between the stained-glass windows. Ali hesitates for a moment, but Jones is away like a sprinter. By the time Ali gets to the door, Geoff is running across the lawn. Jones is close on his heels but then she slips in the mud and falls heavily. She gets up, wipes the dirt from her face and is off again. Ali jogs after her.

She's expecting Geoff to turn left, where the car is parked outside the stables. But instead, he heads for the drive and the main gates. He's about a hundred metres ahead but Jones is gaining fast. She's younger and fitter. Ali is struggling, she has a stitch and her lungs hurt, but she keeps going. The gates open automatically for Geoff. You obviously only need the passcode to get in. Jones manages to get through but they are closed again by the time that Ali is within reach of the sensor. She waits, panting. She can see the two figures silhouetted by the security lights, the rain slanting across them. They seem to be standing still, a few metres apart.

Finally, the gates are open. Ali steps into the circle of light. She sees Jones's Fiat parked on the road. She probably climbed over a wall to get in. In retrospect, Ali should have been suspicious that Geoff had the passcode and a key to the house.

Beyond the road, there's a bench and a grass verge and then . . . nothing. Ali realises that Geoff is standing on the very edge of the cliff.

'Don't do it, Geoff,' says Jones. 'We can fix this.'

'Don't,' croaks Ali. 'If you die there's no proof that Finn didn't do it. He'll go to prison for life.'

Geoff turns to look at her, his face a pale disc in the gloom.

'I've left a full confession in my safe at home. The code is 1703, Bobby's birthday.' His voice breaks slightly. 'The gun's there too.'

'Was it Thomas Creek's gun?' asks Ali. She is dimly aware of the need to keep Geoff talking.

'Yes,' says Geoff. 'I saw him come through the gate instead of you. I chased him, wanting to find out what had happened. We had a struggle and I got control of the gun. Creek escaped.'

'He nearly killed me just now,' says Ali. 'I saw him outside my house too. I think he followed me home from Hawk Street.'

'I'm sorry, Ali,' says Geoff. 'Tell Finn I'm sorry.'

Jones dives forward but she's too late. Geoff steps into the darkness and then the only sound is the crash and sigh of the waves beating against the cliff.

Chapter 43

They have to call the police, of course. The coastguard comes too, the yellow helicopter hovering almost level with the clifftop where Ali and Jones shiver under blankets given to them by the paramedics. DS O'Brien strides over the grass, wearing a yellow cagoule and a determined expression. Her spotty acolyte is there too, seemingly without rainwear.

'DS Dawson, Dr Pellegrini. What's going on?'

'My boss,' says Ali, between chattering teeth. 'He confessed to killing Isaac Templeton. Then he killed himself.'

'He left a confession,' says Jones. She sounds more composed than Ali, although her accent is more pronounced than usual. 'It's in his home.' She gives Geoff's address. Ali is surprised she knows it by heart.

O'Brien clearly doesn't believe a word of it but she ushers them into a police car and, after a whispered consultation with the driver, they go back through the gates of East Dean. Miranda Templeton is standing by the front door.

'What's happening?' she says. 'I got a message from the police telling me to leave the house and take the children with me. When I called to ask how long I had to stay away, I was told that no one from the police station had contacted me.'

'That was me,' says Jones, actually sounding slightly embarrassed. 'I can explain.'

'Well, that's a relief,' says O'Brien. She's quite good at sarcasm. 'Can we come inside?' she asks Miranda. 'I'd like to ask DS Dawson and Dr Pellegrini some questions and I think we should get them somewhere warm as quickly as possible.'

Miranda peers at Ali in the dim porch light. 'Are you Alison Dawson? I was expecting you.'

'I came,' says Ali. 'But it's all a bit complicated.'

Mary O'Brien takes Ali's statement in Miranda's office, a slightly claustrophobic room filled with bookshelves and family pictures. While she is questioning Jones, Ali and Miranda drink tea in the kitchen, which is surprisingly cosy, a stylish mix of old and new, bright pink Aga and antique refectory table. Ali tells Miranda about Geoff confessing to Isaac's murder.

'I never thought that Finn did it,' says Miranda. 'He was always the nicest of the advisors. Chibu's too intense and Piers is just an arse.'

Ali can't help laughing and Miranda joins in. It's as if they've missed out the first five years and have become instant friends.

'Sorry,' says Miranda, wiping her eyes. 'I think I'm a bit hysterical.'

'Me too,' says Ali.

'It's all been a bit . . . a bit much,' says Miranda, with rather touching understatement. 'Did your boss say why he killed Isaac?'

'He didn't want Isaac to tell the prime minister about some secret research our unit is doing.'

'This is going to sound absolutely insane,' says Miranda, 'but did that research have to do with time travel?'

'Yes,' says Ali.

'Wait there a minute,' says Miranda, before darting out of the room. All her movements are swift and sure. She makes Ali feel more than usually lumbering.

Miranda comes back with an envelope and something wrapped in art paper.

'I found these in Isaac's desk this morning,' says Miranda. 'I don't know if he meant to give them to me or not.' Her voice trembles slightly. 'Anyway, it's why I wanted to see you. I won't read you all of the letter. A lot of it's private. We loved each other, whatever anyone says. I know there were rumours of affairs but, honestly, they aren't true.'

'I believe you,' says Ali. She hopes that Miranda never finds out about Helen Graham.

Miranda wipes her eyes. 'There's just a bit at the end that I want to read you. Isaac says, "If anything happens to me, ask Professor Serafina Pellegrini what happened to Alison Dawson at the Department of Logistics. If she tells you it's about time travel, believe her."'

They look at each other.

'I wondered what that meant,' says Miranda. 'I mean, nothing happened to *you*. You're here.'

'It's a long story,' says Ali.

'And then there's this.' Miranda unwraps the paper and reveals a pencil sketch. It's a woman's face, thoughtful and composed.

She's not young but she has a serene beauty Ali did not know she possessed.

'That's you, isn't it?' says Miranda.

Ali peers at the signature. *F. Tremain 1853.*

The coastguard tells them that Geoff's body might never be found, but it washes up on the beach in Newhaven the next morning. Ali is glad for Geoff's parents' sake. By this time, the police have searched Geoff's house and found his confession and the murder weapon, an antique gun containing bullets of unknown calibre. Finn is released the next day, standing beside Ade while he reads out a statement talking about his client's distress and hinting darkly at possible action against the police.

Hugging Finn on the steps of the court is one of the best moments of Ali's life. Right up there with giving birth to him. For a few moments, Ali, Declan and Finn just stare at each other, grinning. Then they go back to Ali's house and order pizza. 'It's so weird to see you two together,' says Finn. 'Almost weirder than being in prison.' Finn seems fine, a little wary and far too thin but very much his old self. The only time he breaks down is when he greets a markedly unmoved Terry. Finn buries his face in the cat's fur and sobs for a few minutes. 'I want a dog,' he says, when he straightens up. 'Don't get a pug,' says Declan, who has one. 'They keep you awake all night with their snoring.' The discussion about dogs lasts until Declan goes home to Nikki and the girls.

Finn leaves after breakfast the next day. Ali understands. He wants to get back to his old life. She knows that he's had calls from Chibu and Piers, both of them anxious to assure him that they had always believed in his innocence. 'I think Chibu is genuinely fond of you. She was just knocked sideways by Isaac's death,' Ali says to Finn over their cinnamon buns (she has discovered an excellent bakery which, pleasingly, has been on the same site since 1849).

'I know,' says Finn. 'Chibu was in love with him but I honestly don't think they had an affair, whatever Piers says.'

'What will you do now?' asks Ali. She has allowed herself one deployment of this question.

'I don't know,' says Finn, hoovering up his last crumbs. 'Go back to the flat. Have my hair cut. Go on the Battersea Dogs Home website. Look for a new job.' Ali wishes him luck with all of these.

After Finn has left, walking with a surprisingly jaunty stride towards the Tube station, Ali tidies away the breakfast things. Getting the dishwasher plumbed in will be number one on her new domestic 'to do' list. Then she feeds Terry and gets her coat. She's going to walk to work. She's dreading the meeting with Bud and Dina.

Last night Declan talked a lot about conspiracy theories. Ali and Finn mostly kept silent (luckily Declan doesn't need much input from his listeners when embarked on his favourite topic) because they knew that Declan's wildest fantasies didn't come close to the truth. Geoff's confession said only that he'd killed Isaac, not why. There *was* a conspiracy. The government had been happy to see Finn charged with Isaac's murder, however flimsy the evidence against him. It diverted attention away from the unbelievable truth about the brilliant scientist and her experiments with time and space. DS O'Brien told Ali that she had been warned by the chief super and the Parliamentary and Diplomatic Protection Unit not to investigate Serafina Pellegrini. 'I went to see her anyway,' O'Brien said. 'I don't like loose ends.' 'I thought you didn't,' said Ali. Mary said that interference like this made her want to quit the force altogether. 'Don't,' said Ali. 'We need officers like you.' But, even as she said this, Ali wondered if she herself could bear to stay.

Ali pauses outside 14 Eel Street. It looks the same, the windows flashing in the sudden early spring sunshine. But how can the team carry on without Geoff? Funnily enough, it's a memory of Clara that eventually gets Ali over the threshold. 'You have to keep on, don't you?' she'd said that night in the kitchen. Ali agrees silently. She has to keep on keeping on. As usual, she avoids the lift and takes the stairs.

Dina and Bud are both in the open-plan office. They are talking quietly together but, when Ali opens the door, Dina rushes over to hug her.

'Oh, Ali.' She's crying.

'I know,' says Ali.

'I'm so happy about Finn,' says Dina. 'But . . .' Her shoulders heave.

'I know,' says Ali again, patting her on the back.

Bud hovers as if he wants a hug too. As if to emphasise the solemnity of the day, he's wearing a plain T-shirt, black with no slogan. Ali pats him on the arm. 'What about a cup of coffee?' Bud brightens immediately, glad of something to do. Drinking the bitter liquid from a *Doctor Who* mug, Ali feels that a thread of normality has returned to her life.

'I just can't believe it about Geoff,' says Dina, for the third or fourth time. 'I thought he loved the unit. I thought he loved us.'

'So did I,' says Ali. She remembers shouting 'I thought you were my friend' at her boss, minutes before he died. But he wasn't their friend and he didn't love them.

'He loved the work,' says Bud. 'That was what he was obsessed with. The time travel. All the rest of it was just a game.'

Ali thinks of Geoff with his diets, his pomposity and his World's Best Boss mug. Was it all an act? Did it disguise a cold-blooded operative who was prepared to kill to save his mission? Or was Geoff obsessed with time travel for a different reason? Last night, probably triggered by the take-away pizza, Finn told Ali what Geoff had said during their drunken evening together, that he'd give anything for just one more hour with Bobby. Did Geoff hope that Jones could take him back to his beloved husband? Did he kill himself because he finally understood the truth? So many impossible things have turned out to be possible, but bringing the dead back to life isn't one of them.

'I don't think it was a game,' she says. 'It was all part of him. He was Geoff – funny and pernickety and all the rest of it – but he was also deadly serious about our work. He thought Isaac was going to jeopardise it. Remember when Geoff said that Number Ten didn't need to know about the mistakes in the 1850 mission? Jones wanted to write a full report but Geoff stopped her. He knew that the PM would shut us down if he found out the whole story.'

'I can understand that,' says Dina. 'But to set Finn up . . .'

'Yes,' says Ali. 'That's what I can't forgive.'

But even as she says this, she wonders if it's true. 'Tell Finn I'm sorry.' Those had been Geoff's last words. Maybe Ali has to accept this apology and, in Clara's words, keep on.

'Have you seen Jones?' asks Bud.

'I was going to ask you that,' says Ali. She hasn't seen Jones since the night on the cliff top. Ali looks across at John's desk and sees Dina doing the same.

'She'll be in,' says Bud, staunch in defence of his mentor. 'She'll get John back for us.'

'I hope so,' says Ali. 'It's starting to feel a little empty in here.'

Dina and Bud want Ali to join them for lunch at a pub Dina has discovered. 'It's called The Bag O'Nails. It's very trendy.' But Ali excuses herself. 'There's someone I've got to see at Queen Mary's.'

Ed Crane is in his office, cataloguing items on a computer.

'Still working on the inventory,' he tells her.

'Can we go upstairs?' says Ali, realising too late that this can have a double meaning. 'And see the Templeton Collection?'

Ed looks at her curiously but says, 'OK.'

They climb the stairs and Ed unlocks the door to the secret room. The fluorescent light reveals the display cases, harmless and functional. But Ali remembers candlelight and Cain Templeton saying, 'Objects can have strange powers, don't you think?' Ali moves between the glass boxes: the Roman skull with a nail hammered into the centre of its forehead, the mummified cat, the Bronze Age jet necklace, the Iron Age torc.

'Where's the writing slope,' she asks, 'where you found my letter?'

'*Your* letter?' says Ed.

'I spell my name like that. You remembered.'

'I'm having the leather restored,' says Ed, 'but it was on that desk there.'

Ali looks across at the desk, a solid walnut structure with a green top that reminds her of the House of Commons. There's a chair in front of it, leather-backed with polished wooden arms that form a half circle around the sitter. She thinks of the chair in *The Pickwick*

Papers, the one that transforms itself into an ugly old man. *If a man sits in a chair all his life, will that seat not retain something of him?*

'Has anything odd ever happened in here?' she asks. 'Anything that seemed a bit . . . well, spooky?'

Ed looks at her for a full minute before replying. 'It's funny you should ask,' he said, 'but last week I was working late and I thought I'd come up here just to check on the collection. I did my usual rounds and everything seemed in order. I was just about to lock up when I turned round for one last look – I don't know why – and there was a man sitting in this chair.'

'A man?' says Ali. 'What did he look like?'

'I only saw him for a minute. Less than that. He was dressed in old-fashioned clothes, they looked Victorian. And he was dark. Foreign-looking, you might say.'

Cain Templeton was dark-haired. Could it have been him in the chair? Was that when he left the unfinished letter?

'As I say,' Ed continues, 'he was only there for seconds. Then there was a flicker, as if the lights were going wrong again, and he was gone. I thought I must have imagined it. People say this place is haunted, but I don't believe in all that stuff.'

'Don't you?' says Ali. 'What about the curse?'

'The curse? Oh, that's just one of those stories that always attach themselves to museum collections. When he was here that time, Isaac Templeton told me some crazy story about a set of cursed chairs, but he had one of them in his house. He can't have believed in it.'

But Isaac Templeton is dead, thinks Ali. She wonders where he was sitting when Geoff burst into the great hall and pointed his gun.

★

What did Jones mean about keeping things between themselves? Did she realise that Geoff would take his own life rather than face justice? Or did she just understand the extent of Geoff's grief over Bobby? Ali thinks about this a lot in the days after her boss's death. But Jones tried to stop Geoff, Ali remembers, chasing after him and pleading with him at the cliff's edge. In Ali's dreams she hears Geoff saying, 'I'm sorry,' and then the silence, broken only by the noise of the sea and the storm.

Ali doesn't try to contact Jones. Instead she makes an appointment at Kelly's salon and has her hair dyed fire-engine red again. She sees Finn for brunch and learns that he's met up with Jones a few times. 'We've been talking about stuff,' he tells Ali. 'It really helps.' Finn also tells her that he's seen Chibu and Piers and is considering a new job with Helen Graham.

Finn seems to want to be on his own these days. Ali doesn't blame him. She remembers the shock of moving from 1850 to 2023 and thinks that coming out of prison must feel very similar. She keeps in touch via gifs and pictures of Terry but she tries to give Finn space. She doesn't ask him about Jones and tries hard not to speculate on the nature of this new relationship. She is waiting for her own message and, when it comes, she surprises herself by bursting into tears.

Chapter 44

Ali stands on the steps of 44 Hawk Street. She presses the top doorbell, intending to ask for Asif, but she is buzzed in without the need for explanations. Those medical students really ought to up their security, she thinks. The hallway is empty but Ali thinks she can sense the same faint electronic hum that sometimes pervades the offices in Eel Street.

The grandfather clock is still stuck at midnight, the imps pushing an unfortunate sinner into the fires of hell. Ali takes one last look around and then closes the door quietly. She stands on the steps looking at her phone screen. It's a slow morning in Hawk Street and, for the next two minutes, no motor vehicles go past. Ali could almost be in the nineteenth century. Apart from the vape shops and Nando's, of course. One minute to go. A young woman in a hijab passes by, holding a toddler by the hand. A pigeon, world-weary and bedraggled, surveys Ali from the railings.

Is there a movement, a parting of the air? Ali doesn't know. She only knows that now she is looking at a man dressed in a long black coat and clutching a top hat.

'John!' Ali runs down the steps and hugs her colleague. He smells of tea-tree and woodsmoke.

'Your hair's red again,' says John, sounding slightly breathless. He's been away for almost two weeks, longer even than Ali. She imagines that the vertigo must be off the scale.

'How are you?' she says.

'All right,' says John. 'It's just . . . strange. A few hours ago I was having breakfast with Frederick and Arthur. Len calls us the three musketeers.'

'Was that book even out in 1850?'

'Apparently so. I was always getting those sorts of things wrong.'

'Me too,' says Ali. 'I can't wait to hear about them all. Did they talk about me?'

'All the time,' says John. 'Tremain thinks you're a woman with a secret. He wants to paint you one day.'

'He's not wrong,' says Ali. Did Tremain paint her? she wonders. Is the drawing only a preliminary sketch?

'What else happened?' she asks.

'Burbage was murdered,' says John. 'Arthur and co say it was the high mob – a sort of Victorian mafia – but I'm not so sure.'

'Oh my God,' says Ali. 'I didn't like Burbage but that's horrible. Who do you think did it?'

'I don't know,' says John, 'but I've got a lot to tell you. I went to a meeting of The Collectors and I saw a man sit on a chair and vanish into thin air.'

'Did you really?' says Ali. Could that be the man that Ed saw materialising at the desk in the museum? She thinks of Creek stopping her sitting in the chair at East Dean. *Oh no you don't.*

'We need to talk about that,' she says. 'Things have been quite interesting here too.'

'Jones told me some of it. About Geoff. I could hardly believe it.'

'We're still getting over it. Things will be easier now you're back. You can take over the team.'

'Oh no,' says John, 'you should be in charge.' This whole 'after you' thing is so typical of John that Ali laughs again, more easily this time.

'What else did Jones say?' she asks.

'She says that, between us, we'll find a way to get her back. Did you know that was what she was planning to do – exchange herself for me?'

'Not until she texted me yesterday. She told me what time to be here.'

'Do you think we'll see Jones again?' says John. 'It was just so incredible to see her just now, all dressed up like a Victorian countess. Far grander clothes than we had, by the way. There was so much that I wanted to say to her, but we had so little time, barely an hour.'

'I think I go back in three years' time,' says Ali. 'I'll tell you later how I know.'

'Three years,' says John. 'Imagine what a woman like Jones can achieve in three years.'

'It's a frightening thought,' says Ali. 'Shall we go?' She takes his arm and they walk down the quiet street into the restless, timeless city.

Acknowledgements

The Frozen People was a new venture for me, a step into the unknown, terrifying and exhilarating. I'm so grateful to my editor, Jane Wood, and my agent, Rebecca Carter, for encouraging me from the very beginning and providing support at every step of the way. Thanks to everyone at Quercus for all your hard work on this book and all the others. Special thanks to Katy Blott, Jon Butler, Charlotte Gill, Florence Hare, Ella Horne, David Murphy, Ella Patel, Emily Patience and Hannah Robinson. Thanks to Liz Hatherell for her brilliant copyediting (are you sure you haven't travelled to 1850, Liz?) and Chris Shamwana at Ghost for the beautiful cover.

Thanks to my American editor, Jeramie Orton, and all at Pam Dorman Books. Thanks to all the publishers around the world who have taken a chance on this new series.

I first worked out the rough plot of *The Frozen People* with my husband, Andrew, sitting outside a King's Lynn pub after visiting the Grime's Graves neolithic flint mines. This book is for you, Andy.

Even though the plot is somewhat fantastical, I wanted to make the details as convincing as possible. Thanks to Graham Bartlett and Tony Kent for advice on policing and legal matters. I also read many books about the Victorian era and am so grateful to all the authors. A select bibliography follows.

Love and thanks always to my children, Alex and Juliet, and to our cat, Pip, who is growing into quite the writer's assistant.

Elly Griffiths, 2024

Select Bibliography

Strange Victoriana by Jan Bondeson, Amberley Publishing

Victorian Things by Asa Briggs, Batsford

The Victorian Home by Ralph Duffy, Bracken Books

How to be a Victorian by Ruth Goodman, Penguin

A Child of the Jago by Arthur Morrison, OUP

The Victorians by Jeremy Paxman, BBC Books

The Order of Time by Carlo Rovelli, Penguin

Gospel Oak

N.W. Fever Hospl

City Prison
Kentish Town

Haver st. H.

ST. PANCRAS

Coll.

Chalk Farm

Camden Tn.

Highb

rimrose ill

ARYLEBONE

Regents

EUSTON STA.

ST. PANCRAS

KING'S CROSS

Angel

Park

Gower Str.

O

N

Portland Rd.

Baker Str.

Holborn Viad.

Farr

Central London Railw.

Ludgate

Hill

S:Po

C

ade Park

CHARING CROSS

Buckingh. Pal.

WESTM.

St. James Park

WATERLOO

on

W.M. Abbey

Ho: of Parliament

VICTORIA

Sloane Sq.

Pimlico

ER

Elephant Castle

LSEA

LAMB